Perdita was in transports of delight while Mrs. Armistead helped her disrobe.

"What a day, Armistead! What a day!"

"What a day, indeed, Madam. And the forerunner of many others like it, I daresay."

"He is so impatient," sighed Perdita fondly.

"The Prince is an ardent lover, Madam."

It was indeed a step forward. Even Perdita knew that now there could be no holding back. . . .

PERDITA'S PRINCE

Jean Plaidy

FAWCETT CREST • NEW YORK

A Fawcett Crest Book
Published by Ballantine Books
Copyright © 1969 by Jean Plaidy

Library of Congress Catalog Card Number: 87-6022

ISBN: 0-449-21658-6

This edition published by arrangement with G.P. Putnam's Sons, a Division of The Putnam Publishing Group

Manufactured in the United States of America

First Ballantine Books Edition: November 1989

CONTENTS

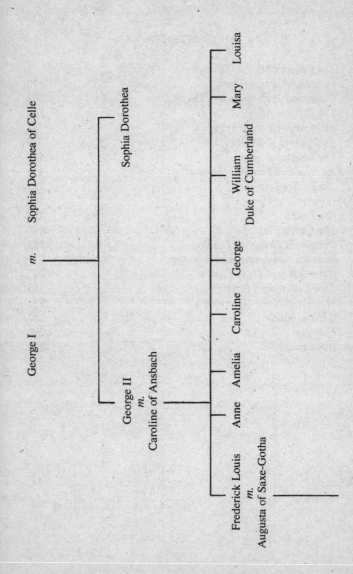

George I   *m.*   Sophia Dorothea of Celle

Sophia Dorothea

George II
m.
Caroline of Ansbach

Frederick Louis
m.
Augusta of Saxe-Gotha

Anne   Amelia   Caroline   George   William
Duke of Cumberland   Mary   Louisa

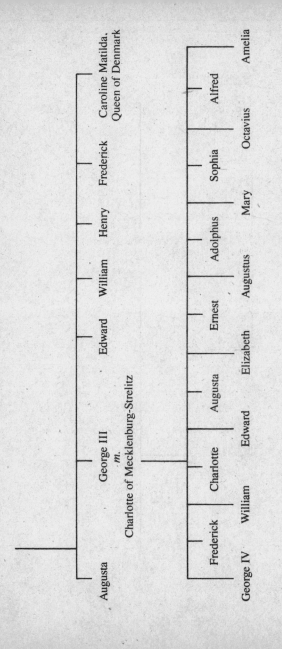

Augusta

George III
m.
Charlotte of Mecklenburg-Strelitz

Edward   William   Henry   Frederick   Caroline Matilda,
                                                                    Queen of Denmark

George IV   Frederick   William   Charlotte   Edward   Augusta   Elizabeth   Ernest   Augustus   Adolphus   Mary   Sophia   Octavius   Alfred   Amelia

The Queen's Maid of Honour

The Prince of Wales stalked up and down his apartments in the Dower Lodge on Kew Green and aired his grievances to his brother, Prince Frederick.

'I tell you this, Fred,' he declared, 'I have had enough. The time is now coming to an end when we can be treated like children. Like children, did I say? Why, bless you, Fred, we are treated like prisoners. Our father, His Majesty . . .' The Prince made an ironical bow which brought a titter to Frederick's lips '. . . is the slave of his own passionate virtue. God preserve us, Fred, from virtue such as that practised by King George III. And our mother? What is she but a queen bee? There in her hive she grows large, she gives birth and, by God, before she has had time to walk a dozen times through her Orangerie or take a pinch of snuff or two, she is preparing to give birth once more. I thought Sophie would be the last, but now we are to have another little brother or sister despite the fact that we have eleven already.'

'At least His Majesty does his duty by the Queen, George.'

'I doubt not that our noble mother would wish him to be a little less dutiful in that direction—although giving birth has now become a habit with her. Really, they are a ridiculous pair. What has the Court become? It is small wonder that people mock. Have you heard the latest?'

Frederick shook his head and his brother quoted:

> 'Caesar the mighty King who swayed
> The sceptre was a sober blade;

1

A leg of mutton and his wife
Were the chief comforts of his life.

The Queen composed of different stuff,
Above all things adored her snuff,
Save gold, which in her great opinion
Alone could rival snuff's dominion.'

'You see . . . that is the popular verdict on our King and
Queen!'

'Kings and queens are always targets for public ridicule,
George.'

'Criticism, not ridicule. *I* shall commit sins . . . royal sins,
Fred. But I shall never be accused of doting on a pinch of snuff
and caper sauce. Oh, when I look back I wonder how I have
endured it for so long. Do you remember the frilled collars I
used to be made to wear until only a short time ago? Frilled
collars, Fred! A man of my age . . . a Prince . . . a Prince of
Wales!'

Frederick put his head on one side and regarded his brother.
Ever since he could remember he had admired George—the
elder brother exactly one year his senior, seeming wise, bold
and brilliant—everything that Frederick would like to have been;
but he bore no malice, no resentment, because George would
beat him to the crown by exactly twelve months; George, in
Frederick's eyes, was all that an elder brother should be, all that
a prince and king should be; the English, in Frederick's opinion,
were going to be very fortunate to have George as their king.

He pondered this now. By God, he thought, for he imitated
his brother's mode of speech as everything else, they are going
to find George IV a mighty change from George III. George III,
The Prince of Wales was contemptuous of their father—so would
Frederick be. Caper sauce! thought Frederick with a smirk.
When the Prince of Wales became king it would be very different. He would not have a plain wife; he would have a beauty,
and perhaps mistresses. Kings should have mistresses; and
George was constantly talking of women. He would sit for hours
at the windows watching the maids of honour pass by, even
though they were not a very exciting band. Their mother had
seen to that. George had imitated her taking her pinch of snuff
and murmuring in her German accent: 'Nothing that can tempt
the Princes!' But there was one pretty one the Queen seemed to
have overlooked. George had noticed her. Trust George.

But George was now thinking angrily of frilled collars, and he began to laugh, and so did Frederick, recalling that occasion when George had taken the frilled collar from his attendant's hand and flung it at him, his pink and white cheeks suddenly purple with rage as he cried: 'See how I am treated! I'll have no more of this.' And he had proceeded to tear the collar into shreds.

'You were at once reported to our Papa,' Frederick reminded him.

'That's my complaint,' went on George, narrowing his eyes. 'We were surrounded by spies then and we still are. I should have an establishment of my own. But they are too mean. That's the point, Fred, too mean!'

'I heard it said the other day that the Queen's only virtue was decorum and her only vice avarice.'

'There! That's the way they are spoken of. They live like little squires, not like a king and queen. I'm heartily tired of this state of affairs.'

'Still, they don't flog us now.'

'No. I put a stop to that.'

'Every complaint that was taken to our father brought the same answer: "Flog 'em." '

'It makes me fume to think of it.'

'But I remember, George, the day you snatched the cane from Bishop Hurd just as he was going to use it on you and how you said very sternly: "No, my lord Bishop, have done. There shall be no more of that!" '

'Nor was there,' said George, laughing, 'which makes me wonder whether if we had not stood out earlier against these tyrannies they might never have continued.'

The two young men began recalling incidents from their childhood. George could remember being dressed like a Roman centurion in a plumed helmet and being painted, with his mother and Frederick, by Mr. Zoffany. Poor Fred was even worse off because when he had been a few months old they had made him Bishop of Osnaburg, which had so amused the people that the child was represented on all the cartoons in his Bishop's mitre. George was particularly incensed by the wax model of himself at the age of a month or two which his mother still kept on her dressing table under a glass dome. This doting sentimentality went side by side with the stern way of bringing up children. 'Completely Teutonic,' said George. 'By God, can't we forget our German ancestry?' Hours of study; shut off from contact with other people; the King's special diet—meat only a few times a week and then with all the fat pared off; fish served without butter; the fruit of a pie without the crust, all specially worked out by the King who might appear in the nursery dining room at any time and discountenance poor Lady Charlotte Finch, who was in charge of them, if these rules were not carried out to the letter.

'What a life we led!' sighed the Prince of Wales. 'And still do!'

'Worst of all,' added Frederick, 'was growing our wheat.'

'Farmer George would make little farmers of the whole family.'

George shivered distastefully, remembering their father's taking them out to show them the little plots of land which he had allotted to them.

'There,' he had informed them as though, said the Prince of Wales, he were offering them the crown jewels. 'There's your own bit of land. Cultivate it, eh? Grow your own wheat . . . make your own bread. Nothing like tilling the land, eh, what?'

Nothing like tilling the land! Going out in all weathers; preparing the soil, sowing the wheat, while the cold winds chapped their hands. The Prince of Wales was proud of his beautiful white hands. The heat of the sun spoiled his complexion. He was proud of that, too, because in spite of a tendency to develop pimples—which would pass—he had a beautiful soft skin, pink, very pink and white. And this precious skin must be burned in the summer sun while the Prince of Wales worked like a farm labourer. They had even been obliged to thresh their own wheat and supervise the baking of their bread.

The indignity of it all! But it had to be done otherwise the cry would go up: 'Flog 'em.' And their parents—the King and Queen of England—would inspect the little loaves of bread that had been made with their own wheat and the Prince of Wales had been infuriated to see that George III paid more attention to this bread produced by his sons than to matters of state.

'I must have an establishment of my own,' declared the Prince.

'It's ridiculous that you should be denied it,' soothed Fred.

'I shall demand it.' The Prince rose and was about to strut across the room when his eye caught a dainty figure crossing the Green on her way to the Queen's Lodge. He was immediately at the window. 'By God,' he cried. 'She's a beauty.'

Frederick murmured agreement.

She was small, dainty and dark; and suddenly it seemed as though by instinct she raised her eyes to the window where the two Princes stood watching her.

George immediately bowed. She stood still for a moment, dropping an enchanting curtsey and then turning away, sped across the lawn.

'One of our mother's maids of honour,' said George.

'How did our mother allow such a charmer to get in?'

'Like Homer, she nodded,' laughed the Prince. 'And let us be thankful for it.'

'Us?'

'I, because I intend to know more of the lady; and you because you will be so delighted in my good fortune.'

'Do you think, George . . .'

George looked astonished. Of course he would succeed with the lady. Wasn't he the most handsome, the most desirable young man in England? Wasn't he the Prince of Wales?

Frederick hastily agreed: 'Yes, of course, George, but our father . . .'

'By God,' cried the Prince, 'I thought I'd made it clear to you that I have had enough of this treatment. Everything is going to be different from now on. I am seventeen years old.'

Frederick, at sixteen, looked suitably impressed.

'Time, dear brother, to have left childhood behind and if our miserly parents will not allow me an establishment at least I shall have a *life* of my own.'

In the Queen's drawing room the royal family was assembled for the evening concert. These concerts took place twice a week, on the King's orders, and every member of the family was expected to attend or the King would want to know the reason why. Only baby Sophie, not yet two years old, was spared. Even three-year-old Mary was there, seated on a footstool at her mother's feet while Queen Charlotte, pregnant with the child who would shortly make its appearance and bring the number of royal offspring to thirteen, industriously worked on her embroidery.

The King was comparatively content on occasions like this. It was while he sat with his family—all outwardly docile—while he listened to the excellent performance of some piece by Handel, that he could forget his anxieties. There were many of these. The trouble growing steadily worse over the American colonies; the conflict among his ministers, the growing truculence of the Prince of Wales; and worst of all the voices in his head which

would not leave him alone, which mischievously mocked him,
starting a train of thought and suddenly snatching it away so that
he could not remember what had been in his mind a moment
before, malicious voices which whispered to him: 'George, are
you going mad?'

But here in the drawing room with his family seated quietly
about him and the Queen looking placid, as she always did when
pregnant, listening to the mastery of Mr. Papendiek with his
flute and Mr. Cramer at the harpsichord and the Cervettos—
father and son—miraculously performing on their violins, he felt
more at peace than at any other time.

He let his eyes linger on the younger children; he sometimes
whished that they did not have to grow up. The arch-trouble
maker was his eldest son and as Frederick was his intimate
companion that made a pair of them. Young William was only
fourteen; he would get him off to sea as soon as possible; that
would provide some necessary discipline. Twelve-year-old Edward should go to Germany—as should the other boys, except
the Prince of Wales of course. There would be an outcry if he
were sent out of England; and he had heard that his son had
expressed very strong opinions about that too. George was anxious to forget that his great-great grandfather, who had become
George I, was a German who could speak no English. The Prince
of Wales was trying to win the approval of the English people
already. The King looked uneasily at his eldest son. A tall,
good-looking boy, quite handsome, fair and fresh-
complexioned; his only physical imperfection being the family
tendency to fat. The King wondered whether the Prince had
cajoled his attendants into leaving the fat on his meat or to giving
him crust with fruit pies. The King was coming to the conclusion that his eldest son was capable of anything.

Why had George turned out so differently from what he had
hoped? The rod had not been spared. He himself had had a hand
in those beatings—and well deserved punishments they were—
but he carried a memory with him of the flushed angry face of
the Prince of Wales, and much resentment at the outrage to his
dignity.

'Necessary,' murmured the King to himself. 'Disobedience
has to be beaten out, eh, what?' And there was young Augustus
with his asthma. That had to be beaten out of him too. He was
six years old, but he was already well acquainted with the cane;
and it certainly seemed to help him get his breath better.

A family could be a great trial—particularly a royal family.

But when they were small they were charming. A great solace, thought the King, particularly the girls. He wished there had been more girls. Dear little Sophie was a delight; and as for Mary sitting there so solemnly at her mother's feet, she looked like a little doll. It would have given him great pleasure to have picked her up and caressed her while he explained to her that Mr. Handel's music was the best in the world. But he must observe the decorum of the drawing room.

His feet tapped in time with the music, but his mind had darted from his children to the situation in America. They'll capitulate, he was telling himself. They'll sue for peace . . . the rebels! Lord North was uneasy and wanted to give up the Ministry, but he wasn't going to let him. Who else was there but North? Chatham dead. Charles James Fox was making a nuisance of himself—he was even more of a menace than his father had been. Nothing went right abroad . . . and at home there was the intransigence of the Prince of Wales. Why could he not be at peace in the heart of his family? Charlotte was dull, but he was accustomed to her by now; it was true he looked with pleasure on other women . . . women like Elizabeth Pembroke, of course, but his emotions were so much in control that he never went beyond looking. His subjects sneered at him for being a good husband. They laughed at his interest in making buttons; in his liking for the land. 'Farmer George' they called him, and 'The Royal Button Maker'. There was scorn rather than affection in these appellations. The people forgot that when he was not with his family at Kew he was closeted with his ministers making decisions on how the campaign against the American rebels was to be conducted, making decisions as to how the armies were to be deployed; discussing naval tactics. Even now he was urging Lord Sandwich to hold the West Indies at all costs. How could we continue to meet our commitments if we lost our revenue from the sugar islands? And what of home defence? What about the aggressive French and the Spaniards?

Problems everywhere he looked, and the voices every now and then whispering in his head: 'George, are you going mad?'

And why shouldn't a king be a virtuous husband? What was there to sneer at in virtue? It seemed to George that whatever a king did he displeased his subjects if he were no longer young. Everywhere that young rascal, the Prince of Wales, went he was cheered. What will become of him, I cannot think, mused the King uneasily. Ideas chased themselves round and round in his head; like mice, he thought of them . . . fighting each other for his attention and when he tried to look closely at them they disappeared; they turned into mocking voices that reminded him of that dreadful time when he had been ill and had lost control of his mind. Pleasant things like his model farm at Kew, his buttons, his gardens, his baby daughters represented safety. If he could have escaped from all his troubles and lived quietly, the voices might be stilled. He glanced at Charlotte . . . good Charlotte, unexciting but safe. Sometimes he was tormented by erotic dreams of women. Hannah Lightfoot, the Quaker girl with whom he had gone through a form of marriage when he had been very young and foolishly romantic, long since dead— for which ironically he must be grateful; for while she lived she represented a threat to his marriage with Charlotte, and that was a matter to shake the whole foundations of the monarchy, for if his sons were bastards . . . well, it did not bear thinking of and set the voices in his head working faster than ever. And then there was Sarah Lennox—Sarah Bunbury as she had become— whom he had wanted to marry, for whom he had as he had told Lord Bute 'burned'; but he had been obliged to marry his plain German Princess because all Hanoverian Kings married German Princesses; it was a duty they must observe and when the time came young George would have to do the same. So instead of his dear Hannah Lightfoot whom he had so dangerously loved in his extreme youth, in spite of flighty Sarah Lennox for whom he had so burned, he was married to Charlotte.

He was a faithful husband, but there were times when his senses were in revolt. Why, he would demand of himself, should he be the one member of the family who observed a strict moral code? His brothers . . . his sister Caroline Matilda . . . He shuddered at the memory of them. Poor Caroline Matilda whom he had dearly loved and longed to protect was now dead—and he could not be sure that her death had been a natural one—after being involved in a storm of intrigue. Married to a near imbecile she had taken a lover and with him had been accused of treason. The lover had died barbarously and she, the Queen of Denmark, had come very near to the same fate, and would have succumbed to it but for the intervention of her affectionate brother—himself, the King of England. He had been deeply disturbed by the death of Caroline Matilda. Such events haunted him in nightmares. Poor Caroline Matilda had paid a high price for her follies.

With his brothers it was a very different matter.

William, Duke of Gloucester and Henry, Duke of Cumberland, had defiantly made their scandals and brazenly shown their indifference to disgrace. Yet they did not arouse half the resentment and mocking scorn which was poured on the King for being a good husband.

Cumberland had been involved in a most disgraceful affair with the Grosvenors because he had seduced Lady Grosvenor and had—young fool!—written letters to the woman which gave no doubt of the relationship between them. George remembered phrases from those letters which made his face burn with shame—and something like envy—even now. Accounts of intimate details when they had lain together 'on the couch ten thousand times'. His brother, who had been brought up so carefully by their mother, watched over, never allowed to meet anyone but the immediate family in case he should be contaminated, had written those words! And as soon as they escaped from Mamma's apron strings, there they were running wild, getting into scandals like that of Cumberland and the Grosvenors. And Lord Grosvenor had had the effrontery to sue a royal duke and to win his case. The jury had brought in a verdict of £10,000 plus costs of £3,000 against the Duke of Cumberland which George had had to find with the help of Lord North . . . out of the King's household expenses.

And as if that were not enough, Cumberland had tired of Lady Grosvenor by the time the scandal broke and was having an intrigue with the wife of a timber merchant—a very wealthy one it was true and fortunately for the royal purse, the timber merchant was too flattered by the royal Duke's attentions to his wife to make trouble; but no sooner had that affair been freely discussed in the coffee and chocolate houses than Cumberland had a new love and this had turned out to be the most serious matter of all, for Mrs. Anne Horton, who was the daughter of Lord Irnham, was intent on marriage, and as she had according to that gossip, Horace Walpole, 'the most amorous eyes in the world and eyelashes a yard long', Cumberland was fool enough to marry her.

This had caused the King so much anxiety that he had done what his mother had urged him to do before her death; he had set about bringing into force the Royal Marriage Act which forbade members of the royal family to marry without the King's consent. Too late for Cumberland . . . and for Gloucester it seemed, for no sooner was the Marriage Act passed than Gloucester came forward to announce that for some years he had been secretly married to Lord Waldegrave's widow—a mésalliance if ever there was one, for the lady was not only the illegitimate daughter of Sir Edward Walpole but her mother was said to have been a milliner!

'Banish them from Court!' George had cried. And Charlotte had declared that she would receive no daughters of milliners. So there was an unsatisfactory state of affairs with his brothers; and since his sons were so wild, the King did wonder what trouble would come through them.

Worry, worry, worry! thought the King, whichever way one turned. Oh, if only life were just living at Kew with Charlotte and the little ones, what a happy man he would be! Well perhaps not happy; he would always think of women like Hannah and Sarah and Elizabeth Pembroke with longing, but while he remained a faithful husband and lived according to his code of honour he could be *serene*.

The Queen was not listening to Mr. Handel's excellent music; she was thinking how handsome her eldest son was looking in his frogged coat and hoping the King would not notice how elegant he was and question the price of his garments. Charlotte was alarmed when she saw the lights of resentment against his father flare up in her son's eyes. She had to face the fact that the relationship between them was scarcely harmonious. She had adored the Prince of Wales from the first time she had first held him in her arms—'A perfect specimen of a Royal Highness, your Majesty . . .' Oh yes, indeed. He had bawled lustily, this wonder infant, and his health had always been of the best—except of course for the customary childish ailments. At the age of four it was true he had given her a great scare by contracting the small pox. But he was such a healthy little rascal, he had even shrugged that aside. She liked to tell her attendants how when he was kept in bed someone asked if he was not tired of lying abed so long and he had replied: 'Not at all, I lie and make reflections.' The brilliance of the child! There was no doubt that he was a genius. He was clever at his lessons. He spoke and wrote several languages, French, German and Italian, fluently; he was familiar with Horace and delighted in Tacitus. He learned with ease and had a command of English which astounded his mother and dumbfounded his father on those occasions, which were becoming more frequent, when they were involved in verbal battles. The Queen was a little anxious about his beloved son and his relationship with his father. Oh dear, she sighed, I hope they are not going to follow the family custom and yet another Prince of Wales is going to quarrel with the King. Not George, she assured herself, not her handsome son George.

She often looked at the wax image on her dressing table and thought of him as a baby. He was no longer that. She sighed, wishing that he would visit her more often and now and then ask her advice.

What would she advise him on? On the sort of shoe buckle he should wear? He was mightily interested in shoe buckles. Or on the colour of his coat? Or about those matters which her woman Schwellenburg was always hinting at—his amours. 'De Prince very much interests selfs in *mädchens* . . .' declared Schwellenburg in her execrable English. 'Nonsense, Schwellenburg, he is a natural gentleman.'

Was he *too* interested in young women? No, of course not. She refused to believe it. She refused to believe anything against George; and though she deplored the passing of his childhood when she had had some control over him, she was glad in a way that he was too old for whippings, for she had suffered to think of that delicate flesh being slashed with a cane.

Oh, George, come and speak to your mother, she implored silently. Not just as a duty. Not to bow, kiss the hand, murmur a few meaningless words and be off as quickly as you can. Not that, George, speak as a son to a mother.

She thought of the next child she would bear; but such happenings were commonplace with her. The thirteenth!

A boy or girl? she wondered. What did it matter now? She already had seven boys and five girls. No one could say she had not given the country heirs. But she had not felt so well with this pregnancy. Perhaps it was time to give up child-bearing. The King would never agree to that, she was sure, and yet what had she been doing in the nineteen years since she came to England?—Bearing children, was the answer. Thirteen of them. Oh, yes, the time had certainly come to call a halt. Not that she could bear to part with any of them. But with fine strong boys like George, Frederick and William at the head of the family— surely they had enough.

The Prince of Wales was pensive tonight. Was he wrapped up in the music? Frederick was beside him. They were inseparable those two and it was pleasant to see two brothers such friends. They seemed now as though they were sharing some secret. They were both watching one of the maids of honour who was in attendance. The Queen heard an echo of Schwellenburg's voice: 'De Prince very much interests self in *mädchens*.' Oh, no, thought the Queen. George is a boy yet. He has always been taught such restraint.

George did not hear Mr. Handel's music, though he shared the family fondness for it. He was thinking: She is exquisite. So dainty. Such little hands and feet. He pictured her delight when he made known to her the fact that he was in love with her. He had discovered her name. It was Harriot Vernon. Harriot, Harriot, he murmured.

Fred nudged him gently with his foot because he had spoken her name aloud.

The music had stopped. The King led the applause and, under cover of it, George threw a glance at the young maid of honour which made her lower her eyes and smile. It was enough for the ardent Prince. His invitation was accepted. They must meet. Where?

'You are watched,' whispered Frederick.

'Always, brother,' sighed the Prince.

He turned to his equerry and friend, Lord Malden, heir to the Earl of Essex.

'I wish you to take a message to a lady,' he murmured.

'At your Highness's service.'

'Come to my apartments,' said the Prince. 'I will give you all instructions there.'

Frederick listened with admiration. This time George was about to involve himself in a real love affair.

'And how?' asked Frederick, 'can you possibly meet Harriot Vernon? You would be noticed. And you know we are forbidden even to speak to the maids of honour.'

George laughed.

'Trust me,' he said. 'I already have an assignation with the lady.'

'Can that be true, George?'

'Indeed yes. Malden has taken a message for her from me and brought one back from her. We are going to meet in the gardens tonight.'

'Where?'

'Why do you wish to know, brother?'

'Because I fear you will be seen.'

'Not us. We shall meet in the most secluded spot . . . not far from the river. You know where I mean. We were saying only the other day few ever go there and you remember I remarked it would be a good spot for a lover's meeting.'

'You think she will come?'

George drew himself up to his full height and looked most princely. 'I *know* she will come, Frederick. I have her promise.'

'And when she does . . .?'

George threw a kiss to his reflection in the mirror.

'She can no more wait with patience for the encounter than I can.'

'So tonight . . . at sunset . . .'

'Tonight at sunset,' echoed the Prince of Wales.

Mr. Papendiek was playing the flute in the Queen's drawing room at the request of the King. Not all the family were present. The Prince of Wales for one was absent. Frederick, seated next to his brother William, was thinking of George sneaking out to that remote spot in the gardens not far from the river. He was going to wear a great coat of Malden's to disguise himself and there he would await the coming of Harriot Vernon and then . . . Frederick's eyes glistened. He hoped that all would go well and George would not be discovered. He wondered what would happen if he were. He looked at his father caught up in the music, and the Queen sitting placidly by. The child's entry into the world could not long be delayed. It has been going on like this for years, thought Frederick; the family assembled there listening to the King's favorite pieces of music; the only difference being that there was a new addition to the family. A new child to sit on the footstool at the Queen's feet while the child who had just vacated it would sit upright on a chair and try not to fidget. So dull! thought Frederick. No change at all.

But a change was coming. He and his brother were growing up. William would soon be sent to sea. And because of this William was half excited, half apprehensive. 'At least,' William had said, 'it'll be an escape from Kew and Buckingham House.' Lucky William, thought Frederick.

The King was in fact giving only half an ear to the music. He was thinking that soon he would have to leave Kew for London. He could not enjoy the sequestered life for long at a time. The dark, clever, rather gross face of Charles James Fox came into his mind. Always plaguing him. The Foxes always had. As though they bore him a grudge for not marrying Sarah. Charles James Fox was her nephew and if ever there was a trouble-maker it was that man.

And the American affair . . . and the French and the Spaniards . . . and the Government . . .

I'll put them from my mind, he told himself. I'll feel all the better for a little respite from affairs. Work all the better when I do get back to business, eh, what? Ought to be on better terms with young George. Can't have trouble in the family. He didn't want to *talk* to George. George was too smart with words. Had an answer for everything. A pleasant game of chess, that was what he would like. Even so, George invariably beat him nowadays. Nevertheless they could get a good game.

Where was George? George ought to be present on a family occasion like this.

Mr. Papendiek's solo was over; the King led the applause and when that came to an end and the musicians waited for his further instructions he declared: 'I should like a game of chess. Tell the Prince of Wales that I wish him to join me in a game of chess.'

Frederick was dismayed. They were going to search for the Prince of Wales and would be unable to find him, unless they went to that remote spot in the gardens and then . . . what would they discover? He had feared something like this. He had wanted George to make some provision for such an emergency, but George had merely shrugged aside the possibility of discovery. And now . . . it seemed inevitable.

'Where is the Prince, eh, what?' the King was already demanding as the chess board had been set out and he himself was putting the ivory pieces in their places.

One of the Prince's attendants came in looking harassed.

'Well, well, where is he? eh? eh?' demanded the King.

'Your Majesty, the Prince is not in his apartments.'

Frederick waited for no more. He slipped out of the drawing room and out of the Lodge and made his way with all speed to that remote spot in the gardens. It was dark now, but there was enough light from the moon to show Frederick the two figures embracing.

'George! George!' cried Frederick. 'For God's sake . . . George.'

The lovers parted and George, seeing his brother cried: 'Good God, Fred, what is it?'

'The King is demanding your presence immediately. He wants a game of chess.'

George cursed chess vehemently and stopped himself in time cursing the King. Harriot, trembling with anxiety, looked appealingly at her lover.

'There's nothing to be done but return with all speed and play this game of chess,' muttered the Prince. 'Here, Fred, take this.' It was Lord Malden's great coat with which he had disguised himself. He turned to Harriot and embraced her warmly. George would be a lover in any circumstances, thought Frederick admiringly. Even now while he was on the verge of exposure he was charmingly protective to the lady. 'Fred, see that Miss Vernon reaches her apartments in safety.' Frederick bowed. If he were involved in this affair he would not blame George. It had always been thus between them. They had always protected each other, at whatever cost to themselves, and took loyalty for granted.

So with Lord Malden's overcoat over one arm Frederick conducted the lady to a back staircase of the maids' house while George hurried to the Queen's drawing room where the King was impatiently glowering at the chess board.

'Takes you a long time to get here, eh, what?' He looked into the flushed face of his son. The elegant boots were just a little muddy. Many eyes noted this. There was a whispering behind fans, a few quietly spoken words among the attendants.

The Prince had for some time been ogling the only pretty maid of honour in his mother's entourage and already someone had reported seeing Prince Frederick sneaking out of the King's presence to warn his brother and later conducting the lady back to her apartments.

The Prince played a reckless game of chess which gave the King the advantage. But the latter did not enjoy this. What's the young blade up to, eh, what? the King asked himself.

And all through the household they were whispering of the Prince's love affair.

The next day in the same spot the Prince successfully accomplished the seduction of Miss Vernon; but by this time the affair was palace gossip.

Harriot Vernon went about her duties with the rapt expression of one who may have lost her virtue but had gained the whole world; and when the Prince of Wales was not seeking private interviews with the lady he was in his apartments writing verses to her.

How could Charlotte have allowed such a charmer to appear in the Prince's orbit, people were asking each other. Because she was about to give birth? Nonsense, this little operation was as normal to her as breathing. Still, she had slipped, and there could be a real scandal if the reckless Harriot should prove to be fertile as well as romantic.

Schwellenburg bustling about her apartments, tending the frogs and toads of which she made pets and kept in glass cages, grumbled to herself about the Prince of Wales. 'Ah,' she muttered, 'you willen zees tricks do.' And she tapped her snuff box and listened to the croaking which followed. She was proud of having taught her little darlings to croak at the tap of a snuff box. 'They vise little frogs,' she would say. 'Very vise frogs. Good little toads . . . not like the Prince of Vales. Must talk to the Queen of bad Prince, little frog. Not talk to self.'

And she did talk to the Queen. The Prince of Wales was having a love affair with that wicked young woman Harriot Vernon whom she had never wanted in the royal apartment, and if the Queen had listened to her would never have been there.

Charlotte was not fond of Schwellenburg, but one must have someone to whom one could speak German now and then. Schwellenburg had been with her ever since she had come to England and in any case was a habit now. The woman was arrogant; she made trouble; she was the most unpopular servant in the royal household . . . yet she remained in the Queen's service, bullying the Queen's women, disgusting them with her 'pets', and insisting on their playing long and tedious games of cards with her.

But she was under the delusion that the Queen could not do without her and that she was in charge of the Queen's household.

'Harriot Vernon is in dream . . . forget all . . . remember nothing. Makes loff with Herr George . . . in the gardens and in his bed. Disgusting.'

The Queen said: 'There is some mistake.'

'No mistake,' contradicted Schwellenburg with the boldness of an old servant. 'Haf seen with self's eyes.'

Charlotte thought: 'Of course it is true. And what will the King say? There'll be trouble . . . great trouble. Of course he is growing up . . . and so handsome. Surely there never was any young man as handsome as my George. It's not his fault exactly. He is so attractive. Oh, why doesn't he tell me what he is doing. He never comes to see me as a son should to his mother. He confides in Frederick . . . and perhaps William . . . But never his mother. This must not come to the ears of the King.'

She was loth to believe the affair had gone very far. He was a boy still. He may have been casting eyes on the girl; but that was as far as it had gone, she was sure.

She sent for her son, who came reluctantly and looked a little sulky, she noticed. He had the Hanoverian rather heavy jaw which unless the Prince was smiling, gave a sullen look to an otherwise charming face.

'I don't see enough of you,' she told him. 'I daresay you are very occupied.'

'Your Majesty knows the plans laid down by my father. It gives us little time to do anything but follow his orders.'

Oh, yes, he was resentful. She wondered whether she dare tell the King that the boys were growing up and they should no longer be treated as children. When had George ever taken any notice of her? When she had first come to England George's mother, the Dowager Princess of Wales, had made it very clear that no interference was expected from her. And George had supported his mother. Bear healthy children and that is all that will be expected of you. And they could not say she had not fulfilled their expectations. But listen to her advice on any subject, treat her like an intelligent being? Never. The only place in which she had any power was her own intimate circle. She could dismiss her maids; she could go over the accounts and find them too great; she could make her economies and take her snuff and look after the younger children. There her duty ended. That had been made clear to her. So it was no use her thinking she could speak to the King about George.

But she could speak to George—and she was going to find out if these rumours were true.

'So you have no time to visit your mother,' she said wistfully.

'Very little, Madam, very little.'

How haughty he was and how she loved him! She had difficulty in assuring herself that his glorious young Apollo was the fruit of her plain little body. She and George between them had produced this beautiful creature! Stolid George and plain Charlotte. It seemed incredible to her. If he would confide in her, if he would show a little affection . . . she would do everything in her power to give him what he wanted.

But he showed so clearly that he had no need of her. Yet she would have to prevent his quarrelling with his father. He would have to be made to realize that even he must not indulge in a love affair under their very noses.

'You find life a little . . . monotonous?' she asked.

He inclined his head and suppressed a yawn.

'I have often thought,' went on the Queen, 'that our maids of honour lead very dull lives.'

'I agree with Your Majesty,' said the Prince. 'How dull merely

to be one of a formal procession from the presence chamber to
the drawing room and never allowed to speak unless one is
spoken to.'

'Some may have nothing worthy to say.'

The Prince had warmed to his subject. 'Poor ladies! What a
life! To make an occasional one of large hoops in a royal coach.
I believe they make two new Court suits a year and now and
then appear in a side box in a royal play.'

'But she does not have to pay for her seat at the theatre,' the
Queen reminded him.

He looked at her slyly.

> *'Save the gold, which in her own opinion*
> *Alone could rival snuff's dominion.'*

he thought. Trust his mother to think a *free* seat compensated
for a good deal.

'I agree, Your Majesty, that a maid of honour goes to concerts
and plays . . . and oratorios *free*. Your Majesty will no doubt
remind me that she does not have to pay her physician and gets
her medicines for nothing.'

'You have forgotten one important thing.'

'No doubt, for the acts of maid of honour formed no part of
my education.'

'I will tell you one,' replied the Queen. 'Perhaps you have
recently had experience of this. She may flirt with Princes and
go to meet them in the moonlight. Is that also . . . free?'

The Prince was for once discountenanced, and his mother
was certain now that Schwellenburg's hints were true. The Prince
had been meeting Harriot Vernon in the moonlight. Heaven
knew how far this affair had gone, but if it reached the King's
ears His Majesty would be furious. She was terrified of the
King's anger; it took him so oddly nowadays and she was always
afraid of where it would end.

She must act quickly, and for once she dismissed the Prince.
It was usually he who pleaded his duty to the King and departed
as speedily as he could.

As soon as he had left her she sent for Harriot Vernon. The
girl stood before her—beautiful, radiant and—guilty.

'I have sent for you, Miss Vernon,' said the Queen, 'to tell
you that your services are no longer required at Court.'

'But Your Majesty . . .'

The Queen looked surprised. 'Call Madam von Schwellenburg,' she commanded.

'Your Majesty . . .'

'I have said, call Madam von Schwellenburg,'

Schwellenburg, listening at the door, had little need to be
called. She swept in.

'Your Majesty calls of me,' she said.

'Miss Vernon is leaving us . . . at once,' said the Queen.
'Pray help her to leave . . . immediately.'

'Vill see to selfs,' promised Schwellenburg, and Harriot had
no recourse but to leave her, and the German woman stood over
her while she packed her bags and herself ordered the carriage.

Within an hour of that interview with the Queen, Harriot
Vernon had left Court.

Encounter in Hyde Park

George mourned the departure of Harriot for a few days and then found a new mistress. He did not have to seek far. He soon proved what he had never doubted; not only was he extremely personable and completely charming, but as he was also the Prince of Wales he was irresistible. More than this his youthful exuberance, his discovery that the most exciting and alluring prospect in life was women made him completely fascinating to that sex; and as he embarked on the lightest of love affairs with the conviction that his partner in the adventure was the one woman in the world to whom he could remain faithful for the rest of his life, even shorn of the trappings of royalty, he would have been a successful lover.

The Queen had given birth to another son, christened Octavius, who was not so strong as his brothers and sisters and almost immediately, to her consternation, she was pregnant again.

It had been impossible to keep the scandal of Harriot Vernon and the inclinations of the Prince from his father, who declared that his eldest son's conduct gave him many a sleepless night.

But George was impervious to scandal. He had discovered the whole meaning of life; he reiterated constantly to his brothers, equerries and anyone interested that if his parents were too mean to give him his own establishment, no one was going to prevent his living his own life.

His confidant continued to be his brother Frederick, who listened avidly to accounts of George's adventures and began to have a few of his own.

The awkward situations which often accompanied these adventures bothered the Prince very little. There were scandals about him; he had discovered a taste for women older than himself—even Harriot had been a few months older—and his fancy often alighted on those who were married. This could mean jealous husbands, for there were some men who failed to appreciate the honour done to the family by the Prince's favouring one of its women. There was no lack of aspirants for his favours and this meant that envy prevailed among those whom he passed over towards those whom he favoured.

After the dullness of his boyhood he found life full of excitement—and he determined to enjoy it.

There were several people who had their eyes on him—apart from women. It was natural that politicians who were out of favour with the King and were extremely ambitious should have the notion of forming a rival faction. It would not be the first time there had been a King's party and a Prince's party; and now that the latter was growing up the time seemed to have come to make plans. Moreover, no one could deny that the Prince was intelligent. There had never yet been such a cultured member of this branch of the royal family. The Prince had taken to learning with alacrity. Perhaps because there had been so little excitement in his boyhood he had sought it in books. The fact remained that he was well versed in the classics, was a good linguist, had a ready wit and was clearly of a very different intellectual calibre from his father.

One man who was watching him with the greatest interest was Charles James Fox. Fox was perhaps one of the most brilliant men in politics and it was galling to him to see the King and Lord North throwing away the American colonies through policies which, it seemed obvious to Fox, were misguided and foolish.

'The King,' Fox had said, 'lowers his head like a cow and goes on chewing the cud, regurgitating over and over again: "They'll come to their senses." If only he would come to his.'

Fox was thirty years old—leader of the Whigs, distrusted by the King—and not only for his political opinions. Fox knew the story of Sarah Lennox. He could remember the consternation in the family when the King's marriage to Charlotte was announced. His mother had been Sarah Lennox's sister and the whole family had naturally hoped the King would marry Sarah. That it was largely Sarah's own fault that he had not, did not relieve the family anguish. Sarah was a foolish girl—her conduct now was proving that; but she could have been Queen of England with a little careful manoeuvring, for the Foxes would

have been a match for the Dowager Princess of Wales and Lord
Bute at any time. But Sarah had lost her chance and George had
married Charlotte. And this was something for which George
could not forgive the Foxes. Every time he set eyes on Sarah's
nephew he thought of Sarah, and quite clearly was resentful
because he had had to take the plain dull Charlotte instead.

'Why he should dislike me,' Charles James told his friends,
'would be inconceivable but for the fact that to do so is in accordance with accepted human behavior. I, with my parents and
the rest of the family, would have been delighted to see Sarah
Queen.'

But the King was a simple man and not accustomed to delving
into the innermost recesses of his mind to understand his own
motives. He merely said: "I can't abide that fellow Fox.' And
never asked himself if his dislike had anything to do with the
loss of Sarah.

Charles James knew that he would never be the leader of the
House if the King could help it, and although the King was
dependent on his ministers, the King's favour was of the greatest
importance to the members of his government.

So the wily Fox had turned his eyes to the young man who
was just emerging into the limelight. If the King would have
none of him, why not cultivate the Prince? Why not *educate* the
Prince in politics. Why not revive the old custom—so prevalent
in the Hanoverian dynasty—of setting son against father. There
could be, as there had been before, the King's party and that of
the Prince of Wales; and as every wise man knew it was more
intelligent to attach one's wagon to the rising rather than to the
setting star.

The Prince was breaking out of his shell; he was indulging
in amatory adventures to the tolerant amusement of the cynical
members of the Court, and although a small part of these rumours reached the ears of his parents and their staid supporters,
very little could be done to prevent the princely exploits. The
Prince was as much a prisoner now as they could make him—
still he managed his secret intrigues. But when he was eighteen
they could scarcely treat him as a child of twelve. The people
would never allow that. And George was only a few months
from his eighteenth birthday.

When he did appear in public the people cheered him wildly.
George was all they expected a prince to be. With his powdered
hair setting off the pink and white of his complexion and making
his eyes look more blue than ever he was indeed a Prince Charm-

ing. Silver buckled shoes, coats of blue and pink satin, white buckskin breeches . . . He was a joy to behold. And while he was young and handsome the people would love him; and was it not always the case that after a period of Puritan rule the people adored a rake? And young as he was, George was show-ing all signs of fast becoming that.

'Reflect,' said Charles James Fox to his friend Edmund Burke, 'how the people welcomed the restoration of Charles the Sec-ond. How they adored him when he promenaded in St. James' Park a mistress on either side and more following behind. And how they loathed poor dull Noll Cromwell because he was a faithful husband and a Puritan. So do they feel about His vir-tuous but oh so dull and just a little stupid Majesty.'

Burke agreed with Fox, but Fox was not going to leave it at that. He had an idea, and like most of his ideas it was a brilliant one.

It was natural that since the King showed no favour towards him he should be on good terms with those who had a grudge against His Majesty and his mind immediately went to the Cum-berlands.

Henry, Duke of Cumberland had, under the influence of his Duchess, the lady whose eyelashes had brought her fame and fortune, smarted under the King's neglect. The King did not wish to see his brother Henry. Whenever he thought of him he remembered the disgusting affair with Lady Grosvenor, and phrases from those very revealing letters which Cumberland had written to the lady, and which betrayed such eroticism as the King had scarcely known existed, haunted his nightmares in which to his dismay women figured so prominently. No, the King could not bear to see Cumberland. It was different with his brother William, Duke of Gloucester, who had made another mésalliance, it was true, by marrying Lady Waldegrave, but although this lady was illegitimate and a milliner's daughter, Gloucester's life was comparatively respectable. Moreover, the King had always been very fond of Gloucester.

This state of affairs made the Cumberlands even more re-sentful, and it was to them that Charles James Fox decided to turn.

He called at the Cumberland House where he was always a welcome guest. Fox was a witty conversationalist, a high liver, a gambler, an amorist—in fact he indulged freely in all the fleshly vices. At the same time he was the cleverest politician in the country and while the Cumberlands could attract such men to their house their parties could be the most amusing in town. Moreover, they could give not only offence but anxiety to the King.

Fox, a stubble on his double chin, for over-indulgence in food and drink had made him fat in spite of the fact that he was only thirty years of age, his coat slightly splashed with grease from his last meal, for he made no concessions to royal dukes, arrived at the Cumberland House, his mind full of the project.

The Duchess, fluttering her long lashes, received him boisterously. There was nothing regal about the Duchess. Her conversation was amusing and droll and not untouched by coarseness, but she was a very beautiful woman.

The Duke was with his wife—a small man with the loose Hanoverian mouth and the rather bulging blue eyes. Charles James had little respect for his intelligence—the Duchess had more—but his position as uncle to the Prince of Wales made him important.

He believed that Fox had come for a gamble, for the politician was a gambler by nature and could never resist a game of chance, but Fox quickly disillusioned him.

'I have come to talk to Your Highness of your nephew.'

'George!' cried the Duchess. 'There is no talk of anything but George. What a rascal the boy is becoming! He'll soon be a rival to his uncle.'

The Duke grinned at her.

'I hope someone will warn him not to write letters,' continued the irrepressible Duchess. 'Love letters can be costly when those who receive them are no longer in love.'

The Duke laughed at this reference to the Grosvenor case. 'Is everyone going to go on talking of that forever?'

'I'm sure it is what His Gracious Majesty holds against you . . . far more than your marriage to me.'

'The Prince will need guidance,' said Fox.

'He'll get it,' laughed the Duke.

'Never fear, dear Mr. Fox,' went on the Duchess. 'Papa keeps him in his gilded cage and Mamma has tied his reins very firmly to her apron strings.'

'All's very well while he's a minor. Your Highnesses forget he will soon be eighteen. Then we shall see changes.'

'Changes!' mused the Duchess. 'He has shown very clearly the way he will go. Ladies, short and tall, fair and dark will lead him by the hand. And, Mr. Fox, is it not charming of him to prefer beautiful English women . . . not like his ancestors who like ugly German ones.'

'He is behaving . . . naturally,' said Charles James. 'Of course he is up in arms against his father.'

'Which does not surprise me,' put in Cumberland.

'It would surprise me if it were otherwise,' said the Duchess. 'The King has treated our Prince like a naughty child in the past and is continuing to do so . . . in spite of the fact that he has shown the world so clearly that he is in possession of his manhood. I don't know the number of seductions to date . . .' She glanced at the Duke. 'Perhaps you do, my darling. But they are too many for a boy. Our Prince is a man.'

'The last one is a rather amusing story,' said the Duke. 'It concerns a certain married lady of the Palace. Yes, His Highness is finding married ladies very much to his taste.'

'Preferring experience to innocence,' added the Duchess. 'Wise young man.'

'There very nearly was a mighty scandal over this affair,' said the Duke.

'There very nearly always is a mighty scandal. Don't look so disappointed, Mr. Fox. We'll have our mighty scandal pretty soon, I promise you.'

'It'll come,' agreed Fox. 'And then he must have someone to turn to . . . someone to help him.'

'He'll get his reproaches from the Queen and a lecture from the King, who'll tell him he wishes he could use the cane on him as he did when he was a bad boy.'

'Alas for the dignity of the Prince of Wales!'

'You've heard what happened, eh?' asked the Duke, and when Mr. Fox and the Duchess declared they had not he proceeded to tell them.

'The Prince's affaire with the lady was proceeding according to the usual pattern. The lady was living on amicable terms with her husband who—unlike some husbands—had no notion of the honour His Royal Highness was doing him by way of his wife. Indeed, he was that kind of a fool of a man who might have resented the honour, so the Prince and his lady refrained from informing him. One day the husband told his wife that he would be away for the night on Palace business, which made an excellent opportunity for the lovers. Alas, the inconsiderate man completed his business that evening and returned at midnight. He was heard knocking at the locked door of his apartment by the Prince who by chance happened to be sharing the connubial bed with the lady.'

The Duchess burst out laughing and cried in delight: '*In flagrante delicto*, I'll be bound. Our future king is such a lusty young dog.'

'Exactly,' went on the Duke. 'But what could he do? Escape was impossible even if he could have scrambled into his breeches in time. Fortunately for the Prince he has loyal attendants, and being of an open nature is apt to confide in them during the various stages of his love affairs. Consequently, one of his gentlemen was aware of the husband locked out and the lover locked in, and knowing precisely what the husband would find if he burst in, took upon himself the duty of releasing his young master from a very embarrassing situation.'

'A good servant,' said the Duchess. 'What was his name?'

'Cholmondeley. You know Cholmondeley.' The Duchess nodded and the Duke went on: 'Cholmondeley went to the husband, told him that the Prince was in some difficulty and he had been asked to summon him to the Prince's apartments immediately on his return that he might be made aware of the Prince's dilemma. Having conducted the fellow to the Prince's apartments Cholmondeley then went to the lady's apartment and released the Prince who hurried off; then Cholmondeley returned to the husband, told him the Prince had retired and that the matter must rest until the morning. And in the morning he told the husband that the matter had been settled and his help would not be required.'

'That is the sort of servant required by all young men who stray into other men's beds while they are away from home,' cried the Duchess. 'Fortunate George. It would be interesting to know what would have happened if Cholmondeley had not been in his confidence and on the spot.'

'Scandal, scandal, scandal and the King would have stormed at his son and suffered more sleepless nights on his account.'

'So all was for the best,' sighed the Duchess. 'The Prince remains blissful in his enjoyment of the lady and the husband in his ignorance.'

Charles James Fox who had been listening without much interest to the story said: 'This brings me to the point of my visit to Your Highnesses. The King cannot long delay giving the Prince an establishment of his own. And when he does, the young man will have his friends . . . not only ladies. He is witty, possessed of intellect and a contrast to his royal father. We will not find our George growing wheat and making butter and buttons. Young George is of a different calibre. When the day comes we should be ready.'

'We?' said the Duchess, her startling black fringed green eyes wide open.

'Yes,' said Fox. He waved his hand. 'Here should be the centre of the Prince's party.'

'You think he'll be a Whig?'

'Certainly, Highness. Is not old George a Tory?'

The Duchess clasped her hands. 'Of course. It is inevitable.'

'His uncle should show an interest in his welfare.'

'And what will H.M. say to that?'

'It will not be the first time Your Highness has acted without the approbation of His Majesty.'

'We'll do it,' cried the Duchess. 'We'll cultivate the acquaintance of our nephew.'

'It will be necessary to go warily.'

'Very,' agreed the Duchess. 'The King won't have us at Court, you know.'

'I know it full well, Your Highness. But the Prince will choose his own friends. He will, I believe, find more to interest him in his uncle's residence than in his father's royal palaces.'

'We should be heading for a real family quarrel.'

'History,' said Mr. Fox cynically, 'has a rather endearing way of repeating itself.'

'A Prince's party to set itself against the King's party,' cried the Duchess. 'We'll do it.'

'I thought Your Highness would wish to,' said Mr. Fox demurely.

George was in love once more. He had found the new paragon in the apartments of his sisters when he had gone to visit Charlotte, Augusta and Elizabeth. He had scarcely been able to talk to them so overcome was he by the charms of Miss Mary Hamilton.

Mary was wonderful. Of all the women he had so far loved there was not one to compare with this new charmer. She had all the virtues and being six years older than he was seemed to him ideal. Nor was she a foolish, simpering girl—as he now thought of Harriot; nor was she a blasé married woman cynically breaking her marriage vows. Mary Hamilton was a pure woman and his love for her was pure.

He confided to his brother Frederick, to Cholmondeley, to

Malden. This was different from anything that had ever happened before. This was a pure affection.

'Do you imagine,' he demanded of Frederick, 'that I wish to seduce this lady?'

Did he not? asked Frederick in surprise.

'Oh, no, you must understand, Fred, this is a *pure* love. But for my station in life I should immediately offer her marriage.'

Was this not a little rash?

In the circumstances, no. This was quite different from any of those other adventures of his.

'Yet at the time . . .' Frederick tentatively pointed out.

'Oh, be silent, Fred. What do you know of love? I have written to her.'

'George, you remember Uncle Cumberland's letters. They cost our father thirteen thousand pounds.'

'Don't mention my Mary in connection with my Uncle Cumberland, I beg of you.'

'But there were letters.'

'Do you think that Mary would ever use my letters against me. Not that I could write as our uncle did. My love for Mary is pure. It will remain so.'

'But will that be very satisfactory?' asked Frederick, who had come to expect a certain line of action from his brother.

George sighed and went on: 'I have written to her telling her that I am in love with a lady of the Court. I have mentioned no names. I have begged her not to be offended by my confidences.'

'Why should she be?'

The Prince of Wales was too blissfully happy to be angry with his brother's obtuseness. If Fred could not see that this was different from anything that had gone before, it was because he was too young to appreciate this strange and wonderful thing that had happened to him.

'I have written to her. You shall read the letter, Fred. I fancy I have a way with a letter.'

Frederick took the paper and read:

'I now declare that my fair incognito is your dear dear self. Your manners, your sentiments, the tender feelings of your heart so totally coincide with my ideas, not to mention the many advantages you have in person over many other ladies, that I not only highly esteem you but love you more than words or ideas can express . . .'

Frederick said: 'But how do you know about her sentiments and the tender feelings of her heart?'

'I spoke with her when I was in our sisters' apartments.'

'But only briefly.'

'My dear Fred, one can fall in love in an instant. I have assured her of my friendship.'

Frederick glanced down at the paper.

'Adieu, dearest Miss Hamilton, and allow me to sign myself him who will esteem and love you till the end of his life.'

Frederick whistled, but George impatiently snatched the paper from him, sealed it and summoned Lord Malden to take it to the lady.

The Duke of Cumberland rode out to Kew, and when he demanded to be presented to the King, none dared dismiss him.

George, being told that his brother was asking for an audience, was uncertain how to act. He thought he had made it clear that he had no wish to receive his brother who had so disgraced the family. And yet how could he send Cumberland away? He shouldn't have come of course. He should have written and, ascertained first that the King would see him.

George paced up and down his chamber. He thought of Lady Grosvenor and the letters Cumberland had written to her. No, he'd not see his brother. Cumberland lived riotously with that Duchess of his and she was a woman he would not receive.

It was sad, of course, that there should be quarrels in the family, but sadder still that members of it should behave as disgracefully as Henry had.

Then George thought of his mother, who had dominated him and with her lover Lord Bute put him into leading strings until he had broken free of them. She had loved him, though; he was certain of that. And she had died so bravely hiding the fact that she was in terrible pain from the cancer in her throat.

'Forgive your brothers, George,' she had said. 'Don't have quarrels in the family if you can avoid it. Your father and his father . . . Your Grandfather and his . . .' Quarrel, quarrel, quarrel . . . Father against son. And it was no good to the family; no good to the monarchy.

Yet he had refused to receive Cumberland although he had accepted Gloucester—but not his duchess.

He called suddenly: 'All right. All right. Tell the Duke I'll see him.'

Cumberland stood before him, a little sheepish, a little truculent. He should be ashamed, thought George, writing those disgusting letters to Lady Grosvenor . . . and making me pay thirteen thousand pounds damages to the woman's husband. And now he had this woman with the fantastic eyelashes. Eyelashes, eh what? thought the King. Who but a fool would choose a wife for her eyelashes?

'Well,' said the King, 'so you've come here to Kew, eh, what?'

'Yes, George. I thought we should make an end to this quarrel.'

So it was George, eh? The brother not the subject. As though it were for him to decide such a matter.

'I said I'd not receive you at Court and I meant it. You understand that, eh, what?'

'At Court, yes. I understand that. I've been involved in scandal, but I am your brother, George.'

'H'm,' grunted the King. 'A regrettable fact.'

Cumberland looked hurt and the King was immediately sorry. 'Scandalous,' he said gruffly. 'Don't you know that? Eh? What?'

'Yes, of course. But it's in the past.'

'And then to marry without consulting me. And those letters.' The King blinked his eyes as though trying to prevent himself seeing those lurid phrases.

'It's over, George. Grosvenor's had his pound of flesh.'

'Yes, at whose expense?'

'You've been a wonderful brother and a wonderful king to me, George.'

The King grunted.

'I've thought a great deal about you. You're a lucky man, George. When I think of your family. Octavius is the thirteenth and the Queen will soon be presenting you with another. A lucky man, George.'

'H'm,' said the King, and thought of young George. What was he up to now? One never knew. And rising eighteen. Something would have to be done when he was eighteen. He'd have to be given a little freedom. And when one considered what tricks he could get up to without it—that was an alarming proposition. Still, he was fortunate to have such a fertile wife even if she lacked eyelashes a yard long.

'I feel deprived, George, not to know my own nephews and nieces. I'd give a great deal to be allowed to visit them.'

Oh, no, thought the King, you are not going to contaminate the children.

'I will conduct you to the Queen,' he said. 'I don't see why you should not pay your respects to *her.*'

Cumberland ostentatiously wiped his eyes. He was succeeding beyond his hopes. He had always known old George was a sentimental fellow. He had told Fox so. It was only because he had made no special effort at a reconciliation that there had been none.

'George, it would give me such pleasure . . .'

'Come this way,' said the King.

Charlotte was sitting at her embroidery, her snuff box beside her, a few of her ladies working with her. She looked startled when she saw her brother-in-law and at a sign from the King dismissed her women.

Cumberland approached her and kissed her hands. 'This is a very happy day for me, Your Majesty,' he said.

'My brother called on me and so I brought him to you,' said the King.

And even as he spoke he noticed how plain she looked and he kept thinking of his brother's wife who, he had heard, was one of the most beautiful women in the country. Charlotte never looked her best during pregnancies—she was so small—and one scarcely saw her otherwise!

It was wrong of him to criticise her for doing her duty. He should be grateful. Cumberland might have a beautiful wife but he did not possess thirteen children and a fourteenth on the way.

'I am constantly hearing of the Prince of Wales,' said Cumberland.

Startled lights appeared in the Queen's eyes. What had George been doing now? What new scandal?

Cumberland saw their alarm and delighted in it.

'The people dote on him. He is so handsome. That is what I hear.'

The Queen breathed more easily. 'He is a very good-looking boy.'

'And a scholar too.'

'He was always good with his books. He speaks several languages fluently.'

'German is one, I hear. Our ancestors all spoke that fluently but George is fluent in French, Italian and English too. And a classical scholar.' Cumberland raised his eyes to the ceiling. 'How did we produce such a genius, George?'

The Queen looked pleased. A discussion of the Prince's perfections always delighted her.

'He's apt to be wild,' murmured the King.

'In that he does not take after his father . . . nor his mother. But it's youth, George, only youth.'

'Then the sooner he grows up the better, eh, what?'

'I am so looking forward to being presented to him.'

The King's lips were set in stubborn lines.

'You cannot see the children,' he said.

'Oh, but . . .'

'I make it clear, eh, what? You cannot see the children.'

Cumberland looked downcast and bewildered. But the King repeated: 'I said you cannot see the children. You heard, eh, what? You cannot see the children.'

Cumberland remembered what a stubborn old mule George had always been. Let him get an idea and there was no moving him. There was something adamant about the way he spoke. So he could do nothing but take his leave and report to Mr. Fox that in spite of being received he had made little headway.

The Prince was developing a great fondness for his sisters and could not let a day pass without visiting them.

'It is pleasant,' said the Queen, 'to know that there is such affection between them.'

Even the King grunted when she told him and said he was glad George was at last realizing his responsibilities.

If they could have seen the Prince's absorption in his sister's attendant they would have felt less satisfaction; but Mary Hamilton was no Harriot Vernon.

She had told the Prince as much.

'No matter what my feelings I should never do anything which I considered detrimental to my honour, Your Highness.'

The Prince had seized her hand and cried passionately: 'Do you think I should ask it? Your honour is more important to me than my own life.'

Chivalry was now the rule of his life and those adventures which had gone before seemed crude and coarse. Pure love was the only true love; it was much better to dally on the road of romance than to reach the climax, for when one did romance very often fled.

Mary was beautiful and so wise, being twenty-three years old, six years his senior. She had enormous eyes, a slightly tip-tilted nose and plump cheeks. She laughed often and infectiously. She was perfect. She admitted to a fondness for the Prince. Was it love? he asked eagerly. Yes, it was love. But not gross love. She would not allow him to demean himself nor her.

Several of the ladies in the Princesses' apartments reminded her of Harriot Vernon.

'The Queen sent for her one afternoon. Within an hour her bags had been packed and she was gone. Be careful, Mary.'

Mary needed no warning. She was going to be careful.

'All that I have to offer you,' she told the Prince, 'is pure, sacred and completely disinterested.'

'I know,' he answered. 'If it were possible I would ask you to marry me.'

'We know full well *that* is impossible,' replied the practical Mary. 'Perhaps you will not be content with what I have to offer.'

The Prince was on his knees. He was fond of extravagant gestures. He asked nothing . . . *nothing* . . . but to be able to serve her for the rest of his life. 'You will forget me in time,' Mary told him sadly.

'Never, never.'

She shook her head wisely. 'If you did forget me I should regret that we ever formed a friendship, but I should not complain.'

'I shall never allow you to leave me,' he declared. 'How could I endure to be parted from one whom I not only love with enthusiastic fondness but dote on and adore beyond everything that is human.'

'It delights me to hear Your Highness express such sentiments, but I must tell you that I could never be your mistress. My honour is dearer to me than my life . . . even than you are to me and . . .'

The Prince interrupted her.

'You need say no more. I would sooner go to immediate perdition than attempt to do anything that would be detrimental either to your reputation or your honour and virtue.'

Mary sighed with happiness.

'Then you truly love me.'

'You could not doubt it. But I must have something. A lock of your hair in a plain setting and on this shall be engraved the date of that most important event . . . your birth. You shall have engraved a message to me and I shall have one engraved to you. Shall I tell you what mine shall be, *"Toujours aimée"* .'

'I think this would be unwise.' Mary was imagining the lock

of hair falling into the hands of Madam van Schwellenburg and being carried to Queen Charlotte. The thought of Harriot Vernon had become an obsession with her. People were dismissed from Court within an hour if they became a nuisance; and the Queen had shown clearly what she thought of those unwise women who allowed the Prince of Wales to become enamoured of them.

The Prince was going on rapturously: 'And you must allow me to present you with a bracelet. Please . . . just a plain one and on it I shall inscribe a message for you. I have decided on it. *"Gravé à jamais dans mon coeur."* '

'This could be dangerous.'

'Dangerous.' His eyes sparkled at the thought. 'I would face the whole world for your sake.'

Maybe, she thought, but he would not be called upon to do so. Possibly only the King, who would reprimand him and tell him to mend his ways. Whereas for Mary Hamilton it would be banishment and disgrace. She did not remind him of this, for she had no wish to spoil the idyll by mentioning such practical matters; but she must never be carried away by the charm of the Prince unless she wanted to rush headlong to ruin.

A passionate but platonic friendship would be delightful, but there it must end.

'You must not be too impetuous,' she warned him.

'Impetuosity. Ardour. No word is too strong to express my feelings. I see beauty, accomplishments . . . in fact everything in you that could make your Palamon happy.'

In his romantic way he had called himself her Palamon and she was his Miranda. And when she thought of the passionate letters—and he loved to write letters, for no sooner did he find a pen in his hand than he must use it, and he enjoyed the flowery sentences which he wrote with ease—she was terrified.

'You must write to me as your sister,' she told him. 'Only then can I receive your letters.'

'No matter what your Palamon calls you, my Miranda, you are the love of his life.'

So fervently did he speak that Mary was deeply touched and a little afraid of her own feelings.

She knew that it was going to be difficult to keep her friendship with the ardent young man on the only possible plane which could ensure her remaining at Court.

* * *

The King's mood had lightened a little. He had been at odds with his government for some time and the friction between them was all due to the disastrous affair of the American colonists.

'I would accept any ministry,' he had said, 'that would keep the empire intact, prosecute the war and treat me with the respect due to the King.'

North was continually pointing out that times had changed. North was a weakling. Always in the background of the King's mind was that blackguard Charles James Fox. Up to no good, thought the King. He likes to plague me. There was a distant kinship between them, because through his mother, Fox was connected with the royal family, on the wrong side of the blanket it was true, for Fox's mother, Lady Caroline Lennox, was the great-granddaughter of Charles II by his Mistress Louise de Quérouaille; and sometimes Fox reminded him of pictures of his royal ancestor.

It was all very disturbing, but he had received news that Admiral Rodney had defeated the Spanish fleet at Gibraltar and that Sir Henry Clinton had had some success in the southern colonies. Fox and his supporters might declare that these were no major victories and it was true that there was nothing decisive about them, but the King was pleased to have news of them and it set his mind at rest a little.

He could go to Kew with a good conscience and give his mind to domestic matters.

What a joy to visit his model farm, to stroll in the country lanes and receive the curtsies of the country women while the men touched their forelocks as they would to any country squire; to visit the nurseries and see the little ones and make sure that Lady Charlotte Finch was obeying his orders with regard to their eating habits; to take the babies on his knee and caress them. Mary and Sophia were adorable; and the elder girls were charming. There at Kew he could be at peace. He could rise early in the morning and light a fire which had been laid for him the night before and then get back into bed and wait until it warmed the room. His servants might laugh at his simple habits but he did not care.

Then he would talk with Charlotte and perhaps walk a little with her in the gardens. She would talk about the children and her Orangerie and how she had found a new way of saving the household accounts.

It was all so . . . soothing.

Of course there was one subject which gave them cause for

alarm—the Prince of Wales—and they must talk of him frequently.

As he sat in the Queen's drawing room alone with her like a simple married couple—he spoke to her of the Prince.

'He is much less wild lately,' said the Queen happily. 'He has become so attached to his sisters. It is most touching.'

'H'm,' grunted the King.

'It is truly so. Augusta tells me he is constantly in their apartments. He is so fond of her and Elizabeth—and so interested in all they do.'

'No more chasing maids of honour.'

'That is all over.'

'I'm glad to hear it. It gave me some sleepless nights.'

He thought of those nights when his imagination had not let him rest, when he had dreamed of women . . . Cumberland's women, Gloucester's women and the Prince's women.

'It was just a little youthful folly, I am sure. He is over that. After all he is so brilliantly clever. Everyone says so.'

'They'll say these things of princes, eh, what?'

'It is true,' insisted the Queen.

'He'll be eighteen soon . . . agitating for his own establishment . . . fancying himself a man. He'll not get it.'

The Queen thought that was a matter for the Parliament to decide, but she refrained from commenting. Long experience had taught her that she was not expected to offer opinions on any political matter—and her eldest son's coming of age was certainly that. All that was expected of her was that she bear children. She might keep her household accounts and had the power to dismiss her maids. That was all.

Perhaps, thought the Queen, if I had not been so busy being a mother I might have insisted on having some say. But it was too late now. George would never allow it; and she was becoming increasingly afraid of upsetting him, for when he was upset his speech grew faster than ever, the 'ehs' and 'whats' multiplied and that queer vague look came into his eyes.

Charlotte was sure that the most important thing was to keep the King calm; and today he was calmer than she had seen him for some time. She must keep him thus.

'We should be seen about together,' said the King. 'Best place to be seen would be the playhouse. We'll have a royal command performance, eh, what?'

'With George accompanying us. That would be an excellent idea.'

'So I thought. I'll send to that fellow at the Drury Lane Theatre. Sheridan, eh?'

'You mean you would command a performance of his play.'

'I don't like the name of it, and I hear it's immodest. The title's enough to tell you that: *The School for Scandal.* It'll have to be Shakespeare, I dareswear. Sad stuff, Shakespeare. Never could see why there had to be all this fuss about it. But it would have to be Shakespeare. The people expect it.'

'Well, you will ask this Mr. Sheridan to submit some plays for your choice.'

'Yes, I'll do this. And we will have a family party, eh, what? Good for the Prince to be seen with us. Friendly, family party . . . I'll send for this Sheridan and when I've chosen the play we'll go the playhouse. It'll show we're a united family, eh? And the Prince of Wales is but a boy yet, what?'

'I think,' said the Queen, 'that it is a very pleasant idea.'

The Prince had shut himself into his apartment in the Dower House to write to Mary Hamilton.

There was one little doubt which was beginning to worm its way into his mind. It was a most romantic love affair this—but he did find that his eyes kept wandering to other personable young women. Not that his eyes had not always thus wandered; but there was a difference. A very disturbing thought had come to him. Would it be very unromantic, while devoting himself to his soulful love, to have a little fun with young women who did not set themselves such a high standard as Mary did?

He dismissed the thought as unworthy. So, this love affair must be perfect. He must stop thinking of indulging in light frivolity with other women. The only one in the world who mattered was Mary Hamilton.

He looked at his reflection in the ornate mirror. It really was a very pleasing reflection. In his blue velvet coat which brought out the blue in his eyes, he was undoubtedly handsome. No one could look more like a prince.

He sat down to write a description of himself to Mary. It would amuse her, he was sure:

'Your brother is now approaching the bloom of youth. He is rather above normal size, his limbs well proportioned, and upon the whole is well made, though he has rather too great a penchant to grow fat. The features of his countenance are strong and manly . . .'

He rose and looked at himself again changing his expression several times, laughing and frowning, looking pleading as he would to Mary and haughty as he would when entering his father's presence.

'. . . though,' he continued, 'they carry too much of an air of hauteur. His forehead is well shaped, his eyes, though none of the best and although grey are passable. He has tolerably good eyebrows and lashes, *un petit nez retroussè cependant assez aimé,* a good mouth, though rather large, with fine teeth and a tolerably good chin, but the whole of his countenance is too round. I forgot to add very ugly ears. As hair is generally looked upon as beauty, he has more hair than usually falls to everyone's share, but from the present mode of dressing it, from the immense thickness necessarily required for the toupees and the length and number of curls it makes it appear greatly less thick than in reality it is. Such are the gifts that nature has bestowed upon him and which the world says she has bestowed on him with a generous hand.'

He stopped to laugh at himself. This *was* amusing. He was beginning to see himself very clearly indeed. But to look in a mirror and write of what one saw was one thing; to assess the character quite another.

He took up his pen.

'I now come to the qualities of his mind and his heart.'

He paused, put his head on one side and began to write rapidly:

'His sentiments and thoughts are open and generous. He is above doing anything that is mean (too susceptible even to believing people his friends and placing too much confidence in them, from not yet having obtained a sufficient knowledge of the world or of its practices), grateful and friendly when he finds a *real friend*. His heart is good and tender if it is allowed to show its emotions. He has a strict sense of honour, is rather too familiar with his inferiors, but will not suffer himself to be browbeaten or treated with haughtiness by his superiors.'

He sighed. What a lot of virtues he seemed to possess. If she believed this Mary would surely find him irresistible. But he would not have her think he was boasting or wished to influence her unfairly. Indeed he would perhaps more likely win her esteem by giving her an account of his faults.

'Now for his vices,' he went on. He hesitated. It was a strong word.

'Rather let us call them weaknesses. He is too subject to give vent to his passions of every kind, too subject to be in a passion, but he never bears malice or rancour in his heart. As for swearing, he has nearly cured himself of that vile habit. He is rather too fond of wine and women, to both which young men are apt to deliver themselves too much, but which he endeavours to check to the utmost of his power. But upon the whole, his character is open, free and generous, susceptible of good impressions, ready to follow good advice, especially when he receives it from so affectionate and friendly a sister as you are.'

He stopped again; the vices had somehow turned themselves into virtues. But that was exactly how they seemed to him. He was a good young man—or he would be to those of whom he was as fond as he was of Mary.

Mary, adorable Mary, who had inspired him with such a noble passion. No wonder he felt good when he wrote to her.

'Adieu for the present. I will finish this in my next. I have been too favourable I fear for my manifold faults, my dearest, dearest Friend; I shall try to correct them, for you shall ever find me ready to lend an attentive ear to your advice. Great imperfections and faults I have, but ingratitude towards you shall never be reckoned among them. My attachment to you shall never cease with my life.'

It was very pleasant to ride in Hyde Park in the company of Frederick. The people recognized him at once and cheered him as he passed. He always acknowledged their acclaim with a bow that was not only gracious but friendly. He wanted them to know that it was his desire to be liked by them. There was nothing of the German about him; he was entirely English. His father was the first of the Georges to speak fluent English, but he had somehow remained a German. There was nothing Teutonic about the

Prince of Wales; he had all the gaiety and charm of the Stuart
side of the family; and the people recognized this in him.

As for Frederick, he was happy as usual to see his brother's
popularity and to take second place, which was one of his most
endearing traits and was one of the reasons why they were the
closest friends.

Now, to ride through the park side by side, made him feel
free. They might have equerries in front and attendants behind
but they could forget them and chat together like two young men
out to take the air, unencumbered.

The Prince was talking of the perfections of Mary Hamilton,
but Frederick was aware that his brother was not insensible to
the charms of some of the ladies who passed by. There were
some beauties. Very different from the young women who made
up the household at Kew—with one or two exceptions of course
like Harriot Vernon and Mary Hamilton. Beautiful ladies in
hoops and feathers, with tight bodices cut low to disclose exquisite necks and bosoms, brocade and silk gowns open in front
or looped as a polonaise to show an ornamental petticoat. They
were rouged and patched and made a brilliant picture in their
big straw hats decorated with flowers and ribbons. And all eyes
were on the elegant Prince who sat his horse so skilfully and
those eyes were so languishing and, yes . . . inviting . . . that
he found his attention straying from his pure love and an excitement possessed him.

'Riding here like this, I feel free, Fred. By God, what the
devil are we doing allowing ourselves to live like children in the
nursery?'

And just at that moment a carriage came bowling towards
them, a very ornate coach bearing the royal arms, and seated in
it was their uncle the Duke of Cumberland who, perceiving
them, immediately called to his coachman to stop.

He alighted and approached the Prince with tears in his eyes.

'Your Highness, my dear, *dear* nephew. Forgive the intrusion, but I cannot pass you by without the greeting due to your
rank when I long to give you a warmer one. When all is said
and done I am your uncle.'

Cumberland! thought the Prince. The rebel. The uncle who
was concerned in the Grosvenor scandal and had such a fascinating wife!

Cumberland had taken the Prince's hand and was kissing it
with emotion.

'And . . . Your Highness Prince Frederick. This is a happy day for me.'

'We are pleased to have an opportunity of speaking with you, Uncle,' said the Prince warmly.

'I knew you would be. I trust this will be no isolated meeting. The Duchess and I have talked of you often . . . with tears in our eyes. We feel for you so much . . . my dear, *dear* nephew.'

Uncle Cumberland was determined to be friendly and the Prince had been right when he had said he was susceptible and ready to accept friendship when offered. Uncle Cumberland had quarrelled with the King and the Prince could well understand that, for his uncle represented the great exciting world outside the royal nurseries. He was implying by his words, his looks and his manner that he felt the Princes were badly treated by the King; they were shut away from the world, treated like children. What could be more humiliating to young men of seventeen and sixteen.

'We hope you will do us the great honour of allowing us to entertain you sometime. There are men . . . and women . . .' Just a little avuncular leer suggesting the delight this could be. '. . . charming men, beautiful women . . . witty, worldly . . . who long to make your royal acquaintance. They have caught glimpses of you now and then . . . in public places, and been enchanted. But it is not enough, nephews, it is not enough. Why at Drury Lane . . . where Sheridan's *School for Scandal* has been playing to packed houses . . . there is the most delightful little play actress I ever set eyes on. Mrs. Robinson is the most beautiful woman in London and London abounds with beautiful women. You should be meeting the world. It's a shame to keep such charm . . . such elegance shut away at Kew. What a coat! What cut! What shoe buckles! I swear I never saw the like . . . Why Your Highness is the leader of the *ton* . . . and shut away at Kew. I have said too much. Why, nephews, I fear I am the most indiscreet man you ever met. But I let my concern for you run away with my tongue . . . and my pleasure too . . . my deep, deep pleasure in this encounter.'

The Duke of Cumberland touched his eye with the corner of his lace kerchief and the Prince of Wales was a little affected too.

'Well, I must not delay you. We are being watched. This will mayhap be reported. I shall be in even greater disgrace. But it's a sad world when a loving uncle cannot have a word with his two handsome nephews. Adieu, my dear, dear boys.'

'Let us rather say *au revoir*,' replied the Prince.

Cumberland kissed first George's hand, then Frederick's; and went back to his coach.

The Prince's eyes were shining as they rode on.

'Why,' he demanded, 'should we be kept shut away? Our uncle is right. We should be out in the world. We should not be living like children. I tell you this, Fred, I'll not endure it much longer. The day is fast approaching when I shall *demand* my freedom. And when I have my rights I shall visit our uncle. It was most affecting, was it not? Why should he be kept from us merely because he fell in love with a woman.'

'Lady Grosvenor was a married woman.'

'Ah, love!' sighed the Prince. 'How can we be sure where it will appear. Is one supposed to wait for it to come *suitably* . . . as our father did with our mother. I hear our uncle's wife is a most fascinating woman, Fred. I should like to meet her.'

'It will never be permitted.'

The Prince pressed his horse into a canter.

'All that, Fred,' he prophesied, 'will shortly be changed. You will see.'

Command Performance at Drury Lane

Richard Brinsley Sheridan, twenty-eight years old, witty, brilliant and the most successful playwright in London and manager of the Drury Theatre, was on his way to Buckingham House for an audience with the King. He knew what this meant: a royal command performance, always good for business. He was well aware that it was no use offering *The School for Scandal*. He laughed inwardly, thinking of some of the epigrammatical gems of that piece, of the screen scene, of his adorable but rather naughty Lady Teazle, and imagining the reception this would get from humorless George and Charlotte.

He was going to offer them *The Winter's Tale*. It would have to be Shakespeare although he knew full well that the King found the great playwright dull. Still, his subjects expected him to see Shakespeare. Shakespeare was respectable, which seemed a little odd to Sheridan as some of the lines came into his mind— but Shakespeare had his place in the literature of the land and his poetry made up for his bawdiness. Any of the Restoration plays with their cynical approach to marriage would be definitely unsuitable for the King.

Arrived at Buckingham House Sheridan was conducted to the King's apartments and in a very short time was granted an audience.

'Mr. Sheridan, it is good of you to come.' The King was always considerate to his subjects, and behaved with an absence of arrogance. The epithet homely was apt.

'At Your Majesty's pleasure,' replied Sheridan with a courtly bow.

'You will have guessed why I asked you to come, Mr. Sheridan, eh, what?' Sheridan was about to speak for one did not realize when first in the King's company that the queries were merely rhetorical. The King went on without a pause: 'We are thinking of coming to the theatre . . . the Queen and myself in the company of the Prince of Wales.'

In the company of the Prince of Wales! Sheridan felt excited. This would indeed be an occasion.

'Drury Lane will be honoured, Sir.'

The King looked pleased. He enjoyed doing good turns and he knew how these theatre people liked a command performance. They were rare. He preferred the opera and a good concert; but it was his duty to see a play now and then.

'The point is,' said the King, 'what will be played for us? It should be something in . . . er . . . good taste, eh, what?'

'The utmost good taste, Sir.'

The King looked quizzically at Mr. Sheridan. He had heard that this young man was a little wild in his habits. There had been some elopement, he believed; though why he should have heard these bits of gossip about a theatre manager he could not imagine. Except of course that Mr. Sheridan had taken the town by storm with that play of his. It was his wife of course. One of the finest singers in the country. Mrs. Sheridan made Mr. Sheridan more respectable in the royal eyes.

'Well,' said the King, 'what would you suggest, Mr. Sheridan?'

'Has your Majesty decided on Shakespeare?'

The King looked scornful. 'Sad stuff . . . most of it,' he said. 'Eh? What?' Mr. Sheridan was pleased not to answer. The King went on: 'But the people of this country seem to have made a god of the fellow. Mustn't say a word against him. He's perfect, so they tell me. I don't see it, Mr. Sheridan. I don't see it.'

'Then, sir . . .' Sheridan's eyes were alight with hope. Why not? Mrs. Abington would have to play Lady Teazle of course. And what a player! And Mary Robinson . . . dear, exquisite Mary Robinson would be Maria . . . as they were before. Mary would want to play Lady Teazle . . . but she wasn't up to the part really . . . lovely as she was to look at; and for all her cruderies Abington was an actress to her finger tips whereas Mary owed her success to that incomparable beauty. Incomparable but not quite. His own Elizabeth, the wife with whom he had eloped . . . had perhaps a greater beauty than Mary Robinson's, but more ethereal. Elizabeth? Mary? Elizabeth would always be first but Mary was so alluring; and a man whose career necessarily brought him into the company of so many desirable women could not be expected to remain faithful to his wife even though she were delightful, understanding, virtuous . . . in fact all that a wife should be. Elizabeth would understand his weakness. But his thoughts were straying. A royal command performance for *The School*. It would be the crowning triumph and what fun to watch the royal disapproval of the wit . . . though would they grasp it? What would prim George and dull Charlotte make of the wittiest play in London? How amusing to discover.

The King had interrupted: 'Yes, it must be Shakespeare, Mr. Sheridan. The people expect it of us.'

Sheridan sighed. 'I believe Your Majesty does not greatly care for tragedy, so I will not suggest *Macbeth*.'

'Can't stand the stuff. People killing each other all over the stage, eh, what? I call that even worse than the rest of the fellow's plays, Mr. Sheridan.'

'Then Your Majesty would perhaps care to see *The Winter's Tale*. A charming story of virtue rewarded, Sir. And we have a very good production of this play. It is a favourite of mine, if Your Majesty would allow me to express my opinion. It is a play for the family, Sir. One could take one's children and not be dismayed.'

'Ah,' said the King. '*The Winter's Tale*. I remember it. A silly story, but as you say nothing to offend.'

'I have an excellent actress in the part of Perdita, Your Majesty. She has been delighting my audiences for some little time and I am sure will please you.'

The King grunted, implying that he was not interested in actresses. But the voices in his head were telling him that he would enjoy seeing this beauty perform.

'She made quite a name for herself as Juliet, Your Majesty; and since then has been a favourite of the public.'

'Good. Then let it be *The Winter's Tale*, Mr. Sheridan.'

'Sir, the players will be enchanted . . . and a little nervous, I dareswear. I shall take the first opportunity of letting them know the honour that awaits them.'

The King smiled, in a good humour. He liked giving pleasure and discussing the visit of his family to the play was more comforting than those interviews with his ministers.

Sheridan went back to his house in Great Queen Street . . . that house which was far more expensive than he could afford. But he was by nature reckless and extravagant.

He went straight to the drawing room, for he knew that he would find Elizabeth there at the harpsichord. She invariably was because it was essential for her to do a great many hours practice a day. She was reckoned by the musical world to have one of the most enchanting voices of all time.

He was right. She was there; and she rose at once to greet him, coming forward her arms outstretched. Even now, her beauty struck him afresh and he had to stifle a feeling of shame for the infidelities he had practised since their marriage. Not that she would not understand. Not that she would ever withdraw the comfort of her serene presence. Elizabeth was a saint—and how could a man like Richard Sheridan live up to the high ideals of a saint?

'Elizabeth my love.' He kissed her hands; he did not have to feign affection; it was there, rising up, swamping all other emotions temporarily whenever he saw her. 'What do you think? I have just come from the presence of His Majesty, King George III.'

'A royal command performance?'

'You have guessed rightly, my dear.'

She drew him on to the sofa and said: 'Come, tell me all about it.' Her lovely face was framed by soft dark hair, the sweet mouth and the lovely long-lashed eyes under delicate but beautifully arched brows, glowed with interest.

Sheridan then gave an imitation of his interview with the King, exaggerating it, mocking both himself and the monarch so that Elizabeth laughed immoderately and begged him to stop.

'The outcome of this historic interview, my love, is that we are to play *The Winter's Tale* for the royal family. And the Prince of Wales himself will be present.'

'This is a sign that the Prince will be seen more frequently in public.'

'Papa holds the knife that will cut the apron strings. It is poised, but the cut has not yet been made.'

'I am sorry for His Majesty. He is so good, really, Richard.'

'Alas for the good! They suffer so much. Unfair of fate is it not? It's the wicked who should suffer.'

He looked at her wistfully and she understood; but she smiled brightly. She would not show him that she often wondered where he was when not at home; that she trembled when she saw the accounts which came too frequently to Great Queen Street. She did not reproach him for those gambling debts which sucked up most of the profits from Drury Lane. But she was constantly worried about money.

'Well, my love,' he said, 'this should bring in the cash. You know what a help these performances are. Everyone will want to see *The Winter's Tale* because the royal family did. And, by God, we need the money.'

She knew it. She helped with the accounts at Drury Lane; and she knew too that they could have lived in comfort—indeed, luxury—but for her husband's wild extravagances.

There could be a way out of their difficulties. She herself could earn money. Her voice could have been her fortune and was on the way to becoming so before her marriage. She had been offered twelve hundred guineas to sing for twelve nights at the Pantheon, but her husband's pride would not allow her to do this.

It was something Elizabeth could not understand. How much more dishonourable to run up bills which one could not pay than to allow one's wife to sing for money. But Richard had his pride. Pride indeed. One of the seven deadly sins. Pride insisted that he must consort with rich men, that he must gamble with them, that he must do all that they did, though they were rich and he must needs earn his living.

But she could not understand Sheridan; she could only love him.

She did not remind him that the theatre was doing well, that he himself had a brilliant future before him. She would have been happy to live as they had in those ecstatic days of their honeymoon in the tiny cottage at East Burnham; but that of course was not what Richard wanted. He needed the gay life of London—the theatrical world, the literary world, the wits, the men and women of brilliance to set off the sparks which lighted his talents.

'It will have to be a superb performance,' he said; and she was astonished at the manner in which he could throw aside all financial anxieties at the thought of the production. 'We must go into rehearsal right away. Nothing but the best, Elizabeth.'

'And will Mrs. Robinson perform?'

He did not meet her eye. He wondered how much she knew of his relationship with the beautiful play actress. He felt angry suddenly. He was a man of genius, wasn't he? She could not expect to apply ordinary standards to him. She should know that however much he strayed he always came back to her. He would never cease to love her; he knew there was not a woman in the world like her. Wasn't that enough? Mary Robinson was beautiful . . . in a different way from Elizabeth. Elizabeth's beauty was of the heavenly variety—'as beautiful as an angel', they had said that of her. But a man of genius must experience the world. He cannot spend his life among angels.

He spoke irritably. 'Of course. Of course. Why not? She's our biggest draw.'

'Of course,' said Elizabeth calmly. 'I merely wondered whether she was experienced enough.'

'Experienced? She's been playing for more than three years. Her Juliet was an immediate success.'

'I see. So she will play Perdita.'

'Perdita it shall be.' He looked at his watch. 'I can't delay. I must tell them of this great honour. We must begin our preparations at once.' He stood up uneasily. Was she wondering whether his affair with the actress was still going on? Did she know it had ever existed?

That was the trouble with these good women. One could never be sure how much they knew because they met all calamity, all disaster and the deceits of others, with a calm tolerance which, although it smoothed out the difficulties of life, could be damnably exasperating.

He embraced her with fervour and her response was immediate. She had sworn to love him and naturally she kept her vows.

'I had to come home to tell my Elizabeth first of all,' he said.

Then he was out of the house and as he called for his chair his anxieties fell from him. It was only when he entered the house that he remembered what it had cost and that a great deal of the furniture was not yet paid for. It was only when he was in the company of his wife that he remembered his sins.

Now to Mary Robinson. He imagined himself telling her the news.

When he had gone Elizabeth returned to the harpsichord, but instead of singing sat silent, thinking of her romantic elopement, of the transcending joy of those days when she had believed that when she and Richard were married they would live happily ever after. At least, she could console herself, she would never be happy without him.

Yet before he had come into her life, she had lived serenely in her father's house where everything was subservient to music. All day long the sounds of music had filled the house. Bath was such a gracious city; often here in London she dreamed of Bath. But Richard must be in London naturally for London was necessary to him. Here he had his theatre and he was in the centre of the gay life; here were the gaming houses, the clubs which he could not resist; here were the brilliant men like Charles James Fox whose company he so enjoyed.

But the old days had been sweet. She smiled to remember singing with her sister Mary; and her brother Tom's playing of the violin when he was in the nursery had been declared nothing short of genius.

And how proud her father had been of his brilliant children—perhaps particularly of her! His 'song bird', he had called her, and she remembered well the day when he had said to her: 'Elizabeth, I believe there never has been a sweeter voice than yours.' How happy that had made her! And she had become famous—or almost—when she had sung in an oratorio before the King. Everyone had been talking of her voice then. And her sister Mary who had a beautiful voice of her own had said it was only a pale echo of Elizabeth's.

Those were happy days when they had all been together in the big house in Bath and their father had taught singing. Then had come that fateful day when Mrs. Sheridan, wife of a teacher of elocution, had come to the house for singing lessons; the friendship between the two families had begun and Richard was a constant visitor to the singing master's house.

She had often thought of going into a convent and when the odious Major Matthews had pursued her and would not be repulsed she had felt the need for the sequestered life more than ever. She had a beauty which almost rivalled her musical talents and she knew that she would be pursued by men. Some in high places had their eyes on her. Horace Walpole had written in one of those letters which so many people seemed to read that the King had been unable to take his eyes from her when she had sung in the oratorio and had ogled her as much as he dared in so holy a place.

A convent promised a blissful retreat in which she could sing holy music for the comfort of its inmates. But Richard was there—the good friend, the gay young man with ambitions of which he talked to her and to whom she was able to confide her desire for the retired life. He was entirely sympathetic and she had wondered how this was possible since his ambitions lay in such a different direction.

When Sir Joshua Reynolds painted her as St. Cecilia she was

famous. None of the angels among whom he had placed her, so it was said, had a sweeter and more angelic face than hers. She was fragile, unworldly; and the desire to go into a convent was greater than ever; and then the doubts had come. Who had planted them in her mind but the young and virile companion of her childhood? What was the attraction between her and Richard? Why should one so worldly find such delight in the company of a woman whose ideal was a convent life?

Major Matthews had come into her life, and even now she shuddered to recall him. How she loathed that man! He was coarse; he was sensuous; and his very remoteness from all that he was made him desire her the more. He was a man of means and persistent and she feared her father would want to make a match for her.

'I must go into a convent,' she told Richard. She knew of a convent in France, and if she could reach it, she was certain she would be given sanctuary there.

Dear Richard. How chivalrous he was! She knew now that he was fighting against his own emotions. He realized the incongruity of a match between themselves; how would such a delicate creature fit in with his ambition? But he could not allow her heart to be broken, her spirit quenched by the hateful Major Matthews. He must save her from that so he had conceived the plan for conducting her to her convent and with only her maid for company and as chaperone they had fled from Bath. It was a mad adventure; and before they had reached London Richard had declared his love for her. At that time it had seemed more important than ambition. And herself? She had made a discovery too. It was not life in a convent she wanted but life with Richard.

'We must marry,' said Richard, 'for even it we did not wish to, now that we have eloped together there is no other course open to us.'

She smiled recalling it; that hasty marriage; the solemn words said before the priest, and no sooner was the ceremony over and they returned to the lodgings Richard had found for them than her father arrived in a great state of agitation, threatened to horsewhip Richard and carried his daughter back to Bath.

'But we are married,' she had insisted.

'Doubtless a mock marriage,' growled her father. 'I know these scoundrels.'

But this was not a scoundrel. This was Richard, the friend of her childhood. Her father must realize this. He did and was somewhat mollified to recall it. He cared so much for me, she thought tenderly. He wanted my happiness above all things. He would never have forced me into marriage with Major Matthews. If she had not been so young and impetuous she would have known that. But perhaps she had deceived herself then. Perhaps at heart she had wanted to elope with Richard, had wanted to marry him all along. Could it be that she had always seen the prospect of life in a convent as an impossible dream?

Richard would always be surrounded by drama. She caught her breath with horror even now as she remembered hearing the news that Major Matthews had challenged him to a duel, that Richard had accepted the challenge and had been wounded. She had wanted to go to him at once but her father had restrained her and Richard had written to her—impassioned letters with that touch of brilliance which playgoers were finding so much to their taste.

And her father . . . her dear father had relented. 'Since you feel as you do, there'd be a proper ceremony and you can set up house together.'

And so they were married in a manner fitting her father's position in Bath; and they went to live in the little cottage at East Burnham.

How many times during the years that followed had she thought of that little cottage and the happiness she had had there! Far more so than in this luxurious house in Great Queen Street. There had been no debts then, no knowledge of what the future with a brilliant man could be like. Romantically innocent she had believed that life would be one long round of bliss.

But he had soon begun to talk of London—wistfully at first. It was his Mecca; it was the centre of the literary world. There was no intellectual life at East Burnham. One *must* be in London.

'And, Elizabeth my love, there is money. It has to be earned you know.' London where the streets are paved with gold, the great city which was waiting to acclaim Richard Brinsley Sheridan, the only place where he could give free play to his talents.

And so . . . goodbye to the cottage where she had been so happy, and to Orchard Street where she learned about debts and witty men who took her husband from his own fireside to clubs where they gambled. To chocolate and coffee houses where men congregated to talk of the events of the day, to read the lampoons which were handed round about the famous and notorious, to laugh at the cartoons. 'To *live*,' said Richard.

It was to her that he read *The Rivals*. She was the first to sit entranced, her hands clasped together, and to call him a genius.

He accepted her verdict. He knew he had genius.

And the people accepted him. They saw *The Rivals* and decided they wanted more of Sheridan. Success came quickly, for he was only in his twenties, and the most talked of playwright and soon . . . manager of Drury Lane.

But oh the debts! The eternal demands for money! Why was it that as he grew more successful his debts increased and the more money he earned the more he needed?

'The company we keep is too grand for us, Richard,' she expostulated.

'Too grand for the Sheridans!'

'We cannot afford to entertain them, Richard. If they need such entertainment shouldn't we tell them it is beyond our means.'

He had laughed at her, lifted her and held her above his head.

'Now you look like an angel . . . looking down on a poor weak mortal. An avenging angel! My dearest St. Cecilia, we cannot reach our rightful place in society unless we mingle with the *ton*. If we did not mingle with the rich and the noble we should soon be relegated to a back seat.'

'It is your plays surely that have made you famous—not your acquaintances.'

But he had laughed at her and said she was his angel; she lived in the rarefied atmosphere far, far above him, so far that she could not see what life was like among ordinary mortals.

And the bills continued to come in and her dowry of three thousand pounds which had once seemed so considerable was quickly swallowed up; and she had asked her father to help them out of their pecuniary embarrassments so many times that she could not bring herself to ask again. She was ashamed to ask, for Richard earned far more money than her father ever had and it seemed so wrong to take his money. When she told Richard this he laughed at her. 'But it is not what one earns that is important, my love. It's what one spends.'

How true . . . how sadly true!

And they could have been so comfortable. She had never wanted luxury . . . luxury that was unpaid for and a reproach to her every time she was aware of it. If she told him that she had been happier in the little cottage in East Burnham he would have laughed that mocking laugh of his. St. Cecilia! he called her. His angel who was too good for ordinary mortal man.

If he would be reasonable . . . if he would give up the worldly life . . . if he would be content to live simply and write his plays . . .

But that was to hope for the impossible. Why had they fallen in love? Why had they not seen that they were so different, that each had their eyes fixed on a different ideal? He was gay, handsome, witty and brilliant—a man of the world. And she asked for nothing from life but her music and his love.

She sighed and turned to the harpsichord.

Yet I would not change him, she told herself. As if I could! For if I changed him he would not be Richard Sheridan—and it is Richard Sheridan whom I love.

Sheridan did not go to the theatre. None of the players would be there at this hour. Instead he directed the chairman to the house of Mrs. Mary Robinson, where the lady's maid, Mrs. Armistead, received him, for Mary Robinson's hired footman had not yet appeared for duty.

His eyes followed Mrs. Armistead as she took him to a small drawing room where he could wait while she went to tell her mistress of his arrival. Mrs. Armistead was so quiet, so discreet, yet one could not help but be aware of her. She was handsome, but in a way which was by no means flamboyant; neatly dressed in her maid's uniform, yet she did not look like a maid. Sheridan had noticed more than once that she walked with unusual grace; and it suddenly struck him that it was her dignity which drew attention to her.

In a short time Mrs. Armistead returned to tell Mr. Sheridan that her mistress would be with him very soon.

'Thank you,' said Sheridan. He was at the point of detaining the woman, but she seemed to sense this and with unhurried dignity left him.

No nonsense, thought Sheridan with a smirk. No flirting with the lady's maid behind the lady's back.

Then he forgot the maid because Mary had come in. He had to admit that every time he saw her she took his breath away. Her beauty burst upon the eye as the sunlight would after coming out of the dark. Mary was a dazzling beauty. Different from the handsome maid—whose looks were of a more subtle nature and had to be discovered gradually; Mary's were so brilliantly obvious that their impact was immediate.

Conscious of the effect she had on people Mary always dressed for the part. Today she wore a pink satin gown, fashionably

hooped and ornamented by a silver pattern. Her hair was dressed
in loose curls and lightly powdered, her exquisite neck and
bosom rather freely exposed.

Sheridan opened his eyes to express the wonder she expected
to see in the eyes of any man; then taking her hand humbly
kissed it.

Mary smiled; she was satisfied.

'Sherry, my dear, *dear* friend.'

'My angel!'

He would have embraced her, but she lifted a hand. Mary
gave herself airs now that she was a well-known actress.

'What an unexpected pleasure to see you at this hour! What
will you take? Coffee? Chocolate? Tea? Wine?'

He would take nothing, he told her; it was enough for him to
drink in her charms.

She laughed—a little refined laugh. Mary was always anxious
that she should be treated as a lady. She liked to think that she
had brought refinement to the stage and as a good business
manager he was ready to humour an actress who had the gift of
bringing in the people. It was enough for them to look at Mary
Robinson, irrespective of the play. And there was no doubt that
she had brought in the nobility too. The Duke of Cumberland
was an admirer, though Mary—wisely perhaps—had resisted all
his offers.

'What brings you, truly? You are not going to tell me that you
could not wait for a glimpse of me at the theatre today?'

'If I told you that it would be true too.'

'Oh, come, come.'

Yes, she was a little imperious. Well, with beauty such as
hers perhaps it was forgivable. Her dark hair was luxuriantly
abundant; her brow was a little high and the deeply set eyes
under the level brows, the straight nose, the perfectly formed
lips, were touched with an air of haunting melancholy which
made her face unforgettable. This was no mere pretty girl. This
was beauty. The contours of her face were perfect; her body
was beautifully proportioned; she moved with the utmost grace;
she was conscious, Sheridan was sure, every minute of the day,
of her beauty.

'Well, my beautiful Mary, there is something else. I was determined to tell you first.'

'A new play?'

He shook his head. A faint irritation had passed across her
face. She had not really forgiven him for not giving her the part

of Lady Teazle. 'Mrs. Abington is so . . . vulgar,' she had declared. Always eager that her refinement should be acknowledged, she invariably called attention to the vulgarity of others.
'Precisely so,' he had retorted. 'That's why it's Abington's part.
Don't forget Lady Teazle was not of the *ton.* You, my dearest
Mary, have only to walk on a stage and everyone knows you are
a lady. And, bless you, you are not a good enough actress to
hide it.' Careful, he had thought. A backhanded compliment.
But one thing he had been determined on: Abington was going
to play Lady Teazle—and not even for beautiful Mary would he
allow his play to have anything but the best. She had not been
reconciled and continued to believe that she had been slighted.

Now he said quickly: 'No, no. Guess again.'

'You are deliberately keeping me in suspense.' She moved to
a sofa and holding out her hand bade him sit beside her.

'Then I will do so no longer. His Majesty sent for me to tell
me that there is to be a command performance.'

'I see.' She was pleased, and tapped lightly with long taper-
ing fingers. A habit, he had noticed, to call attention to them.
They were as perfectly formed as the rest of her. 'And I am to
play before the King and Queen?'

'Of course. How could it be otherwise? And there is something else. The Prince will accompany them.'

There was no sign of melancholy in her face now. Her eyes
sparkled. 'What play?' A terrible fear showed itself. It would
be *The School.* Trust Sheridan to put on his own play. And
Abington would have the better part!

'Shakespeare, of course. His Majesty thinks the "fellow"
wrote "sad stuff" but the people seem to think it's all that's
suitable for royal consumption.'

'Romeo and Juliet?' Juliet had been her first part. He remembered how beautiful she had looked.

'The Winter's Tale. You will be Perdita.'

'Perdita!' She was not displeased, but she was apt to think
Juliet would have been better.

Sheridan disillusioned her. 'Young love in defiance of paren-
tal authority is a sore point with H.M. at the moment. You know
the Prince is apt to give Papa anxious moments on that account.'

She laughed. Perdita. Innocent, wistful, beautiful Perdita.
She was growing more and more excited every moment.

'I have seen him now and then,' she said. 'He's a pretty boy.'

'I feel sure he will be delighted to see *you.*'

Her mind immediately went to costumes. She saw herself in

pink . . . her favourite colour because it became her most. But blue, perhaps. Satin? Velvet?

'We should go into rehearsal immediately,' said Sheridan.

He was looking at her appraisingly. She was even lovelier animated than melancholy, and the most susceptible young man in the country was the Prince of Wales. Surely he would not be able to look on all this beauty unmoved?

Was that what Mary was thinking? She had refused the protection of many rich and notorious men. Suppose . . . But that was looking too far ahead.

He leaned towards her and kissed her lightly.

'Well, think about it, and be at the theatre early. We'll go into rehearsal right away. I want perfection. You must please their Majesties . . . and the Prince . . . Perdita.'

He rose to go and Mrs. Armistead, who had been listening at the door, walked out of sight unhurriedly and with dignity just as he came out of the room.

'Armistead,' said Mrs. Robinson, 'Come here. I'm to play Perdita in *The Winter's Tale*.'

'Is that so, Madam?'

'It's not a bad part.'

'No, Madam.'

'There's something special about this performance though. The King and Queen will be there with the Prince of Wales.'

'That will be a triumph, Madam.'

Mrs. Robinson sighed and looked at herself in the mirror on the wall. She always seated herself so that she could comfortably see into it.

'I am not sure, Armistead.'

'No, Madam?' The cool raising of very well marked brows matched the voice. Armistead was merely respectfully polite to a mistress who wished to confide in her.

'I should never have been a play actress. It is hardly becoming to a lady.'

'No, Madam.'

Mrs. Robinson looked surprised. She had expected contradiction.

'Somewhat higher than a lady's maid,' said Mrs. Robinson, a little tartly.

'Certainly, Madam.'

'And several of my friends have noticed you, Armistead. They say you look too good for a lady's maid.'

'Then, Madam, that makes two of us.'

Mrs. Robinson was a little startled. But then Armistead did startle her now and then. But what an excellent servant she was! Always so discreet! Besides, she could not concern herself with Armistead now. She had Perdita to think of.

The Prince's servants had prepared him for his visit to the theatre and very handsome he looked in blue velvet trimmed with gold embroidery. He was particularly delighted by the diamond buckles on his shoes. All the same he must go with his parents and this in itself was an indication of his position. His father had commanded that there should be a royal visit to the theatre, had chosen the play and selected the date.

What fun it would have been to have strolled into the theatre with his chosen companions: to have gone to see a witty comedy such as *The School for Scandal*. Instead it was to be *The Winter's Tale*. He did not share his father's opinion of Shakespeare, but he would have liked to see a racy comedy of manners all the same, and the fact that his father had chosen the play immediately made him long for something else.

He turned to his equerry Colonel Lake and said: 'I am ready. Let's go.'

Together they went to the King's apartments where his mother received him. Her eyes lit up at the sight of him. This gorgeous glittering creature, her son! She could never see him without recalling the wax image at which she had gazed so often and so fondly. Dear handsome George! In spite of his wildness and all the trouble he caused them he would always be her favourite.

'You look . . . splendid,' she whispered.

'Thank you, Madam,' He wished he could have said the same for her. Pregnant as usual, she resembled a barrel; her face was sallow and she looked old. He thought of Mary Hamilton's rosy face.

Ah, Mary, Mary, I would rather be in my room at the Dower House writing to you than going to the theatre. In one of his pockets he carried the lock of her hair. *'Toujours aimée,'* he thought. Yes, Mary forever. A pure love. If he could have married her that would have been wonderful, but since they could not marry she was right of course to keep their love pure.

The King was ready to leave.

'Ah.' His anxious eyes were on his son. Not so many scandals now, he thought. Settling down, aware of his responsibilities. He could even look with approval on the Prince. He was a handsome fellow, all said and done; and the people liked a handsome fellow. If he would behave reasonably, he would do very well.

People cheered the royal cavalcade as it passed through the streets to Drury Lane. The news that there was to be a command performance at the Lane had been circulating for days and since the Prince was to be present, this won public approval.

At the theatre Mr. Sheridan greeted them. The Prince was interested in Mr. Sheridan. He had heard talk of what an amusing fellow he was—one of the most witty in London; and he certainly liked the look of him, and subtly Mr. Sheridan managed to show that, honoured as he was to receive a royal visit, it was the presence of the Prince of Wales which gave him particular pleasure.

He conducted the King and Queen to their box and the Prince to his.

The theatre was crowded and every eye it seemed was turned not on the royal box but on that one which jutted out over the stage and in which sat the glittering handsome Prince of Wales with his two attendants, Colonel Lake and Mr. Legge.

The curtain went up and the play began.

The Prince was startled. He could not believe his eyes. There on the stage was the most enchanting creature he had ever set eyes on. He could scarcely believe she was real. He could not take his eyes from her. What a figure! It was perfection! Those eyes. Had there ever been such eyes? That dark hair . . . those beautiful teeth, the softly smiling mouth. This was not a woman. This was a goddess.

'Gad,' murmured the Prince. 'The most perfect creature I ever saw in my life. This is perfection. This is beauty. She is a goddess. What charm! What grace! What acting! Stab me—but I would not have missed this for the world.'

He was leaning over the side of the box and Perdita was close to him. She could not help but be aware of him. Beside her was Prince Florizel—but she was far more conscious of the Prince in the box than the one on the stage.

It was as though she spoke to him and not to Florizel. It was as though he were down there on that stage . . . She was his Perdita; he was her Florizel.

He was in a daze of delight. He knew now that he had never been in love before. He would never be in love like this again . . . except of course that he would be in love with Perdita until he died.

When her presence on the stage was not needed, the play had no interest for him, but actresses waited in the wings for their cue and they often contrived to stand where they could be seen by those who had boxes overhanging the stage. So even when she was not playing, he did not lose sight of her, for she stood opposite his box where he might have a full view of her.

It was the custom in the theatre for young men to step up on to the stage while the play was in progress, and make comments on the performance or slip into the wings to exchange a little conversation and perhaps make assignations with the actresses. It was unlikely that anyone would criticize the play while the King was present, but Lord Malden, who greatly admired Mrs. Robinson, could not resist the temptation to mount the stage and slip into the wings.

Malden, a handsome twenty-two—one year older than Mary Robinson—magnificently attired in pink satin and silver, with pink heels on his shoes to match the colour of his coat—was completely visible to the Prince as he chatted with the actress and young George could scarcely bear to sit in his box and see the young viscount in that place where he, above all others, longed to be.

Malden, bewildered by her beauty, was unaware of the jealousy he was arousing, but Mary was fully aware of it and delighted by it. One of the actors had said to her in the Green Room before the performance had started: 'By Jove, Mrs. Robinson, you look more handsome than ever. You will surely make a conquest of the Prince tonight.' And when he had spoken those words and she had caught a glimpse of her reflection, when she realized that it was true, that never before had she looked so beautiful, she had begun to consider what a conquest of the Prince of Wales might mean and the prospect seemed very alluring.

And sure enough there he was, beside himself with jealousy, leaning over the side of the box, paying no attention to the players on the stage, his eyes on her and Malden in the wings while he muttered to his equerries about Malden's great good fortune.

As all eyes were on the Prince, most members of the audience were well aware of what was happening. The King and Queen, however, could not see their son and they were unconscious of his behaviour; what they did realize was the pleasant mood of the audience and the King was congratulating himself that it was a very loyal company.

Perdita came on to play her scene with Florizel and the audience broke into frantic applause, in which the Prince joined, and when she raised her eyes to his box and smiled he was in transport of delight.

'What a night, what a play, what a goddess!' he murmured. 'What a beauty! What Art!' This was said so that she could hear and she blushed becomingly, which delighted him still further.

He could scarcely restrain himself. He wanted to leap on to the stage, to thrust Florizel aside, to cry: 'I am your Florizel from now on—as long as I live.'

When the play was over and the players assembled for the applause, the Prince leaned forward. Perdita lifted her eyes to his and smiled; he inclined his head twice and everything he felt for her was in his eyes.

But it was time to leave the theatre. He was in agony of despair. What was happening back stage? He imagined amorous gallants like Malden storming her dressing room, daring to approach her, talking to her, paying compliments. It was unendurable.

His equerries were waiting. The King was growing impatient. He scowled. He—the Prince of Wales—was not free. He must go home with Papa and Mama like some schoolboy.

He *must* have his independence. It was never so important as now that he had found Perdita, sweet Perdita!

But wait, he thought. I may not see her tonight, but there is tomorrow. And I shall never forget this night.

He spent a restless night. He dreamed of her; he longed for her.

It was no use trying to think of Mary Hamilton. What a child he had been to have imagined that was love. A *pure* love. He laughed. He had grown up tonight, when he had fallen in love with Mary Robinson. He was going to waste no time in letting her know of his devotion.

He was still fond of Mary Hamilton, but this was different; this was real love such as he had never known before.

He would not completely neglect poor Mary. He would still write to her because writing to Mary had become a habit with him. She was after all his dear sister and he her brother.

He could see nothing but Perdita . . . talking in the wings with Malden—pink satin jacket and pink heels! he thought disparagingly, but the rogue had looked handsome and *he* was not treated like a schoolboy—Perdita acting a love scene with the actor who had played Florizel. .

Oh, beautiful Mrs. Robinson, I am a *real* prince. I am your Florizel.

It was impossible to sleep, obsessed as he was by such emotion. So he did what he had done frequently when he needed to be soothed; he wrote to Mary Hamilton. He told her of his visit to the theatre and all that happened there, that on this night he had discovered a goddess. What a comfort for a brother to write to his dear sister.

'*Adieu, adieu, toujours chére,*' he wrote. And added for the sheer thrill of writing that name: 'Oh, Mrs. Robinson.'

Such a tumultuous success must be celebrated and, anticipating it, Mary Robinson had invited a few friends to supper at her house near Covent Garden.

Lord Malden, who was at her side as soon as the curtain had fallen and the royal party had left, begged to be allowed to be her escort, and knowing of his close association with the Prince of Wales graciously she accepted this.

Sheridan was of the party. He was flushed with triumph. The evening had been as successful as the first night of *The School for Scandal*, and he had to acknowledge the part Mrs. Robinson had played in that success.

It was a gay company which assembled in her drawing room. Mrs. Armistead, hovering in the background, never obtruding, noticed a new face among the guests.

We are rising in the world, she thought. Not only Lord Malden but Mr. Charles James Fox himself. Who knows where this might end.

And she was elated, seeing in her mistress's success her own; for Mrs. Armistead knew that she was too handsome, and more important still, too clever, to remain a lady's maid all her life.

Lord Malden whispered to Mrs. Robinson: 'I never saw His Highness so enchanted before, Mistress Perdita.'

And Mrs. Robinson flushed and said he was very young, the dear Prince, and so handsome that she could scarcely believe it was possible.

Everyone was talking of the Prince, how different he was from his father; how elegant, how graceful, how gracious. An Englishman, nothing of the dull German about him.

He was no longer a boy either. They could not keep him in leading strings much longer. And when he attained his majority he would be the most powerful young man in the country.

Mr. Fox was determined to ingratiate himself with the beautiful actress and she was wary of him. She was deeply conscious of his reputation with women; and had no intention of offering him any encouragement—particularly now the Prince had made his interest so clear. It was a pleasant compliment, of course, that the great statesman should visit her house; it meant that everyone of importance would be clamouring for an invitation; especially now that the Prince had noticed her.

Mrs. Robinson felt intoxicated with success and the excitement of the prospect before her.

'You have won on all sides,' whispered Mr. Fox. 'The Queen thought your performance very fine. As for the Prince . . .' He laughed aloud. 'He gave the whole house no doubt of *his* feelings. He could not take his eyes from you. I congratulate you on making the greatest conquest in the world.'

'You are flattering me, Mr. Fox. I daresay he was merely carried away by the play.'

'Carried away by so much beauty, Madam. And it would not be possible to flatter you, for whatever hyperbole one employed one could not praise you more than you deserve. I shall now give a toast to the whole company.'

Mr. Fox had risen and raised his glass. All were silent, listening.

'I give you the Prince—and the beauty and genius he has tonight had the wit to admire. Ladies and Gentleman: the Prince and the fair Perdita.'

The Reflections of Perdita

When the guests had gone and Mrs. Armistead was helping Perdita to bed she lingered over the night toilette longer than was necessary and Perdita did not deter her. It was pleasant to talk with someone—even a lady's maid.

'Madam's success was complete,' said Mrs. Armistead, helping her mistress into her nightgown. 'That much I gathered from the remarks I could not help overhearing from the noble company.'

'Yes, Armistead, the Prince quite clearly enjoyed the play.'

'And admired Madam.'

Perdita laughed lightly. 'He is a very young man.'

'And a prince, Madam.'

'As you say, Armistead, a prince.'

'And the company tonight, Madam . . . it was more brilliant than we usually entertain.'

'It was a special occasion.'

'Madam will no doubt wish to hire a butler if er . . . if we are frequently to have such noble guests.'

Perdita drew her brows together. She had her commitments. A mother, a child and the ever demanding Mr. Robinson who had to be paid to be kept in the background. Her clothes were a vast expense, but necessary, of course, to her profession. A woman with her reputation for beauty must never be seen in public except in the most becoming garments—and these were apt to be the most expensive. But Armistead was right. She would need to hire a butler as well as the footman. If one mingled in high society one must follow their customs. It would never do for them to regard her merely as a play actress. Every

63

moment she must be on her guard that no one should forget she
was a lady.

'I will consider this, Armistead. I think you may be right.'

Mrs. Armistead lowered her eyes and smiled discreetly. She
was looking into the future no less than her mistress.

'Thank you, Armistead.' It was dismissal. And Mrs. Armistead went to her own room where she looked at her face in her
mirror, compared it with that of her mistress, and remembered
the glance that Mr. Fox had sent her way. He was a very dis-
cerning man. It might be possible that he recognized a clever
woman when he saw one, even if she was dressed as a lady's
maid.

How could one sleep on such a night? Perdita asked herself.
From now on she would think of herself as Perdita because
Perdita was a princess—of the rank to match that of a prince.

This was surely the most significant night of her life and all
sorts of glittering prospects were presenting themselves to her.

The Prince was undoubtedly more than ordinarily enamoured. He was young and impressionable and very romantic.
That was what made him so enchanting and the situation so
alluring.

She had heard rumours of palace scandals. Quite clearly he
was interested in women, but from now on he must be interested
in one woman only and to such an extent that he was ready to
go to any lengths for her sake.

Delicious thoughts came into her mind. Impossible, she cried.
But why? Suppose she insisted on marriage. Hadn't the Duke
of Cumberland married the Luttrell woman without the King's
consent? But she was of noble family. And so am I, cried Perdita
angrily. But what was the use of proclaiming it. She had become
convinced that she was the daughter of Lord Northington. Otherwise why should she have been taken to visit him when she
was a child? But of course it was the wrong side of the blanket
and she had had to own Mr. Darby as her father. Well, Cumberland had married without the King's consent—and although
the lady was not received at Court she was married to the Duke
and was a royal Duchess. The Duke of Gloucester had also
married without the King's consent—and Lady Waldegrave was
illegitimate . . . and, it was whispered, a milliner's daughter—
yet that had not prevented her from becoming a royal Duchess
either.

So . . . what of Mary Robinson? What of Perdita?

There was the Royal Marriage Bill which had been brought in not so long ago. And this was the Prince of Wales, the future King. Even Perdita did not believe she could become the Queen of England. Perhaps a morganatic marriage was the answer. She would be the Princess in the beautiful house he would provide for her and to it would come all the most noble and the most brilliant members of London society. And the Prince would adore her; they would have three butlers and six footmen and none of them would be hired!

It was a wonderful dream. It would not be the first time an actress had enslaved a monarch. The Prince was not that yet, but it would come. There had been Nell Gwyn who had enchanted Charles II and had kept her place in his affections from the moment he saw her until he died. Well, if she could not be the wife of the Prince—apart from his station there was also Mr. Robinson, whom she had temporarily forgotten—she would be his cherished and respected mistress, for everyone knew that to be the mistress of a Prince or a King was no disgrace. It was an honour. It would bring the *ton* flocking to her doors; it would mean that the utmost respect was paid to her wherever she went. And her case would be different from that of Nell Gwyn, whom everyone knew was not a lady.

Luxurious thoughts. Was she wise to indulge in them after such as short meeting? Yes, she was certain of it. What a meeting! And everyone had declared that they had never seen the Prince so enamoured. Yes, this was certainly a beginning—from here she would go forward; she would forget everything that had happened to her before this night—all the doubts and fears, the horrors of existence with Mr. Robinson, the great struggle which had brought her to where she was. Mary Robinson was finished; from her ashes had risen the fair Perdita.

But having started to think of the past she could not stop, and scenes which she would rather have forgotten kept coming into her mind, and she saw herself little Mary Darby going daily to school in Bristol and waiting for the return from the whaler on which he was employed, of the man who accepted her as his daughter.

From the first she had given herself airs. Perhaps she had been taught to. Her mother had been very proud of her, very anxious that she should be 'a lady'.

Echoes of the over-refined voice: 'Mary, sit up straight. Don't slouch in your chair. Is that the way a *lady* would sit?' 'Now, Mary, go and wash your hands. Ladies *always* have clean hands.'

That had presented no difficulties. She had been very ready to sit up straight, wash her hands, do anything that a lady would do; for as long as she could remember Mary Darby had been determined to *be* a lady. She had known instinctively whether a dress required a blue or a red sash; she moved with grace; she dreamed fantastic dreams in which her father, some noble lord, came and claimed her and carried her away to his mansion and perhaps to Court. She had heard stories of the royal family, and it was all vitally interesting to her; she had longed to go to London and perhaps catch a glimpse of royalty and the great.

She was a romantic dreamer. She would build up legends about herself; it was inconceivable that she could be the fruit of a union between a Bristol whaler and his wife. Her mother was inclined to foster this belief and now and then gave out dark hints, and when Mary was taken to visit Lord Northington who showed a great interest in her, she was certain that he was her father.

Her mother she accepted, and although she had three brothers—obviously the whaler's children—it was to Mary that Mrs. Darby gave her attention. And small wonder, for Mary was very young when it became obvious that she was going to be a beauty and Mrs. Darby was proud of her daughter.

The boys were of small account. Mrs. Darby spent a great deal of her money on dresses for Mary; and when she visited friends Mary would sing or dance for the company, for she had a sweet singing voice and a natural grace, and if these were not up to professional standards, even as a child Mary had that quality which made people enjoy looking at her.

'You'll have a great future, Mary,' prophesied Mrs. Darby; and Mary would sit and daydream about Lord Northington who, alas, made no effort to claim her.

The family fell on hard times. The whaler went off with another woman and they heard that he had gone to America; he left his family unprovided for, but Mrs. Darby was resourceful; she was connected with the philosopher Locke and she was very proud of this, and from her family came a little financial help without which they could not have managed.

But they could not go on living on their relatives indefinitely and one day when Mary came home from school Mrs. Darby told her that something would have to be done.

Mary was downcast. She smoothed the muslin of her dress—so beautifully white and laundered. She had a picture of them begging in the streets. One could not beg in a muslin dress; one would have to wear something ragged and dirty. She would rather be dead, she decided. She would never suffer the humiliation.

'I could run a school as well as the Mores,' went on Mrs. Darby, for Mary's teachers were the sisters of Hannah More. 'Why not? I'm as well educated. And you could help me and learn at the same time.'

To teach children was not Mary's idea of a career. It was preferable to begging in the streets it was true, but she could feel no enthusiasm for it.

Then her mother said: 'Not in Bristol, of course, where we are known. People would never come to us. We should have to start afresh somewhere.'

'Where?' asked Mary.

The reply enchanted her. 'London, I think.'

London! Chelsea in fact. She could see the school clearly now. There were never enough pupils, but they had not made a bad job of it. Her mother proved to be an excellent teacher—as for herself . . . no one would have guessed she was only thirteen years of age. She looked sixteen . . . possibly seventeen; she already had a well-developed figure and her face was growing more beautiful with every day.

Then her father came home. He had tired of his mistress and thought he would spend a little time with his family. With him came a captain in the navy who promptly did what men were to do from then onwards, fell in love with Mary. She shuddered to remember her innocence. What had she been taught of life and what time had she had to learn! She was thirteen and a half. She had perhaps been a little attracted by the captain. She could not remember very clearly now; and all her memories were rose tinted so she saw rather as she would like it to have happened than as it had.

His embraces! His compliments! So rare then, so common-place now. His talk of marriage and the grand life they would have. He had known how to tempt Mary, and he had almost succeeded in seducing her. Not quite, she insisted, and shut her eyes tightly so that she could not remember too clearly. Then it had been discovered that he was already married, that he had told her lies, had no intention of marrying her as he promised to do, and his one goal was the seduction of this tender maiden.

'A fortunate escape,' murmured Perdita. 'Oh, what a fortunate escape!'

Mr. Darby, after having left his wife and family to fend for themselves, suddenly decided to be righteously indignant because they had done so. He would not have his wife and daughter working, so the school, which had begun to be fairly prosperous, was closed and Mary was sent to a school in Chelsea which was run by a Mrs. Lorrington. This lady was fond of the bottle, but when she was not under its influence was a very good teacher and she took an immediate interest in the strikingly lovely young girl who was so eager to learn.

At Mrs. Lorrington's Mary worked hard, received encouragement and learned fast; not only did she work at her lessons, but in deportment and elocution, for both of which she had a natural flair.

Her mother watched her development with pride and the utmost interest. Mr. Darby, too, was interested in his daughter and, with a little prompting from his wife, agreed that she should go to Mrs. Hervey's Finishing Academy at Oxford House in Marylebone. And there she had met . . . what was the name of the man? He in himself was of little importance to her, except for the fact that he was the ballet master at Covent Garden and had introduced her to David Garrick. Hussey! That was his name. He had taught dancing at Mrs. Hervey's school and had immediately singled her out as his most promising pupil.

She remembered the day he had brought in Mr. Garrick. A somewhat irascible old man he had seemed to her, although she had been overawed by his fame. Very somberly dressed in brown he did not look in the least like any of the great romantic roles he had played in the past. He had been running Drury Lane then, for it was just before Sheridan had bought his share in it. He had grunted at her and made her recite and sing and dance and then he had walked away as though disgusted with her. She had felt so depressed that she had gone home and wept and her mother had been very angry that Mr. Garrick should have failed to appreciate her daughter.

But the next day Mr. Hussey had called her aside from the other pupils and told her she could be a very fortunate girl if she was prepared to work hard because Mr. Garrick—although he found her raw and in great need of tuition—thought that there might be a small talent in her and he was prepared to give her a chance.

What a different story she had to take home on that day. But Mrs. Darby was immediately thrown into a fluster. The theatre! But was it the profession for a lady? She was not at all sure. She was in a terrible dilemma. Mr. Darby had disappeared again, having gone to America, and before he had gone, so impressed was he by the beauty of Mary which was growing more and more obvious every day that he had threatened Mrs. Darby with dire punishment if any ill should befall her.

'I do not think ladies become play actresses,' she reiterated.

'But what should I become, Mother? What *can* I become? Should I teach in school?'

'No, that is no good either. Oh dear. With looks such a yours . . .'

'Mamma,' implored Mary, 'we must be practical. Some actresses have done very well. If one is clever . . .'

'You are not yet sixteen. I should die of fear every time you went to the theatre. You are too young.'

'One must begin. It is really a great stroke of good fortune. Mr. Hussey tells me that Mr. Garrick said I might be trained to play Cordelia to his Lear.'

'How I wish I knew what to do.'

And then Thomas Robinson appeared. Perdita did not wish to think of Thomas Robinson. How much happier she would have been if she had never heard his name. But at the time her mother had rejoiced in that young man because he seemed to provide the soothing answer to her fears.

Marriage was the answer—marriage to a man with good prospects, a man who would provide for Mary, give her a good establishment, servants and keep her in comfort for the rest of her life. Then this dream of theatrical fame could be thrust aside without regret.

And Thomas Robinson would provide these.

Her mother had heard of Thomas Robinson through an attorney whom she had once consulted, a Mr. Wayman. He assured her that Thomas Robinson was a man with prospects. Although he worked in a solicitor's office, he was no ordinary clerk, and had excellent prospects. His father, Mrs. Darby was assured, was a Welsh nobleman who had sent his son to London because he believed it would be good for him to have something to do. In due course he would inherit a vast estate in Wales and maintain a large establishment in London.

Mrs. Darby's eyes glowed at the thought. It was exactly what she would have chosen for her daughter. As the wife of rich Mr. Robinson there would be no need for her to show off her beauty every night on a stage and have people make all sorts of proposals to her.

The first thing was to arrange a meeting with Mr. Robinson, which the obliging attorney was prepared to do.

And Perdita? How had she felt? She liked to think now that she had viewed the prospect with horror, that she had flung herself on to her knees and implored her mother to allow her to take the more honourable line and play for Mr. Garrick. She liked to picture herself weeping stormily, declaring dramatically that she preferred to sell her talents rather than herself.

And over the span of years . . . it was not really so many yet . . . she had forgotten so much; she had coloured here, tinted there, and even she was not quite sure how it happened. Yet even she could not sketch in pretty pictures of what followed.

She saw the meeting at the Star and Garter at Greenwich. She remembered the dress so well. That was the one aspect which remained clear to her in every detail. It was more pleasant to think of the dress—an evening dress, long and flowing, of pale blue lustering; and a big chip straw hat swathed with the same material as her dress.

Thomas Robinson had taken one look at her and was in no doubt. He was conscious of the many eyes turned in their direction—all in homage to the young girl's beauty. Endless possibilities, thought Thomas Robinson, whose greatest ambition was, she had quickly discovered, to live in luxury with the smallest possible personal effort. Through the rich clients who came to his office and a knowledge of the difficulties in which they became entangled he saw a way in which this way of life might be accomplished through a wife of such extraordinary beauty.

So he was eager for the marriage. He was chivalrous and attentive, not only to Mary but to her mother. He visited their home; he made casual references to the family estate in Wales; he talked of running an establishment in London and the names of certain well-known noblemen were scattered lightly throughout his conversation until Mrs. Darby was all impatience for the wedding, and when Mr. Robinson suggested it should take place immediately, she agreed with alacrity.

It was an April day—five years ago. Was it only five years? Perdita asked herself. Could one live through a lifetime of misery, despair and horrific adventure in such a short time? It was a wonder that she had come through with her beauty unscathed—and in fact more dazzling than ever.

St. Martin's Church—and Mr. Robinson looking elegant in clothes for which she later discovered he had not paid—a presentable bridegroom, she had thought then; and knowing little

of the obligations of marriage she had not been unduly downcast.

And so she had become Mrs. Robinson.

Before the wedding he had explained that his father would
have to be *prepared* for his marriage. 'Of course once he *sees*
Mary he will be reconciled . . . enchanted as everyone must
be. But just as first we had better not set up house together.'

How gullible they had been. It had all seemed so plausible.
After all, the heirs of vast estate did not marry penniless girls
without some obstacles being raised by their parents. So Mary
would continue to live for a while in her mother's house in Great
Queen Street and he would spend his nights there, keeping on
his lodgings a few streets away. These humble lodgings were
explained by the story that his father wished him to be independent for a short period, and he was proving that he could stand
on his own feet and as soon as possible he proposed to go to
Wales to inform his father of what had happened.

So during those weeks Mary had merely to receive him in her
own bed in her mother's house each night, which was no great
pleasure to her. She was by no means sexually avid, preferring—
now as then—romantic dalliance to consummation, and she
quickly discovered that Mr. Robinson's habits in the bedchamber were far from romantic.

Perhaps she had begun to doubt him before her mother had.
Perhaps some instinct warned her that this was not the way in
which a gentleman behaved. Disillusionment, however, quickly
set in. There was the discovery that Mr. Robinson's prospects
were non-existent. He was soon proved to be a liar, being but
the bastard son of a Welsh farmer who had no intention of leaving him even his small farm; all Mr. Robinson possessed was
his salary as a clerk and it was for this reason that he had been
unable to set up an establishment for Mary; and until he could
raise money through moneylenders to begin his projects, it suited
him that she should continue to live with her mother.

The truth gradually dawned on mother and daughter, but when
they realized the trap into which they had fallen they were, after
the first shock, philosophical.

They had blundered terribly, but they must now make the
best of it.

Perdita closed her eyes now as though by so doing she could
shut out the memories of the next two years—the shameful memories! She put her hands over her face. 'I was so young,' she
kept repeating to herself. Better to forget those years before she

became an actress. She had hated the life. It was . . . she shivered, besmirching. Even so she could not shut out memories of the joy with which she had contemplated a certain new velvet gown, the pleasure in an exquisitely quilted petticoat, or a hat trimmed with feathers or ribbons. It had given her great pleasure to study the reflection of herself in these garments—which would never have come her way but for the life they led. Whenever she went out people looked at her—so many men showed admiration, so many women envy. This was the tribute to her beauty and it was the knowledge of her beauty which maintained her through all her disasters.

Mr. Robinson had rented a house in Hatton Garden and there had 'entertained'. This meant bringing gentlemen to the place and introducing them to his wife. For this privilege he was able to mix in a noble but extremely rakish society, and because of these friendships was given credit by various tradesmen. Mrs. Darby was allowed to come and live with them to save employing more than one servant and running two establishments. Mr. Robinson had no need now to act so he appeared in his true character—a lecherous man without principles, apeing the nobility to which like his wife, he longed to belong.

And for a year or so they lived on the edge of this society. Men like the libertine Lord Lyttelton—something of a politician, artist and poet, was a constant visitor, his object being the seduction of Mrs. Robinson. Another visitor was the notorious rake George Robert Fitzgerald, known as Fighting Fitzgerald, whose object had naturally been the same as that of Lord Lyttelton.

Because of his beautiful wife these men were ready to treat Mr. Robinson as an equal which meant that they allowed him to accompany them to gaming clubs and brothels. Mr. Robinson had very soon betrayed himself as an unfaithful husband—a fact which had not altogether dismayed his wife since it prevented his pressing his attentions on her too frequently, although she deplored the fact that he slept with their slut of a maid.

That had been a curious year or so . . . when they had lived on the edge of society and Mr. Robinson had tried to make a high class prostitute of her. She would never forget the occasion when George Robert Fitzgerald had tried to abduct her in Vauxhall Gardens. She had resisted him and Mr. Robinson had appeared which put an end to the adventure because the last thing Mr. Robinson wanted was to lose his wife.

Such a life could not go on. Her husband must have realized

that. But he seemed not to be able to think beyond each day. Everything began to go wrong; she became pregnant; the creditors began to threaten; Thomas Robinson's luck at the tables ran out.

No, she would not think of it. She had found a way out of trouble. By her own efforts she had provided for herself, her mother, her child . . . and the means of shutting Thomas Robinson out of her life. She was not to blame. She liked to see herself as virtuous, noble, unscathed by these humiliating adventures. And it was so . . . if she shut her eyes to certain moments . . . and she had shut her eyes; she had quickly learned the necessary art of doing so.

Then . . . the end of the gay life, waiting for the birth of her child, the fear every time the bills arrived. So many of them . . . and the child on the way. What could they do? The birth of little Maria was some comfort; the child was enchanting and although Mary had discovered that being a mother could never be her whole life, she loved the child. But the inevitable result of such riotous living had caught up with them and Thomas Robinson was sent to the King's Bench Prison for debt.

She accompanied him there with her child and there was no doubt that he was a chastened man, although she guessed that if he ever were released he would act in the same way as he had before. He was weak and unprincipled; and it was the unhappiest day in her life when she had married him.

When she heard of the success of Richard Sheridan's *The Rivals* she thought of the chance she had had to become an actress for which many ambitious young women would have given a great deal—and which she had foolishly thrown away. For what? Marriage with a rogue who had attempted to thrust her into a life of sin—and finally a debtors' prison.

The misery around her filled her with horror; it was no use now pining for fine clothes, but there was one comfort left to her: her pen. She discovered then that in times of stress it could give her a great deal. She cared for her chid and grew closer to it, and she wrote poetry.

It suddenly occurred to her that if she could publish this poetry, if people would buy it this might be a source of income. It would not provide the means to live the grand life which she had once believed Mr. Robinson would provide for her, but it would at least be dignified. She immediately built up a picture of the salon she would have. She would be the beautiful poetess. With this in mind she wrote feverishly and very soon she had enough poems to make a book. Now she needed a patron; she would not go to a man—she had had enough of men for a while—and she did not want it said that she was patronized for her beauty. She had heard of Georgiana, Duchess of Devonshire, leader of fashion, lover of the arts.

Was it possible to obtain an introduction?

This presented some difficulties, but not insuperable ones. There were some admirers from that fantastic year who would not be averse to helping her now that she had fallen on hard times. She saw the way out of her troubles. When the introduction was made the Duchess was not only impressed by the poems but by the beauty of the poetess, and when the noble lady heard that she was living with her husband in a debtor's prison and had one young daughter she determined to help such a deserving young woman out of her predicament. So the Duchess not only found a publisher for the poems but brought about the release of the Robinsons.

Free! She remembered the first day when she came out of the prison to find her mother, who had managed to keep the home going, was waiting for her.

There was no need now to placate Mr. Robinson, and both women showed their contempt for him. He had her permission, his wife told him, to sleep with any servant girl he cared for; his visits to brothels were no concern of hers; all she asked was that he made no demands upon her, and that was something she would insist upon.

Mr. Robinson replied that he was not at all sure of that; but he had to remember that his wife had brought about his release from prison and that she was not the pretty puppet he had imagined her to be.

She and her mother ignored him, although he inhabited the house. He had gone back to his clerking, but it was not easy to live on his salary.

'I want independence from him,' said Mary to her mother. 'I should like to walk out of this house and never have to see him again.'

That, Mrs. Darby had to admit, would be a desirable state of affairs. But how could it be achieved?

'I shall never make enough money from writing poetry,' said Mary. 'What a fool I was to reject the offer Mr. Garrick made to me.'

'You'll never have another like it,' sighed her mother sadly; the guilt was hers, she admitted freely. She should have known better. One could not expect a fourteen-year-old girl to recognize a rogue . . . but she was a woman and a mother! What would her husband think when he came home. She remembered his threats before his departure! But he did not come home and Mary was right. The need to find money was urgent, for if they did not they would be back in that prison which they had so recently left and they could not expect such opportune deliverance again.

'Why should I not?' demanded Mary suddenly.

'But . . . Mr. Garrick would never give you another chance. He'd think you were a fool to have rejected him before.'

'I heard that Mr. Sheridan is going to buy him out of Drury Lane and take over Mr. Garrick's share in the theatre and that Mr. Garrick, now that he is getting old, will retire.'

'But you don't know Mr. Sheridan.'

'Not yet,' admitted Mary. 'But why shouldn't I?'

Her success with the Duchess of Devonshire had given her confidence. Why should she not offer her services to Drury Lane? It was a way of life—an exciting way of life; she who was so startlingly beautiful, could dance and sing tolerably well, had had elocution lessons and could recite well—and above all had a strong sense of the dramatic. Surely she was a born actress. She was immediately beginning to believe she was and was already preparing herself to convince Mr. Sheridan, and Mr. Garrick if need be, of this.

'I see no reason of why I should not have another chance,' she told her mother. 'I will seek an introduction to Mr. Sheridan.'

'But how?'

'Well, Mr. Hussey introduced me to Mr. Garrick, did he not? I think Mr. Hussey would be inclined to help me.'

And he had been. The ballet master was a little startled when she called on him, but, in the manner of everyone else, completely enslaved by so much beauty.

'A stage career. Why, with looks such as yours you could not fail.'

'If you would do me the favour of introducing me to Mr. Sheridan . . .'

'It is Mr. Sheridan who will be favoured.'

And so to the meeting which was to change her life and to bring her to this night when she could dream of dazzling possibilities which did not seem absurdly out of her grasp.

* * *

The Green Room at the theatre. She could see it so clearly. Was she not familiar with every aspect of it? But then it had been new to her and there was the handsome Mr. Sheridan taking her hand, kissing it and being so charming because she was so beautiful.

So she wanted to be an actress?

Mr. Garrick himself, she told him, had once offered her a chance.

'And you didn't take it?'

'I married instead.'

'The old man will never forgive you that. In offering you a chance to act with him he thought he was giving you the keys to heaven. And you chose . . . marriage.'

'Unhappily.'

Mr. Sheridan was alert. She knew now, because he had told her, that all the time he was weighing her up, and that almost at once he made up his mind that he wanted her . . . for Drury Lane and himself.

No need to hasten over her memories, to close her eyes and glide over the thin ice which could break suddenly and plunge her into horrid memory. From now on it was success.

At the theatre Mr. Sheridan presented her to Mr. Garrick. He had aged since she had last seen him but he remembered her well.

'I offered you a chance in the theatre and you refused it,' he accused.

'It was madness,' she admitted meekly.

'Madness, folly, stupidity. None of these is a quality that makes a good actress.'

'I know.' She was meek and forlorn; but she knew that he would not have bothered to come and see her if he had not thought her worth a little effort.

'Do you know, young woman, that there are thousands of would-be-actresses who would give twenty years of their lives for the chance you had . . . and threw away.'

'I know it well,' she said. 'It was the biggest mistake of my life.'

He turned away from her as though in disgust and said to Sheridan: 'And you want this young woman to play Juliet.'

'At least she'll look the part,' answered Sheridan.

Without glancing at her Garrick muttered: 'Let's hear you. Begin here:

> '*O Romeo, Romeo! wherefore art thou Romeo?*
> *Deny thy father and refuse thy name . . .''* '

She knew it well. How many times since Sheridan had suggested she might play Juliet had she enacted the balcony scene
before her mirror, seeing herself in some diaphanous garment
leaning over the balustrade in moonlight, picturing the gasp of
admiration from the audience when she appeared.

And as she began to say the words she was on that stage; she
was the young girl in love for the first time.

> ' ''*Or, if thou wilt not, be but sworn my love,*
> *And I'll no longer be a Capulet.''* '

And the old man beside her was suddenly transformed. The
most beautiful voice that had been heard in the theatre for years—
perhaps the most beautiful ever—was answering her:

> ' ''*Shall I hear more, or shall I speak at this?''* '

She went on:

> ' '' *'Tis but thy name that is my enemy . . .''* '

Perhaps she was not word perfect, but she was over-dramatic;
she would need a great deal of coaching, but the fire was there.
He carried her through the scene and then she heard him murmur in that glorious voice of his:

> ' ''*. . . all this is but a dream,*
> *Too flattering-sweet to be substantial.''* '

She knew that she must succeed; that she wanted more than
anything to play Juliet and to play her as she had never been
played before.

Romeo, as if by magic, had become Mr. Garrick—no longer
the passionate and romantic lover, but a carping old man.

He said nothing and had started to walk away.

Sheridan walked after him while Mary stood trembling.

'Well?' said Sheridan.

Mr. Garrick stood still and seemed to consider. Mary thought
he was not going to answer.

She ran to him. 'If you will give me a chance I will work, I will study . . . I will learn . . .'

'You'll need to,' said Mr. Garrick; and walked out of the room.

But that was Mr. Garrick's way. He was not unimpressed; and although she was a mere novice he had discovered that sense of drama in her character without which he would not have considered her. But to Sheridan's delight and her unbounded joy Mr. Garrick said he would coach her himself and this meant that she would make her debut at Drury Lane in the exciting and all important role of Juliet.

Juliet! She would remember that night in every detail. It was worth remembering—even her stage fright just before the curtain rose. She had worn pale pink satin trimmed with crêpe and ornamented with silver and spangles; white feathers were in her hair; and for the tomb scene she had appeared in satin with a veil of transparent gauze; there had been beads about her waist on which a cross hung. She did not have to be told that there had never been a lovelier Juliet. This knowledge had carried her through; she was never unaware of her beautiful image and the very thought of it gave her courage.

She had been eighteen—a few years older than Juliet, but she looked like a child in the early scenes; later in the play when she was in love and loved she matured slightly. Garrick had said this miracle must be subtly conveyed; he had made her *live* Juliet, *be* Juliet, the innocent child and the girl who became a woman overnight. And because the genius of Mr. Garrick was such that made all those whom he honoured with his advice determined to please him and win a word of praise for him, she, knowing he was in the audience that night, made up her mind that she would force the old man to admire her.

Oh, the glory of that never-to-be-forgotten-night when she faced an audience for the first time! There had been a moment of silence and then an audible gasp from the audience. It was the expected homage to her beauty; and what better foil could there have been than the ageing figure of the old nurse!

'How now, who calls?'

She had been afraid her voice would fail her but there it was high and clear—the voice of Juliet.

She was launched. This was her métier.

What an evening, with the excitement rising higher with every moment. An audience that would not have missed a word she said, that could not take its eyes from her. It was Juliet's night. It was an enchanted night. It was her night of triumph. She could not but be conscious of this. Mr. Sheridan had caught her coming off the stage and taking her in his arms had kissed her with reckless passion.

'You're wonderful, Juliet. You're all that I knew you would be.'

And she had laughed and been happy. 'The Happiest night of my life,' she had cried; and he had said: 'It's but a beginning. You will see . . . Juliet.'

And back to play and to sense the excitement in the audience . . . on to the last scene in the tomb . . .

> '. . . oh happy dagger!
> This is thy sheath. There rest and let me die.'

The great sigh as she fell beside Romeo's body and lay there.

The play went on . . . and she was thinking: This is the end of our troubles. I shall make my fortune. I shall be a great actress. And I owe all this to Mr. Garrick and Mr. Sheridan . . . and to my own resolution.

> 'For never was a story of more woe
> Than this of Juliet and her Romeo.'

The curtain had come down and the applause was instantaneous.

Up it went and there they all were with herself in the centre smiling, taking the bow.

Flowers were thrown at her feet, exquisitely dressed men were crowding to the front of the stage. Down went the curtains, to howls of protest and up again . . . and there she was alone and the whole of the theatre going wild with joy.

And in the Green Room, later, they had crowded about her. Names she had heard Mr. Robinson mention with awe. There had been Lord Malden, friend and equerry of the Prince of Wales, in black velvet trimmed with gold. 'Mrs. Robinson, it's an honour to kiss your hand . . .'

His Grace of Cumberland had eyed her with appreciation.

The King's own brother! What society she was climbing into! And being paid for it—not falling deeper and deeper into debt.

'His Grace of Cumberland desires to be presented.'

Lecherous eyes examined her. His Grace had never seen a Juliet he so admired. He trusted she would grant him the pleasure of seeing more of her.

Oh no, my lord, she had thought; I must tread warily. You and others will have to learn that even though I am a play actress I am a lady.

Sheridan was watchful of her. He looked upon her as his creation. He had seen her possibilities; he had persuaded Garrick to coach her; she was going to add to his fortune and his personal happiness.

'Mrs. Robinson is fatigued, gentlemen. I know you will wish her to have the rest she so well deserves.'

And so home to the house in Great Queen Street where she had sat with her mother talking of that night and the triumphs to come.

They *had* come, so quickly and in such number, but she would never again know the excitement of that first night. The theatre became her life. Her mother took charge of little Maria; Mr. Robinson lived in the house but he had no say in the running of it now. He had to be quiet; he had better keep out of his wife's life or he might ruin her chances which would be of little use to him, for with her salary she was able to pay his card debts and make him a small allowance which she told him scornfully, added to his salary, would have to suffice for him and his mistresses.

Mr. Robinson was a subdued man. He had been wise to marry Mary; he had always known it; and now he was proving how right he had been. It was disconcerting to be pushed into the background, but at least she provided him with money and he preferred the kitchen sluts to his lady-like beauty.

'The bad days are behind us,' Mary told her mother.

And so it seemed. With each role she played she improved her acting ability and she grew more and more beautiful. The costumes she wore on the stage delighted her and she gave a great deal of thought to them, and whenever a new play was to be put on playgoers would ask themselves what Mrs. Robinson would wear this time. Of one thing they could be certain; it would be unusual and becoming.

She appeared in public places—the Pantheon and the Rotunda, Vauxhall and Ranelagh, always exquisitely gowned, gaped at, stared at, quizzed—the famous Mrs. Robinson, dressed as no one had ever dressed before.

Sheridan delighted in her and she in him. She had found him irresistible and she could never forget that he had given her her chance. To him she confided her troubles; he knew how she was plagued by Mr. Robinson and the fear of what debts he would accumulate; to him she confided of the horrors she had suffered in the debtors' prison. He knew that that memory would never entirely leave her and being the brilliant playwright that he was, he understood Mary better than she understood herself.

She was a born actress; in fact she acted all the time off stage as well as on. Her life story was one big part in which she was always the wronged or admired but always honest and virtuous heroine. Her motives were always what they should have been, not always what they were. He knew his Mary and she fascinated him. Besides, her beauty was unique. He could not compare it with his own Elizabeth's. Elizabeth's was of the soul. Ah, his saintly Elizabeth! He loved Elizabeth, but he was in love with Mary Robinson and, as he would say, he was not a man to pamper himself with noble sacrifice. She became his mistress. She was coy, feigning reluctance. She felt uneasy about this relationship, she told him, because he had a wife.

And she a husband, he reminded her. 'Which makes us eligible.'

'You jest about a sacred matter.' Dear Mary had little appreciation of humour. But he was enchanted with her faults as well as her virtues.

She had met Elizabeth and that, she had declared, filled her with dismay.

He wondered whether Elizabeth knew. He could not be sure. But Elizabeth had become disillusioned long ago. He would have explained that what he felt for Mary Robinson was a transient emotion. His life was bound up with Elizabeth; he was sure he could have explained it to her had she asked. But she did not. At this time she was obsessed by their baby son, young Thomas; that, her singing, reading plays for him which came into the Lane in hundreds from would-be-playwrights, and helping with the accounts. What time had Elizabeth for suspicions?

But perhaps her family would tell her. Her brother Thomas was musical director of Drury Lane and worked closely with its manager. Thomas was a brilliant musician like all the Linley family and had composed the songs for *The Duenna*. Then there was sister Mary, wife of Richard Tickell, who knew almost everything that was going on and was constantly with her sister.

But Elizabeth gave no sign and the affair went on while Mary Robinson rapidly climbed to fame. She and Elizabeth Farren were the leading actresses of the day; when they played people flocked to see them; they were favourites both of the young bucks and the more sober-minded. To the former they were the loveliest girls in Town; to the latter they were ladies. It was the pleasure of both these *ladies* to bring anew refinement to the stage and to show that the theatre could be entertaining without vulgarity.

What days! What triumphs! She remembered her part of Statira in *Alexander the Great* when she had enchanted the house with her Persian draperies of white and blue, her dark hair unpowdered; and she had played Fanny Sterling in *The Clandestine Marriage*, and Lady Anne in *Richard III*. All successes, every one. What a triumph she had scored in *The Relapse* and *All for Love!* and then Viola in *Twelfth Night*. Only one failure and that was not hers. Sheridan had been at his wits' end for a new play and to deceive the playgoers had put on *The Relapse* under the title of *A Trip to Scarborough*. The audience had quickly detected the deception and had immediately expressed their indignation by catcalls and hissing. What a horrible moment—standing there on the stage and for the first time realizing that the audience no longer loved her.

But even that had turned into triumph, for the Duke of Cumberland, who came often to the theatre to ogle her from his box and to see her in the Green Room afterwards, leaned over and shouted to her: 'Don't worry, Mrs. Robinson. It's not you they're hissing. It's the play.' Then Sheridan had come to the front and told the audience they would get their money back and a riot was so averted.

Yes, she could look back on three years of success; and now . . . Perdita.

In future, she told herself, I shall always think of myself as Perdita.

Incident at Covent Garden

Perdita gazed anxiously at herself in the mirror, but lack of sleep had had no effect on her appearance. Her eyes looked brighter and there was the faintest flush in her usually pale cheeks. Well, although she had not slept she had not been tossing and turning with worry. She had been lying still and relaxed in a haze of contentment and excitement—certain that something miraculous was going to happen while she went over the events which had lead up to this day.

Mrs. Armistead would soon arrive to help her dress. How wise she had been to set up this separate establishment with her mother and child not far off so that she could see them frequently, without having them live under the same roof. Of course the pay of an actress was not so great that she could afford many luxuries. Luxury could have been hers had she been prepared to pay for it. The Duke of Rutland had offered her six hundred pounds a year and a smart town house if she would become his mistress. The Duke of Cumberland had promised even greater remuneration. But she had refused them all, explaining to Sheridan: 'What do they think I am? A superior kind of prostitute . . . because I'm an actress?'

Sheridan had helped her write the letters to these noblemen. 'We won't be too severe,' he had told her. 'The theatre can't afford indignant virtue. We'll be a little coy—perhaps hold out hope . . . but not yet . . . not yet . . . This should ensure their regular attendance at the theatre.''

Sherry was a charming rogue. She was ashamed really that she had succumbed to him; but during those early day in the theatre she had needed support. But when she had known Eliz-

83

abeth . . . Yes, that was how she saw it. It was nothing to do
with his refusing her the part of Lady Teazle. It was because of
her refinement of feeling over Elizabeth.

The point was that they remained great friends although they
were no longer lovers.

Mrs. Armistead was at the door—neat and discreet as ever.

'Madam has rested well, I trust?'

'I slept very little, Armistead.'

'It is understandable. What will Madam wear today?'

Perdita was thoughtful. What might happen today? Who could
say? She must be prepared. Pink satin. Blue silk?

Mrs. Armistead had taken out a white muslin dress trimmed
with blue ribbons. It was one of her simplest.

She held it up so that above the dress her own face appeared
and it was as though she were wearing it. What a handsome
creature she would be . . . *dressed*! thought Perdita.

'One of Madam's simplest but most becoming,' said Mrs.
Armistead.

A simple dress for a special occasion. How did she know it
would be a special occasion? It was a feeling in her bones perhaps.

'I will wear it, Armistead.'

And strangely enough Mrs. Armistead seemed satisfied. As
though my triumph were hers, thought Perdita, which in a way,
of course, it was. For if I fell on hard times how should I
be able to employ her, and if rich people come to my house
she might ingratiate herself with some and find herself serving
a lady in a very great household. It would be a blow to lose
Armistead.

'Armistead, you looked very well when you held the muslin
up . . . as though you were wearing it. It would become you.'

'Thank you, Madam.'

'There is that other muslin . . . the one with the lavender
coloured buttons. I caught it . . . and there's a little tear in the
skirt.'

'I saw it and mended it, Madam.'

Oh, excellent, Armistead! It would be a great loss if she went.

'With a little alteration it could be made to fit you. You may
have it.'

'Thank you, Madam.' No show of pleasure. Just a cool thank
you. One could never be sure what Armistead was thinking; all
one knew was that she was the perfect lady's maid.

As soon as Perdita slipped on the white dress she knew it was right for the occasion. *If* there was a visitor she could play the lady surprised in this dress to perfection. A simple morning gown—and in its simplicity as becoming—perhaps more so in the cold light of morning—than satin and feathers.

She waited for Armistead to put on her powdering wrap, but Armistead said: 'Madam's hair worn loosely about her shoulders *unpowdered* is so becoming.'

Of course; she sat at her dressing table and Armistead dressed her hair. A curl over the left shoulder. How right she was.

Armistead stood back to admire her handiwork and Perdita said: 'Thank you, Armistead. Now pray bring me a dish of chocolate.'

Mrs. Armistead scratched lightly on the door. Perdita knew it was a visitor because she had seen the chair arrive.

'A gentleman to see you, Madam.'

'A gentleman, Armistead.' Her heart had begun to beat rapidly. She must calm herself. Could it be . . . Did royalty arrive in a sedan chair? Did it ask humbly to be admitted? She looked down at her hands and went on: 'Is it someone I know, Armistead?'

'Yes, Madam. The gentleman was here last night.'

She hoped she did not betray her disappointment to the watchful Armistead.

'It is my lord Malden, Madam.'

Malden! The young nobleman with whom she had talked in the wings and who had so obviously expressed his admiration for her. He was at least a *friend* of the Prince of Wales.

'Show him in, Armistead.'

Mrs. Armistead bowed her head and retired to return in a few minutes and announce: 'My lord Malden, Madam.'

Lord Malden entered the room and it immediately seemed the smaller for his presence—so elegantly was he dressed. His ornamented coat was frogged with gold braid, his wig curled and perfectly powdered, his heels were lavender coloured to match his breeches. He was indeed a dandy.

His eyes were alight with admiration.

'Your humble servant,' he said, and kissed her hand.

'Lord Malden, it is good of you to call on me.'

'Madam, it is angelic of you to receive me.' He coughed a little as though slightly embarrassed. 'I trust, Madam, that you will forgive . . . the intrusion. My er . . . mission is one . . .'

He looked at her as though he were at a loss for words and she prompted cooly: 'Pray proceed, my lord.'

'It is a mission which I must needs accept . . . having no alternative, as I trust you will believe, Madam.'

'But of course I believe you.'

'And pardon me, Madam.'

'For what, pray?'

'That is what I have to explain.'

'You are intriguing me mightily, my lord. I shall begin to suspect you of I know not what if you do not tell me what *mission* has brought you here.'

He fumbled in the pocket of his coat and brought out a letter.

'I was requested, Madam, to see that this was put into none but your own fair hands.'

She took it. 'Then now, my lord, your mission is completed.'

He was still looking at her rather fearfully and glancing down she saw that 'To Perdita' was written on it.

She opened it; it was brief. Just a few words to Perdita telling of admiration and a desire to see her again and it was signed Florizel.

'Florizel,' she said. 'And who is Florizel?'

'Madam, can you not guess?'

'No,' she retorted. 'Any young gallant might sign himself so. It is not you, I hope, my lord. Did you write this letter?'

'No, I did not.'

'I am surprised that a noble lord should play the part of messenger.'

'Madam, I beg of you do not despise me for doing so.'

'Well, is it not a little undignified to run errands? Why could not the writer of this letter bring it himself? Why should he *send* you.'

'I dared not refuse, Madam. It was a commission from His Royal Highness, the Prince of Wales. He is Florizel.'

She was silent. She was unsure. This was not the manner in which she had expected to be approached. As she had pointed out, Florizel could be anyone. If the Prince of Wales wished to be her friend he could not do so under a cloak of anonymity. Prince Florizel would not do. It must be Prince George.

She handed the letter back to Lord Malden. 'I do not believe it,' she said.

'Madam, I assure you. His Highness brought the letter to me himself. He commanded me to bring it to you.'

'My Lord Malden, there are men in the world who believe

that because one is an actress one cannot be a lady. They stoop to all kinds of tricks to entrap an actress. I wish to know the truth. Who wrote this letter?'

'I *am* speaking the truth, Madam. I would not dare tell you that His Royal Highness had written this letter if it were not so. You should not feel insulted. There is no insult intended. His Royal Highness merely expressed the wish that you will give him an opportunity of making your acquaintance. He was greatly affected not only by your beauty but by your acting. He admires acting, the arts, literature. He is besides being a prince a very cultivated gentleman.'

'To meet the Prince of Wales is an honour, I am sure, but . . .'

'You hesitate, Madam? It is indeed an honour that the Prince should seek acquaintance. Will you write a note in reply? It is what His Highness hopes for.'

She hesitated.

'But surely, Madam. You cannot still be suspicious.'

She looked at him sadly. 'My life has made me so, I fear. If this letter was truly written by His Highness pray tell him that I am overwhelmed by the honour he does me. I can say no more than that.'

Lord Malden considered. Such a message delivered as he would deliver it could imply success. He bowed low and left her.

In his apartments at Kew the Prince was eagerly awaiting the return of Malden. With him was Frederick, to whom he was confiding his new passion.

'You have never seen beauty until you have seen her, Fred.'

Frederick replied that he had heard of Mrs. Robinson's beauty, for rumour did seep into their quarters in spite of their parents' efforts to keep them unsullied by the world. 'I know she is one of the finest actresses in the theatre and one of the most beautiful women in England.'

'It's true,' cried the Prince ecstatically. 'I cannot wait to embrace her.'

'Will she receive you at her house, do you think? You had better be careful this does not come to our father's ears.'

'You can trust me, Fred.'

'It is a little difficult to get away. What if you were wanted when you were visiting? Remember Harriot Vernon.'

'This is quite different.'

'I know it,' replied Frederick, 'but you *were* wanted when you were meeting her, and it *did* become known and she was dismissed because of it.'

'He could not touch her, Frederick. She is not a member of his Court.'

'But you are, George. You could be *forbidden* to see her.'

George's face flushed with fury. 'It's true,' he cried. 'I'm treated like a child. It will have to stop soon.'

'It will stop soon. When you're eighteen, and that's only a few months away.'

'Yes, then I shall have an establishment of my own. Then I shall be my own master. God speed the day.'

Frederick looked out of the window. 'Malden has just arrived,' he said.

The Prince was beside his brother and was in time to see Malden entering the Palace.

'Now,' cried George, all his ill humour vanishing, 'I shall have her answer.'

'You have no doubt what it will be?'

George tried to look serious, but he could not manage it. Of course she would be ready to fall into his arms. He was the Prince of Wales, young, handsome, popular, the most desirable lover in the country. Mary Hamilton had refused to become his mistress purely on moral grounds. He was well aware that she had had difficulty at times in holding out against him.

How different it would be with Perdita.

He was thinking of Florizel on the stage.

> ' . . . but come; our dance, I pray:
> Your hand, my Perdita; so turtles pair
> That never meant to part . . . '

But it was her voice that he kept hearing:

> ' . . . like a bank for love to lie and play on . . . '

How beautiful those words on her lips; what picture they had conjured up in his mind.

Oh, Perdita, why waste time in love scenes on a stage!

And here was Malden. He strode to him holding out his hand.

'Her letter! Her letter! Where is it?'

'She did not write, Your Highness.'

'Did not write! But you took my letter to her?'

'Yes, Your Highness.'

'And what said she? What said she?'

'She was a little inclined to disbelieve.'

'Disbelieve?'

'That Your Highness had written it.'

'But you told her . . .'

'I told her, but as it was signed Florizel she said she could not be sure.'

'Florizel to Perdita. You assured her?'

'Yes, Your Highness, to the best of my power.'

'And she did not answer the letter?'

'She is no ordinary actress, Your Highness, to come quickly when beckoned.' The Prince's face had grown scarlet and Malden hurried on: 'I think she would wish to be wooed. She is modest, Your Highness, and could not believe she was so honoured. She thought it was some gallant playing a trick.'

'So she wrote no answer.'

'She would not do so.'

The Prince was baffled. Malden said: 'I think if Your Highness wrote again . . . wooed the lady a little, assured her that it was indeed yourself . . .'

'So you think then . . .'

Malden was silent.

He himself had had hopes of the lady, being half in love with her himself. It was a little hard to have to plead another man's cause, even if that man were the Prince of Wales.

Malden went on: 'I think, Your Highness, that Mrs. Robinson wishes to imply that she is a lady of high moral character and does not indulge lightly in love affairs.'

The Prince was momentarily exasperated. He had had enough virtue from Mary Hamilton. But almost immediately he was laughing. Why of course. He would not have wished her to give in immediately. She wanted to be wooed. Well, he was capable of doing the wooing. She had had his letter; she had expressed herself honoured . . . if the letter had in truth come from him.

Very well, he would begin the pursuit and in time she would be his.

He was smiling, thinking of future bliss.

Oh, Mrs. Robinson!

The King had come to Kew for a little respite. How much simpler life seemed at Kew. He woke early, looked at the clock and, getting out of bed, lighted the fire which had been laid the night before by his servants.

How cold it was! 'Good for the health,' he muttered, for he talked to himself when he was alone. 'Nothing like fresh air, eh?'

He lighted the fire and went back to bed to watch it blaze. Soon the room would be warm enough for him to sit in . . . comfortably.

Lying in bed, he started to worry. Even at Kew he worried. Yes when he was with his ministers he felt capable of controlling them and the affairs of the country; sometimes when he was in the council chamber at St. James's he would hear his mother's voice admonishing him: 'George, be a king.'

Yes, he would be a king. He would control them all. Nobody was going to forget who was ruling this country. He would like to see that man Fox banished from the House. There he was . . . popping up . . . always ready to make trouble. His father had been a sly one and so was his son. Sarah's nephew, he thought. And there was Sarah mocking him, laughing at him, as clear in his mind's eye as she had been that summer's morning when he had seen her making hay in the gardens of Holland House as he rode by.

His mind went to Charlotte, perpetually pregnant Charlotte. He would lecture her about her health. Not that she needed the lecture, but he wanted her to know that he was concerned for her. And Octavius, the baby; he was fretful. His nurses said that he cried in the night and wouldn't take his food. He would have to work out a new routine for Octavius.

It was more pleasant thinking of the nursery than state affairs, even though all was not well there. There will always be worries with children, eh, what?

But he must remember that he was the King and he was the last man to shirk his responsibilities. This American affair. If only it could be satisfactorily ended. North wanted to resign, but he would not let North resign. If the Government would stand firm he was sure their troubles would be over. But when had a government made up of ambitious men ever been in unison? Men like Fox . . . 'I hate Fox,' he said aloud. He imagined the fellow—apart from all his political fireworks—was remembering the King's folly over his aunt Sarah. Perhaps Sarah had confided in the fellow. After all, although she was his aunt there was not so much difference in their ages and Sarah had lived at Holland House with her sister, who was Fox's mother. Fox was there . . . to put his mischievous finger in every pie; to laugh and sneer and scatter his wit about so that all wanted to know what Fox's latest quip was.

He remembered Fox at the time of the Royal Marriage Bill which he had felt it urgent to bring in after the disastrous marriages of his brothers Gloucester and Cumberland. Fox had been one of those who had opposed it. 'The Bill to propagate immorality in the descendants of George I,' they had called it. Fox had resigned because of it. 'Good riddance, eh, what?' As if the Bill was not necessary—with the Prince of Wales and young Frederick showing themselves as a couple of young fools with their minds always on women. There'd be disaster from that direction if steps weren't taken. Why even he . . . as a young man . . .

There was Hannah coming out of the past to regard him with mournful and reproachful eyes. But Hannah had never been reproachful. She had been too fond of him. Mournful, yes. She blamed herself. He was but a child, she said, when he had first seen her sitting in the window of her uncle's linen-draper's shop. The follies of youth! And yet at the time they seemed inevitable. But he had lived *respectably* with Hannah . . . as respectably as an irregular union could be. And then for her sake and for the sake of his conscience he had committed the act which had haunted him for the rest of his life. The marriage ceremony . . . that was no true ceremony of course . . . and yet . . .

This was dangerous thinking; this could set the voices chattering in his head even more insistently than thoughts of rebellious colonists, the slyness of Mr. Fox, the pleading of Lord North to be released from office.

He guided his thoughts to North—a safer subject. He had always been fond of him; they had played together in the nursery when they were both young children, acted in plays together— for George's father, Frederick Prince of Wales, had been fond of amateur theatricals—and he and North had been so much alike that his father had remarked to North's father that one of their wives must have deceived them and either he or Lord North must be the father of both of them. Now of course they were not so much alike—or George hoped not; North was fat as the King knew he himself would be—for it was a family failing—if he did not take exercise and watch his diet; North had bulging short-sighted eyes which he appeared to be unable to control so that they rolled about aimlessly; he had a tiny nose, but a mouth too small for his tongue, and when he spoke his speech was slurred and he spat unbecomingly. His appearance was almost ridiculous, yet he was a likable man and because they had been friends for so long the King was fond of him. Poor North, he was extravagant and could never live within his means. As Prime Minister, of course, he had great expenses and it had been necessary for the King to help him out of financial difficulties now and then. North on the other hand would come to the King's assistance when he needed money and would prod the Treasury into supplying it. That unfortunate matter of the Grosvenor case . . . Thirteen thousand pounds for those letters Cumberland had written to the woman . . . And now there he was sporting with a different one; the woman with the eyelashes. Mr. Fox, who had raged against the Royal Marriage Act; Hannah and Sarah; Elizabeth Pembroke, who did not belong to the past but who was at Court now; she was a woman to whom his attention kept straying; American Colonies; little Octavius who wasn't strong; the Prince of Wales. All these subjects raced round and round in the King's mind like trapped animals in a cage.

'Careful,' said the King aloud, 'Eh, what?'

But how could he stop his thoughts?

Now his mind had switched to the riots which had broken out in Scotland and had been going on all during the year. A protest against the Catholic Relief Bill to which he had given his assent the year before. He had been glad to do it; he felt that people should be free to worship in the way they wished—as long as they worshipped; he had little patience with those atheists and agnostics or whatever they called themselves. People should go to church; they should obey the commandments; but high church, low church . . . that was a matter for individual conscience. But up in Scotland the low church didn't like it at all. 'No Popery,' they shouted. Troublemakers. Mob mostly. Seriously minded people *discussed* their differences. They didn't go about burning people's houses because they thought differently on certain matters. Ever since he was a young man he had believed in religious tolerance. He had been lenient to all denominations. Quakers, for instance. And there he was back at Hannah.

No, no, go away, Hannah. I must not think of you . . . dare not, eh, what?

'Pray God the riots don't spread below the Border,' he said.

Time to get up. Yes, the room was warm now . . . or warmer. He would devote himself to going through the state papers and then he would go to the Queen's apartment to take breakfast with her.

When he arrived there he found the Queen already seated at the table with Madam von Schwellenburg in attendance. The Kind did not like that woman. He remembered how his mother, when she was alive, had tried to get her dismissed because she felt she had too great an influence on the Queen; but Charlotte had showed herself remarkably stubborn and refused to let the woman go. It was not that she wanted her; it was simply that she clung to the right to choose her own servants. He had decided then that although Charlotte might have some sway over her own household she should have none in political affairs. No, said George. I have seen what havoc women can play in politics. Look at the late King of France, how he had allowed his women to rule him. Madame de Pompadour. Madame du Barry. And look at the state of that country! 'Not very happy,' murmured the King. 'Not very happy. Would not like to see my country like that. Women ruin a country. They shall never lead me by the nose.'

Charlotte dismissed Schwellenburg. The arrogant German woman was quite capable of remaining if she had not done so.

'Your Majesty looks a little tired,' said the Queen solicitously.

'Eh? What? Not a good night.'

'You have been worrying about something?'

He did not answer that question. She was not going to worm state matters out of him that way.

'Your Majesty should take more than a dish of tea.'

'A dish of tea is all I want.'

'But . . .'

'A dish of tea is all I want,' he repeated. 'People eat too much. They get fat. All the family have a tendency to fat. Young George is too fat, eh, what?'

Charlotte's doting look illuminated her plain face. 'Oh, I wouldn't say that. He is well formed and because he is so handsome and fairly tall he can carry a little weight gracefully.'

'No one can carry too much weight with grace,' declared the King. 'I shall have to make sure that he is not eating too much fat on his meat. Pie crust, I'll swear . . . in spite of my orders that they were not to have it.'

'George is nearly eighteen now . . .' began the Queen timorously.

'Not yet. Not yet. He's a minor. He'll have to remember that, eh, what?'

'But of course, of course,' said the Queen hastily.

'Seems to have settled down, eh? Not so much chasing the maids of honour. There hasn't been one to take the place of that Harriot Vernon, has there?'

'Schwellenburg told me that he was very friendly with Mary Hamilton, but I discovered that it was a very *good* friendship. Mary is a good girl and he regarded her as his sister.'

'Sister. He's got sisters . . . five of them. What's he want with another sister?'

'It was a pleasant friendship, that was all. Mary Hamilton is one of the girls' attendants and he saw her when he visited them. It meant he was visiting his sisters quite frequently and I'm sure Your Majesty will agree that is a good thing.'

'Should have gone to see his own sisters . . . not this young woman.'

'They were just friends.'

'You're keeping your eye on him?'

'I wish I saw more of him.' The Queen sighed.

'Send for him then. Send for him.'

'I would like him to come of his own accord. But when he does come, all the time he seems to be thinking of getting away.' The King frowned and the Queen went on hastily: 'Of course he is so young and full of high spirits. I hear that he only has to appear to set the people cheering. In Hyde Park the people nearly went wild with joy when your brother stopped his coach to speak to them. They were cheering George . . . not Cumberland.'

'Cumberland had no right . . .' The King's eyes bulged. 'I've forbidden him to the Court.'

'This wasn't the Court. It was the Park. After all they are uncle and nephew. They could scarcely pass by.'

'Family quarrels,' said the King. 'I hate them. They've always been. I thought we'd avoid them. But I never could get along with Cumberland. It was different with Gloucester. I'm sorry he had to make a fool of himself. But Cumberland . . . I don't want the fellow at Court, brother of mine though he may be.'

'I must say he lives . . . scandalous . . .'

The King spoke bitterly: 'So even eyelashes a yard long can't satisfy him.'

'I've heard some of the women talking about the house he keeps . . . the people who go there. Fox is a frequent visitor.

Do you think because you won't have him at Court he's trying
to build up a little court of his own?'

The King looked at his wife sharply. This sounded remarkably like interference. Any conversation which brought in Mr.
Fox could be highly political. He was not going to have Charlotte interfering. He'd tell her so; he'd make it plain to her. But
for a few moments he gave himself up to imagining the sort of
'court' there would be at the Cumberlands. Men like Fox . . .
Fox was a lecher . . . Fox had all the vices and none of the
virtues; but he was a brilliant politician, and if he was a habitué
of Cumberland's court that could be very dangerous. For where
Fox was other men of affairs gathered.

The King looked distastefully at the Queen. She was not really an old woman . . . thirty-five or so . . . but having spent
some nineteen years in almost continuous child-bearing this had
naturally aged her. Compared with women like Elizabeth Pembroke she was old and ugly. And she was the woman with whom
he was expected to be content while his brother sported on sofas
with Grosvenor's wife and before that matter was settled was
doing the same with a timber merchant's wife and before very
long marrying the woman he had made his Duchess. Not that
he was faithful to her. He was living dissolutely . . . frequenting
gaming clubs, hanging about the theatres in the hope of seducing
every little actress that took his fancy. Disgusting! The King
could not bear to think about it . . . yet he could not stop himself
thinking about it . . . and when he looked at Charlotte . . .
plain, fertile Charlotte sitting there, smug and so obviously with
child . . . he felt bitter against a fate which had made him a king
with a high moral standard who had forced himself to be a
faithful husband all these years to a woman who did not attract
him at all.

'I will deal with this affair of Cumberland,' he said sternly.

'Do you mean you will summon him to an audience?'

'I will deal with him,' said the King finally.

Charlotte looked disappointed. It was humiliating never to
be able to voice an opinion. She would not have believed all
those years ago when she had come here from Mecklenburg-
Strelitz that she could have been relegated to such a position.
She had been quite a spirited young woman when she arrived.
But of course she came from a very humble state to be the queen
of a great country and that had overawed her a little, and just as
she was growing accustomed to that she had become pregnant—
and she had been pregnant ever since.

So she accepted the snub as she had so many others, and, sighing, thought: It is no use trying to change it now. If she attempted to it would anger the King; it would upset him; and the most important thing to her now was not to upset the King. At the back of her mind was a terrible fear concerning him. At times he was a little strange. That quick method of speech, the continual 'eh's' and 'what's. He had not been like that before his illness . . . that vague mysterious illness, the truth of which his mother and Lord Bute had tried to keep from her. But she had known. During it George's mind had become affected. It had passed, but he had never been the same again; and always she was conscious of the shadow hanging over him. Sometimes . . . and this worried her most . . . she thought he was haunted by it too.

So the last thing she wanted to do was disturb the King.

The King changed the subject to the Prince of Wales.

'I think the people liked to see the Prince with us at the theatre.'

'I am sure they did,' replied the Queen, glad to see him more easy in his mind again. 'It was a splendid evening. I thought the players very good. That actress who played Perdita was very pretty.'

'H'm,' said the King. Very pretty, he thought. Too pretty for comfort. He had seen a young man flirting with her in the wings when she was waiting to go on stage and he believed the fellow was attached to the Prince's entourage. He didn't want young profligates who flirted in public with actresses about his son.

He went on: 'The Prince should be seen more often in public with us.'

'I am sure that is so.'

'But I am not sure that I like to see those play actresses parading themselves before young men. I would prefer something more serious. Some good music.'

'I am sure,' said the Queen, 'that would be an excellent idea and far more suitable than a play.'

Now the King was happier. He could settle down cosily to arrange an occasion when it would be most suitable for the King, Queen and Prince of Wales to appear in public.

The Queen smiled contentedly. After all, she had accepted the subservient role all these years, why complain about it now?

She folded her hands in her lap; she would never complain, she vowed if only all the children remained in good health, her

firstborn did nothing to offend his father and the King remained
. . . himself.

The King had sent for the Prince of Wales and when young
George faced his father, the latter thought: He is handsome.
Looks healthy too. A little arrogant. But perhaps we all are
when we know that one day we will wear a crown.

The King cleared his throat. 'Well, well,' he said. 'I hear
you've been meeting your Uncle Cumberland in the Park.'

'We passed while taking the air, Sir.'

'H'm. And your uncle stopped and behaved very affectionately, I hear.'

'He behaved as one would expect an uncle to.' Just faintly
insolent . . . as insolent as he dared be. Resentful too. No doubt
imagined he was a man already. Well, he was not. His eighteenth birthday was months away—and even then he was not
fully of age. The King started to wonder as he often did in his
eldest son's presence why there was always this tension between
them, as though they were enemies rather than father and son.
When had he ceased to regard the Prince as one of the greatest
blessings in his life and seen him as one of his greatest burdens?
He kept thinking of the pink chubby baby who, everyone declared, was a bold young rascal. Spoilt from his birth, thought
the King. The lord of the nursery, charming everyone with his
good looks and his laughter and his arrogance . . . yes arrogance even in those days. But how they had doted on him—he
as well as Charlotte. This Prince who, he thought then, had
made marriage to Charlotte worth while. He had been almost
as foolish about the child as Charlotte, gloating over that wax
image she had had made of him and which she still kept under
a glass case on her dressing table. In the Park people had crowded
round to look at him, to adore him; and he accepted all this with
a cool disdainful gaze of those blue eyes as the homage due to
him but of which he had such a surfeit that it bored him.

And then the others had come along and they had begun to
realize that the Prince of Wales was headstrong, liked his own
way, screamed for it, cajoled for it—and, the King thought
grimly, invariably got it.

The result: the handsome dandy who now stood before him,
seeking to discountenance him because he was young and handsome and George was old and looked his age . . . because he
was a prince who would one day be King and perhaps resented
the fact that he was not already.

There he was working up a hatred of the boy before he had
done anything to aggravate him, except to stand there with insolence in every line of his—the King noted—slightly too fat
body.

'Your Uncle Cumberland is not received at my Court,' said
the King. 'Therefore I find it unfitting that he should stop to
speak to you in the Park.'

'The people seemed pleased that he did.'

'I have refused to receive him at Court.'

'Yes,' repeated the Prince, 'the people were pleased. They
are not fond of family quarrels.'

'Your Uncle Cumberland has shocked the whole country by
his behaviour.'

'I don't think they hold it against him. Perhaps they were
amused.'

How dared he stand there and say such a thing! He was trying
to behave as a man of the world. Why, he was not out of the
nursery yet!

'You should take more exercise,' said the King. 'You've put
on weight.'

The insolent eyes swept the King's figure and the King was
unable to prevent himself straightening up, holding in his stom-
ach. In spite of all his efforts he did have too much flesh there.

'I would not wish the people to think I was starved as well as
treated like a child,' murmured the Prince.

'Eh? What?' demanded the King.

'I said, Sir, that I should not wish people to think I was
starved.'

'H'm.' The King changed the subject. 'The people were
pleased to see us at the theatre together. It was a pleasant evening.'

A dreamy look came into the Prince's eyes. 'A very pleasant
evening, Sir. One of the pleasantest I have ever spent.'

'The play was well done, though it was Shakespeare and not
as good as some.'

'They do other plays, Sir,' said the Prince eagerly. 'There is
Sheridan's *School for Scandal*, and er . . .'

'I don't much like what I hear of that fellow Sheridan.'

'Sir, he's a brilliant playwright.'

'A bit of a profligate, I fear. He has a beautiful wife and I'm
sorry to see her married to such a man.' It was the King's turn
to look sentimental. Elizabeth Linley with the golden voice. He
had heard her sing several times in one of those concerts her

father arranged. A beautiful voice . . . the best he had ever heard; and she looked like an angel herself. One of the most beautiful women I ever saw, he thought. I'd set her side by side with Hannah . . . or Sarah.

'He's a friend of Mr. Fox and I've heard it said they are the most brilliant pair in the whole of London—and act as a foil to each other.'

'Any friend of Mr. Fox is no friend of mine,' said the King shortly. 'I am very sorry to know that Miss Linley has married that fellow. Nor do I wish to go to his theatre. I was thinking of something more suitable.'

The Prince looked scornful. What a fool the old man was! he was thinking. He deliberately turned his back on the people who would be most well worth knowing. No wonder his Court was the dullest the country had ever known. He was not surprised that his Uncle Cumberland tried to set up a rival court. It was time somebody did.

His own turn must come soon. Was that what the old man was afraid of? The Prince's eyes glistened. He thought of the people he would gather round him when the time came. Mrs. Robinson would be there. What joy! what bliss! Mrs. Robinson in pink satin with feathers in her hair—or simply gowned as she had been in some scenes of the play with her dark hair about her shoulders. He was not sure whether he did not prefer her like that than more grandly attired. Oh, no, he preferred Mrs. Robinson any way. It would not matter how she were dressed. Everything she wore . . . everything she did was perfect.

That was why he felt so frustrated. Here he was unable to behave like a Prince . . . and a Prince of Wales at that . . . forced to present himself to his father whenever he was summoned, to stand before him and listen to his drivel about Mr. Fox and Mr. Sheridan. They were the sort of men he would have at *his* Court. Wait . . . just wait until he had his own establishment. It will be when I'm eighteen. I swear I'll not allow them to treat me as a child any longer.

'More suitable,' went on the King, 'and I have sent for you to tell you what I have chosen.'

Sent for you! What *I* have chosen! Oh, it was humiliating!

'I have ordered a performance at Covent Garden—an Oratorio. Handel's setting of *Alexander's Feast*. You will accompany the Queen and myself there.'

'Oh?' said the Prince of Wales and the King thought he detected a trace of insolence in his voice.

'And now I give you leave to go and visit the Queen.'

'Your Majesty is gracious.'

The King studied his son intently; he always felt the young fellow had the advantage because he was quicker with words than he was himself. That was the pity of it, he had turned all his good points to disadvantage—his good looks, his ready tongue, his scholastic accomplishments which far surpassed those of most young men . . . all these were now turned into weapons to use against his father.

'And don't show her how anxious you are to run away, eh, what?'

The Prince bowed. 'I shall, as ever, obey Your Majesty's commands.'

He retired; and the King said of his son what his grandfather George II had said of his: 'Insolent young puppy.'

When the Prince of Wales returned to his apartments he sent for Lord Malden.

'I cannot understand,' he said, 'why Mrs. Robinson will not agree to a meeting.'

'Sir, Mrs. Robinson is a lady of great sensibility. She is not even sure that Your Highness is the author of the notes she has received.'

'But you have told her.'

Lord Malden lifted his eyes to the ceiling. 'She cannot believe it. She still fears that someone may be signing himself Florizel. What if she agreed to meet you in some place and then found it was not Your Highness after all? I think that is what she fears.'

'Then we must put an end to her fears. I will make her sure. I have it. I am to go to Covent Garden to the Oratorio. She must go, too.'

'Your Highness, the King and the Queen . . .'

The Prince laughed. 'My box is opposite theirs at Covent Garden. See that Mrs. Robinson is in the box above the King's and Queen's. There they will not see her, and I can spend the whole evening gazing at her.'

'Your Highness, what if you betray yourself?'

'Malden, I think the King is not the only one who forgets I am the Prince of Wales. I pray you make these arrangements without delay. Go to Mrs. Robinson. Tell her that I beg her to come to Covent Garden and there I will give her reason to doubt no longer that those notes have come from me.'

* * *

'Lord Malden to see you, Madam.' It was the discreet voice of Mrs. Armistead.

'Show him in at once, Armistead.'

Lord Malden appeared, elegant as ever. What a handsome man he was and his eyes told her how much he admired her, and for a moment disappointment swept over her because she feared he might have come on his own account.

He soon reassured her.

'I come direct from His Highness, the Prince of Wales.'

She forced herself to look sceptical.

'Mrs. Robinson, I assure you this is so. His Highness is most unhappy because he fears that by approaching you he has offended you. He wishes to assure you that this is not the case. He would die rather than offend you.'

'I would not wish to be responsible for the death of the heir to the throne.'

'So I thought, Madam. Therefore I hope you will listen sympathetically.'

'If the Prince wishes to write to me why does he not do so in a manner which could leave me in no doubt that he is the writer of the letters?'

'His Highness is romantic. He thinks of you as Perdita and himself as Florizel.'

'So could a hundred other gallants.'

'His Highness is determined that you shall cast away your doubts. That is why he suggests a meeting.'

She was alarmed. She had heard rumours of the Prince's light love affairs. If she met him clandestinely he would doubtless seek a quick consummation; and in a short time she would be known as Mary Robinson, one of the Prince's light-o'-loves for a week or so. Oh, no. She had too strong a sense of her own worth, too much dignity. Nothing like that was going to happen to her, no matter if the Prince of Wales did desire it.

'I could not agree to a secret meeting,' she said firmly. 'I have my reputation to consider. This happens to be rather dear to me, Lord Malden.'

'Quite rightly so,' said the young man fervently. 'But hear what His Highness wishes. You could, I am sure, have no objection to being in a public place where he might see you . . . and give you some sign of his devotion. I am referring to Covent Garden. There is to be a royal occasion. The King and Queen will be there and the Prince begs . . . implores . . . that you will grace the evening with your presence. All he wishes is to assure you by a look and gesture that he is your fervent admirer and the writer of these letters.'

Her first thought was: What shall I wear? She thought of pink satin and discarded that. Blue! Lavender perhaps. She would have a new gown for the occasion. Because of course she was going.

'Did you say the King and Queen will be present?'

'Yes. The King, the Queen and the Prince of Wales.'

'And before the King and Queen . . .'

'Have no fear. Leave all arrangements to me. I will see that all is as it should be.'

'I have not yet made up my mind whether it would be wise for me to come.'

'Madam, I beg of you. The Prince will be desolate: he is beside himself with anxiety because he receives no reply from you. All you have to do is sit in the box I shall choose for you. He will do the rest.'

'You plead his cause with fervour, Lord Malden. If it were your own you could not do so more earnestly.'

'Ah, Madam. Would it *were* my own.'

She laughed lightly. It pleased her to be so admired.

'Well, I do not wish to disappoint . . . er, Florizel.'

Malden kissed her hand. 'Madam, this will make the Prince of Wales a very happy man. I must go to him at once and acquaint him with his good fortune.'

Mrs. Armistead, listening, heard that her mistress was going to the Oratorio. A step forward indeed, she thought. The Prince will not rest until she is his mistress. He himself will come here.

There would be opportunities; and when Mrs. Robinson was at the height of her ambitions—loved by the Prince of Wales—there would be a chance for a woman who was both handsome and clever to climb a little too. Perhaps not to such dizzy heights as her mistress, but . . . perhaps so. For all her dazzling beauty Mrs. Robinson was scarcely wise; whereas her lady's maid made up in wisdom what she might lack in looks—only compared with Mrs. Robinson, of course, because Mrs. Armistead, by ordinary standards, was a very handsome woman indeed.

Her mistress was calling for her. She must show Lord Malden to the door. He scarcely glanced at Mrs. Armistead so bemused was he by the more flamboyant charms of Mrs. Robinson. But it would not be so with all of them.

As soon as he had gone Mrs. Robinson was calling for her.

'Armistead. Armistead. I have agreed to go to the Oratorio at Covent Garden. The King, Queen and Prince of Wales are to be present.'

'Madam will wish to look her best.'

'I thought of lavender satin.'

'Madam will need a new gown for the occasion. Something which she has not worn before.'

'Exactly, Armistead.'

'I think Madam . . . white.'

'White, Armistead!'

'White satin and silver tissue, Madam.'

'But so pale. I shall pass unnoticed.'

'Madam could never be unnoticed. I was thinking that the simplicity of your gown would be a great contrast to the brilliance of your beauty.'

Armistead stood there, eyes lowered—very neat and quite elegant herself in her black gown over which she wore a white apron.

'The touch of colour could come from the feathers in your headdress.'

Mrs. Robinson nodded. 'What colours, Armistead?'

'Well, Madam, that is a matter to which we should give a little thought. This will be a very important occasion and we must make sure that all is just as it should be.'

Mrs. Robinson nodded. Oh, excellent Armistead.

For us both, thought Mrs. Armistead, who was visualizing not so much the scene at Covent Garden but what would follow . . . the great men who would come to this house, among whom would surely be some who would realize the quite considerable charm of Mrs. Armistead.

Covent Garden! A blaze of Glory. Crowds had gathered in the streets to see the royal cavalcade. The Prince of Wales looked magnificent with the glittering diamond star on his blue satin coat. How different from his poor old father and plain pregnant mother!

'God bless the Prince!' the cheers rang out.

The King was pleased. It was good for any member of the royal family to be popular. Good for the monarchy. As for the Queen, she was proud when she heard them calling for her son. 'He is so handsome,' she murmured.

It was a glittering company. Red plush and gold braid and the

finest musicians in the country; and the most notable people in
the land were present.

There was an atmosphere of anticipation engendered by the
implication that now the Prince was growing up there would be
more of this kind of thing, and there was no doubt that it was
what the public liked to see.

'It was a good idea, eh, what?' murmured the King to the
Queen. 'The family . . . in public . . . together . . . in harmony.'

The Queen thought it was a very good idea.

In her box sat Mrs. Robinson, attracting a great deal of attention,
for she had rarely looked so beautiful. Between them she and
Armistead had decided what she would wear. The white satin
and silver tissue had been a brilliant idea, particularly as her
feathers were of the most delicate shade of pink and green.

How much more elegant she looked than some of the women
in their bright colours. She felt the utmost confidence as she
reclined in her box which was immediately above that occupied
by the King and Queen.

And then . . . the excitement. The royal family were in the
theatre. She could not see the King and Queen, but when the
house stood to attention she knew they were there. And almost
immediately *he* appeared in the box opposite her. The handsome
glittering Prince of Wales and for companion, his brother Frederick.

Perdita's heart began to beat very fast for no sooner had the
Prince of Wales acknowledged the cheers of the people than he
sat down and leaning on the edge of the box gazed with passionate adoration at Mrs. Robinson.

It was true, she thought. But of course she had never doubted
it. She had pretended to give herself time to decide how best
she could handle this enthralling but very delicate situation. Now
she could no longer plead suspicion that the letters were written
by someone other than the Prince. He was giving her no doubt
of his feelings.

The music had started but the Prince's gaze remained fixed
on the box opposite and many members of the audience quickly
became aware of this. Whispers! Titters! Who is this at whom
the Prince of Wales is casting sheep's eyes? Mrs. Robinson, of
course, the actress from Drury Lane. The woman who had had
such an effect upon him when he went to see *The Winter's Tale*.

The audience were far more interested in this byplay between the two boxes than they were in the music. They were a very striking pair for the Prince of Wales in his most elegant clothes with the glitter of royalty was the most handsome young man in Covent Garden and Mrs. Robinson was undoubtedly the most beautiful woman. And the point which was so amusing was that all this was going on right under the noses—literally speaking, one might say—of the King and Queen, whom everyone knew kept the Prince so guarded that he found the utmost difficulty in following his inclinations.

The King noticed nothing; he was absorbed by the music. Handel's setting was perfect, he thought. Not a musician in the world to touch him . . . now or at any time.

The Queen, however, was less interested in the music although she thought it was fine. She had an opportunity of gazing in uninterrupted admiration at her adored first-born. How handsome he looked! How proud she was! Frederick was a good looking boy too, but he could not really be compared with George. She thought of his odd little sayings when he was very young. Old-fashioned he had been, never at a loss for a word. And how proud she had been of his ability to master his lessons! He was really brilliant. He had been a little wayward. What child was not? She had been upset when he had been beaten and the King had told her she must not be foolish, for to spare the rod was to spoil the child. The King would now say that even applications of the rod had not achieved that purpose and none was more aware than herself of the growing animosity between father and son.

She tried to catch his eye to send him an affectionate motherly smile but he would not look her way. His eyes were fixed above their box. She wondered why.

He was smiling now; he was making strange gestures. What did it mean? Now he was holding the programme up to his face; he was drawing his hand across his forehead as though in utter despair. Extraordinary! And all this was directed somewhere over their heads.

He had lowered the play bill and cast off his mournful expression; now he was smiling in a manner which might be described as pleading. He was leaning forward and with his right hand was actually pretending to write on the edge of the box in which he sat. What *was* he doing?

The Queen had now lost all interest in the music; like most people's all her attention was centered on the Prince of Wales who continued behaving in this odd manner, pretending to write;

looking as though he were the most miserable of young men one moment and the most joyous the next.

I believe, thought the Queen, he is making signs to someone.

Every now and then the Prince spoke to his brother and Frederick too was gazing as if spellbound somewhere above the royal box.

Then she understood.

The first part of the Oratorio had come to an end. The King turned to the Queen. 'Magnificent!' he said. 'Handel's setting is perfect. Everything he has written has shown his genius. I find this excellent.'

'I have been wondering about the Prince . . .'

'The Prince, eh, what?' The King shot a glance across the theatre. 'He's there. Glad he likes good music. One point in his favour, eh, what?'

'Oh, he likes good music,' said the Queen, 'but he seems to be very much attracted by something above our box. I have been wondering what it can be.'

The King frowned. Then he summoned one of his equerries who had been at the back of the box.

'Who is in the box above ours, eh?' he demanded.

The equerry who had not been unaware of the excitement in the theatre—and its cause—was able to answer immediately: 'It's a Mrs. Robinson, Your Majesty. An actress from the Drury Lane Theatre.'

The King was silent for a few seconds and the Queen watched him fearfully, heartily wishing that she had not called the King's attention to what was going on.

The King was thinking: An actress from Drury Lane! It would be one of those young women he had seen perform not very long ago. And here she was at Covent Garden and the young fool was ogling her so that people were noticing.

The King again summoned his equerry. 'Tell the actress who is occupying the box above this one that her presence is no longer required in this theatre. She is to leave at once.'

The music was resumed and the King's equerry went to tell Perdita that she must leave at once, for this was the order of the King.

Mrs. Armistead was surprised to see her mistress's chair so early. Could she have left before the performance was over? As soon as she opened the door to receive her she had no doubt that something was wrong . . . very wrong indeed.

Mrs. Robinson said nothing but went straight to her bedroom and there tore off the feathers and flung them on to her bed. She stood looking at her angry reflection, her usually pale face under her rouge was scarlet.

Mrs. Armistead was at the door.

'Madam sent for me?'

Mrs. Robinson was too angry to deny it. Moreover, it was a relief to talk to someone.

'Madam is ill. Allow me to help you to bed. The evening was not a success?'

Mrs. Robinson looked at her maid in sudden suspicion. Was the woman too forward? Did she feel that because her mistress was a play actress she could treat her differently from the way in which she could a noble lady? She was ready to suspect everyone of insulting her.

Mrs. Armistead arranged her features into a look of deep concern, which was not difficult since she believed her mistress's success at this stage was her own.

Mrs. Robinson softened towards her. Armistead was a good servant, good enough to be a confidante too.

'I have been insulted tonight,' she said. 'I have been sent out of Covent Garden. Dismissed. Told to leave. As though . . . as though . . .' Her lips trembled. 'I wish to God I had never gone.'

'But, Madam, surely the Prince . . .'

'The Prince could do nothing. In fact I doubt he was aware of it until it was over.'

'Madam!'

'You may well look startled, Armistead. I have never felt so humiliated.'

'But who would dare, Madam?'

'The King's orders. Very simple. His equerry came to my box. "His Majesty's command, Madam. But he has no longer need of your presence here. I have orders to take you to your chair." And he did.'

'Then . . .'

Her face softened. 'The Prince showed too clearly his devotion to me. I admit it was rather obvious. The King must have noticed. Hence my dismissal. I am deeply sorry that I laid myself open to this insult.'

'Madam, I doubt not that this will but increase the Prince's affection for you.'

'I cannot say. But of one thing I am certain. I shall never put myself in such a position again.'

'Tomorrow it will seem less humiliating. Allow me to help you to bed and bring a dish of warm chocolate. It will soothe you.'

Mrs. Robinson sat at her mirror and Mrs. Armistead let down the dark hair and helped her into her bedgown.

'There, Madam. I will have your chocolate ready in a few moments.'

Preparing the chocolate she was thinking: What airs these play actresses give themselves! Does she think the Prince should marry her and make her Queen of England? Did she think the King would give his consent to that! And what of Mr. Robinson? How dispose of him? But I believe our dear lady feels this is not impossible.

She sipped the chocolate. Delicious. Then she took it to her mistress's room.

Mrs. Robinson was sitting up in bed, the angry flush still on her cheeks.

'There, Madam. Drink this.'

She handed her the cup and picked up the dress and feathers which had been flung aside.

'Take those away,' said Mrs. Robinson. 'I never want to see them again.'

In her own room Mrs. Armistead held the white and silver dress against her and studied her reflection. A little alteration would be necessary. She tried the feathers against her own dark hair. Very becoming. Perhaps at some future date . . .

Lord Malden arrived next day. He brought a letter and a package from the Prince.

'His Highness was most distressed by what happened at Covent Garden,' Malden told her. 'The whole company was aware of his anger. When you disappeared from your box he was quite distraught.'

Mrs. Robinson bowed her head, her eyes on the letter which she was longing to read.

Lord Malden handed it to her. It was addressed to 'Dearest and Most Beautiful Perdita' and begged her to meet him. It was signed as usual Florizel.

Lord Malden watched her while she read it and then handed her the packet. She gasped with pleasure when its contents were revealed. There was an exquisite miniature of the Prince of Wales painted by Meyer, delicately coloured, accentuating his good looks. The Prince had cut a piece of paper into the shape of a heart and on one side had written *'Je ne change qu'en mourant'*, and on the other: 'Unalterable to my Perdita through life.'

'Now, Madam,' said Lord Malden, 'have you any doubt of His Highness's devotion?'

She admitted that she had not; but at the same time she did not think it was wise for them to meet.

'His Highness will never accept such a verdict.'

'And if our meeting should come to the ears of the King?'

'Madam, the Prince will be eighteen in August. Then he will have an establishment of his own. He cannot be kept at the Dower House at Kew after his eighteenth birthday.'

'August!' sighed Mrs. Robinson. 'That is a long way off!'

'There is no need to wait until August.'

'You were at Covent Garden, my lord. You saw me ignobly dismissed.'

'Madam, the Prince will never allow you to be banished from his life.'

'I think that until he is of age he will have to obey his father. You should tell him that much as I admire him, greatly as I appreciate his gift, which I shall treasure until the day I die, I must advise caution.'

'Advise caution to a lover, Madam! And such a lover!'

She sighed and turned away. Then gazing at the miniature she smiled tenderly.

And Lord Malden went back to report to his master.

'A Triumph of Chastity!'

Letters and poems were arriving frequently from Florizel and the theme of these letters was: 'When shall we meet?' But Perdita's answers always showed the same evasiveness. The Prince must be cautious; he must remember his rank; he must not offend his father.

'My fate is in the hands of my Perdita,' he wrote. 'My life is yours to save or ruin. Your Florizel.'

Carefully she preserved the letters, reading them over and over again, soothing her hurt vanity through them; dreaming that this chaste romantic idyll would go on all their lives and be a lesson for the whole world to admire. Lovers parted by two insuperable obstacles—his crown and her husband.

Florizel had different ideas. He raved to Malden. There must be a meeting. She could not go on like this.

The romance was no longer a secret. It was hinted at in the more scurrilous papers. 'A certain illustrious Personage and a famous actress have become aware of each other's undoubted charms . . .' 'A new Florizel for Perdita . . .' And such allusions.

The theatre was doing business such as it had rarely done before, for people wanted to see the actress who had enchanted the Prince. They were more pleased with him than ever. What a change from his dull old father!

Sheridan was delighted with his audiences, but a little apprehensive of the future. Perdita was a very lovely woman but he did not think for one moment that she would be wise enough to hold the Prince of Wales for long.

If she became the Prince's mistress she would continue to

bring in packed houses. He would not be able to accommodate all the people who would be clamouring to get into the theatre to see her; but of course the Prince would never allow his mistress to appear on the stage—and that would be the end of good business for Drury Lane. And if the Prince discarded her? A royal mistress could not return to the stage. The public would come to see her once . . . twice and then lose interest in her.

He decided to speak to her and called at her house to do so, for they could enjoy more privacy there than at the theatre. In her muslin and ribbons she was very appealing. One of the prettiest women he had had ever known. If she would not take herself and her virtue and her ladylike ways so seriously, she would be very attractive indeed. Being frank with himself he admitted that he had quickly tired of her. Beauty alone was not enough. Would the Prince tire as quickly? He was young, and at the moment inexperienced, the prisoner in that Puritan Palace set up by Papa; but when he had his establishment, that would be different. We shall see a change in H.R.H. when that happens, mused Sheridan. And I doubt that our dear ladylike Mrs. R. will then seem to him the ideal of perfection that she does seen through prison bars. Now his—Sheridan's—dearest Amoret (Mrs. Crewe), that sparkling witty creature whom he adored and to whom he had dedicated *The School for Scandal*, would hold any man. If she had been in Perdita's shoes . . . But God forbid. Amoret was too enchanting to be thrown away on a callow prince; only the most brilliant playwright in England was worthy of her.

Fleetingly he thought of Elizabeth. He was sorry Elizabeth had to know of these things. But Elizabeth was a saint and a man of flesh and blood cannot live with a saint.

But here was Mrs. Armistead—that most discreet of women—to usher him in.

'My dear Sherry!' Perdita rose to greet him, so pretty with the faint flush in her cheeks. He knew what that meant. A letter from Florizel. What a correspondent the Prince was! And so was Perdita! She had always been one to pour out her heart and soul on paper, which was probably fanning the flame of H.R.H.'s ardour. Those poems she had written from her debtor's prison! No merit in them but lots of feelings—and that was a commodity the public were often more ready to pay for than a genius.

'My blessed Perdita!' He kissed her hands ardently. It was always wise to feign regrets for a love affair that was over in the presence of the one who had shared it. It was advisable to blame circumstances—'coming to one's senses', 'it is better for you, my dear, and I am thinking of you', 'my own inclinations are of no account'—than to speak of satiety, boredom, a new and more exciting mistress.

'But how enchanting you look.'

She would never grow accustomed to compliments. He wondered lightly what proportion of her life was spent studying her reflection in the mirror and deciding what clothes she would wear.

She sparkled at once—and now she showed some vitality which was more attractive than that look of melancholy which was her usual expression.

'The simplicity of the gown throws up the contrast of your dazzling beauty.'

'This morning gown . . .' she said disparagingly, and he could see that she was wondering whether to order a new muslin to be made . . . one in which she could appear in public, and startle the world of Ranelagh, the Rotunda, the Pantheon by appearing in muslin and ribbon among all the satin and feathers.

' . . . is most becoming,' he finished for her. 'But, my dear, I have not come to talk to you of gowns. I am concerned for you . . . greatly concerned.'

'Sherry?'

'I am thinking of Prince Charming's very public passion.'

'Alas, people in our position cannot live secret lives.'

'That is indeed true and is why you should consider your situation from all aspects before taking any step.'

'I am sure you are right. And that is what I am doing.'

'So far you and the Prince have not met . . . alone.'

'Certainly we have not.'

'But how long do you think he will be content with this state of affairs?'

'The Prince is content that he loves me and I . . .'

'And you, Perdita, adore him. Naturally, all ladies adore Royalty.'

'I don't understand.'

'A simple fact, my dearest.'

'I hope you are not suggesting that I love the Prince because of his rank. You have forgotten how his uncle the Duke of Cumberland plagued me. But you should remember how I repulsed his advances.'

An ageing roué of a duke. A young and charming prince with a crown in view. The one was a much more glittering prize than the other. Moreover, the Duke's character was well known. He had had several mistresses and had merely invited Perdita to join the group. He had not written the sentimental love letters which she had just been reading and which she would tie up with blue ribbons—or possibly pink—and gloat over in her old age . . . that was if she did not use them to financial advantage at some earlier stage. The very fact that Florizel *wrote* to his loved one pointed to his inexperience. The Duke was no scholar; he could not have compiled those flowing phrases had he wished to; but although the Prince might chatter in French, Italian and German like a native, although he was familiar with Horace and Virgil and was reputed to have some taste for Tacitus, he was clearly not aware of the ways of the world or he would never have so guilelessly handed over to an actress those letters which, Sheridan had no doubt, the young fool would in a year's time curse himself for having written. In this Perdita had shown herself wise. She repulsed the roué and encouraged the innocent boy; for much as she might protest, her coy reluctance to become his mistress was the best method of luring him on.

'I remember well,' said Sheridan. 'And that was wise. It would have done your reputation no good at all to be concerned with my lord Duke.'

Perdita shuddered piously.

'And the Prince . . .' mused Sheridan. 'Oh, my dear, dear lady, you must tread very cautiously. What do you think will be the outcome of all this?'

'The outcome? Why, I think we shall learn to content ourselves with our fate.'

Clichés! thought Sheridan. Could she really see a lusty young man being content with letters.

'I think His Highness will become more and more insistent in his request for a meeting.'

'I have advised him to consider his position.'

'And I have come here to advise you to consider yours.'

'That I am doing.'

'I know you well. I shall never forget the day we met. I recognized your ability the moment I saw you and so did Garrick. God rest his soul.'

'Poor Mr. Garrick! Dear Mr. Garrick! What I owe him! It is very sad to think he will never again coach ladies for the stage.'

A short pause to pay respects to Garrick who had died a few months before.

Garrick had said: 'With looks like that, she'll bring in the audiences. If we can teach her to act a little that could be a help.'

How right he was! How right he had always been! He was greatly missed.

'But even now,' went on Sheridan, 'that you have your place in your profession, it could be easy to throw it away.'

'Throw it away? How?'

'By becoming the Prince's mistress.'

She drew back at what she considered an unpleasant word. She would never see herself as the Prince's mistress no matter if he set her up in a house and openly visited her. His friend? wondered Sheridan. The lady whom he favours with his confidences? His wife in name only? Never mistress!

No, he would not give her a long hold on the fickle favour of a young Prince avid for experience, avid for life.

'My dearest, let us face the facts. That is what is in the Prince's mind.'

'I appreciate your anxiety for me, dear Sherry, but I do not think you know the Prince.'

A little better than you do, he thought, for you my dear have not yet spoken to him face to face.

'Listen to me,' he said. 'You know I speak for your good. If you become the Prince's mistress you will lose your place on the stage. You have too much sensibility to become the mistress of a king or a prince. You are too romantic. It would be necessary for you to consider all sorts of propositions which would be distasteful to you.'

'What do you mean?'

'Before entering into such an arrangement you should make sure that some provision was made for the days when it would be over. Tell me this, what would you do if you could no longer act? Don't forget you have a child, a mother . . . and a husband to support.'

She turned away; he was forcing her to see the ugly truth; he was spoiling her romance. And she wanted to go on in her dream.

'My dear Sherry,' she said, 'I know you speak out of your concern for me. But rest assured I shall never do anything which would make you ashamed of me.'

'I should tremble less for you if I thought you would,' he said.

'You must have your quips.' She swept away the unpleasant

discussion with a wave of the hand. 'Now, would you take a dish of tea, a dish of chocolate?'

He declined. Business at the theatre, he pleaded. He had no desire to drink tea or chocolate with a mistress of whom he had tired.

Mistress? he chided himself. No, lady friend . . . the lady whom I favoured with my confidences . . . once.

He took his leave, kissing her hand fervently to assure her that it was her good for which he was concerned and that she should consider very carefully before throwing away a career which had been built up to fame since that night when her Juliet had first enchanted his audiences.

Mr. Fox chose a time when Mrs. Robinson was out to call on her. He had his reasons for this. He had not been unaware of the lady's maid. An extremely handsome woman, he had noted, and he had a liking for handsome women; moreover, there was an air about this one which had specially intrigued him. Not only was she handsome, but intelligent.

It was a matter of some importance to follow the course of Perdita's romance with Florizel, because if the lady in fact became the Prince's mistress and remained in that position when the Prince became a man of independence, Perdita could be a very significant person indeed.

Mr. Fox had been present at the Oratorio and had witnessed the strange behaviour of the Prince; he had read the papers with those hints of the romance; he had heard rumours in Brooks' and other clubs; and he had listened attentively.

But he wished to follow the affair more intimately and believed that if he had a friend inside Perdita's establishment he could be completely in the picture and would not have to rely on hearsay.

A small matter in all his concerns? Not exactly. Because the Prince was destined to be in a position with relation to the Whigs that his father was with the Tories—and Mr. Fox, being an ardent Whig and with nothing to hope for from the King or the Tory Party, was eager to bring back the Whigs to power—and who could be more helpful in this than the Prince of Wales?

The young man could not take his place in the Lords until he attained his real majority, that would be in 1783—more than three years from now; but at eighteen he would gain his freedom and his own establishment and he must be drawn into the right circle before the time came for him to enter the Lords. Three

years was not too long; and if Mr. Fox was not ready, others
would seize the advantage. So therefore the affair between the
actress and the Prince was politics.

'Madam is not at home.' The young woman spoke coolly and
none would have guessed that the sight of the famous politician
had set her heart racing and her hopes soaring because she had
a very strong notion that Mr. Fox had been well aware that her
mistress was not at home and that was why he had called.

Mr. Fox had already entered.

'Perhaps I could wait a while?'

'I am sure that is what Madam would wish.'

'And she would wish you to stay and have a civil word with
me, I don't doubt.'

'It is my duty, sir, to be civil to all Madam's friends.'

'And mighty civil I am sure you are.'

Mrs. Armistead curtsied and turned away, but he said: 'Now,
you promised to chat.'

'I cannot imagine, sir, that a gentleman of your position would
want to chat with a woman in mine.'

He smiled at her. 'And I had imagined you to be a woman of
imagination.'

'What would you wish of me, sir?'

'To ask you first perhaps how a woman of your undoubted
ability should be content to find herself a lady's maid to an
actress.'

'I did not say I was content, sir.'

'Ah.' He smiled at her. He was a strangely fascinating man.
She had thought him the most exciting of all those gentlemen
who called on her mistress. Mr. Charles James Fox who could
make the King uneasy, who was said to be the most brilliant
politician in Parliament, a rival to young Mr. Pitt, to the Prime
Minister, Lord North. He was scarcely attractive to the eye, for
in this age of elegance he was noticeably slovenly. Now she
could see the grease spots on his coat; he was too fat; he had a
double chin and his paunch was obvious; he had not bothered
to shave himself. She had heard that he thought nothing of losing
twenty thousand guineas in a night's gambling at Brooks'. But
he was the great Charles James Fox and it excited her that he
had noticed her.

'Then I'll swear that from your present post you are looking
for a better one.'

'Should not one always keep one's eyes open for advantage,
sir?'

'Wise as well as beautiful.' He moved closer to her and although she did not retreat she conveyed by her expression that she did not expect familiarities and for a moment her spirits sank, for she feared that he had come in merely for a quick physical encounter with the handsome lady's maid who would be ready to serve Mr. Fox in whatever capacity he thought fit for half an hour and then be forgotten. But that was not the intention of Mrs. Armistead; nor must Mr. Fox—famous as he might be—be deluded into thinking this could be.

He understood.

He said: 'Shall we sit down?'

She led the way into the drawing room and with the utmost dignity seated herself some distance from the chair which he had selected.

'I see that you are too clever for me to pretend my mission is other than it is.'

She inclined her head.

'Mrs. Robinson is on the way to becoming the mistress of the Prince of Wales,' he went on. 'I am sure you realize the significance of this.'

'I do.'

'The Prince is young and impressionable. And a mistress could hold considerable sway over such a romantically minded young man. It is very necessary for the heir to the throne to be guided by those who can do him most good.'

'Such as Mr. Charles James Fox?' she asked.

'Exactly. Exactly. The affair is hanging fire, is it not?'

'It is many weeks since His Highness first saw Mrs. Robinson in *The Winter's Tale* and they have not yet met.'

'Why?'

'Mrs. Robinson is a lady of much refinement.' In some way Mrs. Armistead managed to speak exactly as Perdita did in her most refined moments. 'She wishes to be the Prince's mistress but cannot bear to admit even to herself that this is so. She writes long letters telling him of his duty and urging him to consider his position.'

'If she goes on in this way he will soon be considering some other fair charmer.'

'Yes, sir.'

'It would be better if this matter were brought to a logical conclusion.'

'Better for whom, sir? The Prince, Mrs. Robinson or Mr. Fox?'

He looked at her with admiration. 'For all three,' he said. 'And possibly . . . for Mrs. Armistead.'

'Why should this last person be concerned, sir?'

'Because her advancement could well depend on it.'

She nodded slowly.

'Mrs. Armistead, I should be glad to call you my friend.'

'A simple lady's maid is underserving of the friendship of the greatest of statesmen.'

'Not so simple, if I have guessed aright and it is ability at the guessing game which makes a great statesman.'

'What is your wish?'

'That you persuade your mistress to make the Prince a happy man and that you keep me informed of the lovers' progress.'

'Why should I serve you, sir, instead of the mistress who pays me?'

He felt in his pocket and she recoiled in haste.

'I am not asking for money. I should not take it.'

He nodded. 'Then,' he said, 'I would answer your question. You would serve me because you have no intention of remaining in a humble position for the rest of your days. It is you, my dear, who should have a lady's maid. And I am sure that if you are as clever as I believe you to be, one day this will be so.'

She stood up, her eyes were bright, but she lost none of her serenity.

'I know,' he said, 'I can rely on you.'

'It will be an honour to serve Mr. Fox,' she said.

He moved towards her. She thought he was going to embrace her; but again she held him off with her eyes.

He accepted her decision, and when she showed him to the door, he bowed to her as he would have bowed to her mistress.

After his chair had carried him away she went to her room; she held the white and silver tissue dress against her.

Folly! she thought. I am being as foolish as our play actress. But from the way he looked, the way he spoke, it was obvious that he respected me.

On the evening of that day Fox made his way to Cumberland's Mansion in Pall Mall where the Duchess received him with pleasure; and he was genuinely delighted to be in the company of this fascinating woman who had snared a royal duke and had kept her place in his affections because she was twenty times cleverer than he was. One of the most beautiful women in London—and she would have been so without the famous eyelashes—she was also one of the most witty; her wit was spiced with malice, it was true, and often expressed in the coarsest terms, but Fox admired and respected her.

'A game of faro is what you want,' she said.

Of course he wanted a game of faro. He could not see a gaming table without wanting to try his luck. A born gambler always hoping for the success which never came, he had already lost a fortune. It was his sublime indifference to money which had helped to set him in his peculiar position, for it was not only money, but honours which he did not seek. It was enough to be Mr. Charles James Fox—the man recognized as the most brilliant statesman of his country, and not only by his country but by all the courts of Europe. He was bold and independent, aloof from all blandishments, even of the King himself—for George had at one time known that if he could have had Mr. Fox as an ally he could have left the Government in more capable hands than those which guarded it at present. For all his affection for North, the King was well aware of his deficiencies. But Fox had set himself up in opposition to Tory doctrines; Fox was a Whig; and he opposed every Tory measure with the most cutting scorn. Fox declared he was for the people and he was going to maintain their privileges in the face of all opposition.

Such a man could have been an irresistible power in the land but for the fact that he possessed a dual personality. The statesman of integrity was a voluptuary of the most blatant kind. Drink, women and the gaming table were his recreations; and as he was a man of unbounded energy he gave to these activities the same indefatigable enthusiasm that he did to politics. He took a new mistress more frequently than he took a bath; his debts ran into five figures; and it was only because through long practice he could drink most men insensible that he was rarely drunk.

Yet he was sought by all the greatest hostesses in London and now the Duchess of Cumberland had caught the Duke's eye and he, seeing that Mr. Fox was with her, hastened to greet his guest.

'A game of faro?' said the Duke, his eyes glistening.

Fox replied that nothing would give him greater pleasure later; there was a little matter he wished to discuss with the Duke and if it were possible for him and the Duchess to leave their guests for a while, he would like a little serious conversation with them.

The Duchess replied that it should be arranged and if Mr.

Fox would slip into the ante-room near her bedroom they could be quite undisturbed there.

It was not easy for such flamboyant characters as Mr. Fox and the Duke and Duchess to slip away unnoticed, but in due course they met in the ante-room and Mr. Fox came straight to the point.

'The Prince of Wales is making slow progress with his in-amorata,' he said.

'A prude!' retorted the Duke spitefully.

'Dearest Henry must be forgiven a little sourness towards the lady, but he'll make up for it in sympathy towards our nephew,' explained the Duchess. 'He once had a fancy for her. Poor Henry, it was such a waste of valuable time. I told you, Henry, did I not, that many other ladies would have been far more likely to provide a satisfactory end to the chase. Do you know of anything more frustrating, Mr. Fox, than a hunt when the victim gets clean away.'

'None,' said Mr. Fox. 'But the victim must not be allowed to elude the hunter this time.'

Cumberland shrugged his shoulders. But Fox was not going to let personal resentment interfere with his plans.

'He'll soon be eighteen. We should not imagine that we are the only people who are aware of that. We have to get him on our side. If we don't the Tories will have him.'

'He'd be a Whig just because the King is a Tory.'

'I am not so sure. You can be certain that your brother Gloucester will step in if you don't, and don't forget he has the advantage. In spite of his marriage and the fact that his wife is not received at Court His Majesty is quite fond of him.'

'More than he is of me,' grimaced Cumberland.

'So Your Highness will see that it is necessary for us to act promptly.'

'Our little encounter in the Park didn't do much good.'

'I am forced to disagree with your Highness. I believe that the Prince was most touched and thought his uncle a charming fellow. He was more resentful against his father than ever for denying him the company of such fascinating relations. When he is free—and that may well be in a few months' time—he will want to show his affection, I am sure of it. That is why we must be ready for him.'

'Mr. Fox is right,' said the Duchess. 'This must be the house which he must feel is a home to him.'

Fox threw her a grateful glance. Trust Madam Horton to see the advantage. She would deal with her less perceptive Duke.

'Well?' said Cumberland, deferring to the Duchess as always.

'Mrs. Robinson should be your guest.'

'If I asked her she would suspect an attack on her precious virtue.'

'Her Highness the Duchess would be her hostess.'

'The lady shall come,' promised the Duchess. 'Why not with Sheridan?'

'That is no hardship I do assure you.'

'An entertaining fellow. He'll bring a new shine to Cumberland House.'

'And the lady should be persuaded to stop teasing the Prince.'

'Why?' demanded Cumberland.

'Because, my lord Duke, if she does not, our Prince will grow so impatient that he will look elsewhere. We cannot expect a full blooded young man as your nephew undoubtedly is to live on sighs. What if he chose a mistress in the Tory camp? It could be fatal to our hopes. No, it shall be Perdita. But she has to be persuaded that there is more glory to be found in the arms of a Prince of Wales than in prudery.'

'Her prudery could be overcome,' grumbled the Duke.

'How so?' demanded his Duchess. 'How was it that you who are skilled in the arts of overcoming that horrid vice could not overcome it in her case?'

'Every woman has her price.' He looked hard at his Duchess.

That she conceded. 'Even if it's marriage.' She fluttered her lashes, as though calling attention to her big bargaining counter. 'But Perdita could not be such a fool as to imagine she could marry the Prince of Wales. And since she is answering his letters and writing to him as passionately and as yearningly as he is writing to her, somewhere underneath all that display of virtue there must be some small idea of what she would accept.'

'That's it,' said the Duke. 'After all if they're going to make the affair go public—and his behaviour at the Oratorio suggests he will—she would have to give up the stage; and if he tires of her in a month or so, which is not inconceivable, the lady should naturally look for some security.'

'The Prince should offer her bond of some sort,' said the Duchess. 'He should do so in the most delicate terms. The lady will refuse indignantly; then it will be offered again and she will refuse hesitantly; and at the third time she will accept reluctantly. Would you care to take a bet on it, Mr. Fox. A thousand guineas.'

'Done,' said Mr. Fox, 'Although I think you have the better chance. But I'd be so pleased if it happened that I wouldn't mind paying up. But how is the Prince to be made to realize how he should act?'

The Duke and Duchess were silent for a while then the Duchess said: 'Lord Malden is the messenger. Part of his duty as H.R.H.'s equerry is to carry his master's love letters to the ladies of his choice. Malden has been our guest. He shall be so again. Never fear the Duke shall drop a word of advice into Malden's ear. Poor Malden, I fancy he is in love with the lady himself. He will be glad to please his master and at the same time release himself from a mission which, in the circumstances, must be somewhat odious.'

'But if he is in love with the woman will he want to pass her over to the Prince?'

The Duchess looked mockingly at her husband. 'Sometimes the dogs enjoy the crumbs which fall from their master's table. Malden will be waiting, chops slavering, tail wagging ever faithful for the day when Florizel takes on a new role. After all, we must have a change of show sometimes. And when *The Winter's Tale* becomes *The Lady Dishonoured*, Malden will step in with a show of his own, *Patience Rewarded*.'

Mr. Fox said: 'The Duchess as usual has found the solution. Now we will see if this lady—like so many others—has her price. I have no doubt that she has, but it may be marriage, which in her case would be impossible for her lover, however enamoured, to meet. But if she will set her sights a little lower . . .'

'Then,' said the Duchess, 'the Prince shall have his Perdita and Mr. Fox would lose a thousand guineas.'

'In the circumstances,' said Mr. Fox, ' 'tis a consummation devoutly to be wished!'

Perdita was thrown into a state of excitement by the invitation from the Duchess of Cumberland. She called to Mrs. Armistead, for the woman was growing more and more useful and more and more Perdita was taking her into her confidence.

'An invitation from a very illustrious quarter. I confess I should refuse it immediately if it had come from the Duke.'

'The Duke admired you greatly, Madam.'

'He was in the theatre night after night and I remember when we were playing Vanburgh's *Relapse* under the title of *A Day in Scarborough* and the audience showed their annoyance, how he publicly defended me.'

'Madam was wise to spurn the gentleman. He has not a good reputation with the ladies.'

'But since it is his Duchess who invites me . . .'

'Madam will not refuse to grace their company with her presence.'

'I am of a half mind to refuse, Armistead. Perhaps the Prince would not like me to go.'

'But this is his uncle!'

'A well-known seducer.'

'His Highness was pleased to act most affectionately with him in the Park and I cannot help feeling that it would give him a great deal of pleasure if he knew you visited his uncle's house.'

'I am not sure, Armistead.'

Mrs. Armistead, knowing that it was Mr. Fox's wish that Perdita should visit Cumberland House, was determined to persuade her mistress to do so; and Perdita was so bemused with the daily letters from her lover that she allowed herself to be persuaded.

It was with a sense of a good piece of work completed that Mrs. Armistead put on her becoming cloak with its concealing hood—a gift from Perdita and therefore of excellent cut and material—and hurried to Mr. Fox's lodgings in St. James's to tell him that the first step in his mission was accomplished.

Such pleasant company at Cumberland House! And how they had acclaimed Perdita! The Duchess was quite charming to her, and although Perdita was a little uneasy in the presence of such a woman and was a little afraid that such dazzling good looks might draw attention from her own, she could remind herself that the Duchess was considerably older than she was and that she, Perdita, had youth on her side.

There she met old friends. Sheridan was present, enchanting the company with his witty sayings; and with him his Amoret, so he had little time to spare for Perdita. She had no cause to complain. Mr. Fox was charming to her; Lord Malden of course could always be relied upon to play the faithful swain; and the Duc de Chartres paid marked attention.

She was not of course interested. She did not wish it to reach Florizel's ears that she had encouraged the attentions of that notorious roué from across the Channel.

'How pleased I should be,' the Duchess whispered to her, 'if our beloved Prince could be here.'

Perdita blushed becomingly; and the Duchess continued in the most friendly manner: 'Perhaps in the future I shall have the pleasure of being hostess to you both . . . together.'

If that was not an indication that she would be accepted in some of the family circles, Perdita was not sure what was.

She went home flushed with triumph and confided in Mrs. Armistead during her disrobing.

The Prince's impatience was increasing. When, oh when, was he going to see her, to hold her in his arms, to tell her by word of mouth of his devotion. He could not live on letters forever.

'Patience,' she replied. She would not have him act rashly. He must never forget that he was heir to the Crown.

To which he replied impetuously that he was ready to forget— and forgo—everything if he might but be the lover of Mrs. Robinson. It was now May, nearly six months since he had seen her in *The Winter's Tale* and he had not yet kissed her lips. Something must be done.

She was kept busy at the theatre. She played Mrs. Brady in *The Irish Widow* and went on to a stupendous success in the part of Eliza Camply in *The Miniature Picture*. People crowded to the theatre to see her in this part because during it she masqueraded as Sir Harry Revel, which meant that she appeared on the stage in breeches. These set off her fine figure to perfection, revealing her shapely limbs, and the people went mad with joy over her, and demanded Mrs. Robinson in more breeches parts.

When she appeared at Ranelagh or the Rotunda and the Pantheon, she was surrounded by people who came to look at her. She was becoming notorious, for many people believed that she was in fact the mistress of the Prince of Wales.

And then Lord Malden came with a very special gift for her.

'Madam,' he said, 'it is imperative that you give His Highness some satisfaction or I fear for his health. He is pining away. He has sent you this gift as a sign of his devotion and good faith. I beg of you accept it and help to restore His Highness to his former robust health.'

'He is ill?' She was all concern.

'Pining for you, Madam.'

She opened the package and turned pale and then red as she glanced at it. It was a bond for twenty thousand pounds which

His Highness would honour at his coming of age. This was sealed by the royal arms.

Twenty thousand pounds! How long would it take her to earn so much in the theatre with Mr. Sheridan always hinting at cuts in salaries because in spite of full houses he could not make ends meet.

Twenty thousand pounds! It sounded almost as joyous as wedding bells in her ears.

There was a letter from Florizel. He implored her to take this gift because it would show her confidence in him. He hoped he had not offended her by offering it but it was given from the depth of his heart. He would like to lay all he had at the feet of his fair Perdita.

Her eyes filled with tears, but she did not let them fall; they were so disastrous to the complexion and she never for one moment forgot what an ardent admirer Lord Malden was.

'The Prince is the most generous of men, but I could not accept such a gift.'

'But Madam, it will break His Highness's heart if you don't.'

'Wrong constructions could be placed on such a gift.'

'His Highness would be desolate if you placed any but the right ones.'

'I know . . . I know . . . I never for one moment doubted *his* intentions. But if it were known . . .'

'Why should it be known?'

'You must take it away. Tell him the whole notion is repugnant to me.'

'I dare not, Madam. You cannot believe how deeply upset the Prince can be on your account.'

'How I wish he could have all he deserves.'

'It is in your power to give it to him, Madam. I fear he will become ill if he does not see you soon.'

'Take this away!' She picked up the bond. Malden laid his hand lightly on it but did not take it—nor did she release it.

'At least do not make a hasty decision, Madam. Think of the Prince.'

'I am thinking of him . . . constantly. Not what would be best for me but for him.'

'Hold the bond here for a while, I beg of you. To return it now would be such a blow to him.'

'Very well, I will do that. But I have no intention of taking it.'

Lord Malden left and Mrs. Armistead learned from her mistress that she had received the bond. She even was allowed to study it. 'You are so clever at that sort of thing, Armistead.'

A bond sealed with the royal seal, for £20,000 to be paid when the Prince came of age. There was no doubt about it. There it was in black and white.

At the earliest opportunity she reported to Mr. Fox.

'She says she will not take it but she will. She studies it even more constantly than she does his letters . . . and more lovingly. She will accept it.'

'And once she has,' mused Mr. Fox, for he was finding Mrs. Armistead worth a confidence or two, 'the meeting will take place. The Prince will gain a mistress and I shall lose a thousand guineas.'

He kissed Mrs. Armistead lightly on her forehead as though to say Well done, thou good and faithful servant.

Their relationship was changing. Attraction was springing up between them which might have seemed incongruous. She was so neat, fastidious in her cleanliness; he so slovenly; she a servant in the house of an actress and he a welcome guest in high society.

They were both aware of the incongruity of this attraction because it was of the mind as well as the body; but it was none the less irresistible because of this.

She would keep the bond, she explained to Lord Malden, because she feared that to return it would hurt the Prince's susceptibilities.

'It is true,' replied Malden.

'I fear it to be a little indelicate to take it . . . but I see no alternative.'

There was no alternative, Malden assured her.

And she bowed her head.

And each day she looked at it, at those magic words Twenty thousand pounds, and the royal seal. It is after all, she told herself, a measure of his devotion to me. I must try to see it in the spirit in which it is meant.

And after accepting the bond it was a short step to a meeting.

When? the Prince was constantly demanding, and Perdita knew that she could hold out no longer.

She explained to Lord Malden.

'The Prince is asking me to give up my career, my husband . . . my reputation for his sake. Oh, do not mistake me. I would gladly give my life for him. I fear, though, the anger of the King and Queen. And what if he should change towards me? I should have no wish to live.'

Lord Malden reminded her of the paper heart which had come with the miniature. 'Unalterable to my Perdita through Life.'

'Madam, all this time when you have refused to meet him he has been faithful. How much more so will he be when you are his.'

'Do you believe that, Lord Malden?'

'With all my heart,' said Malden.

'And when the world knows what I have done . . .'

'Yours is a triumph of chastity,' he told her.

A triumph of chastity! The expression appealed to her. Yes, she could see it that way. For nearly six months the Prince had sighed for her, implored her to meet him; and always she had replied that he must consider his position, that she must not think of her own desires but what was best for him.

And now at last she was capitulating; and it was a triumph of chastity.

The Meeting at Kew

The Prince was delighted, impatient and angry. The meeting must take place, but where? Never before had he raged so fiercely against the way he was treated. Here he was almost eighteen and a Prince of Wales and he could not freely arrange a meeting with the lady of his choice! Their meeting must be a secret in case it reached the ears of his parents.

He paced up and down his apartments, raging to Frederick and Lord Malden.

'You remember where you used to meet Harriot Vernon,' suggested Frederick.

'I could never meet Perdita there.'

'My house in Dean Street is at Your Highness's service,' said Malden.

The Prince looked hopeful. 'That's a better idea.'

'But,' said Frederick, 'you could never go to Dean Street and it not be known. People recognize you passing through the streets. Moreover, it is too far. You would be away too long. There would be enquiries. What if the King decided to send for you as he did for that game of chess?'

The Prince looked in dismay at his brother. Frederick was right.

'There is only one answer,' he said. 'She must come to Kew.'

'To Kew, sir!' cried Malden, aghast.

Frederick's eyes were alight with excitement. 'We shall smuggle her into the Dower House. She should come in breeches—her Sir Harry Revel costume . . . and no one would know who she was.'

'It's the answer,' said the Prince. 'Fred, you have talent.'

* * *

'In breeches!' cried Perdita, aghast. 'That would be quite out of the question. I should feel so . . . indelicate.'

'It would mean,' Lord Malden explained, 'that you would not be easily recognized.'

'And if I were? Imagine! The scandal! Oh no, no. I could not do it.'

'It was the best plan we could think of.'

'I could never do it,' said Perdita firmly.

Finally it was decided that there was something in Frederick's first idea. The meeting must be highly secret and the only safe spot would be out of doors. The Prince would at least have an opportunity of talking to his love, of clasping her in his arms and making plans for the future; and all he had to remember was that in three months' time he would be eighteen, have his own establishment and then be free to come and go as he wished.

'Your Highness has waited six months,' pointed out Lord Malden. 'In another three all will be settled to your satisfaction.'

The Prince retorted that he had no intention of waiting three more months for Perdita, but they would have a meeting in any case. Lord Malden was to go ahead and make plans without delay.

He came to see Perdita and looking at her with yearning eyes told her of the arrangements.

'I will take you to Brentford and from there row you out to Eel Pie Island. There we will dine and after that I will row you to Kew Gardens where the Prince will be waiting for you.'

'I am glad,' she told him, 'that you will be accompanying me. You will make me feel . . . secure.'

At this Lord Malden dropped to his knees and taking her hand covered it with kisses.

'Madam, all these months when I have been pleading another's cause I have been filled with a mad desire to plead my own.'

'I know, my lord.'

'It has been a well-nigh irresistible temptation to me. If it had been any man but the Prince . . .'

'I know. I know. You have been loyal and faithful. It is something I shall never forget.'

Her eyes filled with tears; she dashed them away dramatically. She could almost hear the applause of the audience, the murmurs of 'None can play a scene like this to compare with Mrs.

Robinson'. In fact she had an audience. Mrs. Armistead had her eye to the keyhole and knew that her lady was to dine with Lord Malden on Eel Pie Island and then be rowed by that self-sacrificing lover to the Prince.

'I have decided that there shall be a meeting between me and the Prince.'

Mrs. Armistead feigned surprise.

'Oh, yes, Armistead. He has pleaded with me so earnestly that I can no longer refuse him.'

'I understand, Madam.'

'And we are going to Brentford tomorrow.'

'*We*, Madam?'

'The coach will call for me and take me to Lord Malden's house in Dean Street where he will join me and together we shall ride to Brentford.'

'You will go alone, Madam, to Brentford with my lord Malden?'

'Why, Armistead . . .'

Mrs. Armistead's features had formed themselves into an expression of horror. Then almost immediately they returned to their familiar respectful state. 'Forgive me, Madam. I forget my place.'

'No . . . no, pray go on.'

'Well, Madam, begging your pardon, I should have thought it unwise for you to go . . . alone with Lord Malden on such a journey. If you were seen and recognized . . . Madam must forgive me. I think of your reputation.'

'But, I have . . .'

'Madam, when ladies travel their maids accompany them . . . not only for reasons of propriety but in case their toilettes should need some attention.'

Perdita was smiling, and yet again asking herself what she would do without Armistead.

In the coach that rattled along to Dean Street Mrs. Armistead sat very upright, her hands folded in her lap. She was not thinking of the excited young woman opposite her, who was deep in her own thoughts.

Could it possibly be, Mrs. Armistead was asking herself. Mr. Fox himself! Many people of humble circumstances had probably been his mistresses . . . briefly. She had no doubt that in the first instance he had decided that she herself was worthy of a brief dalliance. But surely this was something deeper? She could not contemplate it with her usual good sense. She had always been clever, and when the late Mr. Armistead had left her unprovided for she had chosen this profession—for a purpose. As a lady's maid to an actress she would have opportunities. She had briefly before coming to Mrs. Robinson served Mrs. Abington. The possibilities were there; but she had not visualized anything like the present situation. Nor could it have come about if she had not had the great good luck to serve a mistress who had attracted the Prince of Wales. This could bring her into the most exalted circles. She could work so well for Mr. Fox because the outcome of the affair was of equal importance to them both.

Mr. Fox. Oddly enough for all his greatness she saw him as a man in need of care. It was his weakness which appealed to her as much as his strength. She had learned a great deal about him, that some years earlier, his father Lord Holland had paid £140,000 to settle his debts. Lord Holland was dead now and had left Charles James Kingsgate Castle which had had to be sold. There was a jingle sung in the streets about the great man.

> *'If he touches a card, if he rattles a box,*
> *Away fly the guineas of this Mr. Fox.'*

She did not glorify him as Perdita glorified her Prince. She did not wish to clothe him with virtues he did not possess. She would not deny that he was short and fat and rather gross, but there was a look of his ancestor, Charles II, in his face, and his slovenly cravat, his none too clean coat, were forgotten when he talked. One could not be in the company of Mr. Fox without recognizing his greatness and his charm—but it was his weakness that touched the cool serene heart of Mrs. Armistead deeply.

Perdita would have been astonished if she could have read the thoughts of her lady's maid. She would not have been able to imagine that the woman's affairs could be thought of—even by herself—when they were on the brink of this stupendous adventure.

Was her gown suitable? Indian muslin and not too decorated with ribbons.

'So becoming, Madam,' had soothed Armistead. 'I have never seen you look so beautiful.'

And what would *he* say when he say her?

She was rehearsing what she would say to him over and over

again. A woodland scene in Kew Gardens. There was a moon and the weather was fine. It would be like a Shakespearian scene. She would play it with the utmost emphasis on romance.

And the Prince . . . what was he doing at this moment? She pictured his impatience. She could already hear his impassioned words. How handsome he would look and the diamonds flashing on his coat would be real, not paste as worn by mock princes on the stage.

This was romance.

The coach had come to a stop at Lord Malden's door. He was waiting. He seated himself beside Mrs. Armistead so that he could gaze in rapture at Perdita throughout the journey. Very little was said. Mrs. Armistead's presence was a restraining factor; but Perdita saw that although Lord Malden was disappointed that there should be a third member of the party he applauded the wisdom of it.

Silence prevailed for most of the journey; each occupant busy with is or her own thoughts. Mrs. Armistead continued to think of Mr. Fox, Perdita of her Prince and Lord Malden of Perdita; and at length they arrived at Brentford where the boat was waiting to take them over to Eel Pie Island.

At the island inn a room had been prepared that Perdita might use before taking dinner, and to this she repaired with Armistead, 'to rest,' she told Lord Malden, 'for indeed I fear my heart may fail me.'

In the room she gave what Mrs. Armistead later reported to Mr. Fox a study of the doubts and apprehensions of a woman on the brink of taking a mighty decision which she had long since made up her mind to take for the adequate reward.

'Armistead, I cannot do it. Am I right? Don't forget who he is. If the King learned of this night, what would he do? I have to remember that the Prince will one day be the King of this country. It could happen at any moment, Armistead.'

'I don't think Madam should disturb herself too much on that score, Madam. His Majesty is a comparatively young man, Some forty-two years old. He should have many years left to him.'

'I did not mean to be disloyal to His Majesty, but consider my position, Armistead.'

'Madam, I have considered it and it is one which most women would envy you.'

That pleased her, although she struck a tragedienne's role,

putting her hand to her brow. 'The responsibility, Armistead. The responsibility!'

'Madam, I should think only of pleasing the Prince and leave the responsibility of everything else to others. I fear you will crumple your dress. And I think your hair needs a little attention.'

She was ready to listen to such sound advice. She was at the mirror. 'Yes, my hair, Armistead, my hair. Oh how right I was to bring you with me.'

'There!' Mrs. Armistead had arranged the beautiful dark curls in what she considered their most becoming fashion. 'But you look a little melancholy, Madam, as though you are going to a burial rather than to meet a Prince who adores you.'

'It is a solemn moment, Armistead.'

'The Prince will be so happy that he may well consider it a gay one.'

'No, no, he will feel solemn too.'

'I have heard that he loves people about him to be gay. He has lived so long under the eyes of his solemn parents. He will look for laughter, not for tears.'

Perdita had become suddenly aloof. Who was this woman to tell her of the Prince's feelings?

'I am sure the Prince will be ready to fit into *my* mood.'

Mrs. Armistead was alarmed. How long could it last if she were going to weep for her responsibilities and remind him constantly of what *she* was giving up. Oh, what a fool the woman was! Her folly might mean that very soon Mrs. Armistead would be serving a woman who was nothing but an actress.

She hesitated; she had always adapted herself to her mistress's moods.

'He is a great Prince, Madam. The people adore him. He is the most popular young man in the country.'

This was better. Perdita was smiling.

'All his life people will have been fitting themselves in with *his* moods,' ventured Mrs. Armistead. 'Everyone has fallen victim to his charm. The only one who has not is perhaps the King. But the King is important and the Prince has doubtless spent many hours in his father's company; he will be weary of melancholy. I would like to see Madam smiling and gay . . . for so she looks most beautiful.'

Perdita looked at her reflection. There was something in what Armistead said. She would be the woman who laughed and was merry for the sake of her lover and kept her melancholy locked up in her heart.

And so downstairs to dine and afterwards out to the boat which would row them over to Kew Gardens where the impatient lover would be waiting.

The boat was pushed out from Eel Pie Island. Perdita sat back listening to the sound of the oars skimming the water. Lord Malden's eyes were fixed on the approaching bank. Mrs. Armistead sat, the picture of discretion, back straight, arms folded in her lap.

Suddenly Lord Malden said: 'They're here.'

And they looked and saw a white handkerchief waving in the dusk.

The boat touched earth. Lord Malden leaped out of the boat and helped Perdita to land. Mrs. Armistead remained seated.

Two young men had appeared on the bank, one stood a little behind the other. Mrs. Armistead, watching closely, saw the glittering diamond on the coat of the former and her heart leaped with excitement. The Prince of Wales in person; and behind him his brother Prince Frederick.

Then Malden was saying, 'Your Royal Highness, I have the honour to present Mrs. Robinson.'

The Prince gave a cry of joy and gathered Mrs. Robinson in his arms. Lord Malden turned back to the boat and got in. Prince Frederick stepped back a few paces; and the lovers remained locked in a fond embrace.

'Let us walk among the trees,' said the Prince. 'Oh Perdita . . . my beautiful Perdita, how I have waited for this moment.'

Perdita was too overcome by her emotions to play her part.

'But . . . my Prince . . . at last . . . we are together.'

'Never to part,' declared the Prince, quite unconscious of the figures in the boat or Frederick close by. 'This is the happiest moment of my life. But it is only the beginning, my precious Perdita.'

'Only the beginning,' she agreed.

'We must find a way of meeting. I will come to you. In a very short time . . .'

'Oh, my love,' she cried, 'you will soon be of age and then . . . and then . . . there will be no barriers.'

'You will never regret it, I swear. I shall adore you as long as

I have breath in my body. No one in the world was ever loved as Florizel loves his Perdita.'

'George!' It was Frederick's voice, eager, alarmed. 'There are people coming this way.'

'The devil take them.'

'This is the only path. For God's sake, George . . .'

Perdita cried, 'I must go. There will be other times . . . This is only a beginning.'

Lord Malden too had heard the voices. He had jumped out of the boat and was approaching them.

'Your Royal Highness it would never do . . . if this were discovered . . .'

'He is right,' cried Perdita. 'Adieu, my Prince.'

The Prince seemed as though he were going to ignore the intruders and refuse to part with Perdita. But Frederick was pulling at his arm and Perdita was releasing herself.

'We shall meet soon . . .' she whispered.

'When, when?' demanded the Prince.

'It shall be when you wish,' she told him; and with that fled towards Lord Malden and the boat.

Perdita was in transports of delight while Mrs. Armistead helped her disrobe.

'What a day, Armistead! What a day!'

'What a day indeed, Madam. And the forerunner of many others like it, I daresay.'

'He is so impatient,' sighed Perdita fondly.

'He is an ardent lover, Madam.'

'Armistead, did you see him?'

'Not clearly, Madam.'

'He is very handsome. I never saw a man so handsome.'

'I rejoice for you, Madam.'

'Yes, Armistead, what have I done to deserve such devotion?'

Act on a stage, thought Armistead. Possess undoubted beauty. Hold him off for six months talking of virtue while all the time hinting at surrender. Well played, Madam. Yes, you do deserve a small success with His Highness.

'Madam is so beautiful—and I never saw you more so than tonight.'

'Do you think he was satisfied with me, Armistead?'

'There could have been no doubt of it.'

'Ah . . . Armistead. The grace of his person, the irresistible sweetness of his smile, the tenderness of his melodious yet manly voice will remain with me till every vision of this changing scene shall be forgotten.'

'I am sure he would be delighted to hear you say that, Madam.'

'Perhaps he will. I shall write it down so that I don't forget it. But I mean it, Armistead. I mean if from the bottom of my heart.'

'Madame is a poet as well as an actress and great beauty.'

Perdita smiled in a congratulatory manner at her reflection.

And so, said Mrs. Armistead, reporting to Mr. Fox, did she continue to applaud the good looks and accomplishment of her Prince on that night. It was indeed a step forward. Even Perdita knew now that there could be no holding back and she was prepared to become the mistress of the Prince of Wales.

Mr. Fox Calls on Mr. Sheridan

That was the first of many meetings. The Prince declared that never had he been so happy in his life. He lived for the excitement of these encounters; and the knowledge that at any moment during them he could run into disaster only made them the more exciting.

Kew Gardens. Eel Pie Island. For ever more, he declared, these will be paradise to me.

Each encounter was an adventure in itself. Donning a dark coat he would slip out of the Dower Lodge and make his way to the appointed spot; there had been one occasion when it had been necessary to disguise himself—and Frederick—as watchmen. How they had laughed as they had planned climbing the walls and slipping away.

While this provided the romantic adventure it stirred up all the resentment in the Prince's mind. Why should it be necessary? he constantly demanded of Frederick. That they enjoyed it was beside the point. He was the Prince of Wales and he had to leave the Palace like a thief. And why—because of their father—that spoilsport of a king who thought the height of happiness was to go farming and make buttons and plans for the nursery, drink lemonade and play backgammon and who had never been unfaithful to his wife. Not that the Prince believed in infidelity. He would be faithful to Perdita until death, but at the same time Fred had to agree that their father was a dull dog and it would have been more natural—their mother being as she was—if he had a mistress or two.

Frederick agreed as he always did with his brother; and threw

137

himself into the nocturnal adventures as though they were his own.

And then the meetings with Perdita—herself wrapped in a dark cloak—to walk under the trees, arms entwined, talking of the future, stopping every now and then to embrace while Frederick kept watch on one side and Malden and the lady's maid on the other.

This was wonderful at first but it could not satisfy an ardent lover to wander about the leafy glades of Kew, more often than not having to take a hasty farewell because of intruders.

There must be a better arrangement, and between them George, Frederick and Malden decided that they should make use of Eel Pie Island.

'It would be so much easier if Your Highness rowed over to the Island and Mrs. Robinson was there to meet you.'

Frederick said: 'The inn people wouldn't dare. What if it reached my father's ears?'

There were ways and means, Malden pointed out. For instance, need the innkeeper and his servants know. They could be told it was a gentleman of high rank who visited them and if the Prince was sombrely clad and kept his face in shadow as much as possible, need they guess? He, Malden, would make all the arrangements; and it was surprising what a little persuasion could do if it was backed up by the right sort of 'appreciation'.

The Prince said it was an excellent idea. Malden must arrange it right away.

So Malden dropped a few bribes here and there, and a new trysting place was found for the lovers.

In the finest room the inn could provide they met while Prince Frederick sat outside the inn keeping a lookout and Malden, with him, thought enviously of the Prince's pleasure; and Mrs. Armistead took careful note of every little incident so that she might not fail in her report to Mr. Fox.

While the Prince was sporting with his mistress an alarming situation had sprung up. Lord George Gordon who had become President of the Protestant Association of England was stirring the capital to riot. Lord George—brother of Sarah Lennox's lover, the man by whom she had had an illegitimate child—was an insignificant fellow who determined to draw attention to himself by some means, and as he could not do so by his brilliance chose this way. He led his followers with shouts of 'No Popery' and the King was horrified to discover how quickly a crowd of ordinary people defending what they believe to be right can be turned into a mob bent on destruction.

During the hot days of June, the trouble increased. The homes of Catholics were burned to the ground; so were their places of worship; those members of Parliament who had supported the Catholic Relief Bill were similarly treated and many of them lost their homes; then the mob began attacking prisons. It was shocking to discover how quickly a great city could be in the grip of terror. The Palace of St James's itself and Buckingham House were in danger, and the guard had to be doubled.

The King remained in London; he was not going to leave the soldiers to protect his palaces while he remained at Kew. North suggested that the Prince should be in London. He was popular and his presence might have some effect on the people. The implication being, thought the King sadly, that he himself was not popular. What a sad state of affairs when a man who tried to live honourably and virtuously earned the dislike of his subjects while a young rip who thought of nothing but his own pleasure should have their regard!

But he would not have the Prince of London.

'What, heir to the throne placed in danger? You'd have that, eh, what?'

'What of Your Majesty?'

'My responsibility! Let the Prince stay with his tutor at Kew. Only a boy yet.'

Little did he guess that the boy was at that moment stealing out of the Dower Lodge to row over to Eel Pie Island and his mistress.

The King felt ill. A crisis always set his head zooming with hundreds of thoughts and ideas which he could not always comprehend. And such a crisis! Bloodshed. The stupid destruction that a mob of blood-crazy illiterate men and women could bring about, people who scarcely knew what they were fighting against—for it was not the members of the Protestant Association who were causing this trouble; it was the mob that ragtaggle in any big city—beggars, thieves, prostitutes whose mean and sordid lives were brightened by a disaster such as this. He knew this and he had to stop it. But he would not allow the Prince of Wales to risk his life in London.

The King knew too when he went among the soldiers who were guarding the Palace that at any moment someone might kill him. It was by no means a wild impossibility. He thought

of an occasion little over a year ago when, on alighting from his
chair at the back stairs of St. James's a woman had run up to
him and seized him. He had not been afraid. He was never
alarmed at such times. He felt no fear when he showed himself
among the soldiers. It was not physical courage he lacked; there
were things of which he was afraid—the loss of the Colonies,
financial difficulties, government dissensions, the vices of his
brothers and his sons, the voices in his head—but never of sudden death which could come perhaps to a king more likely than
to one of his subjects. And this woman? He had spoken to her
gently. He was always gentle with his poorer subjects, looking
upon them as children to be cared for. 'What do you want, my
good woman?' he had asked her. He would never forget the
wildness of her eyes, the blankness in them. 'I am Queen Beck,'
she told him. 'Get off the throne. It's mine.' Poor, poor creature!
'Do not harm her,' he had ordered. 'She is mad, poor soul.' He
had a passionate desire to protect the mad from those who might
be harsh with them. It was like his desire to protect the Quakers.
Perhaps that was why he had been so ready to give his consent
to the Catholic Reform Bill. Religious tolerance! Hannah had
always wanted it for her own Society of Friends.

But this was not the time for brooding on the past. Action
was needed. The riots must be stopped. If they were not, this
could be the prelude to civil war. A war between Catholics and
Protestants. It must never be. He wanted his country to be known
as one where religious tolerance prevailed.

He sent for North and told him that the disturbances must be
stopped without delay.

'We must get the better of these rebels before further damage
is done,' he declared.

Lord North agreed on this, but was nervous.

George himself was undecided because he knew that only by
calling out the military and proclaiming martial law could the
rioting be stopped. It was a great decision to make and he was
the only one who could make it. He alone could order his army
to fire on his own subjects.

A sleepless night. Pacing up and down. The voices in his
head were silent. There was only one problem with which to
grapple. He forgot his anxiety about the Prince of Wales. He
forgot everything but the need to stop the Gordon Riots.

The rioters were marching on the Bank of England. They
must not be allowed to destroy this as they had Newgate Jail.

The King gave the order. The troops went into action. Several hundred people were killed but the Gordon Riots had been brought to an end.

The riots over, the King was surprised to find that his subjects were ready to give him back a little of that affection which over the years he had somehow lost. His action in giving the order to fire on the mob was approved of because it had been successful in dispersing the mob and ending the riots.

George felt strong. He was indeed that King which his mother had constantly urged him to be. There was no strong man to guide him. William Pitt was dead; he had a son who had yet to prove himself. Grenville was no longer in power, nor was Grafton. Lord Bute had when he first came to the throne stood beside him and he had never felt safe without him; his mother had advised him on every action he took. Now there was only Lord North and, firm friends that they were, the King did not expect great brilliance from North—only loyal friendship.

So he would govern alone, make his own decisions as he had over the Gordon Riots so satisfactorily. He was glad. He would work better on his own.

'Could never abide a lot of magpies chattering round me,' he said aloud. 'I'll stand alone. I'll show them I am their king, eh.'

In such a mood he went down to Kew for a breath of country air and a little peace and quiet.

Charlotte was glad to see him—very obviously pregnant now. He told her about the riots, for now that they were over she could offer no interference.

He sat with the children and told them what had happened. He had played such a decisive part, and it was good for them to learn how affairs were conducted.

He took young Mary on his knee and looking round at the pink faces, the big eyes, the heavy chins—they all looked so much alike and so like himself—he explained how he came to his decision, through prayer and meditation, which was how they should all solve their problems.

The Queen said that Lord George Gordon was clearly mad and in her opinion mad people could not be blamed for their actions.

'Your Majesty will remember when we were driving through Richmond in an open chaise . . . now it would be just after the birth of William . . .' Fifteen-year-old William looked very pleased with himself. 'And Charlotte . . .' The Queen smiled at her fourteen-year-old daughter . . . 'was on the way and had not yet put in her appearance.' She remembered all her dates through the births of her children. 'Yes, we were riding through Richmond, your Papa and myself, when a man and woman began to shout at us. And then . . . the woman threw something at me. It landed right in my lap. What do you think it was?'

'A knife!' shouted William.

'Flowers,' cried ten-year-old Elizabeth.

Augustus, the seven-year-old, began to gasp and tried to hide the fact. He did not want to get a beating for not being able to breathe because the King believed the cane was a cure for asthma.

'Both wrong,' cried the Queen. 'It was her shoe. She had taken it off to throw it at me.'

'Wasn't that wicked?' asked William.

'It was wrong, but your Papa was kind and said there was to be no punishment. She could in fact have been put to death.'

William whistled.

'Pray do not do that,' said the Queen. 'It sounds like a stable boy.'

The King frowned and William immediately tried to efface himself. He did not want to be sentenced to a caning. Nor did the Queen wish him to be, so she immediately began telling another story which she knew would please the King.

'I remember once when a basket was left at one of the gates. I wonder whether His Majesty remembers . . .' Queen Charlotte looked at her husband and went on quickly: 'But of course your Papa has so much to remember . . . affairs of state . . . he can not be expected to remember these little things.'

'What was in the basket, Mamma?' asked William.

'Can you guess?'

The children all had a guess each but none of them was right.

'A little baby,' cried the Queen triumphantly. 'It was about two months old.'

'Was it a present for Papa?' asked Elizabeth.

'Oh . . . no . . . not for Papa specially. But your Papa found a home for it.'

'And did it live happily ever after?'

'If it was good,' said the Queen piously. 'And what do you think it was called?'

The children guessed again, several of them suggesting their own names.

'It was a boy,' the Queen told them. 'George . . . George was the name. The same as your Papa's.'

'And our brother's,' William reminded her.

There was silence. The King looked round the family circle as though he had not before noticed the absence of his eldest son.

'It's a pity that our eldest son does not see fit to honour a *family* occasion with his presence.'

'Frederick is not here either,' the Queen reminded him, as though excusing the Prince.

'Where George is, Frederick will be,' William told them.

The Queen silenced her son with a look.

'Would Your Majesty care for a little music?'

'I want to know why the Prince of Wales and his brother behave as though they are apart from the rest of us.'

'They are growing up,' sighed the Queen.

'They should have been here.' The King looked round him and one of his pages immediately came to him.

'Go to the Dower Lodge at once,' he said. 'Tell the Prince of Wales and Prince Frederick that I command their attendance without delay. Did you hear that? Without delay, eh, what?'

'Yes, Your Majesty.' The page disappeared and the King glowered into space, and neither the Queen's attempts to amuse him nor the chatter of his children could divert him from his irritation with his eldest son.

Nor was his mood improved when shortly afterwards the page returned to report that neither the Prince nor his brother could be found in the Dower Lodge.

The King looked at his watch. 'Is this not the time when they should be doing their private study?'

'On a fine afternoon like this they might decide to do it in the gardens,' suggested the Queen.

The King replied: 'If they are shirking their lessons . . .' And he immediately felt frustrated, for if he attempted to question his sons, George would in a few minutes show him that he was so much more educated than his father and would immediately have the advantage. He had that way with him—which was growing more and more obvious—of mocking his father without saying anything that could be complained of. Young George was clever. He had been able to learn his lesson with the utmost ease; he had actually liked Greek and Latin and languages and literature and poetry; he could talk about pictures and artists in a way his father could not understand. Yet he never seemed to try as his father had. The King's mind went back to those hours in the schoolroom when he had worked so hard and assimilated so little; and there was George, his son, even outstripping some of his tutors as though that was something he did without effort while he went on with the serious business of plaguing his father.

'The Prince is a natural scholar,' said the Queen quietly. 'I don't think he ever shirks his lessons. He likes them. Perhaps having completed their work they have taken a stroll. That is it.'

'There is a time for strolling,' muttered the King. 'I'll speak to the young puppy tomorrow.'

The Queen was relieved. Tomorrow. Yes, tomorrow.

Mrs. Papendiek, the wife of one of the flautists who was in attendance on the Queen, wondered whether she ought to tell Her Majesty that something very strange was going on in the Dower House. She had actually seen the young Princes scaling the wall; and they went off regularly somewhere along the river.

Should I? Mrs. Papendiek asked herself.

The Prince would be annoyed with her. She had mentioned the affair to her husband; he had said: 'Don't do anything to upset the Prince. Once he's of age there'll be no holding him. The King won't have the power to either. See and say nothing. It's safer.'

Yes, thought Mrs. Papendiek, seeing the increased colour in the King's face and noting that he was speaking more quickly than normally, better to hold one's tongue.

The Queen said: 'I am sure Your Majesty would like a little music.'

The King agreed that he would, so the Queen soothed him by her skilful performance on the harpsichord.

It was July.

'Next month,' declared the Prince, 'I shall be eighteen years old. Even the King cannot deny me my privileges then.'

'Ah!' sighed Perdita. 'How I look forward to the day when we no longer have to meet in this clandestine way.'

'You shall have a fine establishment. The best house we can find.'

Perdita sighed and the Prince hurried on: 'You will be so happy in it and I shall be there all the time. The whole world shall know that it is the place where I most long to be.'

Perdita he knew felt her position deeply. She was a good woman and believed that a union could only be perfect if it were legal. The Prince hated legality. Already he was hedged in by rules, and to him no relationship could be as perfect as that which existed between himself and Perdita.

She could become melancholy easily, wondering if, in being with him in this way, she was sinful. The Prince did not wish to consider sin. He was interested only in pleasure. He would do everything in the world to please her, he assured her, but he thought that when they were together they should be happy.

For fear that she would brood on the loss of her reputation, for as soon as she was set up in that establishment which the Prince would provide for her, the whole of the Court—the whole of London—would know of their relationship, the Prince brought in a grievance of his own.

'I could not allow you to continue on the stage.'

She was silent.

'Oh, no, no,' he went on. 'I do not wish you to be paraded for other men to look at, to comment on.'

'But . . . it is my living.'

The Prince laughed. She was not going to *think* about money again. When he was eighteen he would have an income, an establishment. By God, his Perdita forgot that the man who adored her, worshipped her, who would be faithful to the end of his days, was the Prince of Wales. No sordid considerations of money! No talk of working for a living! He would not *allow* her to continue on the stage. She was for him . . . for him alone.

She was not displeased at this display of authority. When the whole of London knew the position it would have been a little humiliating to appear at the theatre, to be gazed at while everyone pictured her with the Prince. No, she was not displeased at all.

But she performed a touching renunciation scene. She told him of how Mr. Garrick himself had prophesied a great future for her; of the days when he himself tutored her; and would Mr. Garrick have concerned himself with anything short of genius? The Prince should have seen her Juliet. 'Pale pink satin. Spangles of silver. White feathers. But the most becoming scene was the last. My transparent gauze veil fell from the back of my head to my feet.'

'Yes, and you looked like an angel. But no more stage. Do you think I will allow anyone to gaze at you in breeches!'

'Ah, those breeches parts! Some thought them my best. But all this I will give up . . . for you.'

More lovemaking. More professions of eternal devotion.

When she was home in her bedroom she told Mrs. Armistead: 'I am looking forward to the adjusting of His Royal Highness's establishment for the public avowal of our mutual attachment.'

It was mid-morning when Mrs. Armistead, after having given her mistress a dish of chocolate in bed, said she must go out as there were several items she needed such as ribbons, rouge and patches.

She might be gone for a couple of hours but in view of Madam's being so late the previous night, she was sure the rest in bed would do her the world of good and she would of course wish to be fresh for the trip to Eel Pie Island.

Wrapping her cloak about her and pulling its hood well over her head she left the house and, instead of making her way to the market, went straight to St. James's Street where Mr. Fox had his lodgings. His servant, knowing that his master always received her whatever the hour, ushered her in and went to tell Mr. Fox that she had arrived.

'Bring the lady in,' cried Mr. Fox; and Mrs. Armistead was a little astonished to be taken into his bedroom.

'I rarely rise before eleven,' he told her; and indeed he was wearing a linen nightgown which was none too clean. Mrs. Armistead wondered angrily why his servants did not take the soiled nightgown away and put out a new one. His hair, which was black and thick, was dishevelled.

He laughed at her dismay for although she had believed she was hiding it, she had for a second betrayed it.

'Yes,' he said, 'If I were female you might with reason call me a slut.'

'Sir!'

He laughed at her and putting his hands on her shoulders studied her face.

'Do you know, Mrs. Armistead, at one time I, my friend Richard Fitzpatrick and my cousin the Earl of Carlisle were regarded as the three best dressed men in London? Times change and we change with them, eh. Look at me now. You could not, in reason, call me the best dressed man in London.'

'I would not call you dressed at all, sir.'

'Stop calling me sir,' he said. 'And I refuse to call you Mrs. Armistead.'

'My name was Elizabeth Bridget Cane before I married Mr. Armistead.'

'Well Lizzie, now you have formally introduced yourself and I am very pleased that we have become good friends.'

'I came to tell you that Mrs. Robinson is going to give up the stage.'

He grimaced. 'Sheridan won't like that. He's playing to excellent business. Everyone wants to see Mrs. Robinson. It's rumoured, but the audience is not certain, that she is the mistress of the Prince of Wales.'

'When the Prince has his establishment he is going to set her up in a house.'

Fox nodded.

'Their little affair goes according to plan. There are other matters.'

He was looking at her intently. She had known it must come to this; and when it did of course this would not be the end. There was more between them than a passing desire for a handsome lady's maid on his side and the need not to offend an important man on hers.

As he came nearer she did not draw back. He took her hand and she let it rest in his.

Sheridan sat in his office at the theatre surrounded by playbills, plays which had been sent in for reading, and bills which he chose to ignore because he knew he could not settle them.

He was surprised when Mr. Charles James Fox was announced. They were acquainted and had an admiration for each other; but as yet their interests had been divergent. Sheridan followed political affairs with a mild interest; Fox was an occasional visitor to the theatre; but Sheridan, himself a Whig, had been impressed by Fox's adroit manoeuvres and Fox by *The School for Scandal* and *The Rivals*.

But why, wondered Sheridan, had the important gentleman seen fit to call upon him?

'Mr. Fox, sir, at your service,' he said.

'At yours, sir. I trust this is not an inconvenient hour to call?'

'Any hour would be convenient to receive a visit from Mr. Fox.'

Fox laughed to imply they could dispense with trite formalities.

'Business is booming, I see,' said Mr. Fox. He was well aware that although business boomed so did Sheridan's debts. Sheridan was a gambler and a gay liver; moreover, he was of an intellectual calibre to match Fox's. Such kindred spirits were rare.

Sheridan, knowing that Fox would be well aware of his financial difficulties, shrugged his shoulders and nodded in the direction of the pile of bills. No need to excuse himself to a man who had been—was constantly—in a similar position.

'So tiresome,' said Mr. Fox, 'to have to pay for one's pleasures!'

'But if one did not make a pretence of doing so we should have every Tom, Dick and Harry scrambling for them. Would there be enough to go round?'

'I do not think it would be beyond the powers of our invention to create new ones, Mr. Sheridan.'

Sheridan opened a cupboard and brought out two glasses.

Without speaking he filled them and handed one to Fox.

'Your very good health, sir, and good fortune to the project you have come here to discuss with me this day.'

Fox laughed. 'Mr. Sheridan, your talents are considerable. Words are your forte. The same thing applies to me. To be brief I have come to suggest that you stand for Parliament.'

'Did I hear you aright, sir?'

'As a Whig. You are a Whig, sir. No doubt of that.'

Sheridan lifted his glass. 'To wine, women and Whigs, sir.'

Mr. Fox drank and said: 'So, Mr. Sheridan?'

'Mr. Fox, sir. I am sitting here among my accounts, doing my theatre business with no thought of taking on the office of Lord of the Treasury.'

'You will not be hurried into that position quite yet, Mr. Sheridan.'

'But no one enters politics surely without dreaming of the Great Seal. It is the Field Marshal's baton . . . it is the Admiral's . . . Forgive me, sir, but what is the insignia of our sea lords? Is it the holy grail?'

'Dream of it then, Mr. Sheridan! Dream of it! You are too clever a man to concentrate all your efforts into one undertaking. Your plays . . . your theatre . . . yes, excellent for an ordinary man. But you are not an ordinary man, Mr. Sheridan. You have a touch of genius. Give it to your country.'

'Are there not too many at this moment offering their genius to the country? See what such genius had done. Lost us the American Colonies, for one thing.'

'Alas, politicians are legion; genius is rare. North is the biggest blundering idiot that ever held the Great Seal. And H.M. clings to him. Why? Because he sees himself as a Supreme Ruler. North and the King. By God, what a pair. I have to put the King and his Tories out of office, Mr. Sheridan; and I can only do that by putting the Whigs in.'

'Surely the people are behind the Government.'

'Mr. Sheridan, you will have to learn your politics. The people will be Tory one day and Whig the next and it is our task to see that they are Whig the day after and the week after and the year after. How do we do it? By teaching them, educating them, by making them realize what a holy mess we're in, what the loss of the colonies mean to us.'

'We?'

'Those of us who have the power to do so. Men who are on familiar and caressing terms with the English language.'

'Like Mr. Fox for instance.'

'Mr. Fox, sir, and Mr. Sheridan.'

'A place in politics . . . a Member of Parliament,' mused Sheridan.

Fox leaned forward. 'If the right party were in power it could be a high place in the Government. It would be a different life from this . . .' Fox waved his hand with a faintly disparaging gesture. 'You would be the friend of anyone you chose to meet. I personally would see that you were a member of Brooks' . . . or any club you fancied. You would be welcome in the most noble houses. Oh, I know these are the outward trappings of power . . . of no importance in themselves. But they are a measure of success.'

'You speak as though Power is the ultimate goal of all men.'

'Men such as you and myself, Mr. Sheridan. We were sent in the world with our talents. Is it not incumbent upon us to use them?'

'I am using mine. I think I have written plays which will be performed a hundred years hence. If the Playmaker Sheridan is not forgotten after he's dead is that not enough?'

'It depends on what talents you arrived with, Mr. Sheridan. A brilliant playwright . . . yes. And the theatre will rejoice in that talent for years. Generations will rise up and call you blessed. But this country is rushing ahead to disaster. Pitt saw it, but he was defeated by the gout and changing his title from The Great Commoner to Chatham. Politicians can't afford to make mistakes. By God, Mr. Sheridan, it's the most exciting game on earth. Loo, Faro, Macao, Hazard! You haven't gambled until you've played politics.'

Sheridan's eyes were shining and Fox knew that he would achieve his purpose.

He leaned forward. 'This, Mr. Sheridan, sir, is a turning point in British politics. Our monarchs carry a certain power. True they cannot act without the backing of their government but the power is there. The King—between men of good sense— is far from clever. I won't say he's a fool . . . not for fear of committing lese-majesty but because it is not entirely true. George is a simpleton. He should have been a farmer. A good man let us say . . . who has never known the pleasures of life, and who feels it his duty to see that these are kept from others. A failing of the virtuous, Mr. Sheridan, as I'm sure you will agree. But what H.M. fails to see is that the pleasures a man indulges in are not his whole life. A man can be a brilliant politician in the House, a lecher in the bedchamber and a gambler at the clubs. A politician can set the country's economy to rights while he's at his wits' end to know how to placate his own creditors. Mr. Pitt happened to be a model husband and a great politician at the same time. That in itself provided his downfall. He didn't become Lord Chatham for his own sake . . . but that of Lady Chatham. And that, one might say, was the end of his career. So you see, Mr. Sheridan, this is the greatest gamble and I know that your fingers are itching to have a throw of the dice.'

Sheridan was silent, turning over the possibilities in his mind. It seemed a glittering prospect because this was not merely going into Parliament—it was going in arm in arm with Mr. Fox.

Mr. Fox continued: 'As I was saying, the King has a certain power and the King is my enemy, and that of the Whigs. But a new star is rising and to this star shall we hitch our wagon. The Prince of Wales will be eighteen in August. He will be to us what the King is to the Tories.'

'The Prince! A young man bent on pleasure!'

'Don't underestimate him. Bent on pleasure certainly. Young, lusty and so far kept under the stern eye of their Majesties. "Eat this. Don't eat that". "Get up at this hour. Go to bed at that." Now what effect is this going to have on a young fellow whose high spirits are higher than average? There is one answer: Rebellion. Believe me, Mr. Sheridan, the Prince has a very good reason to support the Whigs. His father is a Tory. That is the only reason he needs at this stage. Later he will find others. Don't make old George's mistake of thinking that because young George frolics with the ladies, selects his shoe buckles with care, has a passion for gold frogged coats and exquisitely cut breeches, that he's a fool. He has been educated and significantly has made no effort to elude that education. He has the power to make his father feel a dunce in his presence. He is a boy . . . not yet eighteen . . . but time does not stand still. In three years time he will be the most powerful man in the country and . . . our friend.'

'*Our* friend, Mr. Fox?'

'Yours and mine.'

'But I have not yet made up my mind to go into politics.'

'You will.'

Mr. Fox drained his glass and rose.

'So Turtles Pair'

While Sheridan was thinking of Fox's proposition he received
another visitor.

Very different this one—a vision of beauty in muslin and
ribbons and a dark silk coat.

'Perdita!' Like everyone else he called her by that name nowadays. The Prince had given it to her and it was an indication
that everyone was aware of the relationship between them.

He kissed her hands with a fervour which she was too distraught to see was absentminded.

'Oh, Sherry, I have something to say to you, and I fear you
may be a little angry with me.'

'Never,' he declared gallantly.

'I scarcely know how to begin.' A faint smile curled Sheridan's lips. Of course she would have been rehearsing the scene
for hours before she came. He knew his Perdita.

'My dearest, you look distrait. Is all well between you and
the Prince?'

She threw back her head and a smile illuminated her face. By
God, he thought, how beautiful she is when she smiles. She
should smile constantly. What a fool she is to cultivate this melancholy aspect! He won't like it. She won't last if she is not
careful.

'The Prince is magnificent. The grace of his person . . . the
sweetness of his smile . . .'

'Yes,' said Sheridan. He had heard that before.

'He is quite . . . irresistible.' That was the excuse clause, he
thought. She was his mistress—but only because he was irresistible.

'But you have not come to tell me of his perfections, I am sure, because, as you know, I am well aware of them. Come, Perdita. what is on your mind?'

'The Prince can be very masterful.'

'Naturally. He is a Prince and in spite of Papa's restrictions I've no doubt he gets his way with everyone else.'

'Believe me, Sherry, this distresses me. Not on my own account . . . oh, no, I am ready to make any sacrifices . . . but I do wonder how you will receive this news. Oh, my dear, what are you going to say?'

'I will tell you when I hear what it is.'

She lowered her eyes and stood before him in a pose of abject distress.

'The Prince insists that I leave the stage.'

Sheridan was silent. He pictured it; the falling off of business. There was Abington and Farran. Perhaps he could revive *The School*; but although it was a favourite the people were crying out for new plays—though while Mrs. Robinson paraded the boards, particularly in breeches, they did not so much care what the play was.

He could not pretend that this was not a disaster.

'Oh, Sherry, Sherry, what could I do? I remonstrated but he was most emphatic. "No," he said, "I cannot have other men's eyes feasting on the charms of my loved one." You must confess, Sherry, that he has a point.'

'So,' said Sheridan, 'you are leaving the stage.'

'Oh, Sherry, Sherry, you know I don't want to. You know that I fought against it. But the Prince was adamant . . . and in the circumstances you must admit that I could not . . . with decency . . . remain.'

Oh, God, he thought, what a woman! She decided on the angle from which she would view life and made everything fit into her cosy pictures. What was she dreaming of now? One would think from her attitude that the Prince was proposing to marry her. Was she thinking that he would behave as his uncles Gloucester and Cumberland had? Did she realize that their Duchesses were very different women from herself? He could imagine her drawing herself up to her full height and declaiming that she hoped she did not resemble the Duchess of Cumberland whose morals and bawdy wit were the talk of the town. In one thing only, misguided Perdita. She is beautiful . . . and so are you. You lack her mental agility, her wit, her brilliance, her knowledge of the world . . . everything that has put her where she is. And dear Perdita, have you ever heard of the Royal Marriage Bill? No descendant of George I is allowed to marry without the consent of the sovereign. And do you think His Most Holy Majesty will agree to his son's marriage with a play actress? Silly little Perdita . . . moth dancing round the candle. How many months . . . weeks . . . before your pretty wings are singed and you fall to the ground? And then . . . what will you have? A career that is over. Do you think the theatre will allow you to throw her aside and then meekly take you back?

He should warn her, of course. He had been quite fond of her once. Not that it would be of any use. Her mind was made up. She, with all her reluctance, with all her mock propriety, wanted to be set up in that establishment, wanted the whole world to know that the most eligible bachelor in Europe had chosen her. Briefly, Perdita, briefly! But that thought of course must not be allowed to disturb her golden dream.

Sheridan sighed. 'I could almost thank God that Mr. Garrick is not here to see this day.'

'Mr. Garrick? What has he to do with this?'

'What indeed! Did he not teach you what you most needed to know when you most needed it? Mr. Garrick would never have understood your throwing away a great career.'

'Mr. Garrick understood the theatre so well, but did not understand love.'

'I'll warrant he did. Could he have been the greatest actor otherwise? So you will leave us.' He looked at her. He must warn her. He would not forgive himself otherwise.

'Perdita, this is a big step you are taking.'

She nodded dramatically.

'Princes are perhaps more fickle than most men.'

'What are you suggesting?'

'What if this love should not last?'

'He has sworn to be faithful till death.'

'By the moon, the inconstant moon, Juliet?'

'He swore by all he holds most sacred.'

'What a man holds sacred one day he finds profane the next. I am an old friend, Perdita. Take care. Consider before you throw away a certain future for an uncertain one.'

'I cannot grasp your meaning.'

'Because you will not. Has it not occurred to you that the Prince might desire another woman?'

'I see you make the common mistake of presuming this is an ordinary light affair.'

'I hope I am making that mistake, Perdita.'

'But I know you are. And I know you, Sherry. You are angry with me . . . that is why you say these things. I am not ungrateful. I know what you have done for me. Mistake that not. But this is my future. I must obey the Prince.'

'For if you did not he would cast you aside?'

She flushed. 'Never. But I must think of him . . . first. I owe it to him.'

'You mean the Prince's mistress should not appear on the boards.'

'Sherry!'

He laughed inwardly. What a woman. She could not bear the use of that word which was commonly used to describe what she was. He felt an affection for poor Perdita. She was such a fool. And this was particularly noticeable after one had so recently been in the company of Mr. Fox.

Mr. Fox! His mind was alert. This very day Mr. Fox had called to offer a dazzling prospect . . . this day when Perdita had come to offer her resignation.

Could there be any significance in this? Could Mr. Fox have known she would come? But how could he? He was only just acquainted with Perdita. And she would never have confided in him. And yet . . . here was this new proposition side by side with the certainty that theatrical business must suffer a setback.

Suppose Mr. Fox wished no obstacle to be put in the way of this love affair between the Prince and Perdita—suppose it was Mr. Fox's desire that the Prince should set up his mistress in a fine house and the whole world know of the relationship between them? Then he would not wish Mr. Sheridan to persuade Perdita of the follies of leaving the stage, of the inconstancy of princes. He had not *said* so, but politics was a game of innuendoes. And surely it was a strange coincidence that Mr. Fox had called on this very day when Perdita was handing in her resignation?

Had the subtle game of intrigue already begun? It excited him to think so. Rarely, he supposed, had he been so flattered in his life.

Mr. Fox planned to use the Prince . . . and perhaps Perdita.

She was looking at him earnestly. 'If, as you so unkindly suggest . . . But Sherry I know you do not do it from unkind motives for you have always been my friend . . . If the Prince should . . . If the Prince and I should no longer be together . . . why then, Sherry dear, I should most certainly come back to the stage.'

He did not explain to her once more that he doubted she would be able to do that. He was concerned with his own affairs which seemed to him of far greater importance than the amours of a Prince and an actress.

'Thank you, Sherry, for taking it so . . . magnificently.'

She held out her hand for him to kiss, a pretty, wistful expression in her beautiful dark eyes.

Then she returned home to report to Mrs. Armistead: "Mr. Sheridan was certainly distressed, but he took it better than I thought he would. I have always known that he was my very good friend.'

The Duke of Gloucester drove out to Kew to see his brother. When he asked for an audience the King received him immediately. He had always been fond of Gloucester. Cumberland was the brother he detested. But there had certainly been a breach between them over his brother's marriage. The King had been hurt to have been kept out of his brother's confidence, yet he had to admit that had Gloucester asked his permission to marry Lady Waldegrave he would have refused it. He would have told Gloucester that a Prince of the Blood Royal could not marry a woman who was not only illegitimate but was said to be the daughter of a milliner.

So Gloucester had married without his sovereign's consent and kept the matter a secret until the passing of the Royal Marriage Act had forced him to reveal it.

And then . . . George had refused to receive him officially and Charlotte had said she would never make a milliner's daughter welcome at her Court. But the King was a sentimental man, a family man, and although the Duchess was not received, the King was always pleased to see his brother.

'Well, well, William,' said George. 'Be seated, be seated.'

William sat and thought poor old George looked older than when he had last seen him. That affair of the Gordon Riots must have upset him. What a decision to make and fancy old George having the guts to make it. Firing on his own subjects, eh? Right, absolutely right in the circumstances and George had earned the approval of his grateful Capital—which was something rare for the poor old fellow.

William—content with his life and his Duchess—felt sorry for George's hard lot. Not much fun in being the King, particularly for a man like George who took himself seriously. It would be different when the Prince took over. Not for many years yet, he trusted. Couldn't help being fond of good old George although he was a pompous, self righteous old devil now and then.

'I've come to talk with you, George, about the Prince.'

An expression of anxiety crossed the King's face.

'What? Eh? What's he been at now, eh? You've heard something. Rumours . . . rumours . . . there are always rumours. Some of them true too . . . about that young puppy . . . '

'He's been up to nothing that I know of George. Only pleasing the people. I hear nothing but praise for him wherever I go. He's won the people's approval without doubt.'

'Because he's got a handsome face . . . not yet marked with evil living. Because he's been well looked after all these years . . . diet, exercise, discipline. All very necessary, eh what?'

'He certainly does his upbringing credit. The point is, he'll be eighteen in August.'

'A fact I'm not allowed to forget.'

'With his own establishment . . . '

The King grunted.

'I should like to have an opportunity of seeing him, George. It's a long time since I have.'

'People who act rashly take the consequences. Why, your marriage has given offence to all the royal families in Europe. Marrying a woman who . . . '

'I am happy in my marriage, George, and regret nothing.'

The King's eyes were momentarily clouded with emotion. 'Wouldn't have wanted to hear you say aught else,' he said gruffly. 'Still, you must understand. I can't have the Duchess at Court. The Queen wouldn't hear of it.'

'Don't expect me to believe that if the King gave the order, the Queen would not obey.'

'There are some matters she must be the judge of, eh, what?'

Gloucester said: 'I came to ask your permission for an interview with my nephew. Don't you think that we should have a chance to know each other? Should members of families be kept apart?'

'I never wanted to part families. But if people will make reckless marriages there's no help for it.'

'I hear that Cumberland has met the Prince.'

'What, eh?'

'In the Park. They met by chance and there was a touching scene. The people looked on and cheered the avuncular embrace.'

'The fellow's a rogue,' muttered the King, 'for all that he's my own brother. And more so because of it. Ingratiating himself with the Prince. I'll put a stop to that.'

'It still remains that he has spoken with Cumberland and not with me. Don't you think that I should have a chance of congratulating my nephew.'

'There's nothing to congratulate him about, I do assure you.'

'On his approaching birthday. A milestone in the life of a young prince. Eighteen. The age when he ceases to be a boy and realizes he's only three years off his manhood.'

'He has not only just realized it, I can assure you. He's been thinking of it for months.'

'Perfectly natural, George.'

'You seem determined to defend the puppy. Well, you shall see him. I don't see why not. Cumberland waylaid him in the Park. If you come to Kew next Friday, you can call on him and stay for half an hour.'

Gloucester was well pleased.

The Queen sent for Colonel Hotham, one of the members of the Prince's household. She was disturbed because the Duke of Gloucester was going to spend half an hour with her son. The Prince's visits to her were growing less and less: he never came until commanded to do so. It was very sad. When he was in her presence she longed for him to show a little affection. He never did; all he showed was his longing to get away.

And his uncle was going to see him. She would not have allowed it; but the King was weak where his brother was concerned. She imagined how Gloucester would put his case to the Prince: his version of the reason why he had been banished from Court would sound very romantic to young ears. She could imagine the Prince's sympathy; and he would not feel very kindly towards his mother, she knew, if Gloucester should tell him that she had said she would not receive a milliner's daughter at her Court.

Oh, dear, her darling son's growing up did create problems. And just now she was feeling the heat very much, for in a very short time now her child would be born.

'Colonel Hotham,' she said. 'His Majesty has given the Duke of Gloucester permission to see the Prince of Wales. I want you to be in the room during the interview. I want you to tell me *everything* that is said.'

'Yes, Your Majesty.'

'I feel sure that your presence will prevent the Prince's uncle from saying anything that it would not be good for His Highness to hear. But if he should . . . I wish to know.'

Colonel Hotham assured the Queen that she could trust him to be her very good servant . . . now as always.

When the Queen dismissed him Colonel Hotham went back to the Dower Lodge, but on his way there he reflected that if he insisted on remaining in the room where the Prince would meet the Duke he would have some explaining to do. The Prince was on the whole good tempered, but he could fly into rages—particularly if he felt his dignity was impaired. And surely by appointing an onlooker at this interview it could be said that the Queen was treating him as a child.

What a quandry! It was, in fact, a choice between pleasing the Queen or the Prince. The Queen had no power whatsoever. Indeed the King himself might be displeased by the presence of a third party at the interview, and as it would be only on the Queen's orders that he would be there, was he not placing himself in an invidious position?

Family dissensions would make a great deal of trouble—not only for the family but for those who served them. Wise men remained outside them, particularly when a dangerous situation was arising—a powerful king and very soon to be an equally powerful prince.

Yes, he must drop a hint to the Prince *before* the meeting took place.

'What!' cried the Prince. 'You will stay in the room when my uncle calls. But on whose orders, pray?'

'On those of the Queen, sir.'

'So the Queen sees fit to meddle now. And His Majesty?'

'I have no orders from him, Your Highness.'

The Prince smiled slowly, 'I do not think you will be present, Colonel Hotham.'

'Do you not, sir?'

'No, because I will write to the King and ask that you may not.'

'Very well, sir. As you know I shall await orders.'

'Thank you,' said the Prince.

He sat down at once and wrote a letter to his father. The Queen had ordered that one of his servants should be present at the interview between himself and his uncle, and as he was certain that this would give displeasure to his uncle, he was humbly entreating His Majesty to rescind the order.

He had correctly calculated the effect his would have on the King, who heartily disliked the Queen to interfere in any matter, and would think it was presumptuous of her to take it upon herself to give this order to Colonel Hotham. Charlotte had still not learned her lesson; then she must be taught it. No interference. Get on with the task of bearing the royal children at which she was extremely efficient. But certainly she was not when she meddled in matters of state and diplomacy.

The King wrote back to the Prince who for once had remembered *his* manners and written in the respectful way a son should write to his father. Certainly Colonel Hotham should not be present.

Gleefully the Prince acquainted the Colonel with this fact and the Colonel congratulated himself that he had had the good sense to inform the Prince of the matter and so not incur his displeasure.

There was no doubt that the Prince was becoming more important every day. It seemed to the Colonel that today he was only second to the King. And tomorrow? Who could say? But it was as well to be prepared.

The Duke of Gloucester embraced his nephew warmly. There were tears in his eyes which the Prince was quick to notice, and he himself took a perfumed lace-edged kerchief from his pocket and wiped his eyes.

'So long . . . ' sighed Gloucester. 'And you have become a man.'

'I am glad you recognize it, Uncle. It is more than some do.'

'You'll shortly be eighteen. You'll notice the difference then.'

'But still three years from twenty-one. I never knew time could pass so slowly.'

'Ha, there'll come a time when you'll remember those words.'

'So I am constantly told, but I find the passage of time so slow that it infuriates me. You can guess how I long to be of age . . . with my own establishment . . . my *independence*.'

'I can understand it well.'

'I wish my father did.'

'Oh, there is always this difficulty with fathers and sons.'

'You think uncles understand nephews better?'

'I am certain of it.'

They were laughing together. Why isn't the King more like

his brothers? the Prince asked himself in exasperation. When have I ever been able to speak lightly about anything, to have a little joke with him. Never! He has no humour. What a bore the old man is!

'Well, perhaps now you are permitted to come to Court you will be able to drive a little understanding into my father's head.'

'It'll come. He'll realize you are grown up all of a sudden.'

'I intend him to,' said the Prince. 'For one thing, I think it quite absurd that I have not been able to meet my uncles before this simply because my father did not like their Duchesses.'

'We married without his consent.'

'And why should you not? Why should one grown man have to ask the consent of another?'

'Well, his Marriage Bill was fortunately too late to affect us.'

The Prince laughed. 'I'd like you and my Uncle Cumberland to know that I admire you for what you did.'

'I must thank Your Highness for those kind words. But you won't attempt to follow our example will you?'

The Prince was on the verge of confiding his devotion to Mrs. Robinson but decided against it. In any case his uncle probably knew about it. Most people did; the only ears it had not reached were those of the King and Queen.

'If I did,' joked the Prince, 'I would first come to you to ask your advice as to how to set about it.'

Both uncles were so easy to get on with. He enjoyed chatting with them. He asked after the Duchess, for he was not going to follow his father's stupid example. And his uncle was very pleased to speak of her, for there was no doubt that his marriage had been a success.

When the half hour was over, and the Prince took leave of his uncle, he said: 'I cannot see you now without the King's leave, but in three years I shall be of age, and then I may act for myself. I declare I will visit you.'

The King sent for his son. As the rumours and gossip concerning Perdita Robinson and the Prince had so far been kept from him and the Queen, he believed that young George had been behaving during the last months with unusual propriety and had told the Queen that he believed that he was settling down at last. Charlotte was only too happy to agree.

Therefore when the Prince arrived the King greeted him without the usual irritation. The Prince's manner seemed subdued. He was in fact wondering whether the King had sent for him because he had discovered about Perdita; and when he found that this was not the case he was distinctly relieved.

'Your eighteenth birthday will soon be with us,' said the King. 'A milestone, eh, what?'

'A milestone,' repeated the Prince, his hopes soaring. Now he was going to hear of the allowance he would get, the house which would be his. The gates of freedom where slowly opening. 'No longer a boy! Responsibilities eh? Well, it is fitting that you should have an apartment of your own.'

Apartment, thought the Prince; and visualized the fine house which would be his. If he did not like it he would have it altered to his design. He had a distinct flair for architecture and had told Perdita that when his father gave him some noble house it should be a love nest for them both.

'You are not yet fully of age. Another three years before that. But eighteen . . . yes, an apartment certainly. I have decided that part of Buckingham House shall be assigned to you and your staff.'

Part of Buckingham House! How could he and Perdita make their love nest in his father's palace! The Prince was aghast.

The King went on: 'You'll have an allowance that'll be adequate and you shall have your own horses. You'll not be under the same restraint . . .'

The Prince was not listening. A red haze seemed to swim before his eyes. Was this what he had been waiting for?

Rooms . . . rooms in Buckingham House!

He could not speak what was in his mind. He dared not. He was a minor still. Three long weary years stretched out before him. He had expected to gain so much and had gained so little.

One prison door had been opened, but he was not to be allowed his full freedom.

'Rooms in Buckingham House!' he told Frederick. 'Think of it! Under Papa's constant eye. I thought I was going to have my own establishment. I thought I was going to invite my friends.'

'You'll choose your friends now,' Frederick pointed out. 'For instance, you won't have to scale walls when you go and meet them. You won't have to hire rooms in inns surely. You have gained something.'

'By God,' cried the Prince. 'I mean to show them. His and Her Sainted Majesties! I will make them wish they had never tried to put their fetters on me. I shall live as I like . . . do as I like . . . even though it is only in a part of Buckingham House.'

* * *

He determined to show the Court that he would not tolerate restraint. Even the apartments in Buckingham House were not to be occupied until January. But at least he had more freedom and he intended to exploit it to the full. No longer was it necessary to disguise himself as a night watchman and go clandestinely to Eel Pie Island. The Countess of Derby wanted to sell her house in Cork Street and it seemed to him ideal for Perdita. The money to buy it? Who would deny credit to the Prince of Wales?

So the house in Cork Street was his and he met Perdita there and together they went over it planning how it should be decorated. Perdita was all for discreet pastel shades; but the Prince wanted scarlet and gold. It was to be a royal residence; he himself intended to spend much time here. He would furnish it as a surprise for her.

And so he did . . . sparing no expense. On the command of the Prince of Wales, was enough to make any tradesman rush to execute the order. Most expensive materials must be used, everything of the finest—and no questions asked about the price.

The Prince, inhaling the air of freedom, was happier than ever before, he told Frederick; and his ecstasy was reflected in the lovers knots which appeared on the furnishing, the entwined initials G and P, the gilded mirrors, the velvet curtains of the bed.

The Prince's orders were that the work must be completed at express speed. He could not wait to have his Perdita installed in Cork Street.

There came the day when he was waiting there to greet her. There he stood in the hall to embrace her and like an excited child to conduct her from room to room to show her how an ordinary house could be made into a royal residence.

Perdita was delighted with the entwined initials. A kingly custom. She did not recall, if she ever knew, that so had Henry VIII entwined his initials with those of Anne Boleyn in Hampton Court, but that poor Anne had lost her head before the work was completed.

Why should such thoughts occur to her? The Prince was as devoted as ever. He had bought this charming house for her and it was their home; and if it was the grandest she had ever lived in, well then, by his devotion he had lifted her to an eminence which some years before she would not have dreamed of attaining. She had come a long way from the rooms in Hatton Garden which she had shared with Mr. Robinson when they were first married. But she would not think of Mr. Robinson who was an uneasy subject at the best of times.

To the bedroom—with its velvet bed curtains caught up in a coronet under which they could make love.

'Different from that inn room, eh?' laughed the Prince.

'So different. How can I ever thank you, my Prince.'

'If you go on loving me, it is enough,' he answered.

She must be painted, he said. Of course he must have a portrait of her. He would arrange for one of the great painters of the day to come to Cork Street. His very own picture of his very own Perdita.

And so he sent the artist Stroehling to her; and she was painted reclining on a velvet-covered couch—a flimsy gown cut low to give a glimpse of a charming bosom, sloping shoulders and rounded arms. About her lower limbs was wrapped a cloak lined with ermine; and the artist had painted a fountain in the background.

The Prince came to watch the work in progress and was delighted with it.

'I shall keep it for ever,' he declared. 'It will remind me of the day I first saw you, when you came on the stage and changed my whole life. I remember how jealous I was when Florizel came on and you took his hand. How I longed to play Florizel!

>*"So turtles pair,*
>*Who never meant to part . . . " '*

he quoted.

Then he had an inspiration. The artist should paint two turtle doves into the picture.

This was done and when it was completed he was delighted.

As soon as he had his own apartments he would have it hung in his cabinet—a constant symbol of two lovers who were never meant to part.

Cumberland House

Elizabeth Sheridan was apprehensive. She rarely saw her husband now. The East Burnham days seemed so far off that they might never have existed. She feared the future.

The School for Scandal alone could have made Richard a rich man; the theatre brought in a good income; but what happened? The gaming tables claimed a large share of it; and women? She often wondered about women.

How different it was from those days when they had run away together. Richard was not the same man. She had known he had great talent, and had rejoiced in it; but to what had it brought him?

If only he would have allowed her to earn money by her singing, her name could have brought an audience to rival those of Perdita Robinson. But he was too proud, he said. Vanity perhaps would be a more apt term.

But she never showed her fears. She knew that that would have alienated him more quickly than ever. In his way he had an affection for her which went deep and none of his light amours could shake. She must accept him as he was. She must never attempt to change him, for to do so would be to lose him altogether.

Sometimes she thought longingly of the old days in Bath—the happy home, the musical family . . . the carefree days. She had visualized life going on in the same serene way when she had married Richard. She wanted to help him succeed as a playwright and she had thought that would have been the most important thing in the world to them both.

But it was not. He would start a play and tire of it. He did not want to work; he wanted to live in gay society; he was famous for his wit which came to him spontaneously; she had heard him scatter conversational gems to the right and left—to the delight of his listeners—they came and carelessly were lost when they should have been stored for posterity's delight.

He was indifferent to such suggestions; he only lived for pleasure. He caroused half the night and rose late in the mornings; sometimes he did not come home at all and she would lie in her bed wondering where and with whom he was sleeping that night.

And now he had become friendly with Mr. Fox, and she was afraid of where this friendship would lead. Fox was brilliant; Fox was influential; she had no doubt of that. He was also a gambler and a lecher. And . . . she had to admit it . . . so was Richard.

The friendship had begun suddenly and since then had ripened; and it was going to change Richard's career, she knew.

If he had a seat in Parliament he would become the close ally of Fox. She had tried to reason with him when he had come home so excited on that day to tell her that Fox had been to see him. 'You would be drawn into a circle, Richard, where living is high. We could not afford it. We are in debt now.'

'You look at life through your Bath eyes, my darling. You see life provincially. This will be the making of our fortunes if I am clever. And do you doubt that I am?'

'No, no, Richard, but there are your plays . . . the theatre . . .'

And he laughed at her and said: 'St. Cecilia, go back to your angels.'

And if he were successful . . . if he won this seat. She could see it so clearly. He would be reaching for power, he would move among men who had no need to consider money—or if they had, did not—men like Fox who had been bankrupt several times. But Fox was the son of a noble house. His father had been rich Lord Holland; he was connected with the Duke of Richmond. Sheridan could not afford to move in such circles. But he would do so all the same. The mound of bills would become a mountain. The nights away from home would be more numerous; and her anxieties would increase a hundred-fold. But there was nothing she could do.

Sheridan himself came in to interrupt her brooding.

'Elizabeth, where are you?'

She ran to him; he swung her up in his arms.

'Now, my girl,' he said, 'show proper respect to the Member of Parliament for Stafford.'

Prince Frederick was dismayed, and he went at once to his brother to tell him the reason for his concern.

'They are sending me away, George.'

The Prince stared at him in horror. Sending Fred away! Why they had been together all their lives, shared a thousand adventures; George constantly confided in Fred; they were inseparable.

'What are you talking about, Fred?'

'I have just had an audience with the King. He says that before the year's out I am to go to Germany.'

'Whatever for?'

'To start learning how to be a soldier. Colonel Greville is going with me.'

'You could learn that here in England.'

'I know. But they're sending me to Germany.'

'By God,' cried the Prince. 'Can't he forget his ancestors were Germans!'

'I suppose not. There's too much German in the family for that.'

The Prince looked at his brother in amazement, trying to imagine what it would be like without him. He sensed that it would be the end of their close relationship. They would remain friends, but their lives would be so different.

'I believe he does it just to irritate *me*,' cried the Prince pettishly.

'No, because he thinks it's good for discipline.'

'You could have a commission in the army here. We could both have one.'

The Prince saw himself in a dazzling uniform of his own designing. He pictured himself parading before Perdita's admiring eyes in Cork Street.

'That would suit me very well,' he went on. 'And why not?'

Frederick shook his head. He was as desolate as George at the prospect of parting.

The Prince stood before the King.

'I have come to ask you, sir, for a commission in the army.'

'Eh? What?'

'A commission, sir. In the army.'

The King was not altogether displeased by what he considered a show of seriousness.

'Not possible,' he said. 'Government . . . and people . . . would never allow the Prince of Wales to go out of the country.'

'A commission *here*, sir. Germany hasn't the only army in the world.'

How the young dog could anger him merely by a word and a look. The manner in which he said Germany—as though it were some inferior state!

'That's so,' said the King. 'But you will not have a commission in any army. Have you understood that, eh, what?'

'And why not, pray?'

'Are you addressing me?'

The Prince looked round the small chamber with an air of surprise. 'I was not aware that anyone else was present, and as I am not in the habit of talking to myself . . .'

'You insolent young dog!'

The Prince realized that he had spoken to his father in person as he often addressed him in his own private thoughts.

He murmured an apology.

'I should think so, eh, what? And let me tell you this, sir. You have to learn to be a king, not a soldier. You will need all your time and talents to achieve that. And you'll find there isn't time to go chasing young maids of honour round gardens, eh?'

Oh, God, thought the Prince, is he still thinking of Harriot er . . . What was her name?

He said placatingly: 'I had thought, sir, as Frederick is going into the army and we have always been together, we might have both had commissions and as I may not leave the country we might both do our training over here.'

'You think too much, sir,' said the King, 'of matters that are not your concern. You have enough to concern yourself with, eh, what? Now go and do it, and understand once and for all. Frederick goes to Germany; and you stay here and there is no commission for you, understand, eh, what?'

The Prince retired; as he came out into the King's drawing room he kicked a stool across the floor to relieve his feeling.

Bumbling old idiot! he thought. How much longer shall I have to listen humbly to his drivelling nonsense?

Such changes, sighed the Queen, lying in her bed awaiting the birth of her child. Frederick to leave the family circle—and young

William too! Frederick for the army and William for the navy. William was very young, but the King had said a little experience of the sea would do him no harm.

And George—dearest and best beloved—to have his own establishment.

How I wish he would come and see me *without* being asked to. He never did, of course. Perhaps he felt it would not be in accordance with the dignity due to the Queen. Oh, but I am his mother!

It would not be long now before the child was born. She was so accustomed to giving birth that it held few alarms for her. How different that first occasion—that hot August day eighteen years ago when she had prepared herself for her first confinement and prayed for a boy.

And her prayers had been answered—and what a boy she had produced . . . what a marvel of a boy, although a little wayward! But so handsome! She wished she could show them at home what a wonderful Prince she had given to the nation. They would hear of his exploits of course. The whole world talked of the Prince of Wales. She would never forget the welcome sentence: 'It's a boy!' Nor would she forget how Lord Cantelupe had been so eager to tell the King that the child was safely delivered that he had not waited to ascertain its sex and had told him that it was a girl. Cake and caudle for all visitors to the Palace. And what that had cost—because the visitors had been numerous! No cake and caudle for this one. That was a blessing. After all, this was not the Prince of Wales.

Eighteen years ago; and now he was to have his own establishment. She believed he was very happy about that. Oh dear, she did hope he would not be too wild and quarrel with his father. She was terrified of those occasions when the King was displeased with his children. As she listened to his talk growing faster and faster and sometimes a little incoherent because he did not finish his sentences, that terrible fear came to her. Then she would say: It is because there is still much I have to learn about the English language that I cannot catch what he says.

She could hear Schwellenburg's guttural accents not far off.

'*Nein, nein.* Give to me. Selfs will do it.'

The pains were coming frequently. It would be soon now.

'I think,' she said, calmly, 'the time has come.'

Very shortly afterwards she was delivered of a son.

* * *

The baby was christened Alfred by the Archbishop of Canterbury and his sponsors were the Prince of Wales, Prince Frederick and their sister Charlotte, the Princess Royal.

This caused some comment in ecclesiastical circles and the Bishop of Salisbury came to see the King on account of it.

'Your Majesty,' he said, 'the ceremony of the baptism of Prince Alfred has given grave cause for alarm throughout the Church.'

'What's that?' asked the King.

'Sir, the sponsors of an infant take on a solemn responsibility.'

'I am well aware of that, my lord Bishop.'

'And this has been undertaken by people who are scarcely of an age to recognize this. The Prince of Wales himself is but eighteen years of age. His brother and sister younger. I would like Your Majesty to consider authorizing another baptism. Your Majesty could then select persons of a more responsible age.'

The King prided himself on his reasonableness.

'I understand, my lord Bishop, your point of view. But by the time Prince Alfred is of an age to need the guidance of his sponsors, they themselves will have reached an age to give it.'

'Sir, I believe you should reconsider this matter.'

'Thank you, my lord. I believe I have considered it and answered your fears. You have understood, eh, what?'

No one would have dared argue with George I or George II. It was different with George III; although once he had made a decision he could rarely be shifted from it, he was always ready to treat anyone who doubted his wisdom with courtesy.

'The Prince of Wales,' he explained, 'in view of his peculiar position as heir to the throne, is not to be judged by ordinary standards. When in due course he is King of this country he will be the best possible guardian for a brother who is eighteen years his junior. Thank you, my lord Bishop, for raising this point. Now it is explained, eh, what? And you have business to attend to . . . and so have I.'

With that the Bishop had to be content.

But when the Prince heard an account of the Bishop's criticism he was annoyed.

'This is what happens,' he said. 'It is because I am treated like a child that people regard me as a child. I, the Prince of Wales, am not considered worthy to be my young brother's sponsor.'

He could not forget the insult to his dignity; and some days after he had heard of the incident, coming face to face with the Bishop of Salisbury, he stopped him and demanded in a voice which could be heard by all around: 'Have you heard the news, my lord Bishop?'

'What news, may it please Your Highness?' replied the Bishop.

'My father,' the Prince told him, 'has sent to the sponsors of the Bishop of Salisbury to know how they could so egregiously have neglected their duty, as not to have taught their god-child to hold his tongue when it becomes him.'

The Bishop was too disconcerted to reply and the Prince swept on haughtily.

Soon everyone was discussing—and laughing at—the incident.

The Prince of Wales was indeed feeling his independence.

The Prince was biding his time until he could move into his new apartments in Buckingham House. So were others. Meanwhile he had to brace himself for the parting with Frederick and not spend too much time in Cork Street because until he was free of the Dower Lodge he was so close to his parents at Kew that his actions would not pass unnoticed by them; it would be different once he was in his own apartments.

After Christmas the time had come for the brothers to say goodbye.

The whole family assembled; the King wept openly and kept murmuring rather incoherent instructions to Frederick as to how he should behave.

The Prince of Wales felt numb. He was surprised that he could shed no tears, for never had he felt such sadness.

So close was the bond between them that Frederick understood; in fact he himself felt similarly and could shed no tears.

The brothers gripped each other's hands and stared wordlessly at each other. There was in any case no need for words.

Then Frederick left for Germany and the Prince of Wales moved to Buckingham House. Only a round of gaiety could help him to overcome his desolation at the loss of his brother.

Riding in the Park he met his uncle, the Duke of Cumberland. As on another occasion Cumberland called to his coachman to stop, alighted and kissed the hand of his nephew.

'Well met, Your Highness. This is a wonderful moment for me. And now you are indeed a man!'

'I am glad to see you, Uncle.'

'By God, what a fine coat that is you are wearing. I like the frogging.'

'I had it made to my orders.'

'Have I your Highness's permission to copy it?'

'As it is in the family . . . yes.'

'Your Highness, my wife, the Duchess, was speaking of you but yesterday. She had had a glimpse of you and I'll not tell you what she had to say of your charms. By God, I said, Come! come! You can't expect me to compete with the youth of my handsome nephew.'

'I did not see the Duchess or I should have had a word with her.'

'I'll tell her that. By God, it will make the day for her.'

'Pray do,' said the Prince.

'Your Highness's kindness makes me very bold. Dare I? I wonder.'

'You have a reputation for daring, Uncle.'

'So I have. Well, I shall live up to that reputation and say this: If Your Highness should ever see fit to honour us at Cumberland House . . . if by your great good sense . . . which I see exceeds that of some others . . . but my tongue runs away with me . . . If Your Highness should ever be in Pall Mall and have the fancy to be treated like a king, well, nephew, you would make a certain duke and duchess the happiest people in the world.'

'But of course I shall come,' said the Prince. 'If I had had my will I should long since have put an end to these stupid family quarrels.'

'Your Highness! You will indeed!'

'I will. Tell the Duchess that I am curious to discover if she is as beautiful as rumour paints her.'

'She will be overcome with joy.'

The Prince was delighted. After that old fool the Bishop of Salisbury this was the sort of thing he liked to hear.

'And so,' he said gallantly, 'shall I be to meet her.'

'May I tell her this, Your Highness?'

'Pray do.'

'And when . . .'

'I will call on her this evening . . . if that would please her.'

'Please her. She will swoon at the thought.'

'I would not wish to put her to any discomfort.'

'She would swoon with *joy*, Your Highness. I will return to her at once. This is the happiest day since our wedding day. I know she will agree with me. I will tell her of the great honour which awaits her.'

Cumberland returned to his coach and the Prince road on.

Cumberland House! The forbidden territory. What would his father say if he knew he had accepted an invitation to visit it?

He broke into a gallop. To hell with his father's rules and regulations!

It was with a feeling of great excitement that the Prince set out for the home of his uncle. The King and Queen were enjoying a period of domesticity at Kew and were well out of the way. No one could stop him now. If he wanted to visit his uncle he would.

Stepping into Cumberland House was like stepping over the threshold of a new life. All were waiting for him; there was no doubt that he was the most important man in the country.

The Duke was on the threshold to receive him; he bowed formally and then with tears in his eyes embraced him. And there was his Duchess waiting to give a profound curtsey to lift the most famous eyes in England to his face in a look of such adoration that his heart was immediately touched and had he not already been deeply in love with Perdita he would have fallen in love with his newly discovered aunt without fail.

She was tall and slender—like a flower, he thought; her hair was thick and gold coloured and she wore it unpowdered, dressed very high on her head with little curls and tendrils escaping here and there; her face was small, fairylike, almost fragile; she looked angelic but for her eyes which brimmed over with mischief; they were huge and green at the moment because she was wearing a green dress and emeralds sparkling about her person; and fringing them were the magnificent eyelashes—black as night, sweeping her delicately coloured cheek at one moment, lifted up like black feathery fans the next.

The Prince said: 'They are indeed the most fantastic eyelashes in the world.'

'I trust they please Your Highness,' she said. 'If they do not they shall be cut off this instant.'

'Pray do no such thing. I could not be responsible for destroying one of the wonders of the world.'

'How gracious, how charming of Your Highness! And how happy you make me. But we are being selfish. Some of our guests are aware of the great honour that awaits them . . . but not all. We have kept our little secrets . . . and we trust in doing so we have not incurred Your Highness's displeasure, because from now on it shall be *my* pleasure to maintain yours.'

What delightful company! How free and easy! And to think he had been deprived of it all these years. He thought of Kew. Backgammon! Lectures! The only dissipation—chamber music in the family circle.

Oh, life was going to be different from now on!

His bewitching aunt—and he was overcome with amusement to consider her as such—begged for the honour of slipping her arm through his ('for I am your aunt, you know') and conducted him to her guests. And willingly he offered his arm and happily he talked to her, for to tell the truth he was completely fascinated by those eyelashes.

And so, the Duchess on his arm, the Duke on the other side of him, he was led to the company.

This was, of course, how it would be from now on. People—interesting, important and amusing people—would be jostling each other to have a word with him. Beautiful women swept deep curtsies as he passed and lifted their eyes admiringly to him; men bowed low.

It was a glittering assembly at Cumberland House. All the most famous Whigs had been gathered together for the occasion and they all wished to be presented to him.

There was Mr. Fox and Mr. Burke and Mr. Sheridan, and their lighthearted, witty conversation had an immense appeal for him.

And then the surprise of the evening.

The Duchess said: 'There is a lady to whom I feel sure Your Highness would like to be presented. Have I your permission?'

It was granted at once—and the Duchess took him to an alcove and there to his great joy and gratification was Perdita herself.

He took her hand; he kissed it; and she lifted her eyes brimming over with love for him to his face.

'This,' he whispered, 'is the most wonderful moment of our lives.'

It meant that they were at last together in public, that his Uncle Cumberland accepted Perdita. Never again need they meet in secret.

This was indeed independence!

What an evening that was! For the first time since Frederick had gone he ceased to miss him.

He was astonished at the company—the free and easy manners, the talk which could be bawdy and at the same time witty and brilliant. Politics were discussed; so was art and literature. Everyone listened respectfully when he spoke but he had no need to feel ashamed of ignorance, for if he were not as yet fully versed in politics he could compete successfully in discussions on art and literature. There was dancing and gambling. The stakes were high but that seemed to him right in such distinguished company. He played at Faro and watched Loo and Macao; the men who most fascinated him were Fox and the playwright Sheridan. They were the sort of men he would have liked to have had for his tutors. Well, now he might have them for his friends. Might have them? He would if he wished. This night had taught him that what he asked would be readily given, and he was intoxicated with the joy of being the Prince of Wales.

He would come again and again to Cumberland House. There would, said the fascinating Duchess, always be a welcome for her handsome nephew at any hour of the day or night—and for Perdita.

She fluttered her lashes at Perdita who was perhaps a little jealous. She need not have been. He was her faithful lover; but he had to admit that his aunt was a damned attractive woman.

He would, he declared, come again and often.

Cumberland House, he was told, was his home whenever he cared to make it so.

And when he left with Perdita the Duke and Duchess savoured their victory; because it was now quite clear that it was the Cumberlands who were going to launch the Prince of Wales.

The Prince and Perdita went back to Cork Street. He was flushed not only with triumph for he had drunk more than usual.

Perdita had drunk very little and was sober in both senses.

'What an evening! By God, what a house! I declare ours looks like a cottage in comparison.'

He looked round it disparagingly.

'I would rather be happy in a cottage than unhappy in the finest mansion.'

The Prince laughed: 'Well, so would everyone else.'

She stood there, arms folded across her breasts, very pretty but too dramatic, and the Prince was in no mood for histrionics. He had caught the mood of the people he had been with and they would have been very quick to ridicule sentiment—particularly if it were false.

'Come here and stop acting, Perdita. You are not on the stage now. Come and be my turtle dove.'

She came and sat beside him—all grace and willowy draperies.

He kissed her with passion, but his thoughts were still with the company.

'Fox is one of the best talkers I ever heard,' he said. 'And Sheridan's another. By God, they are men I would be happy to call my friends.'

She shivered. 'You promised me once that you would not use bad language.'

'Did I, by God.' He laughed aloud. 'What did you think of Fox?

'I thought his linen was . . . unclean.'

The Prince laughed again. 'You met the most brilliant man in London and the first thing you have to say about him is that his linen is unclean.'

'I cannot see why his brilliance should prevent his putting on a clean shirt.'

'How severe you are. And Sheridan?'

'You forget I know him well.'

'A damned fine fellow. Words! He has a way with them.'

'They're his trade.'

'Perdita, one would think you did not greatly like the company tonight. I trust you did because *I* found it most diverting.'

'There were some ill reputations among that company,' she said, pursing her lips.

'Ill reputations are often the most interesting.'

She drew away from him. 'I do not like to hear you talk like that.'

He was startled. After all the approval he had had tonight this sounded like criticism. Perdita seemed to have forgotten that although he loved her he was still the Prince of Wales.

'That,' he said coolly, 'will not prevent my saying what I mean.'

She was alarmed; she saw the angry lights in his eyes. They were a warning. He had of course drunk more than was good for him. She must be careful, but she would do her utmost to prevent visits to Cumberland House. She did not trust the Duchess—nor the Duke for that matter. Ah, the Duke! How did he feel about *her* now? Did he remember the time when he had done all in his power to seduce her?

If she told the Prince that, perhaps he would not think so

much of his uncle. But not now. This was not the moment, when he was a little peevish.

'No one could prevent the Prince of Wales doing what he wished,' she told him soothingly. 'And as he is a man of great good sense, none but fools would wish to.'

She was on her feet, making a sweeping bow which was somehow reminiscent of a plump lady who had been at Cumberland House that evening. The Prince laughed—his good humour restored. Perdita laughed with him. She was so pretty when she laughed.

'Come,' he cried. 'Let us have a song.'

She sat at the harpsichord and he leaned over her. He had an excellent voice of which he was very proud; she sang well, for when she had decided to go on the stage Elizabeth Sheridan had given her lessons. Their voices mingled perfectly. She wanted to sing a sentimental song of love; but the Prince was not in the mood for sentimentality.

With Sheridan in mind he began to sing the song from *The School for Scandal*:

> *'Here's to the maiden of bashful fifteen;*
> *Here's to the widow of fifty;*
> *Here's the flaunting extravagant quean,*
> *And here's to the housewife that's thrifty.*
> *Let the toast pass*
> *Drink to the lass*
> *I'll warrant she'll prove an excuse for the glass.'*

A little primness had returned to Perdita's mouth; she did not want to be reminded of drink, for she had always known that the Prince was too fond of it.

However, the Prince was in good spirits; and when he had enough of singing, he declared that there was no better way to end a perfect evening than by spending the night with Perdita.

In the Duchess of Cumberland's bedchamber she discussed the evening with the Duke.

She curved her little white hands to make them look like claws and murmured: 'We have him. He is ours.'

The Duke nodded with satisfaction. 'Wait!' he cried. 'Just wait until this gets to old George's ears!'

'He may forbid it to continue. Then I suppose we should have to obey?'

'For a time.'

'For three years. God knows what will happen to our little Prince in that time.'

'You fascinated him. By God, he could scarcely take his eyes off you.'

'Don't play the jealous husband. It's too difficult a role for you.'

'I'll tell you this if you'd like to hear it. I've never seen a woman to come near you for looks.'

'What about Propriety Prue?'

'Who in God's name is she?'

'She goes under the name of Mrs. Perdita Robinson and I can tell you that she was not as pleased with our little entertainment as His Highness was.'

'What! That little play actress.'

The Duchess regarded him sardonically; she knew all about those visits to the theatre which had not been crowned with success as far as the Duke was concerned.

'You will I know agree that she is a beautiful one.'

'I don't doubt she's pretty enough.'

'Pretty enough for a prince . . . if not for a duke?'

'That was long ago. I thought she looked well in breeches.'

'So did many others. But this is beside the point. P.P. does not like us, I fear; and she undoubtedly will have influence with H.H.'

'Propriety Prue! And openly living in sin!'

'With a prince. You must admit that makes it a very *venial* sin.'

'Don't mock, Anne.'

'I'm deadly serious. In fact so serious that I am reminding you of something you may have forgotten.'

'What's that?'

'That women can beg and plead very prettily; they can also very slowly poison a man's mind against those who would be his friends. All these little tricks performed at dead of night in a velvet curtained bed . . . and the curtains, so I have heard, are held together overhead by a coronet, if you please . . . these tricks can be very effective. And I repeat, you should know.'

'Since it was in such circumstances that you forced me to marry you . . .'

'Not forced. I never use force. Only persuasion.'

He laughed. She never bored him in spite of his infidelities. He had given her what she wanted—marriage into the royal family, and she was content with that. He was a conceited little man—by no means the most attractive of the King's brothers, but he had married her and she must be thankful for that. She was not of course of lowly birth like her sister-in-law the Duchess of Gloucester, whose origins were very questionable. They did not meet often; they had so little in common, except that they were married to brothers and had both made marriages which were unacceptable to the King. The Duchess of Gloucester, Lady Waldegrave that was, was dignified, and in spite of her birth played the part of Duchess to perfection. The daughter of a milliner some said and of Sir Edward Walpole—the elder brother of that gossip and writer Horace—her father had supervised her education and in due course married her to Lord Waldegrave; and when Lord Waldegrave had died, Maria, the pretty creature, had taken a fancy to the Duke of Gloucester, and he to her it seemed, for he had impetuously, without consulting his family, rushed into marriage with her.

As for the Duchess of Cumberland—there was no question of her birth. She was the daughter of Lord Irnham and one of the Luttrells; she had married a country squire, Christopher Horton, who had died leaving her very young and ready for adventure. In London she had found it—in marriage with the dissolute Cumberland soon after he had brought scandal on the family through the notorious Grosvenor case.

He didn't regret it. She was the most amusing woman in London besides being one of the most beautiful. She was capable of acting hostess in Cumberland House and attracting all the most brilliant Whigs there—in opposition to the Tory friends of the King. For she agreed with her husband that since the King had refused to receive them at Court they must do everything they could to discomfort him. They would, if they could, have set up a rival court; but this was not possible, for Cumberland lacked the intelligence and his Duchess while not suffering from this lack, while being extremely witty in a malicious way, was so coarse in her conversations that it had been said that one was forced to wash out one's ears after visiting with her. Nevertheless they did attract the Whigs to Cumberland House; and if they could only gather the Prince of Wales into their fold they could at once set up that rival court. The fact that the Prince had no establishment of his own but only an apartment in his father's palace at Buckingham House was in their favour. They would strive to lure him to Cumberland House and keep him there so that until he had a house of his own, this might be his home.

Then they could form the rival court, 'The Prince's Court', 'The Cumberland's Court'—what mattered what it was called as long as it was set up as a rival to the King's Court and would distress that self righteous old fool the King, who had banished them from *his* Court.

'But to get back to Propriety Prue,' went on the Duchess. 'We must watch that young lady or she will persuade our little Prince that Cumberland House is not for him.'

'You think she could?'

The Duchess lowered her eyes and then lifted them—a trick she had long practised to call attention to her eyelashes. If she had persuaded a dissolute Duke to marry her in the face of tremendous opposition, surely a beautiful actress could persuade a susceptible young man to discontinue visiting his uncle.

'He was impressed with Fox . . . no doubt about that,' said the Duke.

'There are other places where he could meet the people he met here tonight.'

'But . . . I am his uncle.'

'That old mollycoddle up at the Palace of Piety is his father, but I don't fancy he is yearning to spend his evenings there.'

'By God, you're right. That woman could spoil our chances.'

She leaned towards him. 'And you know, my dear ducal lord, that we can only have one answer to that.'

He waited for it. He accepted her as the leading spirit.

'Spoil hers,' she spat out venomously, and her green eyes scintillated with malice.

Mrs. Armistead had overheard the conversation between the Prince and Perdita.

What a fool that woman is, she thought. How long can it last? Didn't she understand the Prince at all? He had an eye for a pretty woman. She had even caught his gaze on herself. Of course, thought Mrs. Armistead, if I had gowns of silk and satin and velvet, even muslin and lawn, I could be a fair rival to Perdita.

But who is going to look at the lady's maid? Some would, was the answer, providing the maid was good looking enough. And she was. There was no doubt of it.

And if the Prince was going to tire of Perdita, if they no longer mixed in the highest society, what of Mrs. Armistead?

There was Mr. Fox. She smiled, rather fondly, and she told herself foolishly. It would not serve to be foolish. She had a good example of folly before her now. She would never be guilty of that. Mr. Fox would always have a special place in her life; she knew that. He had wanted to reward her but she would not accept money. Was that foolish? Did she not need money more than most. What would become of her when she was no longer young enough to work, when she had lost her handsome looks? No, she could take nothing from Mr. Fox. What she gave him she gave freely.

She would tell him of course every detail of tonight's conversation and that she believed that the Prince was beginning to tire a little of Perdita—although he was too sentimental to realize this and she too vain and stupid. And when he had tried to give her money she had always refused it. She believed he understood and in a way applauded this. She was his mistress . . . in a casual way. What a strange relationship, yet she would not be without it. It made her in some way long for independence. And how could a woman in her position achieve that? She must either serve a stupid woman, concern herself with rouge and powder, ribbons and patches—or seek to please some gentleman. Was one more degrading than another? It was the end which counted perhaps not the means. She was too young for a celibate existence. Mr. Fox had taught her that—and of course Mr. Fox was the last man to expect fidelity.

Her opportunity to win independence was now. How could she say how long it would last?

Here in Cork Street the richest men in England would be congregating. A clever woman who kept her dignity, could have a chance to win independence and a gracious middle age. All she must do was stifle a few scruples and handle the situations which arose with tact and care.

There was a young gentleman whom she had noticed and who had noticed her. He was Lord Dorset; and she did not think she could demean herself if she allowed the attraction to ripen . . . providing she did so gradually and above all with dignity.

Mrs. Armistead had made a decision.

Now before she retired she would go over the report she would take to Mr. Fox in the morning. Then to bed. But first to take out of her cupboard the white satin gown with the silver tissue and one or two other dresses which had come her way.

She held them against her. Yes, a woman was a fool who did not use the gifts a munificent nature had bestowed upon her.

Visits to Cumberland House had whetted the Prince's appetite for gaiety. A circle was quickly forming around him. It was a wide circle, for he was ready to welcome into it men who were talented in any direction. He had quickly become on intimate terms of friendship with Charles James Fox, Edmund Burke and Richard Sheridan; but men like Lord Petersham and Lord Barrymore were also his close friends. Petersham was the best dressed man in London who would discuss for hours the right cut of a coat or what trimming should be used. He applauded the Prince's taste and assured him that the shoe buckle he had designed was in his opinion the most elegant he had ever seen. Barrymore was a great practical joker and the Prince found this form of releasing his high spirits to his taste. But he had discernment and would not try his practical jokes on Fox any more than he would talk politics or literature with Petersham. The world was opening out for him and with his great gift for falling violently in love, he was in love with his new life. He often said that one should go to the French for fashion and the English for sport; he enjoyed both. He took lessons in boxing and fencing and excelled in them. He rode well and would drive himself in his phaeton at a startling speed. He even drove his Tilbury through the Park with his groom sitting beside him. He was beginning now to be seen not only in various houses but in public, and the people greeted him with affection wherever he went; he was always gorgeously attired and spent a great deal of time planning his toilette, very often with the help of Petersham. He could dance well, sing well, talk well; and he was undeniably handsome. He was, it was said, the finest gentleman in Europe, and the English were proud to own him as their prince.

He kept a mistress, it was true, but very few held that against him. It all added to the gaiety of life and after years of old George—who was not so old but had always seemed so—with his virtuous but oh so dull Queen who did nothing but bear children for the state to support . . . after these two, young George was a source of great amusement and delight.

He was imbibing Whig politics at a great rate from Fox and Sheridan; they had become his closest friends, with Burke a good third. Elizabeth Sheridan was growing more and more anxious at the turn in her husband's fortune. They had been in debt before, but how could they afford to entertain the Prince of Wales? For the Prince insisted on visiting his amusing friend and was enchanted by the beauty of his wife and her singing in which he joined her for many a musical hour. A simple evening at the Sheridans the Prince might call it; but Elizabeth was aghast to realize what it cost to give such an evening to a prince. And there was Mr. Fox with his careless attitude towards debts. Money was something neither of the three ever gave a thought to. It was merely a word . . . a magic sesame to give them what they wanted. One bought and forgot that it was necessary to pay.

The Prince had become a frequent visitor to Cumberland House. Perdita did not care for Cumberland House so she was not often asked, but that not going to prevent the Prince visiting his own uncle. Fox took him along to Devonshire House where he met the beautiful Georgiana, Duchess of Devonshire, another of whom the King would call 'those damned Whigs.'

The Prince was delighted with the Duchess as he had been with his aunt; she was gay, she was witty and there was the same sort of welcome for him at Devonshire House as there was at Cumberland.

Hostesses were vying for his company. He was half in love with Georgiana, half in love with his aunt; and it seemed to him that he was surrounded by beautiful women. If it were not for Perdita . . .

Perdita herself was drawn into the gay world. It was no use thinking she could hide her position. Everyone knew that she was the Prince's mistress and the interest in her was at fever pitch. The papers mentioned her every day. Stories were told of her which at worst had little truth in them and at best were grossly exaggerated.

Tradesmen were constantly at the door with beautiful materials to be made into clothes for her; she bought lavishly. She had always had a passion for clothes, and now recklessly unleashed it, for she believed there was no need to consider the expense. Several seamstresses were working for her night and day; newspaper men called to ask Mrs. Armistead what her mistress would be wearing that day. Descriptions of her dresses were given to journalists and according to their accounts she was always decked out in diamonds, rubies, sapphires and emeralds. 'Gifts,' the public avid for news of the Prince and his affairs were told, 'of his Royal Highness.'

Cartoons were in circulation depicting her with the Prince; they were often ribald, often bawdy. Mr. Robinson was not forgotten either; he was known to the public through the horns without which he was never depicted. Every time she went out it was to find a crowd waiting outside the house; women came forward to touch her gowns, feel the material, comment on its

cost; some would make jocular remarks about the Prince's prow-
ess as a lover. These she ignored and she would return to the
house crying: 'Armistead. I am exhausted! Oh, how vulgar the
people are!'

And Armistead would say: 'Yes, Madam.' And despise her
mistress more than ever. She was so false, thought Mrs. Armistead. No one could have loved this interest she aroused more
than herself. As she did, why not admit it, for this pretence of
finding it tiresome was so stupid. In fact the more Mrs. Armistead felt her independence, the more she despised her mistress.
Lord Dorset had been very kind and considerate. At length he
had prevailed upon her to accept a little present. A *little* present
indeed! She was mixing in the right society, for what was little
to such a gentleman was a great deal to Mrs. Armistead. She
reckoned she had enough to invest in a little house. Why not?
A roof over her head. What could be wiser? And she would
furnish it with simple good taste—and it should be as different
from this gilded mock palace in Cork Street as a house could
be.

It was inevitable that the King should hear not only of his
son's visits to Cumberland House but that he was keeping a
young actress in Cork Street.

'Small wonder,' he said to the Queen, 'that I can't sleep at
night. I have had ten nights without sleep thinking of that young
rake. No good, eh? What?'

'Your Majesty will speak to him?' suggested the Queen tim-
idly.

'No good,' said the King sadly. 'Too late. My eldest son . . .
the Prince of Wales, is a . . . profligate, a rake . . . he keeps a
play actress. You see, he's gone over to my enemies . . . eh,
what? Took the first opportunity. Always knew we'd have trouble
with him. Keeping a play actress! Gambling! Going to see Cumberland when he knows that I . . .' The King was too distressed
to continue. He could only look at the Queen and whisper, 'Eh?
What?' again and again so that she wanted to stop her ears and
shout to him to stop, because she was so frightened to see him
in that mood.

Perdita was faintly uneasy. Was the Prince changing towards
her? Did he treat her with more familiarity? Was he using the
bad language which she so deplored more frequently?

He was constantly at Cumberland House and she was not

invited. Sometimes he talked of his aunt in a manner which disturbed her.

'By God, what a woman! I'm not surprised my uncle flouted my father for her.'

It was as though he were comparing them. Surely he could not compare her with that coarse-spoken woman!

But she was at least a Luttrell . . . a noble family. 'How strange,' she had said, 'that a woman of noble birth should be so coarse.'

'She's damned amusing,' retorted the Prince.

'For those who like vulgarity, yes.'

Had she seen the look he gave her she might have been warned, but she did not; she had a glimpse of herself in a distant mirror and was admiring the blue satin bows on her white dress.

'I personally could never endure it.'

The Prince did not answer; he was studying the buckles on his shoes with a sullen expression.

He left early although she had expected him to stay the night. And he gave no excuse for going.

So she was anxious; but the next time he saw her he was all devotion. Gently she reminded him of all she had given up for his sake. She did not want him to take her for granted. Her husband . . . well he was not much to relinquish, but she had loved her child and although the little girl lived not far away with her grandmother and she could see her now and then, the devotion she gave to the Prince left her very little time.

The Prince would suggest they sing together or perhaps take the air. He liked to ride with her through the Park and the crowds came to watch them, for she must be exquisitely dressed on these occasions; and they made a colourful picture.

Even she was cheered on occasions like that.

Sometimes he would stay away from Cork Street for several days; and then he would come in a mood of such gaiety that she could not doubt that he was happy to be with her. He would stay for several days and nights and declare that all he wanted in the world was to be with his Perdita.

She loved to ride in the Park, St. James's or Pall Mall, in her newest creation—always a different ensemble for she could never appear twice in the same; she would be most exquisitely powdered and patched; her face flowerlike with its contrast of rouge and white lead. Sometimes she was in frills and ribbons, at others she would wear a flowing cravat and a tailored coat, the very masculinity of which only accentuated her femininity. In satin and brocade, in muslin and linen, dressed simply in a hat resembling a sun bonnet or in a fashionable hat spilling feathers down her back and round her face, she always provided excitement for the spectators and there were crowds to see Perdita Robinson as they called her on parade. As she passed some called after her coarse enquiries but members of the Prince's circle doffed their hats and bowed low as they went past on foot or rattled by in their carriages; and members of the King's circle looked through her as though she did not exist.

She would return home as she said 'exhausted' and walked up and down her bedroom declaiming: 'Am I a peepshow for people to peer at? How I long for the quiet and peace of obscurity.' And, as Mrs. Armistead reported to Mr. Fox, savouring it all with relish.

She had ordered a new carriage and when it arrived she was delighted with it. No one could fail to notice it and to realize that its owner must be a very important person indeed. It was scarlet and silver; and the seat cloth was decorated with silver stars. It was lined with white silk and scarlet fringe. On the door had been painted a basket of flowers beneath which was a wreath and her initials M.R. in silver. The wreath had all the appearance, particularly from a distance, of a coronet, which was exactly what Perdita had intended.

She was delighted with her carriage and went everywhere in it. When it was seen outside shops people would gather round it, recognizing it, so that they might have a glimpse of her when she came out.

If the Prince was in love with his life so was Perdita with hers; but whereas he was all gaiety and high spirits, her method of enjoying life was to dramatize it. She would talk to Mrs. Armistead of her child for whom she said she longed; and indeed Mrs. Armistead believed she did miss little Maria, for she was fond of her. But it was absurd, commented that practical lady in her private thoughts, to choose a way of life and then complain because one had not chosen another.

It cannot last, thought Mrs. Armistead. Most certainly it cannot last. And then what? Where shall we be? The debts which were accumulating were alarming, but Perdita was becoming like her lover and gave no thought to them. She was the mistress of the Prince of Wales and no one denied her credit.

Mrs. Armistead often thought how differently she would have behaved had she been in Perdita's position. There would have been no debts. Quite the contrary. Mrs. Armistead would have had a nice little fortune tucked away by now. In her own small way she was not doing badly. Lord Derby had shown interest and the Duke of Dorset had not lost his; so she had her little house in Chertsey very pleasantly and safely waiting for her.

A refuge! How unusual it was for a lady's maid to compare her position so favourably with that of her mistress.

But this was, of course, no ordinary lady's maid.

Blackmail

The Prince had sent word that he would be visiting Cork Street that evening. A quiet evening, he said, merely a few friends, Fox and Sheridan among them.

Mrs. Armistead would arrange the evening; they no longer had to hire their footman, but Mrs. Armistead thought they should have more servants for this occasion. Because of the excellent qualities Perdita was constantly discovering in her lady's maid she was delighted when she had suggested she should take over the arrangement of dinner parties; and Mrs. Armistead performed these duties with distinction. Now she set herself to plan the meal and order the wine . . . plenty of it. What drinkers Mr. Fox and Mr. Sheridan were . . . and the Prince was beginning to rival them.

'Madam,' declared Mrs. Armistead, 'you must rest during the afternoon so as not to be too tired.'

Perdita agreed that this was so.

'The Prince is so full of high spirits,' she said fondly.

'And expects Madam to be the same.'

'Ah yes, indeed. Sometimes I long for a quiet retreat, Armistead. A little house in the country . . .'

'It would not suit His Highness, Madam. He has just escaped from a little house in the country. Kew, to be precise.'

Perdita looked coldly at her maid. There were times when she thought that the woman was inclined to forget her place.

There was no time to reprimand her, for there was loud knocking on the door.

Perdita gazed at Mrs. Armistead. 'Who can it be?'

'The footman will discover, Madam.'

They were soon in no doubt, for the visitor did not wait to be announced but strode straight into Perdita's bedroom. It was Thomas Robinson, his face flushed, his eyes bloodshot.

The creature is drunk, thought Mrs. Armistead.

'Where is my wife, eh? Where is my lady wife?'

Perdita lay back on her pillows looking as though she were about to faint.

'Why have you come here?'

'Why should I not? I have a right.' He looked at the coronet into which the curtains were gathered above the bed and sneered at it. 'So this is the bed where you frolic with His Highness? You don't think of your husband then, I'll warrant.'

'I prefer never to think of him.'

'I daresay, I daresay. So do most whores.'

Perdita flinched and blushed scarlet. 'How dare you! How dare you! Go away.'

'Why? This is where I belong. It's my wife's house . . . and what's hers is mine.'

'No,' cried Perdita, too upset to act. 'Go away, Thomas. Go away, I beg of you.'

'Would you make it worth my while if I did?'

'Yes . . . yes . . . yes . . .'

'Now you're talking. I'm in debt. I want some money. I want it now.'

'Armistead! Armistead!'

That excellent lady was at the door listening, and appeared immediately.

'Bring . . . bring . . .'

'That's right,' said Mr. Robinson, 'bring all you have . . . and that won't be enough. Why should I be jeered at? Why should I see my picture all over the place? And not a good likeness either. Me in horns!'

'We all have to suffer from these scandal sheets . . . I more than most!'

'Well, you deserve to. I don't.'

'When I think of all the serving girls . . . the dirty sluts . . .'

'Compensation, Mrs. Robinson. So you've still got that lady's maid. She's a sly piece . . . and not all that unbedworthy either.'

'Thomas. For God's sake be silent.'

Mrs. Armistead had overheard. So even he had noticed. She was not displeased. She had brought a few pounds for the man and she told him that this was all there was in the house. Perdita shot her a grateful glance and once more asked herself what she would do without Armistead.

When the lady's maid had left the room, Perdita said: 'You have what you have come for . . . now go.'

'I don't intend to go. I like this little place. Why should I live in my little hovel while the wife of my bosom has a snug place like this?'

'Please, *please* go at once.'

But Mr. Robinson sprawled in a chair and regarded the tips of his boots, a sly look of determination on his face.

'I want some compensation for losing my wife,' he said in a whining voice.

'You have . . . as you said. Your kitchen sluts.'

'Even they have to be kept and living's costly.'

'So it's money you want. Well, you've had it.'

'I want it regularly. I want to know where I stand. I want an allowance from you. Why shouldn't I? I've a right.'

'If you will go away you shall have it.'

He nodded slowly, and began to haggle over the amount.

She lay back on her pillows thinking: Go away. Leave me. If he were here when the guests arrived what would happen? The Prince would be annoyed. But Thomas Robinson would never dare. He was a coward. He was a braggart. He would go before they came. But he was in a truculent mood. He had clearly been drinking. And she needed to rest. Late nights with the Prince were beginning to leave their mark—very slightly it was true— but she had noticed faint shadows under her eyes this morning.

Go! she wanted to scream. Leave me in peace.

But the more she showed her agitation the more advantage that gave him. She was ready to promise anything if only he would go.

'Then that's settled,' he said. 'And I want it regularly remember.'

'You shall have it. I must rest now. I am very tired.'

'Yours is an exhausting profession.'

She did not answer that and he continued to sit there leering at her.

At length she said: 'Well, you have what you want.'

'Partly, but not entirely.'

'Pray, what do you mean?'

'I like this place. There's plenty of room here.'

'Are you mad?'

'No, only a husband with rights.'

'Do you think your presence here would be tolerated?'

'Not welcomed probably, but that wouldn't worry me.'

'Thomas, I beg of you to go. If you stay here . . . you will ruin *everything*.'

He still continued to leer at her.

She closed her eyes; she had a horrible vision of her guests arriving to find this unkempt drunken sot sprawling in her house. Mr. Robinson of the cartoons, husband of Perdita.

She was distracted. What could she do? The more she showed her terror the more determined he would be to plague her. She thought of some of the people who were coming tonight—outwardly her friends, but a woman in her position had to face a great deal of envy. It was everywhere—in the lampoons, the wicked verses, the eyes of women who called lewd names after her. Everything she did was noticed. They would say Mr. Robinson has moved in with his wife. *Ménage à trois*. And the Prince would never tolerate it.

And what can I do? she asked herself.

Mrs. Armistead came into the room. She was a little flushed and breathless and looked as though she had been hurrying.

'Madam,' she said, 'Lord Malden is here.'

Perdita looked alarmed and glanced in horror at Mr. Robinson, but Mrs. Armistead said firmly: 'I will show him in.'

Mr. Robinson said: 'So you receive men in your bedroom, do you?'

'Don't be a fool. I am not alone here.'

'No, your husband is here to protect you. Ha! ha!'

Mrs. Armistead appeared with Lord Malden exquisitely dressed as usual in a light brown velvet coat with gold frogging. He kissed Perdita's hand and turned to Mr. Robinson.

However truculent the latter had felt before the entrance of Lord Malden, he could not prevent himself being overawed by the elegance of dress and manners, and as Lord Malden treated him with the utmost courtesy—and interest—his mood changed completely. He was ingratiating and pleased to be noticed.

While Perdita lay back on her pillows exhausted, the men talked and after a while Lord Malden suggested Mr. Robinson come with him to a club he knew that they might continue their interesting conversation.

Mr. Robinson was delighted and both men took their leave of Perdita.

When they had gone, she cried: 'Oh, what a stroke of good

fortune. I shall never be able to thank Malden enough. And the manner in which that creature went . . . as meek as a lamb.'

Mrs. Armistead said demurely: 'It was certainly a stroke of good fortune I found Lord Malden at his residence.'

'You?'

'Yes, Madam. When I saw that Mr. Robinson intended to stay I slipped out of the house and went to Dean Street. As I say it was fortunate that his lordship was at home. I told him that Mr. Robinson was here and in what mood and begged him to come at once and dislodge him. This he did. He will take him to some club or tavern and there ply him with drink. So I do not think we need worry ourselves this evening with Mr. Robinson.'

Perdita sighed. She must endure Armistead's familiarities now and then; she really was a most excellent servant.

The incident had unnerved her. She could not help thinking that but for the prompt action of Armistead Mr. Robinson might be at this moment in the house. The Prince noticed her lack of spirits and chided her affectionately.

'You look tired, my angel,' he whispered.

Oh God, she thought, and looked for the nearest mirror.

'Smile,' urged the Prince. 'You're more beautiful when you smile.'

And she fixed her features into a false smile which could not deceive any.

Perdita was melancholy by nature, thought the Prince, faintly critical. He was comparing her with his aunt Cumberland and the very thought of her made him smile. She could always amuse him. She was so full of gaiety *always* and never failing to come up with a quip which brought tears of mirth to the eyes. And Georgiana, the lovely Duchess of Devonshire—there was another. His eyes grew soft at the thought of her. She was a beauty and no mistake. Of course Perdita was the queen of beauty—but so damned melancholy. Then that lady's maid—Mrs. Armistead—he had asked her her name the other day and she had curtsied so prettily . . . Well, elegantly, he would have said. It was a curtsey that would have become a duchess and she was a handsome woman too. Not perhaps his ideal of beauty; he liked dazzlers like Georgiana, Anne Luttrell . . . and Perdita; but that waiting woman had something.

It was a good evening. The usual practical jokes which he so enjoyed and at which Sheridan was beginning to shine. Sheridan was a great fellow—he loved the man. He had yet to find a friend who compared with Fox or Sheridan. When he was with them he could talk and talk and as they talked they drank and he was beginning to be able to drink as much as they could, which was a good deal. They never bored him; they never wearied him; they were never melancholy, whatever the subject they made it amusing. Cynics both of them—and yet both capable of affection and devotion and they made it clear that they had this for the Prince of Wales. There were sycophants and he was not such a fool as not to recognize them; but these two were his genuine friends. He had never understood the American situation until it was explained to him by Fox, Burke and Sheridan. Fox railed against North's conduct of the affair—and that included the King's because the King and North were together in everything that was done. The more he learned of affairs, the more the Prince deplored his father's attitude. He himself was firmly against the Government and that meant North and his father; the Prince was determined to take his stand with Mr. Fox and the Whigs.

This was the life! He regretted that Fred was not with him to enjoy it. Poor Fred learning army tactics! The use of arms! By God, one thing Mr. Fox had taught him was that words were the finest weapons in the world.

Gambling, prizefighting, horse-racing and loving a beautiful mistress—these were some of the greatest pleasures life had to offer; but he was not sure that he did not enjoy most being in the company of Fox and Sheridan, listening to their erudite conversation, joining with it, growing more and more mellow as the evening wore on. Sometimes of course he was a little hazy after these sessions; sometimes they had to take him back to Cork Street and help him in. This they never failed to do with the utmost care and tact and they would recall similar incidents in their own youth in case he should feel he had not yet learned to take his liquor like a man. He was not a fool. He knew they were wise men of vast experience in all the ways of life which were most exciting to him. He was willing to be tutored. And Perdita would be waiting for him . . . reproachful. Oh yes, she was reproachful even though she might not put her reproaches into words. There he was back at Perdita's melancholy. He'd be ready to swear that that was one thing his lively aunt at Cumberland House never felt—melancholy. Nor would she ever be reproachful. Why she would have to be continually so when one considered the exploits of that wicked old reprobate his Uncle Cumberland.

There was some music and he became proud of Perdita as she sat at the harpsichord in her becoming pink draperies; and a pretty voice she had too. Not as good as Sheridan's wife. Poor creature! There was another. No gaiety, no spirit. Poor Sherry. But he managed to enjoy life in spite of her. She never appeared at these parties. He would never have thought of her being at them—except at moments like this when she might have sung for them. But he liked a gay song—the sort Sherry put in his plays. Elizabeth Sheridan was all for serious music. The King admired her. That spoke for itself.

The Prince must sing, the company declared.

Nothing loth he obliged. He sang by himself and he sang with Perdita. In perfect harmony, he thought, as we shall be all our lives, forgetting that he had only such a short time ago deplored her melancholy and compared her unfavourably with other women.

And afterwards a game of faro, with Perdita's lips slightly pursed, not approving. The stakes were very high. Mr. Fox always played for high stakes and the Prince had lost a thousand guineas in a very short time.

A thousand guineas. What was that added to all he owed? And a Prince of Wales should not concern himself with money. It was so easy to scribble an I.O.U. Mr. Fox did it constantly and with the same abandon as the Prince.

And after that . . . talk, political because after all this, with Cumberland House and Devonshire House, was the centre of Whiggery, and any hostess who could get Mr. Fox to talk was sure of a successful party.

So Mr. Fox talked and of course he talked of America which was the great controversy of the moment. The King, he said, would accept no man who disagreed with him. This was no way to govern. Were the King the most brilliant administrator in the world—which Mr. Fox very respectfully wished to point out that he was not—still this would be wrong. It was through discussion and debate that conclusions should be reached.

'We are going to lose America,' declared Mr. Fox, 'and I say this: Serve us right. There should never have been this conflict with our brothers. Fools . . . fools . . . fools . . . have governed us, have decided on our policies and they are destroying the greatness of this land. This government must go before it is too late. There is a country to be saved.'

The Prince listened entranced. He knew that they were look-ing to him to be the saviour. When he was in control he would

summon men like Fox, Burke and Sheridan to form his government and he would not presume to think that because he had
inherited a crown he was some supreme being. And to think
that the King was that bumbling old gentleman the farmer, the
button maker, the home lover, the man who was only capable
of begetting children and making their childhoods unbearable
with his discipline which was absurd and old fashioned . . . and
should never have been in fashion in any case.

But never mind. The day would come. In three years' time
he would take his place in the House of Lords—and during that
time he would learn his politics and Mr. Fox would be his most
excellent tutor.

Across the room he caught sight of Perdita and Malden. What
a handsome fellow Malden was and that coat of his was of the
latest cut and fashion. He admired the new style of button. He
had not seen them before. In a second he had crossed to them,
but so absorbed were they in their conversation that they had not
heard him approach.

Perdita was saying: 'I shall never be able to show you how
grateful I am to you . . .'

The feeling in her voice was astonishing.

Why? He wondered what Malden had done that she should
be so grateful; and Malden was looking at her with such a look
of devotion that the Prince felt a wave of indignation.

They were aware of him. Perdita's face was transformed by
the most loving smile.

'I trust Your Highness is enjoying the company tonight.' He
was immediately delighted with her. She was so pretty; and
what love for him shone in her eyes. She was merely being
gracious to Malden. Hadn't he been an excellent emissary during their courtship?

He replied that it was an excellent gathering and that there
must be more like them. He had particularly enjoyed her singing
and would like to hear her again.

And she sang once more and they sang together, in harmony.

Mrs. Armistead called at St. James's Street to tell Mr. Fox that
Mr. Robinson had called and was making a nuisance of himself.

'I brought Lord Malden to come and take him away. The
drunken fellow had no notion that it was a plot to get rid of him.
He went with the utmost alacrity to drink with a noble lord.'

'Excellent, my dear Lizzie. You'll make a fine politician.'

She was pleased to please him. His approval was the only

reward she asked. She would have liked to serve him—to see that his linen was washed and a clean shirt laid out for him each day; she would have liked to have sponged the grease spots from his coat.

'And how is it between our lovers? I thought Mrs. Robinson looked less blooming than usual.'

'I think we are moving into the last phase.'

'Is that so?'

'You are displeased?'

'No, no. I had thought in the beginning that she might have carried some influence, but I see she carries none.'

'So it is of no interest to you whether the affair continues or not?'

He shook his head and was thoughtful. Perdita was a most desirable woman, but doubtless he himself would be interested in her for no more than a very short time—but for that short time he would be definitely intrigued. He was rather amused by the manner in which she acted her way through life and would have liked to discover a little of the real woman beneath; but it would probably not be worth the trouble. No, it was not very important that the affair should continue, except of course that if the Prince gave Perdita her congé, there would be another— and perhaps someone who might influence him.

He answered: 'Perhaps on the whole it is better that it should continue a little longer.'

Mrs. Armistead nodded. She would do her best to keep it going. Mr. Fox would understand that but for her prompt action this afternoon there could have been disaster.

He did understand. He could trust her. It was interesting how they could work together.

She told him about the house in Chertsey. He knew, of course, how she had earned the money which had brought it. He advised her about her affairs which he was well able to do in spite of the fact that his own were in disorder.

'Why, Lizzie, you are a woman of property.' And he did not speak slightingly but with admiration.

He talked of the American situation with her for it was very much in his thoughts. He believed that if the Colonies were lost it could bring down the Government.

She listened, made intelligent comment, and later spent an affectionate hour in his company.

The Queen Plots

News of the life the Prince was leading came in time to the King's ears. He could not sleep at night for thinking of it. George . . . young George . . . little more than a boy and keeping a play actress! The King's mind went back to the days when he himself was eighteen. He thought of that establishment in which he had set up Hannah, where their children were born. But it was discreet. No one knew. It was wrong, it was foolish, and he deeply repented it; but it was *discreet*. That was the first quality a prince who would be king must acquire. It was not generally known about his affair with Hannah, although it had been rumoured and whispered of here and there. This was different. This was blatant. Going out together . . . her in her carriage . . . painted like a harlot—although the women in the Prince's set all did the same. Rouge and white lead, bah! Didn't they know it stopped up the pores and caused consumption?

And the company he kept. That was the real source of trouble! He was a frequent visitor at Cumberland House. Nothing he could have done could have been more designed to flout his father. To go . . . as soon as a little freedom was granted him . . . to that hotbed of Whiggery which was in complete opposition to everything his father stood for. To choose *them* as his friends. If it had been the Gloucesters it would have been different. But it was not. It was Cumberland, that lecher who had made a scandal with Grosvenor's wife—Cumberland and that woman with her eyelashes. George must have set out deliberately to defy his father.

He summoned Gloucester to Kew and told him of his anxieties.

'You've heard, of course,' he said.

'The whole town is talking of it,' replied Gloucester. 'He's there every other night. Sometimes with his play actress, sometimes without her. He's constantly in the company of Fox and Sheridan.'

'Rogues, both of them. Fox would do anything to plague me. As for Sheridan, he's a drunkard and a lecher and I think it the greatest shame that he should have married that charming Miss Linley.' The King's eyes clouded momentarily with sentiment. 'I shall never forget hearing her sing in an oratorio. Never heard singing like it. Sang like an angel, looked like an angel. I'm sorry to see her married to a fellow like that.'

'They say he's talented. I heard it said that on the first night of his *School of Scandal* a journalist passing the theatre ran for his life because he thought the thunder of the applause would bring the roof down.'

'Bah! Pandering to the senses! Low taste. The man's a drunkard and a gambler and he and Fox are teaching George to be the same.'

'What are you going to do about it?'

'What can I do? The young dog's eighteen. They say that's the time for a little independence. Fox, Sheridan, Cumberland . . . Cumberland most of all.'

'I wonder you allow them to meet.'

'I don't care to part relations.'

Gloucester looked surprised considering the manner in which he—as well as Cumberland—had been kept from their nephews and nieces for so many years. But old George was behaving oddly nowadays; one could never be sure of him.

The King began to pace up and down, his face growing scarlet.

'What would you have me do in my present distress?' he demanded. 'Eh, what? If I attempt to put a stop to this I shall drive my son further and further into the arms of the opposition. And that would increase my distress.'

Gloucester agreed that taking into account the Prince's age and the freedom he had already had it would be difficult to intervene now. Perhaps if he had not been so rigorously controlled beforehand he would not have rushed so madly into freedom. But he did not distress his brother still further by telling him this.

'He comes to see you, I suppose?' said the King.

'Not often.'

'But he is fond of you?'

'Yes, I think so. But when I have tried to remonstrate with him he has hinted that he does not care to be preached at.'

'You see. You see. What can you do with such a young dog? Tell me that, eh, what?'

'It may be that after a while he will grow less wild.'

'Less wild! Less wild! I hear that he is beginning to talk like that woman . . . that coarse creature with the eyelashes. I hear that he drinks to excess . . . that he has actually been carried home to that place where he lives with the actress. A pleasant story to be set about the Prince of Wales.'

'Many princes have behaved in similar fashion,' soothed Gloucester.

'I won't have my sons doing it. I won't, I say. But how can I stop it? Tell me that, eh, what?'

The Duke of Gloucester could give no answer. 'I fear Cumberland may be attempting to blackmail me into receiving that woman of his,' went on the King.

'Well,' retorted the Duke of Gloucester speaking for his own Duchess, 'she is after all a member of the family.'

'Eyelashes, bah!' said the King.

When Gloucester left he went to see the Queen. She was a little worried about the health of the baby, for young Alfred had not picked up as her older children had and as little Octavius had never really been strong there were new anxieties in the nurseries.

She was sitting in her drawing room at her embroidery, her snuff box beside her, some of her women with her, contented apart from her anxiety about her family, to be staying at 'dear little Kew'.

She gave the order for dismissal because she saw at once from the King's expression that he was upset and she knew that if he talked too quickly or incoherently some of these women would gossip about it, so she took every opportunity of keeping them out of the King's way.

She did not have to ask what was wrong. She guessed the American Colonies might have something to do with it, but he would not of course come here to discuss those with her. She was supposed to be unaware that any conflict was taking place. If she had offered an opinion it would have been received with cold surprise. She had grown accustomed to this, and only resented it now and then.

But the family was a different matter. So it was family affairs of which he had come to speak.

'The baby?' he asked.

'As well as we can expect. He grows a little stronger each day, I think.'

'I'm glad of that. And Octavius? Eh! What?'

'He has had a little cold but it is better,' soothed the Queen.

Now to the subject which had brought him here; George, Prince of Wales.

'It's young George,' he said.

The Queen put her hand involuntarily to her heart.

'Up to his tricks,' went on the King. 'Gambling, drinking and keeping a play actress.'

'No!' cried the Queen.

'But I say it is so and something will have to be done about it. He'll have to be taught his duties to the state, to his family . . . eh? what?'

'There are always people to gossip . . . to lie . . . about us.'

'These are not lies. I've heard from too many sources. He's wild. He's set this woman up in a house . . . He lives there with her. His friends are my enemies. Fox is always with him. He goes to Cumberland and that woman of his. He's with the Whigs . . . he's with the Opposition. His bosom friends are the people I most dislike. He does it to spite me, eh, what?'

'A play actress,' murmured the Queen. 'George with a play actress.'

'I'm afraid our son is too fond of women.'

The Queen was silent.

'If that were all . . . I'd understand.' The King seemed as though he were talking to himself. 'Young man . . . hot blood. It happens now and then. They grow out of it . . . become sober . . .' He looked at Charlotte with her big mouth and her lack of eyelashes. 'They do their duty, are faithful to the wives that are chosen for them . . . But he has deliberately gone to Cumberland. My brother is teaching him to despise everything that I wish him to respect. That's what is happening to the Prince of Wales and what am I going to do about it, eh, what?'

The Queen did not know. She wanted to soothe him, to stop him talking too rapidly. She knew her son well enough to realize that if his father tried to direct his actions he would be more rebellious than ever.

And as the King walked up and down murmuring half sentences to himself she was more concerned for him than for her son. Loving young George she believed that there was nothing really wrong with him. He was a little wild, it was true. But he would grow out of that. The fact was that he was so attractive that he could not help being the centre of attraction, but he would settle down.

She was a little worried about the play actress, though. That was the woman who had made a scene at the Oratorio when George had attracted so much attention by staring at her.

She sighed. But young men would be young men and until they found a wife for him he must she supposed have a mistress.

She wished though that he would choose some good quiet young woman—someone at Kew so that he could call and see his mother often—and perhaps confide in her.

She had to prevent the King becoming too excited and she said something of this to him.

'Young men will be young men. They must not be judged too harshly.'

And oddly enough this did seem to soothe. Then she suggested a little walk or a drive in the carriage round 'dear little Kew which I know Your Majesty loves as much as I do.'

This was indeed a success, for he agreed to go. It was so pleasant riding in Kew, for the place was like a little village with the houses round the Green which were occupied by the children's governesses and tutors, the ladies in waiting, doctors and gardeners. '*Dear* little Kew,' murmured the Queen; and the King echoed her sentiments, for to him this little world seemed far from the ceremonies of St. James's or Buckingham House; and here George was the Squire—the benevolent landlord, beloved of his tenants. Farmer George, in fact, who delighted in the people who came out of their cottages to curtsey and pull a forelock as he and the Queen rode by.

The river flowed peacefully by and there on Strand-on-the-Green the Queen saw Mrs. Papendiek about to go into the painter Zoffany's house where she had lodgings, but when she heard the royal carriage she turned and curtsied; the King raised his hat and inclined his head. He liked Mrs. Papendiek and Charlotte could see that he was forgetting his troubles momentarily, as she had intended he should.

The Queen thought a great deal about the play actress, trying to remember what she looked like. She recalled the performance of *The Winter's Tale* in which the woman had played Perdita. What a pity they had ever gone to see that play! But then they would have seen something else and it would probably have been another play actress.

If only he could have found a *nice* lady—not an actress. There had been Mary Hamilton to whom he had been devoted and had written charming letters and looked upon as a sister. And that had taken him often to his sister's apartments and no one could say that wasn't a good thing! But a play actress! Suppose he had fallen in love with someone in the Queen's household and it was all very discreet. The Prince would visit his mother often—and that could do nothing but good.

How pleasant if he would break this association with the play actress and find a kind, clever and above all *discreet* lady in his mother's household.

At the Queen's robing Madam von Schwellenburg was ordering the women to do this and that in her hectoring manner.

Charlotte had been helped on with her gown and her powdering robe was being put about her. While her hair was being dressed she read the newspapers and looked for references to the Prince and Mrs. Perdita Robinson. She always tried to keep these from the King.

She was well aware that her women discussed this matter; in fact she believed that the whole Court was discussing it.

Perhaps she should ask Schwellenburg. Not that she wanted to talk of it, but at least Schwellenburg was German and she would be honest. She never chose her words with much care and would be as outspoken to the Queen as to anyone else.

While her hair was curled and crimped she was thinking of the women of her household. It would have to be someone young and there was no one young. It would have to be someone beautiful and there was no one really beautiful . . . at least not that a young boy of eighteen would think so; and most important of all *discreet*. The trouble was that people who possessed youth rarely had discretion and vice versa.

Should she speak of the matter to the King? She imagined his dismay at the thought of providing a mistress for his son. She wondered at herself. But she was desperate; and she proved in the past that, docile as she might seem, when she was determined she could act boldly.

She wanted to save the Prince from folly and the King from anxiety; and surely it was worth while stepping outside one's usual moral code to do that?

The thought of intrigue was exciting. This was one of the rare times in her married life when she was not pregnant. And the King had agreed with her that in view of the fact that Alfred was their fourteenth and that neither he nor Octavius were as strong as the others, perhaps the time had come to call a halt to child-bearing.

Just suppose she were successful in finding the right sort of woman who would lead the Prince away from his wicked uncle and bring him back into the family circle? What ever means were necessary, the result would justify them.

She decided that she would choose an opportunity to speak to Schwellenburg to discover what was being said among the women; and she might even find out through her if there were any women of the household who combined enough beauty to please the Prince and enough discretion to satisfy his mother.

Madam von Schwellenburg was in her room surrounded by her caged toads when Madam Haggerdorn came to tell her that the Queen requested her presence.

Before obeying the summons she insisted on Madam Haggerdorn's witnessing the cleverness of her favourite toad by tapping on his cage with her snuff box.

'He know. He know,' she cried animatedly. 'Listen . . . see, he croak. You hear?'

Madam Haggerdorn said it was a wonderful performance, for like everyone else in the Queen's household she was afraid of offending Schwellenburg. The woman was heartily disliked; the King had made two mild attempts to have her sent back to Germany; but for some reason the Queen—although she herself did not greatly care for the woman—had insisted that she stay; and because the King was determined to keep his wife out of important affairs he conceded her complete sway in her own household. Consequently Schwellenburg remained, growing more objectionable and arrogant every week.

Schwellenburg's repulsive face was softened by her affection for the animals—the only living creatures who could soften her; and Haggerdown reminded her that the Queen was waiting.

'Go when want,' said Schwellenburg and deliberately went on tapping the cages and listening ecstatically to the croaking of her pets.

When Haggerdorn had left, with a studied leisureliness, Schwellenburg made her way to the Queen's apartments.

Charlotte was alone and invited her Mistress of the Robes to be seated.

'I want you to talk to me about the Prince of Wales,' said the Queen.

Schwellenburg's features formed themselves into the sort of smile she bestowed on her pets. She liked to think she was the confidante of the Queen.

'Is vild,' she said. 'Very vild. Drink too much; too much gamble; too much vimen.'

'I fear so,' mused the Queen. 'And the King is most distressed.'

Schwellenburg nodded, well pleased; she was glad the King was distressed. He had tried to send her back to Germany.

'What have you heard? That he keeps a play actress?'

'Everyvon talk. Everyvon know. Is dronk . . . has house in Cork Street. Herr Prince very vild.'

'I fear there is truth in the rumours. Do the women talk much about it?'

'All the time. Everyvon talk.'

'Do any of the women er . . . envy this play actress?' Schwellenburg opened her eyes in surprise. And the Queen went on: 'Perhaps some of the younger and prettier ones . . . perhaps they feel that they would . . . like to be in her place.'

'There vos von. Harriot Vernon . . .'

'I know about her. She was dismissed from Court.'

'He like very much Mary Hamilton . . . but no more. Never see now.'

Mary Hamilton! thought the Queen. Oh, no, that was no use. One could not expect to revive an old attraction. He had given up Mary Hamilton when the play actress came along; he could not go back to her.

'I do not like his friends. I think this play actress is having a bad effect on him, taking him to his uncle. If there was someone here at Court . . . at Kew . . . I am not condoning immorality, of course, but young men are such that they need a . . . a friend, a female friend. You may know what I mean, Schwellenburg.'

Schwellenburg knew. She muttered: 'These girls . . . they are vild. Like Herr Prince. All they think is . . . dance . . . and patch and rouge and white lead . . . That is English girls. German fräuleins do as told. Much better.'

The Queen was suddenly excited. A German mistress for the Prince. What an excellent idea. But where? The King had dismissed all the German women who came over with her—except Schwellenburg and Haggerdorn. There might be one or two others, but they were old, old as herself. No, what they wanted was a young, buxom German girl who was disciplined and discreet and would do as she was told.

'Thank you, Schwellenburg.'

She was indeed grateful. Schwellenburg had given her an idea.

When the Mistress of the Robes had retired she sat down and wrote home to Mecklenburg-Strelitz. In that poor little province there were always people who were longing to get to England and enjoy the patronage of Queen Charlotte.

In Cumberland House the Duke and Duchess were discussing the Prince on similar lines.

'Do you fancy,' asked the Duchess of her husband, 'that he is quite so happy in our company as he was?'

'He comes here.'

'But not so often. And he is always in a corner with Fox or Sheridan. They often leave early together to go off to Devonshire House I believe.'

'I'm sure we have entertained him lavishly.'

'He's certainly lost a lot of money at our tables.'

'It's at his wish.'

'But he is drifting. I sense it. And I think that Propriety Prue is at the bottom of it. She doesn't like us.'

'She fears you outshine her.'

'And she remembers that you once chased her. She may still think you have designs on her virtue. Have you?'

'Pah!' cried the Duke. 'Does she think she's so irresistible?'

'I'm sure she does. Otherwise she might be a little more careful with H.R.H. Because I think that we are not the only people who have had the misfortune to weary him now and then.'

'You mean Prue is on the way out.'

The Duchess nodded slowly. 'I have seen the writing on the wall. She won't last more than a few more months.'

'And then?'

'That is what we have to be prepared for.'

'And knowing you, my love, I am prepared to stake a thousand guineas that you are already prepared.'

'Dally the Tall,' she said.

'What?'

'Why so surprised? Have I not seen your lustful eyes studying this tall one appraisingly? You must admit your tastes are not dissimilar to those of your amorous nephew.'

'Well, Dally's a charmer.'

'I know you think so; and I am sure the Prince will too.'

'What do you propose to do?'

'See that they have the opportunity they desire.'

'You mean that *you* desire.'

'Dally has a reputation for er . . . pleasing men.'

'So has Perdita.'

'And I'll tell you something else. I am not the only one who has noticed a falling off in His Highness's devotion. The jackals are gathering round . . . hopefully. Malden is ready to leap in as soon as H.R.H. retires. Poor Malden. His faithful service should be rewarded. And Fox is biding his time. Malden should take care. He is rather lamblike and what chance has a lamb against a fox?'

'And such a fox! So he is waiting to drag Perdita into his lair, is he?'

'And I hope you, my lord, will have enough respect for your Ducal rank not to join the patient throng.'

'What are you going to do about Dally?'

'From now on she should be treated with respect. Mrs. Grace Elliott, one of the most amusing and beautiful young women in London! She is perfect in every way. Three years his senior— as Propriety Prue is. Have you noticed how His Highness likes his women to be older than himself? And she will be a complete change from Prue because there is no propriety about Grace Elliott.'

'When does the battle start?'

'Tonight, my love. We dare not delay. Don't imagine because you are blind to what is happening about you others are. Depend upon it, many people are noticing that the chains of love are slackening. But she could do harm to us before she goes. And others will be bringing forward their candidates for his approval. It is always best to be the first, my love. Leave this to me.'

This the Duke was very happy to do.

Perdita was far from tranquil. Mr. Robinson was constantly threatening and he demanded his payments promptly. She wished that she could have had her mother and daughter to live in Cork Street. What a comfort that would be! The little girl adored her and Mrs. Darby was so proud of her beautiful daughter and on her visits to them, taking costly presents, Perdita was really happy.

Then she would come back to Cork Street and rest for a while and submit herself to the ministrations of Mrs. Armistead to be prepared for the night's company. There were times when she would have given a great deal to go to bed and stay there. But the Prince's energies were unflagging.

She had returned from a visit to her mother and daughter and had rested and been powdered and rouged and dressed in a gown of rose coloured velvet when the Prince arrived.

He kissed her absentmindedly and made no comment on her appearance, but sprawling in a chair said he had only come to stay an hour or so.

She was disappointed, although a short while before she had been longing for a restful evening. What she had meant was a quiet evening with the Prince.

She said: 'I had hoped we could have been together . . . just the two of us . . . for one evening. I have a new song I want to sing to you. We can sing it together, too.'

'Another time,' he said.

She looked mournfully up at the ceiling and pressed her lips slightly together to imply resignation and restraint. This annoyed the Prince. He would rather she had openly protested. He was becoming a little exasperated now and then with this martyr's role which was such a favourite one of hers.

There was a pause. The Prince was thinking it was a mighty long hour.

She said: 'I saw little Maria today.'

'I trust she is well.'

'And so delighted to see me. She wept when I left. Sometimes I wonder . . .'

The Prince said nothing.

'It was a great sacrifice to make,' she went on. 'Perhaps I was wrong to give her up. After all, I am her mother. I think sometimes she wonders . . . One day I shall tell her of how I suffered because I could not give her the time which most mothers give their children. I hope she will understand.'

The Prince yawned. It should have been a warning.

'Yes.' She was warming to her role now. She had risen, and putting her hand to her throat gazed before her. There were tears in her eyes. 'It was a great decision to make . . . this renunciation. Husband, child . . . and virtue . . . all I abandoned.'

'I did not know,' said the Prince coldly, 'that you so regretted leaving your husband.'

'He was not good to me but at least he was my husband.'

'Then perhaps Madam you feel you should return to him?'

Danger signals. She changed her tactics. 'I would never return to him. You must know that better than anyone.'

'Yet you sounded as though you regretted his loss.'

She went to him and put her arms about his neck. 'You . . . you are handsome . . . all that a Prince could be. How could any woman be blamed for not being able to resist you?'

This was more like it.

'My angel,' said the Prince, but he was still a little absent-minded.

'Pray come and sing a little.'

'Not now. There is not the time. I but called in to see you for an hour.'

'You used not to be so eager to get away.'

'Eager? I'm not eager. Or if I am it's because of all this damned melancholy.'

'And you promised me not to use bad language.'

'I only do so in your presence when goaded.'

'Goaded!'

'Oh, Perdita, stop being the tragedy queen. You came here because you wanted to. And there's an end to it.'

She was silent, and going over to the harpsichord played a melody. Even her tunes were melancholy, thought the Prince. Why be melancholy when there was so much in the world to be gay about?

She looked over her shoulder. 'And where are you going to in such haste? Or would you rather not tell me?'

'I have no reason to hide my actions. I am going to Cumberland House.'

Cumberland House! And they had not invited her. She knew they called her Propriety Prue and mocked her behind her back. And when she thought that the Duke had once pursued her so relentlessly and had admired her so! Of course it was the Duchess. The woman was jealous.

'My dear George, do you think you should go to Cumberland House?'

'In God's name, what do you mean?'

'I do not think the Duchess behaves in a manner which could be called ladylike.'

'She doesn't have to ape ladies. She's a duchess . . . and a royal one at that.'

'I still think she is a little coarse. And I do not like to hear you talking as she does.'

'Madam,' said the Prince, incensed now, 'I have been treated like a child by my father for eighteen years. I have no intention of allowing my mistress to do the same.'

Mistress! That dreadful word which always unnerved her. She felt the tears brimming over on to her cheeks. They were splashing on to the red velvet. She hoped they would not mark it. It was too good and too new to be given to Armistead just yet. But she could not hold back the tears.

The Prince saw the tears and said in a shamefaced way: 'Well, you should not attempt to dictate to me, you know.'

She could never stop play acting; she wanted all the best lines. So she said: 'I have angered you, but I cannot let that influence me when I speak for your own good. The King and Queen do not wish you to go to Cumberland House. This distresses them.'

'So you are in Their Majesties' confidence?'

'Everyone knows it.'

A suspicion came into his mind. 'They have not given you some command to stop my going to Cumberland House, have they?'

'Do you think they would notice me! They despise me as so many do . . . because I gave up my home, my husband, my daughter . . . everything . . . for you.'

Because the Prince had known his fancy was straying, because he realized the inconstancy of the vows of constant devotion, he was ashamed of himself and sought to shift the blame to her.

'I believe,' he said, 'that you wish to be rid of me.'

'Oh, no . . . no!' That at least was genuine.

'I have seen men here . . . with you. Malden for instance. You are so grateful to him. I overheard you telling him so.'

'That was because he had helped us to come together. Why should I be grateful to him for anything else?'

'So you are grateful for that, are you?'

'More than I can say. Oh, if you but knew . . .' She was smiling through her tears; and now she was very appealing. He wanted to be the faithful lover; he did not wish to break the vows he had made. If only she would not be so melancholy, if only she would not talk so much about her sacrifices.

He kissed her.

'Please don't quarrel with me. It breaks my heart.'

He quarrel with *her*? But she was the one who made the quarrels. Still, she was loving and sweet now, declaring that it was only her anxiety for him that made her so sad.

So they embraced and when she said: 'Is everything as it was,' he answered: 'Nothing has changed. Constant unto death, my Perdita.'

So she was relieved and not sorry too that she had voiced her disapproval of his going to Cumberland House. Lord Malden had told her that that was what had upset the King more than anything and that if the King and Queen believed that she kept him from Cumberland House they might begin to take a much kindlier view of her relationship with the Prince.

But in spite of the reconciliation the Prince would not linger. He went, as he had said he would, when the hour was up.

Saucy Grace Elliott was delighted at the prospect of taking Perdita's place. The Duchess of Cumberland had explained the position quite frankly for Grace Elliott and Anne Luttrell were of a kind and understood each other perfectly.

Grace was very tall but slender and willowy; her hair was of a delightful gold colour, fine and abundant; she had large grey eyes; the manner in which she walked, gesticulated and talked betrayed her sensuality. A glance from Grace was an invitation and a promise, and as she kept her promises she was constantly surrounded by would-be lovers.

Perhaps her father, Hew Dalrymple, a Scottish Advocate, recognized this, for at a very early age she was married off to a Dr. Elliott, who at forty looked fifty, and in any case in years was quite old enough to be her father.

In her mid-teens she was already a lusty creature and marriage with Dr. Elliott was not her idea of bliss and as shortly after the marriage she made the acquaintance of Lord Valentia, she became his mistress and eloped with him.

This caused a great scandal because Dr. Elliott decided to divorce Grace and at the same time demand damages from Lord Valentia, which he was granted. The escapade with Grace cost Lord Valentia £12,000 and the case was compared with that of the Grosvenors and the Duke of Cumberland. Lord Valentia's expensive escapade proved to be impermanent, and when he left Grace, unprotected and ostracized by society, there seemed only one course for her to take. She announced her intention of going into that French convent where she had received her education and left the country.

Grace's character was not exactly suited to convent life and very soon she left this refuge and, living on the fringe of the

Court of France, met Lord Cholmondeley who was on a visit from England.

Lord Cholmondeley was gallant, and Grace was homesick, so they comforted each other and Cholmondeley brought her back to England . . . and to Cumberland House.

Grace was gay and unscathed by her adventures. She knew herself well enough to realize that though men were necessary to her full enjoyment of life, she would never remain faithful to one for any length of time. She would flit from one to another, enjoying each encounter to the full because she knew that when it was over there would be no regrets, no looking back and sighing over the past; Grace could only live life in the present; it was this quality which many found so attractive and Golden Dally the Tall was welcomed into society such as that at Cumberland House.

She had seen the Prince of course and could imagine nothing more desirable than to be his mistress for a while. She was growing a little tired of Cholmondeley in any case.

So she listened to the Duchess's plans and agreed at once that if she did not win His Royal Highness from Perdita it would not be her fault.

Cumberland House looked gayer than usual after the scene with Perdita.

There was dancing and gaming as usual, as well as good talk. The Duchess had a word in private with the Prince when he arrived, asking if all was well. 'Your fond aunt fancies you look less contented than usual and she is concerned for you.'

'I'm not discontented.'

'But it is not enough that you should merely be not discontented. I must see you basking in complete contentment.'

'My dearest aunt!'

'So tell me what I must do for your delight.'

'What more could you do?'

She fluttered her eyelashes at him. 'Anything in the world you asked of me, dear nephew. And I will tell you this: I certainly feel very angry towards any who disturb you.'

It was a reference to Perdita, he knew, for she suspected that Perdita was playing the injured woman who had given her 'all'. She had told him an amusing story about a woman who had left her husband for a lover and who comically dramatized the situation. He had laughed with the rest of the company and it was not until later that he had realized how those timeworn clichés she had put into the woman's mouth were the very ones Perdita would have chosen.

She was frowning, which was rare with her. 'I am a little disturbed, dear nephew. So disturbed because I know it is my duty to speak and wondering whether it will make you angry with me.' Again one of those coquettish looks. 'Could you imagine circumstances in which you would be angry with me?'

'Impossible because none exist.'

'Not only the most elegant, the most handsome, but the most gallant of princes!' She was laughing again. 'I have found my courage and I will speak. You should take care. I believe your father has set a spy very close to you.'

'To report on my actions! The newspapers do that very well.'

'More than that. He wants to guide your actions. He is trying to stop your visits here.'

'He'll never do that.'

'Poison works slowly sometimes, but it can kill in the end. I know that your father deplores the fact that you come here. He hates Cumberland because he married me. He's never forgiven him. And that you should choose to visit us infuriates him. He wants to stop it.'

'He has not commanded me to stay away.'

'No, because he realizes he could not do that. If you refused, the people would be on your side. There is Fox or Sheridan to mention it in Parliament. It is not the wish of the people, dearest nephew, that you should be treated like an infant in arms.'

'That I will resist at all costs.'

'The King wishes you to live as he does. Early to bed, early to rise. Lemonade your drink; a little backgammon your sole dissipation. Lucky nephew, to have two Holy fathers—one in Heaven and one on Earth.'

'He knows it's hopeless to force me to live the kind of life he does.'

'Does Propriety . . . Does Perdita ever mention your coming here?'

The Prince hesitated.

'Oh, you are too honourable to tell, but of course she does. This is why it is so difficult. She wishes you to stay away because the King wants it. He would be even ready to accept the fact that you keep a mistress if he could stop your coming here and break up your friendship with your uncle and myself and Fox and Sheridan.'

'Nothing would induce me to break up the friendships I most

treasure. You cannot mean that the King has approached Perdita . . .'

'I do not mean that His Majesty has been visiting Cork Street nor that your mistress has been summoned to St. James's or Kew. But there are ways of communicating messages, and I know for certain that the Queen believes that although it is deplorable that you keep a mistress it is not the first time an heir to the throne has done so. The King is more concerned with your politics and the fact that you have made a friend of the brother he refuses to receive than your association with a mistress.'

'Is this so?'

She laid a hand appealingly on his arm. 'Do not believe me until you have proved this for yourself.'

'I will prove this. I will ask her if she is doing the King's work for him.'

'She would deny it. Imagine her. "Do you think I would allow myself to be the King's spy!" ' The Duchess had put her hand to her throat and was staring before her in a perfect imitation of Perdita. ' "Do you think I would work in the dark against the man for whom I gave up husband, home and child?" '

It was cruelly similar and he felt ashamed and yet not as angry as he should have done. There was almost a feeling of relief. Once again he felt that the door of a cage in which he was locked—and this time he himself had turned the key—was slowly opening for him to escape if he wanted to.

The Duchess was quick to sense his mood. 'Don't blame her too much. She would naturally wish to please the King, and if it meant that her liason was not frowned on in those circles, imagine how relieved that would make her.'

'It is certainly a disturbing thought,' he said. 'But I believe your zeal for my comfort has perhaps led you to the wrong conclusion.'

She was smiling happily. 'Oh, I do hope so, for your happiness is the most important thing to me. I do want all to be well. The King may banish *us* from Court if he wishes. Who wants to visit the Palace of Piety? But if you should withdraw *your* presence . . . well, then Cumberland House would hang out the mourning.'

He laughed. 'You'd look very well in purple and black.'

'But better wrapped in smiles.'

'Dear aunt!'

'And I have not offended? I have not been too outspoken?'

'As if you could ever offend.'

'Then I am happy. But, Prince of Princes, you will be watchful.'

He promised that he would.

He was thoughtful when Grace Elliott was presented to him. He could not help assessing her charms though. She was exciting. But he kept thinking of Perdita, perhaps receiving a message from the Court. Could it be Malden? No, Malden had been a good friend. Yet if the King commanded Malden to tell Perdita his pleasure, who could blame Malden?

An uneasy thought. Spies in the very house which was to have been his refuge!

He danced with Grace. He complimented her on her dancing and her beauty.

She conveyed as she could so well that she had other attributes which she would be pleased to put at the Prince's service. He was aware of this but his attitude was vague; and Grace knew that she was not going to step into his bed immediately.

The next day the Prince called at Cork Street, his mind full of the accusations he had heard on the previous night.

Perdita had had a sleepless night; when he had left her she had gone over everything that had been said and she remembered those early days when he had contrived to be with her every possible moment and had never left her side until he was forced to. Nowadays he merely announced that he was going to Cumberland House or Devonshire House, to neither of which households was she invited.

She had thought the Duchess of Devonshire might be her friend since when Perdita had been in the debtor's prison the Duchess had helped her. But while the Duchess was ready to help a poor woman of talent, she was not prepared to receive a play actress in to her house. Perdita had been very angry and instead of making it tactfully known to the Prince that she longed to go to Devonshire House—for had he asked that she should go his request would have been immediately granted—she had tried to outshine the Duchess in public at such places as the Rotunda, the Pantheon and Ranelagh. She had dressed herself in magnificent gowns, colourful and dazzling, certain to attract the eye and wherever the Duchess was there was Perdita—always calling attention to herself, determined to oust the Duchess from her position as the leader of fashion.

And when she had, coming face to face with the Duchess,

bowed, the Duchess had looked through her as though she did not exist and the crowds had seen the snub.

That had sent her home in tears, railing against her position and all she had given up for the Prince; and she continued with the theme when the Prince called to see her.

So, after that near quarrel Perdita was uneasy. She lay in bed thinking not so much of her child as of the changing attitude of the Prince. There was one other subject of which she refused to think. Every time it came into her mind she pushed it away. This was Debts. She did not know how much she owed but she knew the amount must be considerable. The cost of entertaining at Cork Street was enormous; her dresses cost a fortune; her wine bill she dared not think of—the Prince and his friends were heavy drinkers. No, she dared not think of money. And while she had the Prince's affection it was unimportant.

She must keep that affection; so when he arrived that day she was all charm and sweetness and he was obviously deeply affected by her beauty.

During his visit he mentioned Cumberland House.

'Why,' he said, 'do you dislike the place so?'

'Because I think it is not a worthy setting for you.'

'My uncle's house!'

'But an uncle who, in the King's eyes, has brought disgrace on your royal family.'

'So you would side with the King against me?'

'I would never side with anyone against you. They could torture me . . . they could do anything they would with me . . . but I would always stand by you.'

It was the answer he wanted. In fact when he thought of his father's approaching Perdita he saw how improbable that was. Dear Aunt Cumberland! It was her concern for him, of course . . . and her fear of losing him. She need not have feared. He would remain faithful to her *and* to Perdita. As for the King, he could go to the devil.

It reminded him that the King's Birthday Ball would soon be taking place. He told Perdita of this and said: 'You shall come.'

She clasped her hands in ecstasy. Pink satin? White perhaps as she had worn at the Oratorio. Lavender? Blue?

'Why not?' cried the Prince. 'You cannot join the dancers, but you will be watching in a box of course . . . and you will be there.'

The Prince specially noticed Mrs. Armistead that evening. A strange woman who while she did not immediately catch the eyes remained in the mind. How gracefully she moved! And there was an air of assurance about her. He had often wondered why a woman who had such an air of breeding should be a lady's maid. A disloyal thought occurred to him. One would have thought she was the lady of the house rather than Perdita, but for Perdita's fine clothes.

And then a thought suddenly struck him.

He called at Cumberland House to see the Duchess, who received him with arms outstretched.

'Prince of Princes!'

'Most enchanting and incongruous of Aunts.'

The embraced.

'I have come to speak to you about our recent conversation.'

The black feathery fans shot up to disclose the glitter of the green eyes.

'There may well be a spy in Cork Street.'

'So you have discovered . . .'

'The lady's maid. Her name is Mrs. Armistead.'

The Duchess threw back her head and laughed. 'Now there is a woman.'

'You know of her?'

'She is becoming rather well known.'

'For what reason?'

'The usual reasons.'

'Dear Aunt, pray explain.'

'Dear Nephew, certainly. She is a very unusual and attractive lady's maid, is she not? You think so. So do our gentlemen . . . Mr. Fox, Dorset, Derby . . . so I've heard.'

'By God, but why does she continue to serve Perdita?'

'She is no ordinary woman. She wishes to preserve her independence.'

'In being a lady's maid!'

'In rather special circumstances. I . . . who make it my pleasurable duty to keep a close watch on all that concerns my Prince. . . .'

'At least a very charming spy.'

She curtsied. 'But I love you as a mother, as an aunt . . . as anything you care to name. And so I learn these things. No, you must look elsewhere for your spy. It's not the lady's maid. She is a Whig . . . a good Whig. A friend of Mr. Fox. She would never spy for the King.'

The Prince was laughing. 'I had always thought there was something unusual about her.'

'So you must look elsewhere, dear one.'

She was thinking: Armistead. Not a bad idea. If Grace cannot do, why not Armistead?

It was a scene of splendour at the Haymarket theatre where the King's birthday ball was being held, and although as many members of the royal family who were of an age to attend were present, it was the Prince of Wales who attracted all the attention. As usual he was dressed in the height of fashion, augmented by inventions of his own which would be copied immediately to become the very pinnacle of good taste and elegance.

Watching him from her box Perdita's feelings were mixed. Pride, pleasure, gratification, apprehension and humiliation. She herself came in for a good share of the attention; in fact it was divided between her and the Prince and whenever he gazed up at her box, which he did frequently, many were aware of it.

It had been most galling to arrive to find that she was to share a box with Mrs. Denton who was the mistress of Lord Lyttleton. It was, she felt, a humiliation—as though she were judged to be of the same calibre. Why, when she had been at the theatre Lord Lyttleton had pursued her and offered her a luxurious house and a good income if she would become his mistress, and she had refused him. Mrs. Denton had accepted—and here they were in a public place—grouped together as it were.

Mrs. Denton was leaning forward in the box pointing out this person and that, excited and *honoured* to be present. How difficult life was! sighed Perdita. She wished she had not come.

'There is the Duchess of Devonshire,' whispered Mrs. Denton. As if I did not know the creature, thought Perdita. 'Is she not beautiful? And her gown! No wonder she is the leader of fashion.' Is she! thought Perdita. Indeed she is not. I can outshine her any day. And I will. The arrogant woman snubbed me in Pall Mall. I shall not forget it.

And the Prince was talking to the Duchess and showing so clearly that he admired her and was delighted with her company.

'Of course she is very clever and her house is the meeting place for the Whig opposition. His Majesty won't be too pleased to have her here, but it's clear the Prince is delighted. And look . . . Oh, is she not beautiful! The tall one with the golden hair.

I know who she is. Mrs. Grace Elliott. There was a big scandal about her. I wonder the Queen allows her to come to Court.'

'She is too tall,' said Perdita.

'Do you think so? They call her Dally the Tall. It's because her name was Dalrymple before she married Mr. Elliott . . . who divorced her, I might say.'

Perdita pursed her lips. Such a woman could mingle with guests while virtuous people must be seated in boxes!

'Oh . . . look.'

Mrs. Denton had no need to direct Perdita's attention for she had already seen. The tall Mrs. Elliott had selected two rosebuds from her corsage and had approached the Prince, curtsied and offered them to him.

'What . . . blatant impudence!'

'They say she is very free in her manners, but . . . at a public ball . . . !'

'It is quite shocking.'

'He's taking them.'

'He's too chivalrous to do anything else.'

The Prince was standing smelling the rosebuds while Grace Elliott remained before him, smiling complacently. Then the Prince looked up at the box and caught Perdita's eye.

He called to one of the members of his suite and handed the rosebuds to him.

'What does it mean?' twittered Mrs. Denton.

Perdita was silent. It was a direct insult to her. This tall woman with the golden hair was telling her, and the Court, that she was ready to be—or already was—the *friend* of the Prince of Wales; and the fact that he had taken the flowers was almost an acknowledgement of this.

There was scratching on the door of the box.

Perdita did not look round; she felt too mortified.

Then a voice said: 'Er . . . Mrs. Robinson . . .' And she saw the gentleman of the Prince's suite to whom he had handed the flowers standing there in the box and holding in his hands the rosebuds.

'With the compliments of His Royal Highness, Madam.'

Perdita felt almost hysterical with joy. She took the roses. She was well aware of the watching eyes. Dramatically, as though acting for an audience, she put the rosebuds into her corsage making sure that they were very prominent.

She sparkled. It was a successful ball. No matter that she

must sit in a box while others danced with her lover. He had shown his regard for her publicly.

She was happier than she had been for some time.

The King and Queen were at Windsor—not so homely and comfortable as 'dear little Kew' but preferable to St. James's.

The Queen was pleasantly excited and the King was pleased to humour her.

She explained to him: 'It is always pleasant to see people from one's native land even though it has ceased to be one's home.'

The King could see this point.

'Herr von Hardenburg and his wife are charming people. I trust you will honour them with an audience.'

'Pleased to, pleased to,' said the King.

'They have with them a young woman . . . about eighteen years of age. She is very pretty and of good family. I wish them to be comfortable during their stay here.'

Any such problem pleased the King. There was nothing he enjoyed more than planning domestic details. So he threw himself wholeheartedly into the matter and questioned and cross-questioned the Queen about the arrangements which had been made for the Hardenburgs.

She had asked that a house be found for them in Windsor; and she believed that they were very happy there. They had several small children and Fräulein von Busch, the young lady whom they had brought with them was such a pleasant creature . . . very handsome but modest; the Queen was sure that His Majesty would find her a pleasant change from some of these garish women who seemed to be considered so fashionable nowadays . . . women like the Duchesses of Cumberland and Devonshire . . .

'Dabbling in politics,' grumbled the King. 'Never should be allowed. Women . . . in politics, eh! what?'

The Queen did not answer, but her resentment on that score was appeased a little. There were ways in which women could play their part in state affairs—for the amours of a Prince of Wales could be state affairs, witness the way he had fallen into the hands of Mr. Fox—subtle ways; and because she was not pregnant she now had the time and energy to exert herself in her own particular brand of statescraft. And the King knew nothing about it. Comforting thought.

She suggested that they go for a drive and ordered the coach-

man which way to go. This took them past the house occupied
by the Hardenburgs and as Frau von Hardenburg was in the
garden with her children and swept a most demure and becoming curtsey, the Queen ordered the coachman to stop.

'Would Your Majesty allow me to present these pleasant people to you?'

The King was happy that this should be so. Beaming with
goodwill he even condescended to dismount and go into the
house.

It was pleasant to talk in German again. Even the King spoke
in it as though it were his native language. The Hardenburgs
were delighted and honoured. The wife, the King noticed, was
a very pretty woman indeed, and as for the children they were
quite enchanting. The King sat down and took several of them
on his knee, questioning them and smiling at their bright answers.

'Charming, charming,' he muttered.

And there was Fräulein von Busch. What a pleasant creature!
Plump, pink and white, golden haired and so modest.

When the visit was over and they rode off the Queen was
smiling complacently. As for the King he declared himself to
have been enchanted.

'Must make friends from Germany welcome. Very nice people. Homely . . . pleasant . . . eh, what?'

The Queen agreed that the Hardenburgs—and Fräulein von
Busch—were indeed homely and pleasant and she could wish
that there were more like them.

The Prince came down to Windsor. This was what the Queen
had been waiting for. The King had gone to London on government matters, and she had taken advantage of his absence to
summon the Prince.

Windsor; thought the Prince. What was there to do in Windsor? There was only one place to be and that was London.

He was bored; he could not think why his mother had sent
for him.

Did she want to chatter to him of what a bonny babe he had
been while she did her tatting or sewed for the poor (Pious
Person in the Palace of Purity). If so he would return to London
at the earliest possible moment. He would do that in any case.

'You should drive with me,' said the Queen.

'For what purpose?'

'Because the people would like to see us together.'

So he rode with her and the carriage stopped at the Harden-burgs' house and there was Frau von Hardenburg in the garden making a pretty domestic scene with her children which would have delighted the King. But the Queen feared it would not make the same impression on the Prince of Wales.

'I should like to present you to these visitors from Germany.' She spoke quickly knowing that the Prince did not care to be reminded of his German ancestry.

The Prince was however extremely affable—and how charm-ing he could be when he wished to!

He stepped down from the carriage and went into the house; and there was the enchanting Fräulein von Busch, flushing with her realization of the honour and looking so pretty and modest.

The Prince was clearly impressed. On the drive back he asked a great many questions about the Hardenburg *ménage*.

The Prince stayed at Windsor to make arrangements, was his excuse, for his birthday ball in August. He would be nineteen—only two years off his majority. In the last year he had changed considerably; in the next two years there would be more changes.

In the meantime he was happy—yes, really happy to stay at Windsor, and the Queen was so pleased with the success of her little bit of diplomacy that she was looking forward to telling the King about it when the Prince had given up that playacting woman and his Whig friends and settled quietly down with that young German girl who would do as she was told and help to guide the Prince to a better life. How amazed his Majesty would be! Perhaps he would realize then that women were not such fools. After all it was the Duchess of Cumberland who was the leading light in Cumberland House. But one did not have to be a bad woman to be clever.

She knew that the Prince was calling frequently on the Har-denburgs, and about two weeks after she had introduced the Prince to them, Schwellenburg came bustling into her room in a state of some excitement.

'Haf news. Said vill tell Her Majesty selfs. Herr and Frau von Hardenburg left . . . is gone.'

'Gone?'

'To Germany. The childs are there. He come back for them.'

'You mean that Herr von Hardenburg and his wife have gone away and left their children behind?'

'Come back for them. Fräulein von Busch stay and look after them.'

'So Fräulein von Busch is here. But how strange. Why have they gone?'

Schwellenburg looked sly.

'Herr Prince,' she said.

'What do you mean?'

'He likes too much vimen.'

'But . . . Fräulein von Busch . . .'

'It is Frau von Hardenburg he likes . . . so her husbint say. There is von I can do . . . I take her vay from Herr Prince. So he go in night . . . and come back for the childs.'

The Queen could not believe it. She called for her carriage; she went to the house. There she found, as Schwellenburg had said, Fräulein von Busch looking after the children.

She explained in German that Herr von Hardenburg had thought it wiser to leave at once for he feared that their Majesties would be as displeased as he was by the Prince's too fervent attentions to his wife.

The Queen was dumbfounded. Frau von Hardenburg! When there was this fresh young girl brought over for one special reason.

She could not understand it. Her little effort at diplomacy had failed. And that day the Prince, bored with a Windsor that did not contain Frau von Hardenburg, returned to London.

Danger on Hounslow Heath

One thing he was sure of, he was tired of Perdita. Her continual hints of sacrifice, her frequent tears, the theatrical tones in which she talked of her position and her wrongs, the turgid sentimental poems she was fond of writing—and they were all addressed to him—these were more frequent than the gay times. He was beginning to make excuses for not calling at Cork Street. And when he did call, his visits were enlivened by the brief chats he indulged in with Mrs. Armistead.

He was discovering how handsome she was, and she always seemed so sensible when compared with Perdita. When he kissed her hand in an excess of gallantry she did not protest or show any surprise but accepted this attentions as natural. Even when he went so far as to kiss her lips she returned the kiss in a sensible way.

He was greatly intrigued; and one thing the Hardenburg affair had taught him was that he no longer had any intention of remaining faithful to Perdita.

He had already accepted Grace Elliott's invitation to be her lover. She was amusing—just what he needed as an antidote to Perdita. A little cynical, extremely worldly; and a woman to whom one did not have to swear eternal fidelity every few minutes. He knew what his affair with Grace meant. It was good while it lasted and when it was over there would be no recriminations on either side. He knew that Grace had several lovers. He believed Cholmondeley was still one. There was St. Leger, Selwyn, Windham . . . Safety in numbers. He could be gay with Grace.

But he was tremendously intrigued with Mrs. Armistead. In

fact it was an unusual situation. He visited the mistress and desired the maid. Opportunities would have to be made for they could not very well make love under Perdita's nose.

She would be different from everyone else, he was sure.

His Aunt Cumberland knew that Grace had become his mistress and was delighted.

He talked of Mrs. Armistead.

'Intriguing creature,' agreed the Duchess; and thought how amusing it was that under her very roof Perdita was housing a rival. If she but knew! And she would, in due course. Silly little Perdita had some shocks coming to her. 'A meeting with Mrs. Armistead could easily be arranged.'

'It's a devilishly ticklish situation.'

'You will not have to consider it so much longer, I gather.'

The Prince looked startled. Of course he would not! How much longer was he going on with this farce of being Perdita's devoted lover? Why should he not meet the interesting Mrs. Armistead if he wished?

'Why not invite her to Windsor. You could meet at an inn there. That would be discreet. I am sure the good woman would wish for discretion.'

'An inn at Windsor. Why not?'

'You will have to go there for your birthday celebrations.'

He was thoughtful. He could not help remembering the inn on Eel Pie Island to which he had gone in such a state of ecstasy.

His uncle appeared.

'Ha, so we have the pleasure of His Highness's company. Looking well and debonair. Better to be the lover of women in the plural than in the singular.'

'He speaks from experience,' said the Duchess coolly.

'Am I right or wrong, eh, Taffy?'

Taffy? thought the Prince. Oh, Wales, of course. It struck a discordant note. *Taffy*.

It occurred to him for the first time that his uncle was a very crude man and that he did not really like him very much.

Perdita was not at home. Gorgeously painted and patched she had gone out for one of her morning drives. She had not felt in the mood for such an outing, she told Mrs. Armistead; the Prince's attitude lately had worried her. But she did not want people to notice that she was less happy than she had been. The Prince was young and gay and he had fallen into bad company;

and as she naturally had tried to make him understand this, it had caused a little lovers' quarrel.

Mrs. Armistead, who had overheard the lovers quarrel, thought it far from little. She had already decided that Perdita had not very many weeks left to her in which to bask in the glory of the Prince's favour. Let her dress in her silks and muslins, her fantastic hats. Poor creature, she would very soon be dislodged from her position.

So she had driven out in the ostentatious coach with the wreath of flowers which looked like a coronet and she would be gone for at least another hour.

Mrs. Armistead, reviewing her mistress's position, was in fact thinking of her own. Things will change mightily when we have lost His Highness, she thought. Would that be the time to retire to Chertsey? She had not only her house but enough money to live on in modest dignity. Mr. Fox was her friend. He would visit her there and they would talk politics together; he had paid her the compliment of actually letting her share in a discussion with him and although perhaps she could not go so far as to say he had taken her advice, he had listened to it.

The footman came to her room to announce that a Mr. Meynel had called from the Prince of Wales.

'Mrs. Robinson is not at home, but perhaps I should see him. Bring him in,' she ordered.

Mr. Meynel appeared and bowing asked if he had the pleasure of meeting Mrs. Armistead.

'I am Mrs. Armistead. But I'm afraid I have to tell you that Mrs. Robinson is not at home. Any message you care to leave . . .'

'I have not come to see Mrs. Robinson, Madam, but yourself.'

'Indeed?'

'Yes, Madam. His Highness the Prince of Wales asks that you take supper with him.'

Mrs. Armistead flushed a faint pink. 'Is this really so?'

'Yes, Madam. His Highness is shortly leaving for Windsor; he wishes you to take supper in an inn near that town, and wishes to know whether you accept this invitation.'

'His Highness does not issue invitations but commands.'

Mr. Meynel inclined his head in acknowledgement of the truth of this statement.

'Then, Madam, I am to understand you accept His Highness's command?'

'Being fully conscious of the honour, indeed I do.'

'I will tell His Highness, who I am sure will be delighted.'

'And when . . . ?'

'Madam, you may leave these arrangements to me. A carriage will pick you up and take you to the inn. All you must do is hold yourself in readiness. You will have notice.'

'Thank you, sir. I shall await His Highness's instructions.'

Mr. Meynel departed and Mrs. Armistead sat down, for once without her usual serenity. So it had come! Fox, Derby, Dorset and now the Prince of Wales.

Oh, indeed Perdita's day was done.

In the days which followed, Mrs. Armistead was busy. During one of Perdita's absences she moved many of her belongings to the house of a friend. They should be taken to Chertsey at the first opportunity.

It would not be possible for her to stay with Perdita after taking supper with the Prince. At least she would not deceive her and remain under her roof. There should be a complete break. A friend of the Prince of Wales could not remain the lady's maid of his ex-mistress.

It was a very extraordinary situation, but she would be able to handle it.

The message would come any day now for she knew that the Prince would most certainly be going to Windsor soon to celebrate his nineteenth birthday there.

She had no illusions. This would be no grand passion. She was not the sort of woman to inspire that; nor did she wish to be. Perdita was a sad warning to any woman who might have such dreams. No, she and the Prince would have a quiet discreet friendship which would go as far as he wished and be terminated at his desire—which was the best in the long run. Only a fool would expect fidelity from such a young man; she did not even expect it from Mr. Fox and her feelings towards him were different from any she felt towards anyone else.

She was excited. She knew now that she was an extremely attractive woman. She guessed she would last as long as Dally the Tall; and she had no objections to running simultaneously with that notorious lady.

Perhaps she should warn Perdita. She imagined the effect that would have because the vain creature was beginning to learn how much she owed to her maid, and the more she considered the matter the more certain she was that once she had supped

with the Prince she could not come back to Perdita. It would be
undignified to do so; and her dignity had been her most char-
acteristic trait; it had helped to bring her to the position in which
she now found herself.

Meanwhile Perdita was growing more and more melancholy.

There were hints everywhere about the Prince's friendship
with Mrs. Grace Elliott.

'Friendship!' cried Perdita. 'That creature is so impertinent
that she would presume on any friendship.'

'She is certainly a very bold lady,' agreed Mrs. Armistead.

'How do you know, Armistead?'

'I have seen her, Madam. She is constantly showing herself
in her carriage.'

'And doubtless you have heard rumours?'

'Yes, Madam, there are rumours.'

Perdita went into a mood of morbidity; and Mrs. Armistead
chose this moment to hint that she might be leaving.

'Personal affairs are beginning to intrude a little, Madam. I
may find it necessary in the near future to give up my post and
attend to them.'

'Personal affairs,' murmured Perdita vaguely.

'Yes . . . my own affairs, Madam.'

Perdita looked at Mrs. Armistead. How strange! One had
never expected her to have *personal* affairs. They sounded very
vague. Perdita could not pay much attention to Mrs. Armistead's
personal affairs; she had so many of her own. Then it suddenly
struck her. Armistead wanted more money. This was her way
of asking for it. Of course she should have it.

She offered it and it was gratefully accepted. Mrs. Armistead
had done her duty, she considered; she had warned Perdita.

Perdita was in her room; she was weeping undramatically. She
was too unhappy for drama. It was true; he had a mistress. She
was this woman who had been divorced by her husband for
eloping with Lord Venetia. Mrs. Grace Elliott—Dally the Tall—
the golden haired beauty who had dared to give him rosebuds
while she, Perdita, had looked on.

Of course she had opportunities of seeing him which were
denied to Perdita. But they need not have been. He could have
been constantly at Cork Street if he had wished. But he did not
wish; he came less frequently and when he did come he stayed
for such a short time. Why? So that he could hurry away and be
with Grace Elliott at Cumberland House. For she had no doubt

of this. Her enemies were the Duke and Duchess of Cumberland. The Duke hated her because he had wanted her for his mistress and the Duchess hated her for the same reason. They had been against her from the first. It was they who had brought this Grace Elliott to his notice. But he had been ready enough to be unfaithful to her.

And she had given up everything for him!

She had shut herself in her room; she could not bear to see anyone. She had not even sent for Armistead to dress her. She could only lie in bed and contemplate her misery.

What would this mean? Humiliation. The whole world would know. One could not hope that it would be a secret. The papers would be filled with cartoons and lampoons; when she rode out people would laugh at her. There would be no more of those rides along the Mall when people stopped to stare at her, and gallant gentlemen doffed their hats and almost swept the ground with them to do her the utmost homage.

And the Prince would flaunt another mistress. And . . . hideous thought and one which she tried to shut out altogether . . . the creditors would demand their money. They would not humbly request payment as they had in the past; they would make ugly demands. And what would she do? Where would she find the money to pay?

She thought of the cold stone walls of the debtors' prison . . . the hopelessness, the despair of those within.

No! she thought. Never, never! Anything is better than that.

The Prince was going to Windsor for his birthday celebrations. There would be beautiful women there . . . women of the Court. But she was shut out. She was not received. At one time he would have deplored this. He would have said: 'I will go to Windsor for the birthday ball because I needs must and then I will fly back to my Perdita.'

But now he was going to Windsor days before the ball; he was going to make the arrangements himself. He had no desire to be where Perdita was.

Oh it was so different; it was all that the moralists would have told her that she must expect.

So she lay in bed all day, too limp to get up, to care, and it was a measure of her misery that she did not care what she looked like.

There was a scratching at the door.

'Is that you, Armistead?'

Mrs. Armistead entered. 'A letter, Madam.'

Eagerly she took it because she saw that it came from the Prince.

Her fingers were trembling as she opened it. She could not believe those words. They could not be true. He was telling her that their idyll was over and that they should not meet again.

She lay back on her pillows, her eyes closed. Mrs. Armistead picking up the letter, took the opportunity to read it.

She understood. The moment had come.

'Madam has had bad news?' she asked soothingly.

Perdita nodded vaguely.

'I will make you some chocolate.'

'Chocolate!' cried Perdita bitterly.

'Then, Madam, a dish of tea.'

'Leave me, Armistead. Leave me alone.'

Mrs. Armistead quietly shut the door, leaving Perdita to her misery.

The Prince she guessed was on his way to Windsor. Soon now, if it were coming at all, the summons would come.

She went to her room—bare of all her private possessions. The beautiful gowns which Perdita had given her were all safely stored in Chertsey.

All day long Perdita stayed in her room, wanting nothing but to be left alone with her misery.

What a fool she is, thought Mrs. Armistead. She will ruin her looks with weeping—and there is Lord Malden, and a host of others who will cherish her. She could discover that it is not such a bad thing to have been the mistress of the Prince of Wales.

Mrs. Armistead looked at her own reflection in the mirror and smiled secretly.

There was an air of waiting about the house in Cork Street. The servants knew. Perhaps like Mrs. Armistead they had seen it coming; they knew how infrequent were the Prince's visits, they had heard his voice and that of their mistress raised in anger against each other. Doubtless, thought Mrs. Armistead, they imitated those in higher circles and wagered how long it would last. They would know that their mistress had shut herself in her room and that she refused to eat or see anyone.

Mrs. Armistead stayed close to the window. Every time she heard carriage wheels she was intent.

And at length a carriage stopped at the door of the house and glancing out of the window she saw Mr. Meynal step from it.

She was at the door and herself let him in.

'The time has come, Madam,' said Mr. Meynal.

'Now . . . this minute?' she asked and her serenity amazed Mr. Meynal.

'The carriage is waiting, Madam. We should leave in ten minutes. It's a long journey to Windsor.'

'Pray go to the carriage, Mr. Meynal, and wait for me there. I will be with you in ten minutes.'

Mr. Meynal bowed his head. He could see that she was a woman of her word.

Mrs. Armistead scratched lightly on the door. Perdita did not answer, so she opened it and looked in. Perdita lay in her bed, her lovely hair in wild disorder, her face devoid of rouge, powder and patches looking strangely childlike. She did not glance at Mrs. Armistead, but stared before her as though she were in a dream.

'Mrs. Robinson, Madam.'

Perdita shook her head. Her lips framed the words Go away, but no sound came from them.

'It distresses me to disturb you with my affairs at such a time, Madam. But I have to leave.'

Perdita did not speak.

Very well, thought Mrs. Armistead, if she did not wish to hear there was no need to force an explanation upon her. She had done her duty. She had told her that she was leaving. This was an easy way out.

Mrs. Armistead shut the door and, putting on her cloak, quietly left the house.

The following day Perdita roused herself and saw ruin staring her in the face. The Prince had deserted her; he no longer wished to see her. She picked up the note he had written and read it again and again.

The fashionable world would know by now: Perdita's day is over. Now he would be flaunting that woman—riding with her, dancing with her in Cumberland House and even perhaps at his own birthday ball.

He was at Windsor now. And he would not be thinking of her; but would he not? He had cared for her so deeply and that was not so long ago.

She had done everything to please him. Where had she failed? When she thought of what she had spent in this house to entertain him in the manner to which he was accustomed . . . !

Oh God, she thought, bills! Those outstanding accounts which she had thrust away so impatiently because there had been no time to consider the cost. All her energies had had to go into keeping her Prince happy. There had been no time for anything else. But when the dressmakers, the wine merchants, the butchers, the pastrycooks . . . when they all knew that the Prince had deserted her, they would lose their patience.

She was a frightened woman.

She got up from her bed. She could not allow him to treat her like this. Where was her confidence? She thought of how not so long ago she had been able to change his mood to one of peevish dissatisfaction to one of adoring contentment.

She was being foolish. All she had to do was see him, to tell him she adored him, that she could not live without him. That was all he needed. After all he was such a boy, a spoilt boy. Of course he was a spoilt boy. There were so many people around him showing him how important he was. Would he not one day be king?

Then she must see him. But he was at Windsor. Well, what was to prevent *her* going to Windsor?

She felt better now that she had decided on some action.

She leaped off her bed, looked at herself in the mirror and gasping with horror covered her face with her hands. What a fool she was! What if he had repented and called and seen her like this? The damage must be repaired without delay; and she would go to Windsor. She would take Armistead with her and it would be rather like the old days on Eel Pie Island.

She pulled the bell rope for Armistead and went to her wardrobe. Now what should she wear? A becoming gown and a cloak in a contrasting colour. Her hair dressed simply as he had liked it best, perhaps with a curl over the shoulder.

Why did Armistead not answer her summons? It was unlike Armistead.

She frowned and brought a blue silk dress from her wardrobe. She was feeling better already. Once Armistead had done her work she would have transformed this pale and sad creature into the most beautiful woman in London.

Hurry Armistead! What has happened to you.

It was five minutes since she had rung.

She opened her door and called: 'Armistead.'

She went along to Armistead's room. The footman was on the stairs. He looked flushed and it occurred to her later that he must have been at the wine.

'Where is Armistead?' she asked.

'She left, Madam. Yesterday.'

'Left!'

'Yes, Madam. She went away. She said she was leaving and had told you.'

'Leaving . . . But . . .'

The footman shrugged his shoulders . . . insolently, she thought. What had happened? Armistead . . . gone!

Then she remembered that the woman had come to her yesterday and said something. What had she said? She, Perdita, had been too unhappy with her own affairs to listen to Armistead's account of hers.

The footman was watching her covertly. Of course he was seeing her as he never had before . . . unkempt, carelessly dressed, her face unpainted.

He knows, she thought. He will tell the servants that the Prince has deserted me.

So she *must* see her lover. She must go to Windsor without delay.

She went back to her room. It was mid-afternoon. Why had she not realized before what she must do. If it had been morning she could have reached Windsor in daylight.

But first she must make herself beautiful. Oh, how she missed Armistead! And where had Armistead gone? Some family matter . . . was that what she had said? Why hadn't she listened? Why hadn't she insisted on retaining Armistead's services at all costs?

Because she was taking some action she felt better. After all, she was capable of choosing the most becoming and suitable of her dresses, capable of applying the patch close to her eyes to call attention to their brilliance.

Dressing took a long time and she could not arrange her hair as effectively as Armistead could, but at length she was ready. Perhaps she should start tomorrow morning. No, she could not endure another night of suspense. She must see the Prince—and the sooner the better.

She sent for her young postilion—he was only nine years old—and told him that she wished to drive her small pony phaeton to Windsor, so he was to saddle the ponies and bring it to the door.

The boy looked astonished, but when she told him to be quick he went away to do her bidding.

How long it seemed while she waited there! The time seemed

to have flown by since she had made her decision; again and again she looked at her reflection and thought of how much better a job Armistead would have made of her toilette.

At length the phaeton was waiting and she climbed into it while her youthful postilion took his place and they set off. Preparations had taken so long that it was getting dark when they reached Hyde Park Corner.

As the coach rattled on she was rehearsing what she would say to the Prince when she saw him; but first she must make sure that he would see her. This thought made her shiver with sudden anxiety. What if he refused? He had sounded so insistent in his letter. 'We must not meet again.' But he could not really have meant that. He had written it in a sudden passion. Perhaps inspired by Grace Elliott or her enemies at Cumberland House.

They had reached Hounslow and pulled up at an inn.

The innkeeper came out to welcome her and usher such an obvious lady of quality into the inn parlour.

She declared that she could take nothing. She was only eager to continue her journey as soon as possible.

'Whither are you bound, Madam?' asked the innkeeper.

'To Windsor.'

'Madam, you cannot cross the Heath at this hour. Stay here until morning.'

'I must press on.'

'I must tell you, Madam, that every carriage which has crossed the Heath these last ten nights has been attacked and rifled.'

'I must take that chance.'

'But you . . . a lady and no one to protect you but that young boy!'

She smiled. 'I am not afraid,' she said.

'There are some dangerous men about.'

She was immediately dramatic. She threw back her head and smiled. Let me be murdered, she thought; and then he will be filled with remorse. For the rest of his life he will remember that my death was due to his treatment of me.

'I do not fear dangerous men,' she said.

'You will be risking your life.'

'Perhaps I have no great desire to save it.'

The innkeeper looked at her oddly. Her face was vaguely familiar to him. It could not be. Not *the* Mrs. Robinson! But of course, and she was going to Windsor because His Highness had lately arrived there.

All the same, if she were to encounter a highwayman he

wouldn't care if she was the Prince's mistress; and now he knew who she was, the innkeeper believed that that was a diamond she was wearing at her throat. She was asking for trouble, she was, but he could do no more than warn her.

As she rode off into the darkness he stood at the door of the inn scratching his head and watching until the phaeton was out of sight.

Perdita rode on. Hounslow Heath! Notorious as the haunt of the most desperate highwaymen. Her little postilion was frightened; she could sense his fear. The Heath stretched out before them—ghostly in starlight. At any moment from behind one of those bushes a dark figure might rise up, flourish a pistol and call 'Stand and deliver.'

She herself caught the boy's fear. All very well to act a part before the innkeeper, to pretend that she did not care whether she was murdered or not. That was a part she played. But this was reality. Deep emotions, such as fear and misery penetrated the mask. She suddenly knew as they crossed the Heath that she did not want to die at the hands of some rough murderer.

She heard something like a sob from the little postilion; and then she saw the masked figure on the road.

Providence was with her, she was sure, for just as he was about to grasp the reins, the phaeton bounded over a hump in the road which threw the man backwards and gave her the chance she needed. She whipped up the horses and before the highwayman had a chance to recover his balance she had a start. He was running behind them, calling them to stand and deliver, shouting that he wanted their money or their lives.

Perdita did not heed him; the ponies seemed to sense the danger and galloped as never before, and after some moments of intense anxiety with great relief she saw the lights of an inn. She decided that if she reached it safely she would spend the night there for in any case it would be too late to get a message to the Prince at Windsor now.

The poor little postilion was white with fear and a little resentful, wondering why they had had to risk their lives by crossing the Heath only to pull up at the Magpie.

The landlord received them with pleasure and when she recounted the adventure assured her that she was a very brave lady and lucky to escape not only being robbed but with her life.

She was exhausted she said, and would have food sent up to her room. Her young postilion needed food too; he had acted with courage in an alarming situation and she wished him to know that she was pleased with him.

When the food was brought to her room she found she was very hungry and remembered that it was long since she had last eaten. She ate and lay down on her bed and was soon fast asleep.

She was awakened after a while by the sounds of commotion in the inn yard, where there was a great deal of running to and fro; visitors she supposed, and slept again to be awakened some hours later by more noises. This time it sounded like departures.

The busy life of an inn, she supposed, and slept again.

She was awake early and immediately became anxious to continue the journey to Windsor. She washed and dressed, put on her rouge and patches to the best of her ability, sighing for Mrs. Armistead who would have done so much better than she could.

Then she went down to take a little refreshment before leaving.

This was brought to her and when she had eaten and had made her way out of the dining room, she saw a woman descending the staircase. At first she thought she was dreaming.

Mrs. Armistead!

But what could her lady's maid be doing here at the Magpie Inn at this hour of morning?

It was a mistake. It could not be Mrs. Armistead. It was her double.

For a few seconds they stood perfectly still looking at each other. Surely that calm handsome face could belong to no one else.

Then the woman turned and unhurriedly, and with the utmost dignity, made her way back the way she had come.

Perdita cried suddenly and imperiously: 'Armistead.' But the woman did not look back as she disappeared round a turn in the staircase.

Impossible, thought Perdita. I must be dreaming.

The innkeeper was at the door rubbing his hands, trusting she had spent a good night and had had a good breakfast.

She assured him she had and he told her that the phaeton was ready to leave when she was.

And then she received her second surprise. A man sauntered across the yard. She knew that man. He was a servant of the Prince's. His name was Meynal. He had on one or two occasions brought messages to her from the Prince.

How strange. It was like a dream. First she imagined she had seen Armistead—but she *had* seen Armistead—and then the Prince's servant.

The innkeeper was beside her.

'Is that man attached to the household of the Prince of Wales?' she asked.

The innkeeper looked sly. 'Oh, Madam, we entertain the quality here. I could tell you . . .'

She did not answer. She went out to the phaeton. Mrs. Armistead! Meynal! How very strange.

All the way to Windsor she was thinking of the strangeness of this encounter. A suspicion had come into her mind. The Prince had shown an interest in Armistead. She had caught him watching her now and then. There had been an occasion when she had seen his arrival and he had been a long time coming into her room. And Armistead had left her . . . after all those years . . . so oddly.

Armistead! An assignation with the Prince!

'Oh no, no,' she murmured.

But in her heart she believed it was true; and something told her that if it was, this was indeed the end.

The next day she arrived in Windsor. She gazed wistfully at the castle and thought of how happy she could have been had she been a princess who might have married him. Everything would have been so different then. There would have been none of the anxieties which had led to friction between them.

She saw herself as a princess arriving from a foreign country, startling him with her beauty.

But encroaching reality was so alarming that it robbed her dreams of any substance; at such a time even she was forced to recognize them for the fancies they were.

She would be brisk and practical; so she pulled up at an inn where she wrote a letter and sent the postilion to the castle with it instructing him to find Lord Malden who, she was sure, was with the Prince, and when he had found him to tell him from whom the note came and beg him to deliver it into no hands but those of the Prince of Wales.

The boy was away for a fretful hour and a half before he returned and said that he had at length been taken to Lord Malden and given the note to him.

'You did well,' she told the boy.

The waiting was almost unbearable. At one moment she was assuring herself that the note would bring the Prince to the inn full of remorse; at another she pictured his becoming angry with her for following him to Windsor, but soon to be placated by her soft words and beauty. One thing she would not visualize and that was that he would not come at all.

It was Lord Malden who came, looking melancholy and anxious. Dear Lord Malden, who had always been such a good friend!

She greeted him eagerly. 'The Prince . . .'

Lord Malden shook his head.

'You gave him my note?'

'I did.'

'And you have a reply for me. Why did he not come himself when I begged him to?'

'The Prince is determined not to see you.'

'But why . . . why . . . what have I done to deserve this? Did he read my note?'

'Yes and . . .'

'What? Pray do not hide anything.'

'He tore it into pieces and said he had no wish to see you again.'

'But . . .'

Lord Malden took her hand and looked into her face. 'You should return to Cork Street. You will find you have many friends . . . many friends . . .'

He was regarding her with that hungry expression which she knew so well.

She withdrew her hands impatiently.

'I must see the Prince.'

Malden shook his head. 'He is determined.'

'And so am I.'

'But . . .'

She seized his hand suddenly. 'Promise me this, that you will do your best to persuade him . . .'

Lord Malden replied tenderly: 'You know that if there is anything on earth I can do to add to your happiness it shall be done. You have lost the Prince of Wales but you have friends left.'

She felt so sickened with anxiety that she turned peevishly away. She had never known Malden not to plead his own cause! She knew what he was hinting. Don't mourn because you are no longer the mistress of the Prince of Wales. There are many other men who are ready to take you on.

The shame of it! she thought. That was what they would be saying and thinking now.

'I will go back to Cork Street now,' she said. 'There is nothing more to be done here.'

Malden bowed his head.

And Perdita, sick at heart and defeated, climbed into her phaeton. How much better if she had never come.

She rode back to London, bruised and wounded—yet thinking not so much of the Prince of Wales as the bills which would be coming in as soon as the news leaked out that the Prince had finished with her.

How would she meet them? It seemed to her that as she rode across the Heath—in daylight this time—a shadow loomed over her. Not a highwayman, but the debtors' prison.

Birthday Celebrations at Windsor

In the great drawing room the Prince stood beside his father receiving congratulations on attaining his nineteenth birthday. He looked magnificent in his elegant coat, on which flashed the diamond star as brilliant as the buckles on his shoes.

Handsome enough, thought the King. But getting fat. Have to speak to him about it. If he shows signs at nineteen what will he be at my age?

The King felt that he was an old man although only in his early forties. The weight of state affairs, the trials of a family . . .

The Queen looked on almost complacently for having produced such a handsome son; she was pleased, too, because although her little scheme to provide him with a nice comfortable German mistress had failed, there were rumours that he was not nearly so friendly with that dreadful play actress.

He'll settle down, thought the Queen.

The Prince was thinking of women. He was free. Dally was amusing and how experienced! He was enjoying his encounters with Dally; and as for the rather sedate Mrs. Armistead, she was a treasure. It was amusing to ride out to the Magpie when he felt in the mood and there she would be, never reproaching him, always pleased to see him, so different from Perdita that she reminded him of her—most pleasantly. Reminded him of what he had escaped, of course. That virago-saint! How had I endured her for so long?

There were going to be changes when he returned to London. He was not going to Cumberland House so frequently. He did not like his uncle and he was not going to pretend he did. The fellow was an ignoramus. The more friendly he became with Fox and Sheridan the more he realized this. Insolent too! *Taffy!* He would have his friends remember that although he liked to be on terms of intimacy with them he was still the Prince of Wales. No one was going to call him by familiar epithets without his permission. Taffy indeed!

Yes, there would be changes.

The celebrations were to last several days, and it was enjoyable to be the centre of them. He was behaving with such propriety that even the King had nothing of which to complain.

When they met they talked of politics, which at the moment meant the affair of the American Colonies which occupied the King's mind almost exclusively. The Prince did not set forward his views which, having been acquired through Charles James Fox, were in exact opposition to those of the King.

The King was a little optimistic.

'The French,' he told the Prince, 'are not so ready now to help our rebels. And I'll tell you why. They have troubles of their own, big troubles. I would not care to see the finances of this country in the same condition as those of France.'

The Prince nodded.

'You should take an interest in these affairs. They concern the country. More important than gambling or running after maids of honour, eh?'

Oh dear, the old fool hadn't advanced since Harriot Vernon—and he himself had almost forgotten her name and certainly could not recall what she looked like.

'I do take an interest,' said the Prince coolly. What if the old man knew about those long discussions he enjoyed with Fox and Sheridan over innumerable glasses of wine! That would startle His Majesty. But of course Mr. Fox could bring a lucid and brilliant mind to the subject; not like poor old muddled Papa.

'Glad to hear it, glad to hear it. Don't forget you'll be taking your place in the House of Lords in two years' time.'

'Two years,' said the Prince ironically.

'Seems far ahead. Not so. Not so. I know what it's like at your age. I was young once myself, you know.'

Indeed, thought the Prince sarcastically. Your Majesty surprises me. But he merely smiled sycophantishly. There was no point in antagonizing the old man further at this stage. That would come when he did take his part in politics and ranged himself beside Fox against his father.

'Well, well, this has all the appearance of a long contest that will end as it ought by the colonies returning to the mother country and I tell you this: I will never put my hand to any other conclusion of this business.'

No point in telling him that Mr. Fox thought differently, that Mr. Fox believed that there would never have been any conflict between the mother country and her colonies if it had not been for the stupidity of the King and certain of his ministers.

It was irksome indeed to be still under the jurisdiction of such a bumbling old fool. Two more years before he could hope for complete freedom! In the meantime he had to be content with a little more than he was allowed as a boy. His cage was opened now and then; he was allowed to fly out provided he made sure of returning.

The King, thought the Prince—and he believed this because Fox had told him it was so—was a monarch who believed he should have supreme power in the country. He treated his Prime Minister, Lord North, as the man who should carry out the royal orders. This, according to Fox, was the reason why the best men in the country—Fox implied men like himself—would not serve the King. That was why they must put up with the mistakes of a second-rate politician like North. The troubles of the country were largely due to this attitude of the King's and it was one which no government worthy of its name would allow. A government headed by Fox would never allow itself to be dictated to. Pitt's had been such a government and it was under Pitt that England had gained an Empire; it was during North's ministry that England was losing one.

Oh wait, thought the Prince. Wait until I am of age. Wait till I take my place in the House of Lords. Wait till I show my hand. Then it will be Fox and the Prince. Men of intelligence at the head of affairs, not two old idiots like North and the King.

The King had now started on a lecture about the evils of gambling, drink and women. The Prince must remember his position. Never gamble. It meant heavy debts. (The Prince mildly wondered what he owed.) Drink ruined any man—physically and mentally. As for the company of light women that meant scandal; and that was something of which royal family had to beware more than anything.

'That play actress . . .' said the King gruffly. 'It's over now, is it?'

The Prince could say truthfully that it was.

'Good thing. Hope you realize now . . . those women can be

dangerous. Grosvenor's wife and your Uncle Cumberland. Shouldn't go there, you know. They're not received and it looks bad.'

'I don't intend to go there so much in future.'

'That's good . . . that's good.'

'And that fellow Fox. He's sharp. I don't trust him. Hear you see something of him. And Sheridan. They say he's a clever fellow. Can't see it. Writes a few plays . . . just words . . . words . . . and married that good woman and treats her badly. These people are no good to you. Understand, eh, what?'

The Prince changed the subject. 'Several people have invited me to their houses. I thought I would do a tour of the country. It might be interesting and the people like to see us in other parts of the country besides the south.'

He was thinking: It would be an excellent idea. He would get right away from Perdita in case she became importunate. She had dared come to Windsor to see him. Impertinence. But Perdita could be persistent and she was not going to be easily cast off. He remembered the protestations he had made of fidelity. Well, it was the usual lovers' talk. And how was he to have known that she would be so melancholy and write those dreadful poems about how she had suffered and all she had given up. It had become unendurable. No one could have endured it—few would as long as he had.

'Oh,' said the King, 'where have these invitations come from, eh what?'

The Prince told him, enumerating some of the most well-known families in the country.

The King grunted. They would entertain him lavishly. There would be drinking and gambling and women. He did not think that this was the time for his son to go gallivanting all over the country. Not until he was a little more mature . . . and the King was a little more sure of what was going on in his mind. He seemed to have improved a little but he could not be sure.

'When did they wish you to go, eh, what?'

'Almost immediately. Before the summer is over. Travelling up to the north would present difficulties later.'

'H'm. Have to think about this. After all, Prince of Wales has his duties. Have to be careful. Go to one, and another wouldn't like it. Understand, eh, what?'

'No,' said the Prince. 'I hope to visit frequently and if I don't take in some this visit I'll do another later. I think it is wrong for us to stay in the south all the time as though we hadn't a country outside this area.'

'Oh, you do, do you? Well, we'll see. I'll look into this and let you know my decision.'

The Prince's face was pink. He could not keep on friendly terms with the old man for long. He was impossible. How much longer must he be treated like a child. He knew the answer to that. Two years. Not until he was twenty-one could he escape.

But the visit to Windsor had its compensations.

At the dinner which preceded the birthday ball he found himself seated next to the lovely Lady Augusta Campbell.

The banquet was held in St. George's Hall and to accommodate the eighty members of the nobility who were the guests of the royal family three long tables had been set up. At the head of one of these sat the King and Queen and at another the Prince of Wales.

Lady Augusta was young and charming and she talked gaily of the review in the Park which had taken place that afternoon as part of the birthday celebrations. The Prince talked to no one else and this was noticed—and not without some dismay by Lady Augusta's mother, the Duchess of Argyll.

As soon as the banquet was over and the ball began the Prince danced with Lady Augusta and it was clear that he was reluctant to partner anyone else.

There were whispers and sly glances. He has finished with Perdita Robinson. Will Lady Augusta be the next? And what of Dally the Tall? Was she going to stand aside and see the prize snatched from her by this young inexperienced girl.

Lady Augusta was certainly a lovely creature. She lacked the art of beautifying herself which a woman like Perdita Robinson possessed; but beside the actress she would seem young and pure.

During the evening the Prince persuaded her to leave the ballroom and walk in the moonlit park, but when he attempted to kiss her she was a little reluctant.

'Why?' he demanded. 'Don't you know I have fallen in love with you?'

'Oh yes,' she answered. 'I know that—or you have for me what passes for love. But where could it lead? My parents will never allow me to be your mistress and yours would never allow you to be my husband.'

'Ah, my dearest angel, I am not so easily defeated.'

But she was firm, and although she was undoubtedly attracted by him she was not so much so that she would forget discretion.

The Prince was not going to lose heart because he had failed after one banquet and ball. He had a new excitement in his life.

He had amusing Dally; intriguing Mrs. Armistead; and now he sought to add Lady Augusta to his reason for finding life enjoyable.

The Prince sat in his apartments at Windsor writing a poem to Lady Augusta Campbell.

> *'Oh! Campbell, the scene of tonight*
> *Has opened the wound of my heart;*
> *It has shown me how great the delight*
> *Which charms of thy converse impart.*
> *I've known what it is to be gay,*
> *I've revelled in joy's fleeting hour,*
> *I've wished for the close of the day,*
> *To meet in a thick-woven bower.'*

He laid down his pen and thought of Perdita whom he had met not exactly in a thick-woven bower; but an inn room on Eel Pie Island could be as romantic.

When Lady Augusta succumbed to his pleading would it be the beginning of a great love affair, such as he had once believed there would be with Perdita?

He forced himself to believe it would be so. He was at heart romantic. Fox might imply that he would be much more content if he did not allow himself to become deeply involved with one woman; but he knew that it was something more than a passing appeasement that he desired. He enjoyed being in love, being ready to die—or at least renounce a great deal—for love.

So he would continue to write letters and poems to Lady Augusta and if she returned his passion he might insist on marrying her. The Argylls were a great family; but his father, he knew, would never consent to a marriage; it would be some plain German frau for him.

He shivered at the prospect and picked up his pen.

> *' 'Twas there that the soft-stolen kiss,*
> *'Twas there that the throb of our hearts,*
> *Betrayed that we wished for the bliss*
> *Which love, and love only imparts . . .'*

He sighed, thinking of her beauty.

He did hope she was not going to remain aloof, insisting on preserving her virtue as Mary Hamilton had. In any case she with Grace Elliott and Mrs. Armistead were helping him to forget Perdita; and that was what he wanted almost as much as Lady Augusta's surrender—to forget Perdita completely, to forget her reproaches, her sacrificial sermons; he wanted to wash all memory of Perdita from his mind for he was heartily tired of her.

But as the days passed it became clear that Lady Augusta would cling to her virtue.

'There could be no future for us,' she said. 'Your Highness cannot imagine that my parents would allow me to become another Perdita Robinson.'

By such words she irritated him. The very thing he did not want was to be reminded of Perdita.

So he decided to give up the pursuit of Lady Augusta and devote himself to those ladies who appreciated his attentions. There was no doubt that Grace did—gay abandoned creature. Though she was not entirely satisfactory because she kept on her old lovers at the same time.

Mrs. Armistead was perhaps the more comforting of the two. She was always so delighted with some small diamond trinket that he found pleasure in making her little gifts.

Perhaps Charles James Fox was right. It was better not to become too involved.

The King sent for his son to tell him that he had come to a decision.

'I cannot give my consent to these proposed trips of yours.'

'But why not?' The King looked surprised that the Prince should address him so curtly. 'I can see nothing wrong in visiting some of Your Majesty's most highly respected subjects.'

'I have a treat for you,' said the King. 'Something you will enjoy more than these rounds of draughty country houses.'

'A treat.'

The King nodded smiling. 'You'll see, eh? Patience . . . a virtue, eh, what?'

The Prince was disgusted. Treats? As though he were a boy.

His frustration was strengthened when he reminded himself that he could not disobey the King and accept invitations which His Majesty did not wish him to.

It was maddening. Let him wait, thought the Prince, until I'm twenty-one.

The 'treat' which the King was offering his son as a compensation for refusing his permission for the country visits was a trip to the Nore.

When the Prince heard of this he was disgusted. This in place of those country visits where he would have been fêted and treated according to his rank, entertained lavishly and enjoyed good conversation and the company of pretty women.

But such was his position that it was useless to protest. The King had decreed that he should go and go he must.

The King and the Prince rode in their separate yachts down the river and were saluted by the ships they passed. Through Woolwich, Tilbury and Gravesend they went accompanied by numerous small craft and cheered along the way until they anchored in Sea Reach for the night. They set off again at five in the morning for Blackstakes; and here the King and Prince left their yachts and toured the dockyards, then proceeded to the Nore where they went on board Admiral Parker's flagship.

There officers and men were presented to the King and the Prince and after these ceremonies, which were somewhat tedious in the Prince's opinion, he and his father returned to their yachts. This, fumed the Prince, was his treat for being denied the ability to accept invitations when he wished. It was too humiliating. Particularly as before long what had happened was the talk of the town. A verse was circulated to commemorate the occasion.

> *'The King and the Prince went to the Nore,*
> *They saw the ships and main;*
> *The Prince and King they went on shore*
> *And then came back again.'*

The people were laughing at the King. Couldn't he see it? And until the Prince was considered of an age to make his own decisions and cut himself free of his father's control he would be laughed at too.

Returning to Windsor he went to the Magpie for the solace of Mrs. Armistead's company. She might lack the obvious beauty of Lady Augusta Campbell but she never irritated and she always knew how to soothe him.

No *grande passion* this—but eminently satisfactory.

Humiliation in Hyde Park

Bills! Every day they were coming.

'Madame Duvernay regrets she must call Mrs. Robinson's attention to this long overdue account.'

Perdita frowned and read the long list of articles. That pelisse which she could well have done without. The muff. The cloaks. The gowns . . . numerous gowns. They had all seemed so essential at the time. And Armistead had been so good at planning them.

Armistead! She did not wish to think of that woman. Traitor. Spy in her own house. Going off for *personal reasons . . .* which meant to the bed of the Prince of Wales!

Bills for wine. How could they have consumed so much? The poulterers, the butchers, the bakers . . . There was no end to it.

She started to attempt to add up the amounts but she was no good at it and it was so depressing in any case. And what good would it do to know how much she owed? There was one fact which she knew well enough now. She had not the money to pay them.

Oh, God, she thought. What shall I do?

There was Malden, dear faithful Malden; he would be the Earl of Essex one day but he had no money now. He could not help her.

Cumberland?

'Oh, no, never, never,' she cried dramatically. 'I would rather die.'

And then suddenly she was aware of the desperate position she was in and broke down and wept.

* * *

Lord Malden called. He looked very anxious.

'Have you any news?' she implored.

He could only shake his head.

'You have seen him?'

'I have.'

'And has he spoken of me?'

'I'm afraid not.'

'But that does not mean he does not *think* of me.'

Lady Augusta Campbell the elusive one; Dally the Tall the gay one; Mrs. Armistead the cosy one . . . How could he tell Perdita that the Prince no longer needed her? And that all he asked of her now was that she should cease to bother him and forget him as quickly as he was forgetting her.

'If I could but *see* him,' sighed Perdita.

'He will not see you. He was annoyed that you came to Windsor.'

'I risked my life in doing it.' Dramatically and with some embellishments she told the story of how she had crossed Hounslow Heath and had by a miracle escaped.

'Surely if he knew I did that for him . . . '

Lord Malden sighed. How could he tell her that all the Prince wanted was that she should go out of his life and stay out.

'My dear lord,' she said, 'if I could only *see* him. You are close to him. You could do so much . . . if you would.'

'You know there is nothing in my power I would not do for you.'

'I know it. And you will arrange a meeting. If I could but see him *once* . . . '

She might be right, thought Malden. She was very beautiful. Dally and the Armistead women were nothing compared with her. Nor was Lady Augusta. Surely he must be moved if he could see her looking as appealing as she did now?

And if he could bring them together again . . . if they could be happy together. And surely Perdita would have learned her lesson. Then they would both be very grateful to him.

'Rest assured that I will do everything . . . everything.'

'But you will speak with him?'

'I will take the first opportunity, and if it is at all possible I will bring about that meeting.'

When he had gone Perdita felt greatly relieved. She thrust all the bills into a drawer out of sight and gave herself up to the contemplation of what she would wear for the meeting and rehearsed what she would say. She would not reproach him; she would be humble, pleading, assuring him of her complete submission and devotion.

She was sure then that he would find her irresistible.

A few days later Lord Malden called again.

'I have good news for you. The Prince will see you.'

'My dear friend, how can I thank you!'

What should she wear? Lilac satin . . . pale green silk . . . one of the many dresses which had not yet been paid for? No need to worry herself on that score. All would soon be well. No one would worry her for money when they knew she was back with the Prince of Wales.

'When is he coming?' she cried. 'I must have time.'

'He will not come here.'

'But why not?'

'Er . . . I think it better if you were to come to my house in Clarges Street. The Prince could see you there.'

She took his hand and kissed it. 'Oh, how can I thank you.'

His ardent gaze was enough to tell her how. But he could say nothing as yet, of course.

Surely she was as beautiful as ever. Hope had restored the beauty she feared she had lost. Her carriage rattled through the streets and she was happy for the first time since she had quarrelled with the Prince and been aware that she was losing him.

That should never happen again. She would be so careful. She would never reproach him again; she would be sweet and loving and ever grateful for being given a second chance.

Lord Malden received her with the admiring looks which he had never failed to bestow upon her. What a good faithful creature he was! Especially as by being her friend he incurred the displeasure of the King—and perhaps would risk losing the Prince's favour if all did not go well between him and her. Dear, good faithful Malden, who would even now have paid her debts for her had he been able!

'His Highness is here,' he whispered.

And he took her into his drawing room where, his back to the door, stood the Prince.

She stood waiting and he being aware of her slowly turned.

'My . . . Prince . . . !' she cried and went towards him, her hands outstretched.

As he took them and kissed them, great floods of relief swept over her.

'I . . . I feel as though I am alive again,' she said.

'I am happy to see you,' he told her. And taking her hand drew her to a couch where they sat side by side.

'I have been so unhappy,' she told him.

'My dear Perdita!'

'I thought you would never forgive me. I thought you hated me.'

'Do you think I could ever hate Perdita?'

'But you went away . . . ' Careful, she thought. No reproaches.

'It was a state affair in fact,' he said easily. 'My birthday had to be celebrated in the heart of the family at Windsor.'

'Of course.'

He began to chat of the festivities at Windsor, describing the public celebrations and the review in the Park; the banquet and the ball; but he made no mention of Lady Augusta.

She was longing to ask him questions about Mrs. Armistead but she dared not. She had learned one lesson at least.

They talked of mutual friends and it was a most pleasant hour. Then the Prince said he must go; he had an engagement. She suppressed the desire to ask if it was at Cumberland House; and he said an affectionate goodbye to her in which she was certain that he meant to imply the would meet again soon.

Lord Malden conducted the Prince to his coach and came back to Perdita.

'I can only tell you how grateful I am.'

'His Highness was friendly.'

'Extremely so.'

'That I can see, for you are radiant.'

'It was just a little misunderstanding. I shall see that it does not happen in the future.'

Poor Perdita! thought Malden. She did not know how difficult it had been. The Prince had most certainly not wished to see her and Malden was sure had no intention of renewing the acquaintance.

Still let Perdita be happy for a little longer.

She returned to Cork Street, played a little on the harpsichord and sang softly. She retired to bed and lay listening, wondering whether he might call.

The next morning she dressed with the greatest care. She

wore one of her fantastic hats, all ribbons and feathers; and a lavender silk gown which was exquisite. And taking her carriage with the coronet-like wreath went into the Park.

She felt intoxicated by the sunshine. It was a beautiful morning; the grass had never seemed so green, the flowers so beautiful. People gazed at her, nudged each other and whispered together. Perdita was about again.

And suddenly she saw him. He was walking with a crowd of his friends about him laughing and chatting; and as usual he was the centre of attraction. Now the moment was at hand. He would come to her carriage, take her hand, kiss it, perhaps ride with her. They would be together again.

She stopped the carriage. The Prince and his group were approaching. She smiled. He looked at her blankly as though he did not know her; and then turning his head began to talk animatedly to one of his companions.

She was stunned. It was a deliberate cut, a deliberate insult.

He had seen her and pretended he did not know her. He had shown her publicly that he had finished with her.

But after their meeting yesterday . . .

She could see it all now. He had been persuaded to it; it had meant nothing. He did not wish to resume their relationship. More than that he did not wish to know her.

No one could have been told more clearly.

She was aware of curious eyes on her; she could hear the sounds of laughter floating back to her. His laughter! And she wanted to die.

Love Letters of a Prince

Back to Cork Street.

This is the end, she said. He will never come back now.

She took the bills from the drawer and looked at them. It was better to do something than nothing.

How can I pay all these debts? she asked herself. They were all incurred for him. But for him I should be a famous actress, earning a good living from the theatre. I gave up everything for him. Everything.

She forced herself to add up the amounts she owed. No, it was impossible. Seven thousand pounds. They could not be so much. She had been extravagant . . . for him, she repeated bitterly. But surely not as extravagant as that.

'Where can I find seven thousand pounds?' she asked herself. Where indeed?

And then she remembered. She took a key from the drawer and opened a box which she kept in her bedroom.

From this she took a piece of parchment. It was the Prince's bond for £20,000, and it was sealed with the royal seal.

She remembered his giving it to her, and how she had declared she would not have it and he had had to persuade her to accept it.

It was the answer, of course. It would be the only way in which she cold pay her debts.

And yet she shuddered to think of asking him to honour it.

Yet . . . £7,000! How could she produce that sum of money unless he did.

If it were possible I would work, I would do anything, she

told herself. I would not take a penny of his . . . if I could help it.

Work. There was a possibility.

In a feverish haste she put on her cloak. She could not bear to sit down and think quietly. The only way in which she could endure to live through this terrible day was by taking action.

She sent for her carriage and drove to Bruton Street.

The Sheridans had moved to Bruton Street when Richard had become a Member of Parliament and so frequently entertained the Prince of Wales.

Perdita asked if Mr. Sheridan was at home, for she wished to see him urgently. She was taken into an elaborately furnished room and while she waited there the door opened and Elizabeth Sheridan came in.

Perdita had not seen her since she had become the Prince's mistress and was shocked by the change in her appearance. Her beautiful eyes looked enormous, her face thinner which did not detract from its beauty, but in fact, accentuated the exquisite bone structure; and the flush on her cheeks.

Perdita rose and held out her hand uncertainly.

Elizabeth Sheridan took it and said gently: 'Are you well?'

'I am . . . distraught,' replied Perdita.

'I am so sorry.' She said it as though she meant it and there was a world of understanding in the musical tones.

Poor Elizabeth Sheridan, who had suffered no less than Perdita herself, and there in that room Perdita—which was rare for her—ceased to think of her own tragic situation in contemplating that of this woman. Elizabeth, fragile and clearly not long for this world, for the change in her appearance could only mean that she was consumptive, had suffered even more at the hands of her husband than Perdita had at those of her lover.

I might have expected it; I broke the rules; I loved a feckless boy and expected fidelity; I was extravagant and vain. But this woman was a saint . . . and she had married a man of genius and had looked forward to a life with him which could have been perfect.

But Sheridan was ambitious. Not only did he wish to write immortal plays, he must be a statesman, friend of the Prince of Wales, lover of many women . . . And because he believed these glittering prizes to be more valuable than the love of his wife he had thrust her aside to reach them.

Ambition, thought Perdita. By that sin fell the angels.

'I must see Richard,' said Perdita.

Elizabeth nodded. 'He will shortly be with you. I am so glad that you have found him at home. He is rarely here now.'

'You have a magnificent home,' said Perdita.

Elizabeth looked about the room sadly.

Perdita understood. Debts, she thought. Living beyond their means. But then he always had. And Elizabeth was not the woman to thrust the bills into a drawer and forget them. She imagined her brooding over them. I am not the only one to suffer.

And then Richard Sheridan came into the room.

How he had changed from the handsome man whom she had known when she first went into the theatre! It was not such a long time ago. Four years . . . five years. He had coarsened, grown fat, and his face was an unhealthy red. Too much drink; too many late nights. Would the Prince grow like this in time?

She could see at once that he knew why she had come. He had been a good friend to her even after they had ceased to be lovers, and she felt an uneasy twinge of conscience. How much did Elizabeth know of that episode which she, Perdita, would rather forget?

'I will leave you together,' said Elizabeth. 'You will have business to discuss.'

She took Perdita's hand and pressed it. 'May God go with you,' she whispered.

Perdita faced Sheridan; was she right and did she detect a faint impatience in his expression?

'Sherry,' she said, 'I had to come and see you. You know what has happened?'

'The whole of London knows,' he said. 'The whole of the Court.'

'Does the news travel so fast?'

'It is some time since he left you. He has other mistresses now.'

She winced and he smiled a little sardonically. So after all her adventures she still could not bear to hear the word spoken. It was ironical to him that an act should be less repulsive than the words which described it. He thought there was an idea there for a *bon mot*. He should make a note of it and use it some time . . . but like all his ideas they came to nothing and he lost them because he would never put himself out to record them.

But the theatre took second place now. The future stretched

out brilliantly before him as the politician, friend of Fox and the Prince of Wales.

'I have debts, Sherry.'

'You are—as always—in the fashion, Perdita.'

'But I cannot pay them.'

'Still in fashion.'

'Because of all this . . . they will not wait. I must earn money quickly. My creditors must be made to understand that although I cannot pay them immediately I intend to do so . . . in due course.'

'And how will you convince them of these noble intentions?'

'By going back to work. I want to come back to the theatre.'

He looked at her blankly. 'You couldn't do it, Perdita.'

'Why not?' she demanded shrilly.

'They would never let you.'

'Who . . . Who? Do you mean *you* would not?'

'I have to consider my audiences. They would jeer you off the stage.'

'Why, why?'

'Because of the past. They would crowd the theatre for the first night and like as not there would be a riot. I could not risk it.'

'How can you be sure if you will not give me a chance?'

'I tell you I *know* it. It is not the way. I warned you. Remember? Do you remember?'

She nodded somberly.

'Did I not tell you that you should never have become his mistress?'

She was too shaken to wince now. Poor Perdita, denuded of her mask. She was herself now, and that was a desperate and frightened woman.

She nodded. 'Yes, you warned me.'

'And I told you then that afterwards you could never return to the theatre.'

'You mean you won't have me?'

'Willingly would I, if it were possible. But it is not possible. You must find some other way.''

'How? How can I pay my debts?'

'I wish I could answer that one. Most willingly would I use the information.'

'I owe seven thousand pounds.'

'I wish I owed as little.'

'But *I* have no means of paying it.'

'I too am living beyond my means.'

Did she imagine it or was he bored? Oh, God, she thought, this is how people will be towards me in future. I am no longer of any consequence.

Then she said: 'There is no help for it. I have his bond.'

'What bond is this?'

'The Prince's bond for twenty thousand pounds. He gave it to me and I have kept it. I shall need this money . . . badly. I had hoped not to touch it.'

Sheridan was silent. A bond for £20,000! The Prince would never honour it. He happened to know that His Highness had a mound of debts of his own which would make his, Sheridan's let alone Perdita's, seem paltry.

'It has his signature and seal,' she said. 'He would have to honour it.'

'You mean . . . you would insist?'

'Please tell me how else I can pay my debts.'

Sheridan was silent.

Then she said wearily: 'I will go. I see that you cannot help me.'

'If I could . . .'

'Yes, if you could you would. But you cannot give me this chance in the theatre.'

'Perdita, if it were possible . . .'

'Is it not possible to give it a test?'

'No,' he said firmly. 'No.'

She hesitated. 'You are the Prince's friend. Perhaps you could make him aware of my plight. I did not wish to ask him for money, but in the circumstances, what else can I do?'

Sheridan was alarmed. He did not wish to be the man who conveyed to the Prince the information that his discarded mistress was demanding the money he had promised her. That was not the sort of entertainment the Prince looked for from Sheridan. He wanted to be amused, not disturbed.

She laid her hand on his arm. 'You will do this for me?'

What could he say but: 'You may rely on me to do what I consider best for your welfare.'

'For old times sake,' she said with a return of her old manner.

And Sheridan nodded and conducted her to her carriage.

He called on Fox in St. James's, and without preamble came straight to the point.

'Perdita Robinson has been to see me.'

Fox nodded. He knew how the affair had ended. His good friend Mrs. Armistead visited him now and then and let him know the Prince's attitude to various matters not excluding that towards his old mistress. He was well aware of the meeting between the two women in the Magpie and how the Prince's own relationship with Mrs. Armistead progressed.

'She is in a desperate situation. Her debts amount to some seven thousand pounds and the creditors are making a nuisance of themselves.

'They've heard of course that she is now discarded.'

'She is a desperate woman.'

'And came to ask you to allow her to resume her career as an actress, I'll swear.'

'Which I have most definitely refused.'

'Naturally, naturally. The poor improvident creature!'

'Well, Charles, we are two fine ones to talk of improvidence.'

'We are not the Prince's mistresses, my good fellow. Perdita should have made herself very comfortable on the gifts she received.'

He thought of his friend Mrs. Armistead who was fast becoming a woman of some substance, with a house of her own most tastefully furnished, and she was now building up a pleasant little fortune. But Perdita was of course no Mrs. Armistead. Such excellent creatures were rarely met with. All Perdita had accumulated were debts.

'He gave her a bond for twenty thousand pounds and she is talking of claiming it.'

Fox was alert at once.

'She will never get it.'

'No, I daresay it's completely invalid.'

'She'll put herself into an unfortunate position if there is a scandal over this. Does she realize this?'

'The poor woman is too frantic to realize anything but that she has debts of seven thousand pounds and it seems her only possession is this bond for twenty thousand pounds. She has asked me to convey to H.H. that she intends to claim the money as her due.'

'And what was your answer?'

'I prevaricated. I was vague. I should certainly not like to be the one to pass such an item of news to the Prince.'

'It would scarcely make him jump for joy. Imagine the news reaching the Hall of Purity. It would be as bad as the Grosvenor affair. Worse! This is not a mere duke but the Prince of Wales.'

'That is why I came to see you immediately.

'I think,' said Fox, 'that I must, immediately, go and see Mrs. Perdita.'

Sheridan was relieved. If anyone could handle this situation it was Fox; and Fox's great attraction for his most ardent admirers—among them the Prince of Wales—was that he never sought to curry favour with anyone. He stated his views frankly. The Prince had accepted this and had the intelligence to know its worth. Other men might fit their words to suit a royal mood. Fox never did. It was strength and his dignity.

Frantic with grief Perdita was going through the latest bills to arrive accompanied by demanding letters—insolent letters— when Mr. Fox was announced.

She thrust the bills out of sight, hurried to a mirror and hastened to compose herself when he came in.

How gross he was! He was growing more so each week: his swarthiness was not attractive and his chins rested on his soiled cravat. One would never have thought that he was the great Mr. Fox, who was received with delight in all the noblest Whig houses, until he bowed and began to speak. Then the regality and charm which he had no doubt inherited from his ancestor King Charles II was obvious.

'My *dear* Mrs. Robinson.'

What a comfort to be treated so respectfully by Mr. Fox after the veiled insolence of servants and the truculent manners of creditors.

'Mr. Fox, welcome.'

He was holding her hand and seemed reluctant to let it go. She flushed a little. Everyone knew Mr. Fox's manners with women. He was as fond of them as he was of wine and gambling. And in spite of her misfortunes she was a very beautiful woman. 'Pray be seated,' she said.

He sat down heavily, legs apart, surveying her.

'It is good of you to call, Mr. Fox. People do not call so frequently now.' Her lips trembled.

He said: 'Had you asked me to call, Madam, I should have been here at once.'

'How kind you are, sir.'

'Who would not be kind to a beautiful woman? But let us speak frankly. I do not care to see beauty in distress. Sheridan has talked to me.'

She flushed. 'If he could be persuaded to give me another chance . . .'

'If those beautiful eyes could not entreat him, the case is hopeless.'

'Mr. Fox, I am desperate. I owe a great deal of money.'

Fox nodded lugubriously. 'A situation with which I can heartily sympathize. I am in such a one myself at this time . . . in fact I have rarely been out of it. But you spoke of a bond.'

She hesitated and Fox went on: 'Madam, I have come here to help you. I can only do this if you trust me.' He rose and coming to her chair laid his hands on the arms and brought his face close to her. 'Shall I tell you this. I have long admired your beauty.' He kissed her on the lips. She gasped and drew back and he thought: Not called Propriety Prue for nothing! He laughed. 'Forgive the impertinence, Mrs. Robinson, I wished to show you that admiring you as I do, I am ready to do what is within my power to help you. The kiss was a bond. Perhaps as significant as that of His Royal Highness. Would you let me see this bond so that I can assess its value.'

'I cannot understand, Mr. Fox, why you who are His Highness's friend should wish to help me.'

'Madam, I am the friend of you both. And I see this: I may best serve you both by helping to bring this little matter to a satisfactory conclusion. If you will show me the bond I promise you . . . on this new understanding which is between us two . . . that I will do all in my power to help you.'

Perdita said. 'I will get it. I will be back with it shortly.'

In her bedroom she went first to the mirror. Her eyes were brilliant and there was a faint colour in her cheeks. She had not had time to paint her face but perhaps it looked more attractive without rouge and white lead. It certainly did with that faint rose-like flush. And the gown she was wearing . . . it was not one of her best but quite becoming. And Mr. Fox? He was repulsive. How different from the Prince. And yet he was so clever. If anyone could help her he could. And what had he meant by that kiss? Was it a suggestion? She knew of his reputation. She was trembling as she opened the box and took out the bond.

When she returned Mr. Fox was sitting back in his chair as though deep in thought. He took the bond from her without a word and studied it.

'He won't honour it,' he said.

She cried in horror, 'But what can I do? I must have money.

All these debts . . . Do you think I should have incurred them but for entertaining him and his friends?'

'My dear lady, creditors alas are never interested in why debts are incurred . . . only that they are.'

'But, Mr. Fox . . . what am I to do.?'

Mr. Fox said nothing for a few moments; Perdita began to pace up and down the room wringing her hands like a tragedienne on a stage. Fox watched her and thought: She acts naturally without knowing she is doing it. Poor creature, she will be demented if she goes on like this. And so pretty. He thought of all the jackals who would be waiting to step into the Prince's place. There would be many of them. That old reprobate Cumberland was one. He only had to set her up and the creditors would be ready to wait. The jackals could wait. Meanwhile the Fox would step in. He had always thought that it would be rather amusing to share her with the Prince of Wales. Such beauty was rare and he never liked to miss anything. But although as the mistress of Mr. Fox she would be able to hold her head up again in some circles—for he flattered himself that it was in fact no step down from the Prince to Mr. Fox, her creditors would view the move with disfavour. Whereas Cumberland—royal Duke that he was—would not displease them.

A piquant situation.

'Madam,' he said. 'I pray you do not distress yourself. We will put our heads together . . .' He smiled at her. He was giving her hints enough. Did she grasp them? She must. However innocent she was of financial matters she was well versed in dealing with the advances of men.

'But Mr. Fox, I am a desperate woman. I did not wish to take this bond, but the Prince insisted. I gave up a lucrative career for his sake. He insisted that I accept this recompense. I must pay my debts. Mr. Fox, I have lived in a debtors' prison. I will never go back to such a place. I will die first . . . I will do anything. Why should he not honour his bond? Everyone knows of the relationship which existed between us. Everyone knows what I gave up for him. If they do not . . . I have his letters to prove it. I would publish those letters. I would . . .'

Mr. Fox sat up very straight. 'Letters, you say, Madam? Letters? Ah, now that might be a very different matter. You have these letters . . . here?'

'Indeed I have them and I must pay these debts. I will never again . . .'

Mr. Fox interrupted. 'Madam, show me these letters.'

She was not a fool. She had noticed the change in the atmosphere, the change in Mr. Fox. The letters made all the difference. The letters were more important than the bond.

She hesitated. Fox was after all the friend of the Prince. What if the Prince had sent him to get the letters?

'I cannot help you,' said Mr. Fox gently, 'if you will not show me the letters.'

She went to her bedroom. She unlocked the box and took out the letters tied up with lavender coloured ribbon. How many times had she read them and treasured them . . . and wept over them. She hesitated. What if he took them away. What if he took them to the Prince. She could no longer trust the Prince.

No, she would not give Fox the letters. She would select one and that would be a good sample.

She untied the ribbon. There was one in which he had referred to his father in the most disparaging terms, also of his great devotion to herself. She glanced through it, remembering every word. Oh, he would regret he had ever humiliated her in the Park!

She was elated. These letters were the answer. Let him throw the bond in her face. There were still these most valuable letters.

Mr. Fox read the letter she gave him and even he could not hide the fact that he was deeply impressed.

'Only one letter, dear Mrs. Robinson?'

'There are many more.'

'And all in this strain?'

'Yes, Mr. Fox.'

He smiled at her. 'And you do not propose to let them out of your hands. I rejoice in your wisdom, Mrs. Robinson, which in this matter almost equals your beauty. You should keep those letters under lock and key. They are very valuable.'

'And what shall I do, Mr. Fox?'

He rose and still holding the letter in his hand approached her.

'Will you trust me, Mrs. Robinson?'

She hesitated, and he laughed. 'Again you show your wisdom. But in view of our growing er . . . friendship . . . I think you might trust me . . . a little. Not too much as yet. But remember that such is my position that I am one of the few people who could approach His Highness personally and believe me, Mrs. Robinson, this is not a matter which should be handled with anything but the utmost tact.'

'I am certain of it.'

'Then allow me to take this one letter. For what is one among
so many? If you will allow me to do as I think fit, I believe we
shall together drive those braying dogs of creditors from your
door.'

'Oh, Mr. Fox, if that could happen I could never be grateful
enough.'

'And I should be a very happy man to earn that gratitude.'

He took his leave of her; and she felt better than she had for
some time.

Fox! she thought and shuddered. In a way he was so repulsive
and yet not without attraction. And if he could only extricate
her from this frightening situation she would indeed do anything
to show her gratitude.

Sitting in the chair which took him to Buckingham House Fox
read the letter again. By God, he thought, how could he have
been such a fool!

He was not thinking so much of the Prince's dilemma, nor of
Mrs. Robinson's gratitude to come—although both these matters
were in mind—but the effect the publication of those letters
would have on the Party. The Prince was to be the leader—in
name only of course. It would be Fox's party. But if these letters
were published there would be a Grosvenor scandal all over
again and it was clear that the Duke of Cumberland had lost
much prestige through that affair. But he had not spoken in
derogatory terms of the sovereign as this foolish young man had
done. What would ministers think of a prince, a leader of a
Party, who could be so indiscreet to a play actress who was his
temporary mistress? Those letters would spoil the plans Fox had
been making for that time when the Prince attained his majority
and took his seat in the Lords. It was not the Prince's morals
which would destroy his prestige as a leader, but his indiscre-
tion.

Putting the letter carefully into a pocket of his waistcoat Fox
alighted from his chair and went to the Prince's apartments where
he was immediately received and with the utmost pleasure.

'Apologies for disturbing Your Highness at such short notice.'

'No need to apologize for giving me pleasure, Charles.'

'I fear this visit will not give Your Highness much pleasure.'

'Oh, Charles, what have you on your mind?'

'Perdita Robinson.'

'Oh, no. That's all over.'

'I fear not, sir. I wish to God it were. I have been to see her.'

'You, Charles? Good God, don't tell me you and she . . . '

'Your Highness! How could such a lady step so quickly from a handsome Prince to a seedy politician.'

'Well, if the politician were Charles James Fox . . . '

'But the Prince was His Royal Highness the Prince of Wales. However, allow me to get to business. She is in dire distress. Her creditors are bothering her.'

'Charles, have you any idea of the size of my own debts?'

'A rough idea, sir, and it appals me.'

The Prince laughed. 'I fear I cannot give her money.'

'She has a bond.'

The Prince turned pale.

'Your Highness should not be distressed on that account. I have seen the bond and I think it is useless. It's not to come into effect until you are of age and that's two years off, in any case. I don't think we need concern ourselves with the bond.'

The Prince's relief was obvious. 'Charles, how glad I am that she showed this to *you.*'

'Yes, well I heard of it and thought I should see it without delay. But there is another matter which gives me cause for great disquiet.'

'What is this?'

'The letters you wrote to her.'

'Letters . . . I wrote?'

'Your Highness has a ready, fluent and eloquent pen. With such a gift it often seems a sin not to use it. I could have wished Your Highness less gifted in this direction.'

'But these letters . . . ' The Prince wrinkled his brow, trying to remember.

'I have one here,' said Fox, and took it from his waistcoat pocket. He handed it to the Prince who read it, flushing.

'It is not so much the tender and explanatory terms used as the references to His Majesty. I fear this would be judged a most damaging letter to the sovereign.'

The Prince flushed and was about to tear it in two.

'Stop . . . please. I beg Your Highness's pardon, but that would be unwise. Mrs. Robinson would never part with the others . . . moreover she would realize even more than she does now their value.'

'So she has been hoarding these letters . . . keeping them until she could use them. The cheat. The blackmailer!'

'Your Highness . . . forgiveness again . . . but this will not solve our problems. We have on one side this frail lady who is—let us be fair—in a desperate position. I do not believe she would wish to sell those letters if this were not the case. I feel she would prefer to keep them tied up with ribbons to read to her grandchildren in the years to come and so recall those days of romance and passion. But she is in debt. She lives in terror of the debtors' prison of which she has had a taste. Let us see Mrs. Robinson as she is. It will help us. A blackmailer? Well, perhaps. But she is in a corner and she has to fight her way out.'

'Well, Charles, you make a good advocate for the woman. I thought you were on my side.'

'On your side in the past, now and for ever. But my plan is to settle this matter as speedily as possible. To have those letters where they belong—and that is consigned to the flames . . . before they have done irreparable damage.'

'What damage could they do?'

'They could hold you up to ridicule, they could place a strong weapon in the hands of your enemies; they could rob you of the popularity you now have and which is so important to you and our plans. Your Uncle Cumberland is an instance. He is not greatly loved by the people. They have heard passages from those letters he wrote to Lady Grosvenor and they will never forget them. Moreover, there is your father to face. He is after all the King. What have you said of him in those letters? You cannot even remember, but in this one you have been damaging enough. Even those with whom he is not popular recognize him as the King. The criticism of him, to a light woman . . . I know of course how deep your feelings towards Mrs. Robinson were when you wrote those words and that you did not see her in this way, but that is how she will be looked upon . . . will be frowned on, not only by his friends but yours. Discretion is the first quality men look for in a leader and, my Prince, you are soon to be our leader. I know you understand.'

'Yes,' said the Prince heavily. 'I understand that I have been a fool.'

'Well, so are we all in our times. And Your Highness could turn this affair into valuable experience. But first we have to deal with this situation. We have to buy these letters from Mrs. Robinson. We have to see that they and the bond are safe in our hands.'

'Do you mean pay her twenty thousand pounds *and* buy the letters?'

'I think she can be persuaded to hand over the bond; but the letters are what concern me. Any young man in love might give a woman a bond he finds it difficult to honour; but the letters are our concern.'

'Charles, I know you are right. But I cannot raise the money. You know how short my father keeps me. It is easy enough to run up debts. People are only glad to serve me. But I cannot raise this money.'

'I have thought of this. There is only one thing to do.'

'Yes, Charles, yes?'

'You must go to the King, confess your folly and ask him to buy the letters.'

'What! It's the last thing I could do.'

'Maybe, sir, but as I see it, it's the only thing you can do.'

'I never will.'

Fox shook his head sadly and said: 'Then, Your Highness, I must leave you to settle this matter your own way.'

'Charles . . . how can I? You *must* help me.'

'Everything I have is at Your Highness's service. Unfortunately I have no money or it should be yours. I am in the same position as Your Highness. I can run up debts but raise no cash. I have nothing to offer you but my advice.'

'Which is the best in the world, I know.'

'It is disinterested, that much I can tell you. I have thought of this problem as though it were my own—and indeed it is my own, for apart from my affection and friendship for Your Highness my future plans are concerned in it. I dream of that day when Your Highness takes his place in the affairs of the nation and I want nothing to spoil that. But I can see only one way out. These letters must be bought back from Mrs. Robinson and the only way this money can be raised is through the King. Your Uncle Cumberland was in a similar position. I pray this affair will not be so public. Nor need it be if we act with care and speed. But there is not time to lose. Let Mrs. Robinson go to a lawyer . . . and she is desperate . . . and we are lost. We have to find that money quickly and settle this matter once and for all.'

'Charles, you must help me.'

'I am asking Your Highness to place this matter in my hands; but if I am to be your adviser you must perforce follow my advice.'

'To go to my father . . .'

'To confess the whole affair, your folly, the realization of what you have done, your growing responsibility to your position. The King is not an a ogre.'

'You don't know him as I do.'

'He is a sentimental man . . . and I'll swear at heart he is fond of you. Be tactful. He must supply the money. It is important to him that there should be no more family scandals. Do as I say and in a short while when this unfortunate matter is over you will see that it was the only way in which you could have acted.'

'And Charles . . . you will be my ambassador with Perdita?'

'I will. And I'll swear that if you will face up to this interview, painful as I know it is going to be, you will very soon be able to put this matter behind you—and little harm will have been done.'

'Charles, I rely on you.'

'In which,' said Mr. Fox with a bow, 'Your Highness shows your wisdom.'

The Prince humbly requested an audience with his father, which the King willingly granted. The terms in which the request was written pleased him. His son showed a proper—and unusual—respect.

He's growing up, thought the King. He was wayward at first . . . but so are most young men.

He was in a mellow mood as he greeted the Prince who, he noticed, had what might be called a hangdog expression.

'You have something to say to me, eh?'

'Yes, Father, and I am going to ask Your Majesty's indulgence for the follies of youth.'

'What's this, eh, what?' The King shot a suspicious glance at his son. Such humility was a little disturbing. 'Go on, go on,' he commanded. 'What are these follies, eh?'

'I have to confess that I have formed an . . . an association with an actress.'

'I know. I know.'

'A Mrs. Robinson who played at Drury Lane with Sheridan's company.'

'Can't abide the fellow,' said the King. 'Drinks, gambles . . . leads that nice woman a life. Pity she married him. He's not faithful to her. Rackets about the town. Don't like the fellow. Friend of Fox.'

The Prince saw it was a mistake to have mentioned Sheridan.

'Well, Father, this woman is no longer . . . my friend.'

'Come to your senses, eh? Perhaps time you were married. Bit young. I was young myself . . . but perhaps it's best.'

The interview was going badly. The outcome might be that his father would discover some plump German princess for him. That he would stand out against with all his strength. If his father would wait until he was twenty-one he would have some say in the matter . . . but if he should produce the woman now . . . But he was straying from the unpleasant point and the sooner this was reached the better.

'I wrote her letters . . . foolish letters.'

The effect on the King of that word letters was great. His mouth slightly open, he stared at his son.

'It was foolish,' admitted the Prince. 'I know that now. I've learned my lesson.'

'Letters?' breathed the King. 'It's like that fool Cumberland all over again. What possessed you, eh? Letters! Don't you know better than that, eh what?'

'I do now,' said the Prince.

'Letters,' murmured the King. He looked at his son and thought of the folly of youth; and Hannah Lightfoot's image rose up before him. Remember your own youth, George. Were you so wise? 'Not letters,' he mumbled.

'Yes, Father, I fear so. She has them and she is threatening to publish them.'

The King closed his eyes.

'There is only one thing to do. We must buy those letters from her.'

'This woman . . . she has a husband?' The King could not get the thought of Lord Grosvenor out of his mind.

'Yes . . . a low fellow . . . a clerk of some sort.'

'Shocking! Disgusting! You realize that, eh, what?'

'I realize it fully but I know something has to be done.'

'What sort of letters, eh? Love letters? That sort?'

'That sort,' admitted the Prince; 'and I fear that I was a little indiscreet about . . . family matters.'

'Family matters! You mean you discussed your family . . . the royal family . . . with this . . . this . . . woman. Eh! What?'

'I fear so.'

'And she wrote you letters?'

'Yes.'

'And where are they?'

'I destroyed them.'

'So you destroyed hers and she kept yours, eh?'

'It seems so.'

'It seems so! How do you know she has these letters?'

'I have been shown one . . . and that itself is enough to . . . er . . .'

'I know, I know. Letters!'

'I gave her a bond.'

'What?'

'A bond for twenty thousand pounds.'

'You are mad.'

'I fear I was at the time, sir. But the stipulation was that I could not honour it until I was twenty-one.'

'I doubt it's valid. And you've another two years to go. I trust you learn a little sense by then.'

'I trust so, sir.'

'Letters,' mused the King. 'Damning, humiliating letters! What have I done to be cursed with a family like this?'

'We are not so bad, sir,' said the Prince soothingly. 'It is only when compared with Your Majesty's high code of morals and blameless existence that we appear so.'

The King looked sharply at his son. The young dog was too free with words—always had been. One never could be sure what he was driving at.

'Go away,' he said. 'I'll think of this.'

'Sir, we must get those letters.'

'Do you think I don't understand the trouble this sort of folly can bring to the family?'

'I did not think that for one moment, sir, that was why I plucked up my courage to bring the matter to your attention.'

'You'd do better to consult me more often.'

'I know that now, sir.'

'Then go and I will consider this in due course. But I'd have you know that I am preoccupied with weighty matters of State which one day perhaps you will know something about. And you have to disturb me with your follies. I tell you this, sir, I am displeased. I am disgusted and this sort of thing will have to stop. You understand that, eh, what?'

'I understand it well, sir; I admit my folly. We all have to learn by the mistakes of youth, sir.'

For one moment the King could almost have believed that this son of his, who knew so much, was aware of that period of his father's life which all this time the King had been striving to forget.

It was on occasions like this that one remembered and the

past came up to mock. It had the effect though of making a man more lenient than he might have been.

He said in a milder tone: 'If it's taught you a valuable lesson then perhaps it is not such a disaster as it appears. Go now. You will hear more of this from me.'

The Prince knelt and kissed his father's hand. There were tears of real gratitude in his eyes—but tears came easily to the whole family. Yet, this had changed the young dog. He was worried, and there was no doubt that it had brought him to heel.

Charles James Fox was a constant visitor to Cork Street. Perdita had also received a visit from Lieutenant-Colonel Hotham who had told her that he came on the King's business.

Perdita was thrown into a state of great anxiety by the visit of this gentleman who pointed out to her that in attempting to blackmail the Prince she was placing herself in a very dangerous position. The Prince had confessed to the King the fact that he had written indiscreet letters to her and the King was most distressed, first that his son should have written the letters and secondly that he should have so far forgotten the dignity due to his position as to become involved with a woman who could offer to treat them as merchandise.

So terrified had Perdita been that she had almost agreed to hand over the letters; but the thought of her debts and her interview with Mr. Fox sustained her; and she had told the Lieutenant-Colonel that she could do nothing without consulting her friends.

Thank God for Mr. Fox!

He listened gravely to all that Hotham had said and had told her that she must act with the utmost caution and not allow herself to be bullied. He would tell her exactly what she must do.

She was very ready to lean on him. He was so clever. She had never known such a clever person. Of course his appearance was a little repulsive—particularly if one were as fastidious as Perdita undoubtedly was—but even that was a little piquant. On each visit he became a little more familiar; and she could see, of course, to what he was leading. No, she told herself. Never. Yet what would she do without him? He only had to appear and she could forget those hideous bills. Moreover, it was known that Mr. Fox was visiting her and this meant that the tradespeople were not so insolent. They were holding off a little. Mr. Fox was making some arrangements for her, therefore they would be patient for a little longer.

Mr. Fox persuaded the Prince of Wales to allow her to remain in the house in Cork Street until some other arrangement could be made. That was a great comfort.

And now there was this terrifying man, Hotham, who wanted to know the extent of her debts and how many of the letters there were and to see some of them (but not to let them out of the house, said Mr. Fox) and with whom she could never have bargained, if Mr. Fox had not been in the background telling her exactly what to do.

There came a day when Hotham arrived, stern and disapproving and not even glancing at her as though she were some ordinary woman and not one of the most beautiful in London.

'I have an ultimatum from His Majesty, Mrs. Robinson,' he told her. 'You will be paid five thousand pounds and on accepting this you will hand to me the bond given to you by His Royal Highness the Prince of Wales in addition to the letters he wrote to you and this will be an end to the matter.'

'My debts alone amount to seven thousand pounds,' she told him.

'This, Madam, is no concern of His Majesty nor the Prince of Wales.'

'But indeed it is. The debts were incurred for the Prince's pleasure; and for this also I gave up a lucrative career.'

'The King's last words are five thousand pounds or, Madam, I fear you may publish the letters and take the consequences.'

'I will take the consequences.'

'They will hardly bring credit to you, Madam, I assure you. If you are wise you take this money, sign these papers and hand me the bond and the letters.'

'I will consider this,' said Perdita. 'Call back tomorrow.'

Mr. Fox came to Cork Street. He embraced her with passion. The consummation could not be long delayed. Mr. Fox very clearly showed that he had worked indefatigably on her behalf and that her gratitude was the natural course of events.

She told him of Hotham's ultimatum.

'Five thousand pounds,' he said. 'Not a bad figure.'

'But he promised twenty thousand pounds.'

'I told you to put the thought of the bond out of your beautiful head. It's practically worthless. The five thousand pounds is for the letters. I think we shall have to consider this very closely.'

He gave the impression that if he stayed the night they could discuss it at greater length. He would have more time for working out a satisfactory conclusion, for although they must not say no to the £5,000, they should make it a bargaining point towards a solution.

'What solution?' Perdita wanted know.

Mr. Fox said he had no doubt he could work that out.

They had a pleasant supper. Perdita was excited, for she reminded herself that he was an unusual man, and there was nothing to be lost by being his friend. Perhaps if they became more and more friendly she would give him a hint about changing his linen more frequently and bathing now and then.

'You're thoughtful,' he said.

'I was thinking of the future . . . when this terrible anxiety is no more.'

'Our future?' asked Mr. Fox.

And then he began to talk of what he envisaged as his future. England was going to lose America and this would bring down the Government. Then those who had deplored the way affairs had been conducted would come into their own. Mr. Fox would doubtless lead a new ministry.

Perdita saw herself queening it in a salon in which she would receive all the most important people in the country. It was a wonderful dream. She saw herself in velvet and feathers. Society's leading hostess. The Prime Minister's dearest friend and adviser. Had she really stepped down when she lost the favour of the Prince?

She toasted the future with Fox. For the first time since the Prince had deserted her she was really happy.

And everything depended on this man who was clearly going to be her lover.

In the morning a gratified Mr. Fox had the solution. She would surrender the bond and letters on these terms: Her debts were to be added to those of the Prince (which were so enormous that hers would not make much difference in any case) and paid by the Treasury; instead of the £5,000 she would accept a pension of £500 a year for the rest of her life and on her death her daughter was to receive £250 per annum until the end of her life. To these terms and these only would she agree.

Mr. Fox was a wonderful man.

She was not surprised that he was so universally admired.

The King wrote Lord North:

'I am sorry to be obliged to open a subject to Lord North that has long given me much pain, but I can rather do it on paper than in conversation; it is a subject to which I know he is not quite ignorant. My eldest son got last year into a very improper connection with an actress and woman of indifferent character through the assistance of Lord Malden and a multitude of letters passed which she has threatened to publish unless he, in short, bought them off her. He has made very foolish promises which undoubtedly by her conduct to him she entirely cancelled. I have thought it right to authorize the getting them from her and have employed Lieutenant-Colonel Hotham on whose discretion I could depend to manage this business. He has now brought it to a conclusion and has her consent to get these letters on her receiving £5,000 undoubtedly an enormous sum. But I wish to get my son out of this shameful scrape.'

The King sat back and put his hand over his eyes. Memories came to him. Hannah would never have attempted to blackmail him. Hannah had been a good woman. Why should he be reminded by this 'scrape' of his son's of that episode in his life?

But he was and the last few days Hannah had begun to haunt him as she had years ago.

He was weary. This continual conflict among the ministers; Fox standing threateningly with the opposition; the family—Frederick in Germany, William at sea. Were they going to confront him with similar episodes like this?

There was no peace . . .

'Uneasy lies the head that wears a crown . . . '

Didn't that fellow Shakespeare say something like that? Not that he admired the poet. Too much fuss made of him and he had always said so; but now and then he would say something which was true—and by God, he had when he said that.

What sort of king would young George make when his time came? It was years away. He himself was not old. It was the Prince who made him feel old. He was in his early forties. That was not old.

And yet somewhere at the back of his mind there was an uneasy feeling, a foreboding of disaster.

There had been a time when a mysterious illness had overcome him, changing him while he was in its grip. It had terrified the Queen so much that she never spoke of it. But he had seen her looking at him oddly sometimes when he became too excited.

It was nothing. It would pass. It was just at times like this . . . times of great anxiety when his head started to buzz with strange voices and ideas darted in and out of his mind and escaped before he could catch them.

How dared his son add to his troubles! As if he had not enough.

But George was young yet. He had to learn his lessons, and what of himself? Had he lived so blamelessly?

He picked up his pen and added to the letter he had just written to Lord North:

'I am happy at being able to say that I never was personally engaged in such a transaction which perhaps makes me feel this the stronger.'

Mr. Fox's agruments carried weight and Perdita's terms were accepted.

She was happy. She was no longer bothered by her creditors. The Prince would take on her debts. She could live in Cork Street until other plans could be made; she had an unusual lover, and the whole world knew it. She could still ride out in her carriage and people stopped to stare at her.

'Mrs. Robinson has quickly found a new protector in Charles James Fox,' they said.

When the Prince heard that his old love was Fox's mistress he was very amused.

'Why, Charles,' he cried. 'if you have done me the honour of taking on my mistress, I have done the same by you, for I believe you were once on very friendly terms with Mrs. Armistead.'

It was amusing, said Mr. Fox; and more than that, most convenient.

But when he returned to his lodgings in St. James's he thought of Mrs. Armistead and he was surprised that he had not enjoyed hearing the Prince discuss her as though she were a woman of the town, lightly to be exchanged from one man's bed to another.

Yet he had felt no such resentment at the mention of Perdita in the same connection.

He had known from the start that he was quickly going to tire of Perdita. She had little to offer him but her beauty. She was undoubtedly a pretty creature and she had a certain slender talent both for acting and writing. She liked to read her poems to him—sentimental stuff, but a pleasant enough jingle.

Thinking that the day would come when his sojourns at Cork Street would be less frequent he had taken some of her poetry along to various newspapers with whose proprietors he was on excellent terms.

As a result poems were appearing now and then under the name of Tabitha Bramble and the little money they earned was greatly appreciated by Mrs. Mary Robinson.

Poor Perdita, thought Fox. So soon to be deserted again. Well, at least I arranged that she should have five hundred a year and see her poems profitably in print.

Not poor Perdita. Lucky Perdita. There were many who would be eager to supplant the Prince and Mr. Fox.

Mr. Fox and the Government

Perdita was sad to lose the companionship of Mr. Fox, but he eluded her so skilfully and so gradually that she scarcely realized he had gone.

Even when their relationship was at its closest, there were so many matters to which he must give his attention and Perdita had made up her mind that she would make no demands on him. Therefore she never reproached him when he did not appear. He had done so much that she must be grateful to him for ever. She would never forget the horror of the debtors' prison from which with a few deft arrangements he had delivered her. He had brought interesting people to her house; and he allowed her to play the hostess as she had dreamed of doing.

Among the guests had come one of the most interesting men she had ever met. This was General Banastre Tarleton who had just returned from the most exciting adventures in America. He entertained the company with accounts of his exploits and at that time everyone was talking about the Colonies.

In fact it was because of them that Charles absented himself so often; great disasters meant great opportunities; and perhaps she had always known that Charles would rather lose a mistress than an opportunity.

Banastre Tarleton was so gallant. He told her that she was the most beautiful woman he had ever met; and it was perfectly clear that he was only waiting for Charles to move out before he moved in. It seemed a delicate touch which she would have expected of Banastre. He understood that she was not the sort of loose woman who would have more than one lover at a time.

So although she had not been able to have the political salon of which she had dreamed, there was something comforting about a soldier's return from the wars. And when Charles was no longer her lover she slipped gracefully and happily into the protective arms of her soldier lover

Fox often rode out to Chertsey to Mrs. Armistead's comfortable little residence. He found it very pleasant to sit in her garden or at her fireside whichever the season warranted, and talk to her. She had kept herself informed of politics and he was astonished at her insight. Not that she was inclined to put forward an opinion unless asked. She preferred to listen.

He could talk to her about the worsening situation which he saw developing.

The King and North he said would be remembered by future generations with contempt. It was their policies and nothing else which had lost the American Colonies—for lost they were whatever these two blind dodderers might think.

'He thinks Cornwallis will beat Lafayette and that he'll link up with Clinton and together they'll fight the main force under Washington. My dear Lizzie, it is easy to win battles in an armchair.'

'How can they be so foolish as not to beg you to take charge of affairs.'

'But it is precisely because they are foolish that we are in our present dilemma. If we had had wise men in the Government we should never have allowed this quarrel to reach this point. Poor old George! He means well, you know. But how many well-meaning people have fallen into disaster. He babbles about our troops being excellent fellows and he talks of the justice of our case and he is quite certain that God is on our side.'

'Do you think he is seriously worried and that is why he talks like this?'

'I think there is a great deal in what you say. Our gracious king while decrying the deceit of the French is guilty of the most damning deceit of all—self deceit. Where is this policy leading us? Holland declares war on us. The French have blockaded Gibraltar; and France and Spain have captured fifty of our ships in the West Indies. This Empire which Pitt built up is disintegrating.'

'And when we have lost the Colonies will the Government fall?'

'Undoubtedly the Government will fall.' Mr. Fox looked as

sly as his name, and Mrs. Armistead knew that he was thinking that that would be the time for Mr. Fox to realize his dream.

Meanwhile Mrs. Armistead could enjoy the realization of her own. She would never again serve other ladies; she would have her own lady's maid. The Prince was her friend; this passion was less intense than it had been, but she was prepared for that. He had been a generous lover and she was growing if not rich extremely comfortable.

The most interesting days were those when Mr. Fox called to talk politics; and she was very happy on those occasions to be able to entertain him not as a mistress entertains a lover, but as a friend in whom he could confide his ambitions, and the extent to which he did this was a measure of his trust.

The King could no longer deceive himself and was forced to admit the loss of the Colonies. He shut himself into his bedroom and buried his face in his hands.

'What will become of me?' he asked himself; for in times of crisis he felt the old sickness returning to him and he was afraid.

All these months he had been deceiving himself. He had defied those men who had cautioned him, who had suggested a conciliatory policy; he had believed he knew; he had forced poor North to follow his line . . . and he had lost.

Mary Tudor had said that when she died Calais would be found written across her heart; and what was Calais compared with the loss of America!

Future generations would say: 'George III! He was the King who lost us America.'

He was the most unfortunate of men. No ruler could have tried harder to do what was right. No man could have tried to lead a better life.

And there was his son who cared for nothing but frivolity, adored by the public, smiled at indulgently in spite of the fact that he had got into difficulties with a play actress—which little scrape had cost his father a small fortune.

The Colonies gone; the voices back in his head, and the future spread out before him . . . dark and unpredictable.

The Government had fallen. Rockingham had formed a new ministry and in it were men whom he personally disliked. The Duke of Richmond, Master General of Ordnance; Grafton, Lord Privy Seal; and the two Secretaries of State where Lord Shelburne and . . . most bitter blow of all . . . Charles James Fox.

The only friend of the King's in the cabinet was the Lord Chancellor Thurlow.

A King of England must bow to his parliament. There was plenty to remind him of that. So there was nothing he could do but take up the reins, of course, and try to forget that he was surrounded by men whom he regarded as his enemies.

The Prince longed to play a part in politics.

'The time will come,' Fox told him. 'Wait . . . just wait until you take your place in the House of Lords.'

'There is more than a year to wait,' the Prince reminded him.

'Nothing sir. It will soon be with us.'

'An establishment of my own!' sighed the Prince. 'Freedom.'

'Let us drink to it,' said Fox. 'The Prince's Party.'

'Whiggery and women,' echoed the Prince. 'How is Perdita?'

'The answer to that question will best come from General Tarleton. He is a very great friend of the lady.'

'It is well that she is comfortably settled.'

'Most comfortably, I believe.'

'A pretty creature but a dull one. And to think that I once thought her all that I desired on earth.'

'Your Highness has found the world to be full of desirable projects.'

'True, Charles, true . . . but until I am out of the cage how can I pursue them?'

'Patience. A year or so . . . and all that Your Highness desires will be yours.'

'An establishment of my own . . . an income worthy of my rank . . . a place in politics . . . '

Fox laughed. 'And all you have to cultivate now is . . . patience.'

There was no sense in not enjoying life during the waiting period. He had his mistresses. Dally was pregnant and swore he was the father but everyone said it could as well have been Cholmondeley. The Prince shrugged his shoulders; the idea of being a father rather appealed to him and when the child was born she was christened Georgiana. There were several light affairs which pleased him; he dared not become deeply involved as he had been with Perdita. His visits to Mrs. Armistead were growing less and less frequent. He would always remember her with gratitude and he really believed that she was one of his few mistresses with whom he could remain friends, but he needed change; he needed variety. He sighed for the surrender of his dearest Duchess Georgiana of Devonshire, but while she remained one of his best friends she declined to become his mistress.

Life was full excitement and passing as quickly as could be hoped. Politics with Burke, Fox and Sheridan; visiting tailors with Petersham; studying the art of fencing and boxing with Angelo; going about the town by day and night—often incognito.

Those were the exciting times.

One night he with several of his friends attended a masquerade in the costume of a Spanish Grandee. Heavily disguised he always enjoyed luring people on to talk of the Prince or the King and sometimes he would reveal his identity but not at others.

On this particular occasion he saw a tall willowy girl in the costume of a nun and decided that she should be his partner. As he went to claim her a masked sailor stood in his way and told him to move off for the lady was not for him.

'That,' said the Prince, 'is where you are wrong, my dear fellow.'

'It is you who are wrong, fellow,' was the reply. 'Now you will leave us if you are wise.'

'It is you who need to be wise. Come'

The Prince seized the nun about the waist, but the sailor had pushed him aside, and put his arm about her.

'Is that the manner in which you treat a nun?' asked the Prince.

'Your opinion was not asked!' was the retort.

The nun moved closer to the sailor and this annoyed the Prince. He believed that even disguised as he was all ladies should prefer him.

'And you, Madam,' he said, 'does your character fit the robes you wear as well as your charming shape does? I doubt it . . . I doubt it . . . indeed.'

'Sir, you are insulting a lady.'

'Sir, you are insulting me.'

The sailor let out a burst of laughter, which angered the Prince.

'Where did you find her?' asked the Prince. 'On Portsmouth Point?' As this was the notorious spot where prostitutes waited for the sailors the lady uttered a shrill protest and several other sailors came up to ask who this fellow was who was daring to insult the navy and their ladies.

One of the sailors moved menacingly towards the Prince, his attendants immediately closed around him, but the sailor escort of the nun came forward and struck the Prince in the chest. The Prince, well versed in fisticuffs by Angelo's expert tuition, immediately retaliated and a crowd gathered to see the fight.

There was a general uproar and constables were called. Everyone began talking at once and the ringleaders—the Spanish Grandee and the sailor—were seized and marched off to the watch house, much to the consternation of the Prince's attending squires.

But the Prince was in fact enjoying the adventure.

In the watch house he and the sailor were ordered to take off their masks.

The Prince did so with a flourish and the gasp of dismay which followed delighted him. It was the turn of the sailor; and there standing before the Prince was his brother William.

They stared at each other and burst out laughing.

'So, William, it is you!' cried the Prince.

'So, George, it is you!' echoed William.

They fell into each other's arms and embraced and laughed until the tears ran down their cheeks while the constables looked on, not knowing what to do.

'You young rip,' cried the Prince, 'what were you doing at a masquerade?'

'Exactly the same as you were.'

'And what were your intentions regarding that nun?'

'The same as yours, brother.'

This seemed so funny to the brothers that they could not stop laughing; and when the Prince's attendants arrived breathless and anxious at the watch house, the Prince cried out that he wished all the people concerned in this adventure to receive a guinea a piece to compensate them for their trouble.

The brothers went off arm in arm; but of course it was impossible to keep such an adventure secret; and since the King had commanded that nothing regarding the Prince's conduct should be held back from him, he eventually had an account of it.

He talked to the Queen about it. What was the world coming to? America lost; and the Prince appearing in brawls with his young brother. If the others went the way of the Prince of Wales, he did not know what would become of them all.

'I have not slept for ten nights, thinking of them. Not ten nights. You understand that, eh, what?'

The Queen nodded sadly, She understood too well.

There was no end to trouble, it seemed to the King that year.

Just as he had become resigned to the new ministry, Rockingham died and it was necessary to appoint a new Prime Minister, Fox—recognized to be the ablest man in the Government—naturally expected to be appointed. But the King would not have it and sent for Lord Shelburne. Those Whig supporters of Fox known as the Foxhounds showed their indignation by resigning, Fox at their head, and Burke and Sheridan—who had a minor post in the Government— among them. Fox, however, still held control over a considerable number of votes in the House of Commons and was in the strong position of holding the balance between North's opposition and the Government. The King knew that his wily enemy would not rest until he had ousted Shelburne from his place.

The wrangling went on as to how the ignoble peace with America should be settled; and that August a great family tragedy occurred. Little Alfred, who had been ailing since birth, died.

The King was desolate; so was the Queen; and the fact that little Octavius was so delicate added to their anxieties.

The Prince followed these political events with the utmost interest. And all during the trying times when the King was in conflict with Fox, the Prince was seen with him in public places—arm in arm with Fox, gambling with Fox, drinking with Fox.

As soon as he was of age he would openly side with Fox— and that meant, of course, against his father.

And so the King grew more and more melancholy; and the Queen wondered where it would all end; and she often said that she wished the Prince would come and talk to her as any son might be expected to visit his mother.

And the months of his minority were passing; and at last it was the year 1783 when, in August, he would be twenty-one.

Carlton House

'I have not slept for ten nights,' said the King. 'Ten nights. Twenty nights. Thirty nights. I doubt I shall ever sleep peacefully again. I wish I were eighty, or ninety, or dead.'

The Queen tried to comfort him. It was alarming when he talked in this way. But he had never allowed her to share his burdens so how could she do so now? She could only talk to him about the family—and God knew that was a depressing enough subject. Little Alfred gone; Octavius ailing; the Princes indulging in brawls . . . and the approaching majority of the Prince of Wales.

'Thirty-nine thousand pounds owing to tradesmen!' wailed the King. 'And a good proportion of it for wine . . . When I think of the way I ordered their diet . . . Why did my son become a drunkard?'

'It is because he is young.'

The King ignored her. 'I was young, Madam. But I was never a drunkard. Tailors, trivialities, jewellers . . . Wine and women . . . He thinks of nothing else. Can you make excuses for that, Madam, eh, what?'

The Queen looked sad. It was no use blaming her for the Prince's wildness.

'It is his companions, I doubt not.'

His companions! The King nodded. Fox—that man who haunted his dreams, who mocked him in his secret thoughts, the nephew of Sarah Lennox, the man with Stuart blood in his veins, who was a distant connection of his from the gay feckless charming side of the family. And the Prince had chosen this man for his companion. No, it was Fox who had chosen the

Prince. The King knew why. To turn him against his father; to make a rake of him, a drunkard, a womanizer, a politician in direct opposition to his own father. And Sheridan was another as bad as Fox. The King could imagine their witty conversation, the barbs which would be directed against the Palace of Piety. Oh he knew what they called his Court; he knew how they jeered at him and the Queen. And the Prince with them!

It was intolerable. But what did he do when he wanted to buy his indiscreet letters from a play actress? Come to his father! What did he do when he wanted an allowance, his own establishment? Come to the King!

He was asking for £100,000 a year—and Fox would try to help him get it.

'He'll not have it,' said the King, his eyes protruding.

'What's that?' asked the Queen fearfully.

'One hundred thousand pounds a year he wants. To spend on wine and women.'

The Queen looked shocked.

'He'll not get it. He'll not get it. You understand me, eh, what?'

The Queen nodded sadly and the King was a little mollified. At least she caused him no anxiety.

He almost confided his worries to her over the Government. He had felt stricken since North had formed a coalition with Fox. The idea of his trusted 'good Lord North' going over to the enemy. A coalition with Fox! He had thought North loathed the man as he did. But North for all his good qualities was a weak man. But to side with that man whom he knew the King hated, whom he knew was working with the Prince!

He felt so angry about this sometimes that he told himself it would be better if he abdicated and let his son rule in his place. Then 'they' would see what would happen to the country.

'A strange thing,' said the King sadly, 'when a man's son is against him, eh, what?'

'It is not that he is against Your Majesty. He is in the hands of bad companions . . .'

She trailed off ineffectively. How could she comfort him? And when she saw him lashing himself into a state of anger her one thought was to do so.

'An establishment, he wants. He wants his own house. You know what that means, don't you, eh, what? It means that he'll set up in rivalry to St. James's. There'll be two Courts before we know where we are! People are already likening this to the quarrel between my father and grandfather. They are saying it's a royal custom for fathers and sons to quarrel.'

'I suppose there are little upsets in all families.'

'This is the royal family. This is politics. Something of which you know nothing.'

No, thought the Queen, and whose fault is that? I wanted to know. I wanted to help you, but I have been kept in the background. I have been allowed to hold no position but be the mother of your children.

She was resentful, and yet in a way sorry for him. She did not love him. How could she when he had never taken her into his confidence, when she had always known he had married her under sufferance. Her compensation in life had come through her children, not through him.

But she was alarmed when she saw him working himself into a state of tension because she was terrified that one day he would lose his reason.

The King said: 'He wants his own establishment. Buckingham House is not good enough for him. I have decided he shall have Carlton House.'

'Carlton House! But no one has lived in it since your mother died. It's almost a ruin.'

'It's good enough for my lord Prince,' said the King vindictively.

Carlton House. A house of his own.

The Prince could not wait to take possession.

He went in with a group of friends; they ran up the staircases and in an out of the rooms. Cobwebs clung to the Prince's fine velvet coat, and rats hurried out of the way. Beetles scuttled across the floor. There were patches of damp on the walls and the banging of a door brought down a ceiling.

The Prince stood in the garden among the battered statues and folded his arms.

'It's a ruin,' he said, 'but I never saw a house with greater possibilities. Carlton House will be in a few months be the most elegant residence in town.'

He brought Georgiana, Duchess of Devonshire, to look at the place. She caught his enthusiasm. She went from room to room and decided what furniture should be needed.

'Henry Holland is the architect we need,' said the Prince, 'and I'll have that Frenchman Gaubert for the inside decorations. And of one thing I am certain: there shall be no delay.'

Nor was there. The Prince was kept informed of how the work progressed—and it did so at a great pace.

No expense was spared. Why should it be? This was for the Prince of Wales and Parliament had voted a sum of £39,000 to pay his debts.

The Prince was happy and excited.

He had visited his Uncle Cumberland who had a house by the sea and he found the place enchanting. Brighthelmstone—Brighton for short. He spent his time supervising the alterations to Carlton House, designing his clothes, dancing, drinking with men like Fox and Sheridan, making love with his mistresses, gambling, horse-racing, attending prize fights and driving down to Brighton. He had designed his own phaeton with which he always used three horses one before the other like a team—a postilion mounted on the first and himself driving the other two. It was the speediest vehicle on the road.

Artists, mercers, tailors, furriers, shoemakers, waited on him daily. He discussed with Gaubert the pillars of porphyry he would have erected in the hall; he chose yellow Chinese silk to line the walls of his drawing room; he even had a bathroom installed and this was to lead from his bedchamber.

All the alterations he planned could not be completed before his twenty-first birthday, but the house must be made ready for his occupation by that time. And this would be done.

He was contented. Even when it was decided he should receive only £62,000 a year instead of the hoped for £100,000, he was not unduly dismayed. He would go on making plans for Carlton House for a long time to come—but in the meantime he would live there. At last his dream had come true. He had his own establishment. He was independent. Now he would do as he liked. Not even the King should curb the Prince of Wales.

In November 1783 three months after his twenty-first birthday, the Prince took his seat in the House of Lords.

It seemed as though the whole of London had come out to see him ride through the streets on his way from Carlton House.

And it was well worth it. The Prince was a dazzling spectacle dressed in black velvet embroidered with gold and sprinkled with pink spangles; the heels of his shoes were the same pink as the spangles; and his hair was frizzed and curled.

The people cheered him wildly. They were greatly interested in the work going on at Carlton House. The Prince was extravagant, but this gave work to thousands and the builders and mercers, the tailors and hairdressers could not speak too highly of him. He was setting new fashions, and fashions were good for trade.

The Lords—in the traditional scarlet and ermine—were astounded by the unconventional but spectacular appearance of their Prince.

His maiden speech was greeted with loyal cheers. All forward looking men, he believed, had their eyes fixed on him.

He existed, he announced, by the love, the friendship and the benevolence of the people. He would never forsake their cause as long as he lived.

When he left the House of the Lords he went to the Commons where his friend Fox was speaking in defence of the East India Bill, the object of which was to put the Company under the jurisdiction of directors who should be selected by the Government.

Fox—whose Bill this was—spoke passionately in its favour, but he had a strong opponent in young William Pitt, a boy of about twenty-four who had all the fire and shrewdness of his father, the Great Commoner. The Prince knew that young Pitt had to be watched for the King was taking him into favour—largely because he was an opponent of Fox's.

When the Prince entered the Commons and took his place in the gallery all eyes were on him—and not only because of his black velvet and pink spangles; but because this was a gesture. He had come to hear Mr. Fox, to applaud Mr. Fox and to show parliament that he stood with Mr. Fox against his enemies even though the chief of these was the King.

Mr. Fox looked ruefully about his lodgings at St. James's. He would have to sell every piece of furniture that was left if he was going to fight this election. He could no longer stave off his creditors; his gambling debts were enormous. If he were going to fight this Westminster election he must have the money to do so.

And there was no question of his fighting. He *must* fight.

This was one of the rare moments when he forced himself to think about money. Lucky Prince of Wales, he though ruefully, with a parliament to take care of his debts.

But there was nothing he enjoyed like a fight—so he must call in the dealers and sell his home—and after that? He would trust to luck which had never really deserted him so far.

The Coalition had fallen on his East India Bill which although it had passed through the Commons was thrown out of the Lords. Fox knew how this had happened. The King had written to Lord Temple telling him to make it known that he would consider as his enemy any man who voted for the Bill. Although not all the lords were intimidated by this threat, the Bill was defeated by a narrow margin; and this had brought down the Government. With what joy had the King commanded Fox and North to return their seals of office!

The King had then summoned young William Pitt and appointed him Prime Minister.

'We have a schoolboy to rule us,' was the comment, for Pitt was twenty-four years of age.

But he was the son of the great Pitt and had already shown signs of having inherited his father's powers.

And then . . . Pitt demanded a dissolution of Parliament— and the result was this election which Fox could ill afford to fight.

While he sat wondering where he would go when he had sold up his home, his manservant announced a visitor.

He rose to greet Mrs. Armistead.

She looked very elegant. There was no sign now of the lady's maid.

'My dear Lizzie,' said Fox, taking her hand and kissing it.

'I hope I have not called at an inconvenient time?'

'It is in fact most convenient. Had you called a few days later that would have been another matter. Then I might not have had a chair to offer you.'

'Ah, yes, this election. You have to fight it.'

He nodded. 'And to provide the means I shall sell all my possessions.'

'And then?'

'I shall win.'

'Of a certainty, but I was thinking of your home.'

Fox shrugged his shoulders.

'You will need somewhere to live.'

'I have friends.'

'Devonshire House?' she asked. 'But your stay there would be temporary. You must have a home, Mr. Fox. There is one waiting for you at Chertsey.'

He rose and took her by the shoulders. He was visibly moved, which was touching in a man such as he was.

She looked at him steadily. 'I think,' she said slowly, 'that when I bought my home, when I accumulated my little fortune,

I had something like this in mind. You are a brilliant man, Mr. Fox, but a somewhat feckless one.'

He raised those bushy eyebrows which added to his unkempt appearance and said: 'My dear dear Lizzie, are you sure that you are not at this moment being guilty of the one feckless action of a hitherto sensible career?'

'I am quite sure, Mr. Fox, because if you decide to come to Chertsey the purpose of my sensible career will have been achieved.'

He was silent for a moment and then he said: 'I cannot understand why this good fortune should be mine, for even if I lost the Westminister election I should still be one of the most fortunate men on earth.'

'But you will not lose, Mr. Fox.'

'No, I shall win the Westminister election—and I hope I shall be worthy of my electorate . . . and my sweet Liz.'

There had never been such excitement. The whole of Westminister seemed to be in the streets and taking sides over the election. Georgiana, Duchess of Devonshire, canvassed for Fox wearing a cape of fox fur and carrying a fox muff, giving kisses in exchange for promised votes. The Prince of Wales toured the streets dressed in a blue frock and a buff waistcoat—dull for him but an exact replica of the clothes Fox wore for the House of Commons; and great was the excitement when Fox was returned.

The Prince determined to celebrate. It was to be a special occasion in Carlton House. Six hundred guests were invited— all Foxites. Nine marquees were erected in the grounds and four bands played constantly.

The Prince himself was a brilliant figure in pearl grey silk decorated with silver, and crowds gathered in the Mall to listen to the sounds of joy.

The King rode down the Mall on his way to open Parliament.

'What's the fuss at Carlton House?' he wanted to know.

'It is the Prince, Your Majesty. He is celebrating the victory of Mr. Fox at Westminister.'

The young dog! The traitor to his father!

'He never loses a chance to plague me,' muttered the King. 'And Fox is still in the House. Thank God for good Mr. Pitt. He'll be a match for him, eh, what? But why did I have a son like this? Who would have thought he would turn out to plague

me.' The people scarcely glanced at him. They were all for the
Prince. They liked the rip-roaring, hard-drinking, gambling
lecher. They could not appreciate a good man. These people
were a feckless crowd. 'I don't belong here,' thought the King.
'We ought never to have come.'

He fell to wondering what life would have been like if the
English had never driven the Catholic Stuart away, or if they had
decided to take him and send the Germans back to Germany. It
could have happened in 1715 or more likely in 1745. But the
Germans had won and they had stayed . . . and as a result he
was the King of England and one day that reckless young fool,
that gambling, that deep-in-debt pursuer of women would be
their king.

'Serve them right,' said the King aloud. 'By God, serve them
right.'

And the sounds of revelry from Carlton House kept echoing
in his ears as he rode on to Parliament.

EPILOGUE

In the year 1800 Perdita Robinson lay in her bed and because she knew she was soon to leave it for ever, thought over the events which had made up her life.

Crippled after rheumatic fever, she had yet made a place for herself in society with her poems and novels and for a time had reigned over that salon in which she received distinguished guests who came attracted by her fame.

But this was the end; and she was not sorry. She was forty-two years old and still beautiful; but she felt she had lived long enough and she could never endure the prospect of old age.

Sometimes she thought of those days of glory when she had appeared in the Pantheon or the Rotunda in some fantastic concoction of ribbons and feathers for all to gaze at. The Prince's beloved mistress, the famous Perdita.

It was so long ago and she had ceased to regret, ceased to reproach. There had been a time when she had railed against a lover who had so quickly tired of her and gone to other women, who had given her but a mere pittance (for £500 a year seemed a pittance when her carriage alone had cost £200 to maintain). But all that was over.

Banastre Tarleton had been a good friend and had remained faithful all these years. It was for his sake that she had gone to France in winter and suffered so acutely from the dreadful cold at sea that she contracted rheumatic fever which had left her paralysed.

Since then she had never walked again. Oddly enough—and this surprised her—she had borne her misfortune with fortitude. Looking back she wondered how she had endeavored to be so calm, so philosophical. When she remembered all the men who had sought her favours she would tell herself she was a most remarkable woman.

Malden—dear Malden—who had loved her from the first; Cumberland who longed to add her to his retinue of mistresses; Mr. Fox, to whom she had surrendered and, she would confess it, been a little piqued at the short duration of a relationship from which she had hoped for much; the Duc d'Orléans had sought her, had implored her to become his mistress; and she had refused him. Queen Marie Antoinette had sent her a purse which she herself had netted because she had refused Orléans. And that was long ago. The revolution had come to France and Marie Antoinette had gone to the guillotine and Orléans had become known as Philippe Egalité . . . That was long ago.

She had seen a great deal happen about her, but now she remembered most the personal incidents. She had been fortunate. Maria, her daughter, had come to live with her when Mrs. Darby had died and bore no resentment to her mother for deserting her when she was a child.

They had grown closer with the years and it was to Maria whom she read her verses and the chapters of her novels as they were written; and Maria herself had displayed a talent for literature.

As Tabitha Bramble, called by some the English Sappho, Perdita had had her salon; she had received her guests; and she had felt no bitterness—not even when she heard that Mr. Fox had married Mrs. Armistead and that they lived together afterwards as before in harmony.

Sometimes she wondered whether the Prince ever thought of her. She liked to imagine his recalling that gilded nest in Cork Street, those meetings on Eel Pie Island.

She would let herself dream that he came to her salon and knelt before her.

'I have come back, Perdita,' she imagined his saying. 'There has never been anyone to compare with you.'

And she found pleasure in acting scenes of reconciliation which she knew would never take place.

But there was Maria, dear Maria, who was happy to wait on her and she herself was not strong. Maria would not live long after her she was sure, and she was glad that she would get her £250 a year which had been a part of the settlement Mr. Fox had arranged for her.

Mr. Fox, dearest Banastre, they had been good friends to her. The Prince too.

Ah, the Prince! He was never far from the surface of her mind. How could he be? She constantly heard news of him. It was inevitable. His exploits were on everyone's lips. He must soon be the King of England.

She wished that she had been able to keep those letters he had written her. How she would have enjoyed reading them again! But they had been sold for the pension she now enjoyed and which would continue after her death to be paid to Maria. At least she need not worry about Maria—her dear daughter who had nursed her and loved her over the years of her affliction.

And to think that Maria had come from her union with the hated Mr. Robinson who had long since through death ceased to trouble them.

Such, she thought, was life.

But it was death which was now her concern.

She called Maria to her, for she knew there was not much time left.

'Maria, my dearest daughter,' she said, 'I should like to be buried in the churchyard at old Windsor . . . close to the river. I have always loved the river.'

'Do not speak of death, Mamma,' begged Maria.

'My dearest, we cannot ignore it. It is coming soon, I know.'

She could not bear to see Maria's tears yet she could not prevent herself playing the part of the dying woman. It was natural for her to act. She knew this was so and wanted to explain to Maria. Her mind was wandering a little. She talked of Mr. Garrick who had been so brusque but who had promised to teach her; she talked of Mr. Fox and the Prince.

'Is that someone at the door, Maria? He's come. I knew he would come at last.'

Maria shook her head, but Perdita was already seeing him—not as he was now but as a charming prince, eager and loving.

'Maria love, give me the paper heart . . . "Unalterable to my Perdita through life." He meant it then . . . He will remember . . .'

'No, Mamma,' whispered Maria gently.

But she did not hear.

She was quoting to herself the poem she had written and which Maria had always known referred to the Prince of Wales.

'Thou art no more my bosom friend,
Here must the sweet delusion end,
That charmed my senses many a year
Through smiling summers, winters drear,'

Ah, yes, thought Maria, here must the delusion end. The Prince of Wales deeply immersed in his own tempestuous life could scarcely be expected to be aware of the passing of one who had amused him briefly twenty years before.

Perdita was smiling. Perhaps, thought Maria, she believes he has come to her. Perhaps the sweet delusion is still with her.

Maria put her arms about her mother and Perdita lay in them, smiling as life passed away.

BIBLIOGRAPHY

George IV	Shane Leslie
George IV	Roger Fulford
George, Prince and Regent	Philip W. Sergeant
The First Gentleman	Grace E. Thompson
Portrait of the Prince Regent	Dorothy Margaret Stuart
Memoirs of George IV	Robert Huish
Life and Times of George IV	The Rev. George Croly
The Diary and Letters of Madame d'Arblay	
The Great Corinthian	Doris Leslie
The Good Queen Charlotte	Percy Fitzgerald
Life of George IV	Percy Fitzgerald
George III	J.C. Long
The Four Georges	W. M. Thackeray
The First Gentleman of Europe	Lewis Melville
Memoirs of Mary Robinson	Edited by J. F. Molloy
Life and Letters of Lady Sarah Lennox	Edited by the Countess of Ilchester and Lord Stavordale
Loves of Florizal	Philip Lindsay
Memoirs and Portraits	Horace Walpole
Memoirs of the Reign of George III	Horace Walpole
George III, Monarch and Statesman	Beckles Wilson

George III, His Court and Family	Henry Colburn
In the Days of the Georges	William B. Boulton
The Four Georges	Sir Charles Petrie
The House of Hanover	Alvin Redman
The Dictionary of National Biography	Edited by Sir Leslie Stephen and Sir Sidney Lee
British History	John Wade
National and Domestic History of England	William Hickman Smith Aubrey

About the Author

Jean Plaidy is an extremely popular author who is also known as Victoria Holt and Philippa Carr. She resides in England and has written over twenty novels for Fawcett, including both the Georgian Saga and the Plantagenet Saga series.